## Titles by Marliss Moon

**DANGER'S PROMISE**
**BY STARLIGHT**

# By Starlight

## MARLISS MOON

**BERKLEY SENSATION, NEW YORK**

## BY STARLIGHT

A Berkley Sensation Book / published by arrangement with the author

PRINTING HISTORY
Berkley Sensation edition / July 2003

Copyright © 2003 by Marliss Arruda
Cover art by Daniel O'Leary
Cover design by George Long
Book design by Kristin del Rosario

The Berkley Publishing Group,
a division of Penguin Group (USA) Inc.,
375 Hudson Street, New York, New York 10014.

ISBN: 0-425-19103-6

A BERKLEY SENSATION™ BOOK
Berkley Sensation Books are published by The Berkley Publishing Group,
a division of Penguin Group (USA) Inc.,
375 Hudson Street, New York, New York 10014.
BERKLEY SENSATION and the "B" design
are trademarks belonging to Penguin Group (USA) Inc.

PRINTED IN THE UNITED STATES OF AMERICA

10 9 8 7 6 5 4 3 2 1

For all the members of my big family, especially my incredible parents. Thank you, Mom and Dad, for encouraging your dreamer to dream.

As always, for Alan, my best friend. And for our new baby, whose coming we've anticipated with joy! Welcome to the world, Elizabeth Grace!

# *Prologue* ～

## The Outskirts of Jerusalem, A.D. 1130

THE sun had just plummeted behind the low mountains to the west, drawing the veil of night behind it, when Luke reached the summit of the hill near his home. Determined to catch the first debut of the magical star, he'd raced up the hill as fast as his thin little legs would allow. Out of breath, but happy to have arrived in advance of the star's appearance, the boy collapsed on a large rock to catch his breath.

As yet, no stars pierced the darkening canopy above. Luke glanced downhill toward his home, a pathetic structure standing alone by the roadside. Beyond it, torches flared to life along the walls of Jerusalem. His mother would worry about him, coming home so late. But he had bread in his satchel, taken from a merchant who'd unwisely turned his back, and he'd found a silver trinket on the ground that could be pawned for food. His findings would ensure his mother's forgiveness.

Casting his gaze upward, Luke gasped in delight as the first needle of illumination pricked the dark sky, followed immediately by the winking of thousands of others. With eyes of a lighter hue that betrayed him as the child of an Englishman, he searched the heavens for the cluster of stars his father had once pointed out to him.

*See the bright star at the top there?* His father's voice

returned to him, speaking in Norman French, a tongue Luke hadn't overheard in five months now. *'Tis a magical star. If you make a wish on it, your wish will come true.*

Until this morning, Luke had forgotten all about the magical star. But the trinket shimmering in the dirt today had reminded him, and he'd looked forward eagerly to the opportunity to put things right again.

James d'Albini had filled Luke's head with hopeful visions, like magic stars. He'd regaled his son with stories of a land lushly green and shaded with enormous trees, of meadows watered with silvery streams and studded with castles made of stone. He'd drawn pictures for Luke, read him books about kings and mighty warriors, men whose links of armor protected them from the Saracen's blades; men of such strong faith they had traveled great distances to subdue the disbelievers.

Those stories had become such a part of Luke that the land his father called England seemed more real to him than the dusty, arid country in which he lived. His father had promised Luke they would return home together, when his peacekeeping duties were done. Five months ago, he'd abruptly died, leaving his son and his Saracen mistress destitute.

Luke had mourned the promise of England, lost to him at his father's death, nearly as much as he'd mourned his father. His life became a wretched blur. Threatening to stone his mother to death for her shame, her people had cast them from the walls of the city. Esme built them a hut of palm fronds and dug them a garden, hoping to eke a living from the stingy soil. When their goat ate weeds and died, she sent Luke into the city to beg and to steal.

Neither of those tasks suited him well. His father had raised him to be an honest boy, proud of his Norman heritage. He suffered the scorn of the Saracen locals, endured their mockery and name calling, knowing all the while that he was an outcast, that he would never belong.

Tonight he would change all that.

For a panicked moment, he searched the glinting stars above, fearing he had lost the magical star forever. But then his gaze fell upon the brightest illumination at the height of a starry cluster, and he exclaimed his joy out loud.

"Magic star," he whispered, his heart thumping urgently

within his chest, "I wish . . ." He cut himself short. Nay, he could not afford to be hasty, for he had but one wish, a wish his father had advised him to save for a time when it was truly needed.

He put a hand to his mouth to keep from blurting anything rash. It was selfish to consider only himself while making his wish. After all, his mother suffered even more than he, being shunned by her family, unwelcomed within the city's walls.

He would think of a wish that saved the both of them.

"Magic star," he said again, speaking slowly and with care, "I wish for a better life for the two of us, for Mother and me."

He wondered if he ought to say more, but the star gave a wink and dimmed, as if to say it was too late to tack on specifics.

With a trembling of anticipation, Luke craned his neck to peer into the valley below. If his wish had come true, there would be light in the window and a fire for cooking.

To his disappointment, the hut remained dark.

Reality brought Luke's trembling to a hopeless calm. A gnawing emptiness filled his belly, reminding him that he'd not eaten at all that day. Touching the loaves in his satchel, his only comfort, he scolded himself for depriving his mother of food, and turning toward home, plodded heavily downhill.

THOUSANDS of leagues away, in a castle made of stone, the earl of Arundel clutched a missive in his trembling hand. The letter, like those that James had sent before, was stiff from the many months it had taken to arrive from the Holy Lands. But this letter was not penned in James's distinctive scrawl but in the hand of a stranger, informing Sir William that his only son and heir was dead.

Through eyes blurred with tears, Sir William's gaze fell upon these words, words that rallied him from complete despair:

*Sir James left a son by the name of Luke. He remains with his mother, a Saracen woman named Esme. They live on the outskirts of Jerusalem.*

"Steward!" Sir William bellowed, rising from his chair on knees that quaked. "Prepare for a lengthy journey. We go to Jerusalem to collect my son's remains . . . and to find my grandson."

# *Chapter One* ❧

*North Yorkshire, A.D. 1154*

WITH a rustle of black robes, the Prioress of Mount Grace stood between her colleagues, the Abbot of Jervaulx and the Rector from Richmond, to deliver the verdict. Her broad wimple blocked the sunlight beaming through the slit behind her, yet even with her face in shadow, there was no mistaking the eager gleam in her slate gray eyes.

The nuns who had gathered for the verdict hushed themselves into silence. It was late September, yet the refectory hall felt as cold as if it were winter. A shiver crept up Merry's spine. She stood before the dais braced for condemnation, knuckles white, knees locked to keep her standing. With every shallow breath, her heart beat a tattoo of premonition.

In desperation, Merry glanced at the clerics on either side of the prioress. Nothing in their darting gazes gave her comfort. The prioress, with her business acumen, had made the diocese wealthy. The jury would vote as Mother Agnes decreed.

"Sister Mary Grace," the woman began in a voice as dry as fallen leaves, "you blaspheme the name you were given when you took your vows. Henceforth, I will address you as Merry of Heathersgill, for you have proven yourself a nun no longer."

Merry's heart beat faster. *Not the rope*, she prayed, dreading a hanging sentence. A drowning she might survive, for she swam quite well.

"After lengthy interrogation and deliberation," continued the prioress, "we find you guilty of attempted murder, of heresy, and of malefaction."

*Guilty!* The word reverberated in her head like a death knell. She had come to Mount Grace to avoid persecution for her healing art. Yet in this supposed sanctuary, she'd found anything but tolerance.

The trial had been a farce, from beginning to end. The eye-witnesses to her crimes had clearly been coerced. One had seen her frolicking under a full moon. Another had caught her copulating with the devil. Others still had espied her with a black cat, most likely her familiar. Tales of fancy! Those same nuns would have thanked her if the Mother were dead.

Only she wasn't. At the last minute, Merry had put only two leaves of henbane in the prioress's wine instead of three. Now she wished she were more hard-hearted. Her reluctance to kill might ironically be the death of her.

"Malefaction is a grievous crime committed against God and the Holy Church," the prioress added, savoring her victory.

Merry's jaw came suddenly unhinged. "And what of your crimes, Mother?" she challenged boldly. "Are they not grievous, having been committed against mere girls?"

The nuns behind her gasped in awe. The Abbot of Jervaulx and the Rector from Richmond shared a common look. All of them knew the prioress's perverse pleasure in wielding her whip. She ruled her abbey with a heavy hand, seeming to enjoy the inhuman punishments she inflicted on her nuns.

"Silence!" Agnes cut in, raising her arms to resemble a great, black bird. "The accused is not to speak! How dare you malign me when you have proven yourself an abomination in the sight of God?" She narrowed her gaze at Merry. "I was going to display Christian tolerance by reducing my sentence to a whipping of twenty lashes, but I have changed my mind. We condemn you to burn at dawn tomorrow, and tomorrow you shall burn!"

*Burn!* The sentence was absurd. Burning was common on the continent but rarely executed in England. Merry widened her stance, determined not to swoon as the floor seemed to shift.

'Twas not too late to beg forgiveness. Still, twenty strokes of Agnes's whip were as likely to kill her as any fire.

And for what crime? All Merry had done was shield her sister nuns from Agnes's wrath. Whenever the Mother whipped them, Merry ensured there was a consequence: A seizure that made the woman bite her tongue; a rash that wouldn't go away; warts upon the hands—all designed to make Agnes hesitate ere she raised her whip again.

The prioress was subdued but not reformed.

Her most recent victim suffered an infection that had killed her. In reprisal for her death, Merry had put henbane in Agnes's wine, and the prioress suffered a purging of the bowels so violent it might have left her dead. Alas, it hadn't. Now Agnes wanted justice.

"You will have to notify my family," Merry stalled, gasping for breath.

Agnes eyed her with false sympathy. "Your family isn't the least concerned with your fate, else they would have written long ago," she pointed out.

It was true, her elder sister, Clarise, and her mother, Jeanette, had declined to visit after delivering her to Mount Grace. Given the trouble she'd caused them, it was unlikely they would wish to save her now. Only Kyndra might wish to save her, but her younger sister was still flowering into womanhood and therefore powerless.

She would suffer death alone. Since the day that had changed Merry's life forever, she had found no justice, no peace anywhere, not even in a priory. What matter if she died tomorrow?

"Well, have you something to say for yourself?" the prioress prompted. "Are you sorry for turning from the Church and making a pact with Satan? Come, where is your penitence?" In her eagerness to hear her, Agnes leaned over the high table, her face pulling out of shadow.

Merry drew back at the Mother's countenance, struck by the resemblance between this tyrant and her stepfather, Ferguson. Both had hooked features and chilling eyes. There was an ugliness about them that went beyond the sneer of their lips, the heaviness of their jowls. Thank God Ferguson was dead. At least there was one less tyrant to torment meeker souls.

As the flame of righteousness flickered, Merry found her tongue. Her tone was anything but penitent as it rang out in the vaulted chamber. "I will see you in hell, Agnes," she replied, drawing gasps of admiration from her sister nuns. "If I am to burn now, then you will burn for eternity for scarring innocent women. Burn me if you must." She lifted her chin, demonstrating a defiance she did not fully feel. "I would sooner die than remain in this hell on earth with you."

SIR Luke le Noir, captain of the prince's royal army and grandson of the earl of Arundel, never suffered the infirmities of mortal men. He urged his army to ride through the night, setting a pace that made sleeping in the saddle impossible.

Erin, his groggy squire, considered him sidelong, amazed to find his lord's posture still erect after all these hours. Against the backdrop of a violet dawn, Sir Luke's proud silhouette contrasted sharply with the slouching figures of his men. His armor, kept in immaculate condition, glowed silver in the purplish light. His dark head was helmless as usual; his ears alert to sounds more menacing than the chirping of insects.

His army had pledged a year of service toward the destruction of adulterines—strongholds built without royal sanction. Nine months out of twelve were already spent. They'd destroyed one castle in Drax and another in Lincolnshire. With only three months remaining, one might question whether they would complete their final task. Erin suffered no concern. Sir Luke would set a grueling pace, bloodying his fingers, inspiring his men to match his expectations. One look of approval from his burning eyes and anything was possible.

Yet Erin sensed the captain's heart was no longer in their labors. A missive had come by courier a week ago informing him of his grandfather's continuing debilitation. No one would have blamed Sir Luke had he turned home with his work undone. Yet, loyal vassal that he was, he set aside personal concerns in the name of duty, fording moor and mountain to convey the full reach of Prince Henry's arm.

At times like these, Erin pitied his lord, though it made no sense to pity him. Sir Luke was wealthier and more powerful than most nobles, and yet he was not only baseborn, he was also half Saracen. With two marks against him, 'twas a marvel he had risen so high in rank as to become Prince Henry's favorite.

Of course, he had saved Henry's life in a fire, when the prince was but a boy. His bravery had earned him the nom de guerre, the Phoenix, by which name his fame had spread. He was Henry's most cunning military leader. To the benefit of his enemy, he preferred to strike a truce than to fight. Abroad and at home, with this tenuous matter of tearing down unsanctioned structures built in Stephen's rein, Sir Luke's diplomatic skills made him indispensable.

Like the Phoenix, whose name he bore, Sir Luke seemed immortal, imperturbable. He emerged from battles unscathed, his dignity and poise intact, utterly unaffected by whatever drama seethed about him.

Even now, he did not look like a man who had ridden through the night. Tirelessly, his sharp gaze scanned the distance for their destination—a priory where at last his men could rest. Glancing over his shoulder like a shepherd, he kept watch over his men, lest one of them should tumble from the saddle, fast asleep.

The moment he spurred his sorrel to a canter, Erin knew his lord had spied the priory in the distance. He would arrive at the gates before his men, smoothing the way for them, as was his custom. Erin prodded his mount to follow, eager for a meal and a pallet, in that order.

Built on the edge of the fells, the priory was a small, sullen enclosure. With the sky turning silver behind it, it seemed cold and unwelcoming and shut tight as a tomb.

Sir Luke dismounted and tugged at the bell rope.

The peephole cracked open. "Who's there?" inquired a girl in a frightened voice.

" 'Tis the prince's royal army," the Phoenix gently conveyed. "We seek rest and a meal behind your walls."

To their mutual surprise, the peephole slammed shut. Sir Luke sent a startled look at his squire then tugged the bell rope a second time.

It seemed a very long time before the peephole opened once

again. "I'm the prioress. Why are you here?" barked a dry, unfriendly voice.

"We serve His Majesty, Prince Henry," the captain said, tersely this time. "We need a place to sleep and a meal." *Now.* The command was unspoken but clear nonetheless.

"You've picked a poor time to ask," groused the woman. "There's an infection within these walls. We're quarantined," she added. "This morning we will burn the bodies of the dead."

Erin wondered at the strangeness of her words. There was no black flag tied to the gate in warning.

"What manner of illness is it?" his lord inquired, taking a precautionary step back.

"A pox of some sort," said the prioress. " 'Tis horridly contagious. You had best be off." With that she shut the little door between them.

Erin felt sorry for his lord again. But mostly he felt sorry for himself, for he had *so* looked forward to a few hours' sleep. He eyed the Phoenix's stiff back and wondered what his lord would do now. The men were just catching up to them. The relief in their faces was not something any captain would want to disappoint.

He turned around, slowly, his expression guarded. "Take your rest on the ground," he called. "We've been denied entrance."

As the soldiers lamented loudly and slithered off their horses, Sir Luke drew a length of rope from his saddlebag, his movements betraying no inner strife. His gaze rose to meet his squire's. "Come with me, Erin," he instructed. "Sir Pierce, I am going to take reconnaissance," he added, addressing his sergeant.

Erin hurried after his lord's tall form as they rounded the priory's wall. The grass, brittle from the summer's drought, crunched loudly beneath their boots. At last, the Phoenix paused. He shucked his mailed gauntlets, unbelted his sheath so that his sword dropped to the ground and began unlacing the stays of his surcoat.

"Are you climbing the wall, my lord?" Erin guessed, with dawning appreciation. Clearly, his lord suspected something amiss within the priory walls, and he meant to discover what it was.

"Help me get this mail off," he said simply.

As Erin struggled with the iron coat, Sir Luke divested himself of his remaining armor, until he wore only his padded shirt, armored hose, and boots. Even without his armor, he cut an impressive figure, his body honed from years of intense physical duress.

The first pale rays of sunlight fingered the rough wall. "I may not need the rope," said the captain, studying the stones.

Erin watched as his lord crooked his fingertips over projections and found footing in crevices below. Inch by inch, he scaled the wall, nudging Erin's respect still higher. His lord's climbing skill had made him famous in Rouen ten years before. Now Erin knew why.

In less time than it had taken to undress, the Phoenix was peering over the partition.


TO Luke's grim satisfaction, he had an unfettered view of the priory's courtyard. His gaze went at once to the figure at the center of the stake, and a cold blade of shock bisected his spine. It wasn't a dead person at all, but a woman fully alive and tied to a stake!

*God's blood!* The prioress meant to burn her alive!

His jaw muscles flexed. *A pox, indeed.* He'd smelled something illegitimate from the moment the frightened nun had answered his summons.

The girl at the stake was also a nun, dressed from head to toe in black homespun. She was scarcely a woman by the looks of her, her young face narrow and pale, her eyes enormous. She stared at the sky to avoid watching the workers sprinkle straw at her feet.

Luke simmered with disgust. Ecumenical law forbade the Church to enact such punishments. The word *sanctuary* would mean nothing if the Church wielded such terrible power!

He focused his resentment on the prioress, a tyrant whose isolation led her to the false belief she was all-powerful. He would confront the woman at once and demand the girl's release. He prepared to leap from the wall, when an imposing nun swept into the courtyard, whipping a torch about like a banner.

"Hurry!" she commanded. "I want more tallow on it!"

He knew her by her voice. She was determined to get the matter done swiftly, no doubt wary of the army outside her walls. There was no time for negotiation, he surmised.

That left just one course of action, an alternative with grave ramifications. No one, not even a tenant-in-chief to the future king, had the right to enter a holy house uninvited. On the other hand, he was honor-bound to save the girl. To walk away now would make him as much a murderer as the prioress.

Figuring his odds for success, Luke glanced down.

"What d'you see, my lord?" Erin prompted.

"A girl being put to the stake," Luke said evenly.

Erin gasped. "Is she a witch?" he asked, crossing himself.

Luke sent a thoughtful look at the victim. He couldn't tell much about her, enveloped as she was in black robes and a wimple. "There are no such things as witches," he replied, curbing his squire's imagination. The workers had finished splashing tallow on the straw. He would have to devise a plan quickly.

The prioress's brittle voice drew his gaze. "Don't think you can beg now, girl," she taunted her victim. "You mocked my offer of charity, remember?"

Luke cut his gaze to the girl, curious to hear her reply.

"I don't require your forgiveness, Agnes." Her voice was as steady as steel. " 'Tis you who should ask forgiveness of me."

Luke's eyebrows rose in admiration. Such bravery deserved reward, no matter the consequence.

He threw a quick look at the assemblage. With only a handful of men present and a clutch of nuns in one corner, he would face no serious resistance.

"Erin, throw me my sword," he called, making a swift decision.

The youth complied with a grin, and Luke caught the broadsword, laying it soundlessly on the top of the wall. "Return my armor to the horses," he added, "and do so quickly. Tell Sir Pierce we must get away from here at once. Look for me at the gate. Now hurry!"

Erin knew better than to question his leader. He tossed the gauntlets, guards, and belt onto the mail and began to drag the armor behind him. Luke put both hands on the top of the wall and hoisted himself on the ledge.

No one had seen him, for all eyes were fixed on the prioress as she tossed her torch with flourish onto the pyre. The kindling exploded into flame.

Black smoke billowed upward then dissipated under the morning breeze. So too did the victim's bravery. Her eyes went wide with terror. Her slender body strained against the ropes.

Luke had less time than he'd wagered. As the flames roared higher, he braved the enormous leap to the ground, rolling to break the fall. Broadsword in hand, he sprinted toward the pyre.

MERRY had shut her eyes against the encroaching flames. She clenched her fists, feeling her fingernails break the skin of her palms. The heat took her breath away. She pressed herself against the wood at her back, dreading the first contact of flame against her bare feet. *Be brave,* she counseled herself, but she could feel the screams welling inside her.

Suddenly the platform shuddered, and a breath of cool air hit her face. Her eyes shot open, and she found a man balanced on the stage beside her.

She stared at him, disoriented. The ropes slipped from her wrists, fell from her hips.

"Hold on to me," he instructed.

She threw her arms around him, gladly. Given his handsome visage, he could only be an angel come to deliver her soul. God had been merciful, after all. *Glory be!*

The ropes at her ankles parted. In the next instant, the world turned upside down as the angel hefted her over one shoulder. He leaped down the face of the pyre, managing to dodge the flames. They rose up, however biting into Merry's wimple, singeing her hair. She snatched off the headpiece and threw it down.

It was then that she realized she was still alive. The angel hadn't taken her soul, but rather her mortal shell. He jogged toward the gate, now, his hard shoulder pummeling her belly. Gasping for breath, Merry craned her neck to see the Mother pursuing them. Agnes had snatched up her braided whip and was coming after them, teeth bared like a she-wolf. The abbot and priest followed close behind.

Merry's savior beat them to the gate. He threw it open, and suddenly she was surrounded by milling horses and gleaming weaponry.

*"Ride!"* he said with authority, and the horses leapt into thunderous motion.

Strong hands spanned her waist, and Merry landed jarringly atop a saddle, the sky once more above her. No sooner had she caught her breath than the prioress's voice raked over her.

"Stop!"

The tip of a whip whistled by her cheek, and Merry lurched back, fighting to keep her seat. "Hand her over to me at once!" the prioress insisted, threatening them both with her whip.

Agnes was a formidable woman, but Merry's rescuer was taller still, with shoulders twice as broad. He gripped his sword with accustomed ease, frowning at the Mother's unseemly rage.

Clearly he wasn't an angel, but a warrior of some sort. His voice reached her ears, steady and dignified, as he addressed the prioress. "As the prince's right arm, madam, 'tis my duty to intervene. You said you would be burning the bodies of the dead this morning. This girl does not look dead to me."

He flicked Merry a glance, his gaze running through her like a sword of fire.

"She is dead of spirit, dead to the Church!" the prioress raged. "How dare you interfere in matters of religious concern! This witch tried to poison me!" She glared at Merry.

"Indeed," said the warrior smoothly. "Then I will convey her to the nearest abbey to be tried there. It seems to me you have forgotten whom you serve."

*Conveyed where?* Merry's heart stopped dead. Nay, she could not endure a second trial!

"I will not stand for it!" the Mother seethed. "What is your name? I intend to bring a formal complaint against you. How dare you breach my wall!"

" 'Tisn't your wall," the warrior corrected softly. " 'Tis God's wall. The name is Luke le Noir," he answered. "Complain all you like, only be prepared to account for your actions if you do." He dismissed the Mother with those words and positioned himself to mount behind Merry.

The prioress drew back her whip.

"Beware!" Merry cried.

The sword flashed by her eye, severing the lash in two. With scarcely a pause, the warrior dropped into the saddle, pulling Merry snugly against him. They leapt into a gallop, riding into the golden trail of dust the army had left behind.

A hundred paces down the road, he placed his sword across her lap. "Hold this," he requested, taking the reins with both hands.

Merry's fingers closed about the heavy weapon. She registered the smooth, cool quality of the blade, its razor-sharp edge. Her senses were strangely heightened, so that the newly risen sun blinded her, the grass filled her nostrils with dusty perfume, and the wind whistled through the weave of her nun's attire, cooling her skin. Those details roused her to the realization she was still alive!

Yet she felt nothing but despair. She had come so close to death that she'd welcomed its oblivion. How much better for an angel to have taken her soul! Now, according to this man, she would be made to stand another trial.

She had endured too much in her previous trial—allegations that the devil had tricked her; questions as to the properties of herbs; how had she come by the mark on her backside; had the devil put it there? By heaven, she was weary of it! She simply could not live through it again!

A quiet rage began to burn in her, overtaking the shock of her reprieve. Merry looked wildly about her. She could see that they were gaining on the army ahead of them. It hadn't escaped her notice that her rescuer wore no armor. Finally, she looked down at his sword, lying across her lap.

She curled her fist around the odd-shaped pommel. The steel had been beaten into the shape of wings. If only she had wings herself to fly away!

It wouldn't be right to kill the one who'd saved her. Neither could she wound him, though it might allow her to thrust him off his horse and gallop away. Still, where would she go after that? The prince's soldiers would be on her in an instant.

'Twould be easier just to kill herself. The rolling movement of the horse alone might send the point sliding between her ribs.

God's teeth, only the sword was too long! She struggled a

moment, extending the pommel as far as she could. The tip slipped under her arm, pricking the man behind her.

"What are you doing?"

He wrenched the sword from her grasp and, at the same time, brought the horse to a sudden standstill.

Merry relinquished the weapon with disgust. She should have known oblivion would not come easily. And now she'd angered the one behind her. She cringed, preparing for a blow.

"Were you trying to kill yourself or me?" he demanded incredulously. Having slid his sword beneath a strap on his saddlebag, he captured her jaw and angled her head back so that she was forced to meet his gaze.

The strength in his fingertips astounded her. She realized he could break her neck without calling upon even a portion of his power. A familiar terror rose up in her and seized control of her muscles. *His motives for saving her could not be pure. No man was that noble.*

She gained her freedom by sliding abruptly from the saddle. Unmindful of her bruised knees, she scrambled up again, deaf to the warrior's command that she stop. The dry grasses pricked her feet like a thousand needles. She could not understand why it pained her so to run, but her usual speed was hindered.

She felt only dismay, not surprise, when two powerful arms snatched her from behind and lifted her off her feet.

She kicked him mightily, making painful contact with his armored hose. After a moment of useless struggle, she realized she was wasting her strength. Better to conserve it for a later time. She went suddenly limp.

How miserable her existence, she marveled. She'd avoided being raped by her stepfather and beaten by the prioress only to face ruin at the hands of a warrior too powerful to overcome. Again, she was at the mercy of a warrior. What she knew of such men, she had learned firsthand. They were bloodthirsty barbarians who used women ruthlessly and cast them aside. Her own mother had been raped by such a man.

"If you force me," she warned, calling upon the unique defense that had kept her chaste this long, "your member will shrivel and fall off, I swear it. I am a powerful sorceress," she added raggedly, "and you will rue the day you ever did me harm!"

# Chapter Two

A *powerful sorceress?* The girl's warning froze Luke, though not because he believed her. What indication had he given that he meant to force her? He'd just saved her life, for God's sake!

Yet her heart beat like a bird's beneath his forearm, telling him her fear was real. He relaxed his hold a bit.

"You mistake my intent, lady." He forced himself to sound calm but, in truth, he was offended. "My army awaits," he added. "Shall we return to the horse, now?"

"I won't stand trial again!" she said in a rush. "I won't!"

*Ah.* Now he understood her fear, so strong that she'd tried to stab herself with his sword. Or had she been hoping to skewer him? "There will be no trial," he reassured her. "I said so only to appease the prioress. I mean to return you to your family. Now let's return to the horse."

As the tension flowed out of her, he took advantage to swing her up and across his arms. She balked at being held like a baby, her small hands pushing at his chest.

"Your feet are burned," he rapped out, impatient with her irrational fear of him. "You shouldn't walk on them."

Her gaze widened with surprise, and he saw that her eyes were intensely green. Her hair, though sprinkled with ash, appeared to be red. Add to that her pointed chin and soot-blackened face, and she certainly looked the part of a sorceress. Of course, there was no such thing.

As he strode with her back to his horse, replacing her upon the saddle, he saw his men waiting at the edge of a forest. Even at a distance, he could discern the resentment in their postures. And no wonder, for he'd denied them rest at the priory, and now he would burden them with the need to return this girl to her family. He was beginning to regret his impulse to save her. With the deed now done, he could only wonder at the ramifications.

He mounted behind her a second time. "Sit back, lady," he warned, starting them briskly forward. She fell against his chest, as rigid as a pike.

The soldiers had paused by a stream that separated the fells from a forest.

"What now, my lord?" Sir Pierce inquired, testily.

*It would be better to distance ourselves from the priory,* Luke thought, glancing over his shoulder, yet he couldn't ask his men to ride a furlong farther. "We take our rest in these trees," he decided, nodding at the rowans on the other side.

He led the way himself, driving his horse through the rushing water.

Merry knew this forest well. It was here that she gathered raw materials for her herbal, foraging by moonlight, as her right to work in the priory gardens had been denied. Bilberries, licorice root, and Saint-John's-wort abounded here.

"I apologize for stopping so soon," said her rescuer in her ear, "but my men are weary. After a few hours' rest, we'll continue."

Merry nodded. She didn't fear that the prioress would raise an army and pursue them. Nothing short of an act of God could wrest her from a troop this large. It was now her rescuer whom she feared, yet he'd spoken more kindly, his voice as deep and resonant as the forest itself.

She recalled the name he'd given to the prioress. Luke le Noir, the right arm of the prince. His name meant, simply, Luke the Black. It was not the name of a nobleman.

Then how did he come to lead so many men? With a chorus of groans, they all dismounted. Looking weary, they stumbled

about, some collapsing onto bedrolls, others pausing first to
care for their horses. Most wore purple surcoats with a golden
emblem of a phoenix. The others were more shabbily dressed.
Vassals and mercenaries, she supposed.

Their leader dismounted also. With his feet firmly planted
on the groud, his head still topped her waist. He gave her a
quick, enigmatic look, from which she gained the feeling that
he was at a loss as to what to do with her. She looked away, cha-
grined for having called herself a sorceress. She should have
thanked him instead, only she wasn't particularly grateful.

"Your armor, my lord," announced a youth whose voice
cracked midsentence. He pulled a packhorse in his wake.

"Excellent. Fetch some water for the lady, will you?"

The flaxen-haired youth could not have been a day over fifteen. He stared up at Merry, curious to the point of being rude.

She ignored him, disliking his open stare. His cheeks were
ravaged by angry pustules common to adolescents. She thought
of a remedy that would clear his complexion within a week.

"She's only a girl," the boy determined with amazement.

Merry flicked him a patronizing look. "I'm older than you,"
she corrected him.

"Kindly fetch the water," the leader repeated, an edge to his
tone this time.

The boy stomped off, bearing a wineskin to the stream.

That left Merry to bear the warrior's scrutiny. "Show me
your feet," he requested, reaching for her right heel.

She steeled herself to endure his touch, yet it was not
unpleasant and it remained gentle. The black streaks of his eyebrows came together, and she was struck by the contrast
between his hard expression and his tender touch.

She dropped her gaze to her feet, surprised to see the blisters that ridged them. "I can't feel anything," she marveled.

"You will," he answered gravely. "What about your hands?"

She held them out for his inspection. As he cradled them on
fingers that were warm and sure, a strange thrill chased up her
arms, speeding her heart rate.

She bore welts from the ropes and four crescent punctures
on either palm, but her hands had been spared from burning.

"You may sit on the log here whilst I find a salve for your
feet. Gervaise," the captain called, summoning a squat man

who had just lain down on his bedroll. "Find a salve for this lady's burns." Turning back, he held up his arms to Merry to help her down.

Bracing her hands on his broad shoulders, she let the warrior take her weight. As he lowered her, their bodies brushed, giving her a shockingly anatomical image of his hard man's body. She sank bonelessly onto the fallen tree. For her sake, he had best be trustworthy, she considered with alarm.

The squire reappeared with the wineskin. "Water, my lord," he said, handing it to his master. He resumed his stare at Merry. "How old are you?" he inquired, picking up the dialogue where they'd left off.

"Nineteen," she said, hoping it would quell his interest.

"You're a witch, aren't you?" he persisted.

The cork popped free of the wineskin, drawing both their gazes. "I'll ask the questions," the leader said, putting an end to the boy's interrogation. He sprinkled water onto the cloth in his hands.

"What is your name, lady?" he inquired, handing Merry the wineskin.

"Merry," she said warily, taking a quick sip.

"Mary," he repeated, flicking a meaningful look at his squire. She interpreted the look to mean: *She can't be a witch with a name so devout.* She refrained from correcting his mistaken assumption.

"I'm Sir Luke le Noir, also called the Phoenix," he said. "This youth is my squire, Erin. My horse I call Suleyman. You have tallow on your face," he added, handing her the cloth.

Merry took the cloth and self-consciously wiped her cheeks, only to discover he was right. No wonder the men had looked at her so strangely.

The man Gervaise approached them, bearing an earthenware vial. "A salve for burns, my lord," he announced.

Merry eyed the vial suspiciously. "May I ask what it is?"

"Sheep's fat boiled with the rind of elder," said the man.

She had no wish to wound his pride, but it wouldn't do. "Thank you," she said, "but the fat will only inflame the burns. I'll look to them myself."

Puffing out his chest, Gervaise glanced at his lord for instruction.

"Go and take your rest, Gervaise," said the Phoenix evenly. Only the coolness of his tone betrayed his irritation.

Discomfited, Merry continued to scrub her face.

"Erin," the warrior added, addressing his squire, "find my shin and knee guards, if you will."

The boy began pulling armor off the packhorse. It crashed to the ground, accoutrements spilling in all directions. Merry sensed rather than saw the Phoenix stiffen.

"Have I got the soot off?" she asked Luke to save the boy from a scolding.

His perusal was courteous, yet unnerving. "Not quite," he said, holding out his hand. "May I?"

She relinquished the towel without realizing that he meant to scrub her face himself. Before she could scoot away, he seized her chin in a firm grasp and ran the cloth along her nose and under her lip. Merry held her breath until her lungs ached.

His eyes were the color of a stream, she realized, a clear brown hue, flecked with gold. The lashes that rimmed those eyes were long and thick, the same shiny black as his hair, which he kept shorn. His straight nose and square chin were ruthlessly masculine. She admitted with reluctance that he was interesting to look at.

Erasing the last black smudge from the young woman's face, Luke realized he had overlooked her beauty. True, her nose had an impudent tilt and was dusted with freckles; her face was narrow and her chin pointed. But her deep green eyes were appealing, as was the curve of her lips. He found her an odd combination of puckish and sensual.

Erin, who was laying chunks of armor on the log beside him, also noticed the color of her eyes. "I've heard witches have green eyes," he volunteered, leaning forward to regard her.

The girl went rigid at his observation. "I know of an herb that will cleanse those pustules from your face," she said in a biting tone.

Erin reared back, clearly mortified that she had pointed out his flaw. "Mind your own business!" he snapped, scowling and turning away.

"Just so," muttered the girl, her cheeks tinged pink.

Impressed with strength of character, Luke kept his mouth

shut. Erin had deserved a reprimand for his rudeness. "Take your rest," he instructed his squire. "I'll manage the armor on my own."

The boy turned full circle and sighed. "I can't find your other knee guard, lord," he admitted, hanging his head.

"Look around for it," Luke instructed.

As Erin retraced his footsteps, scuffling about in the dry leaves, Luke went to put the towel away. A sound like the cry of an infant had them both spinning about. A small animal streaked through the undergrowth and bounded onto the lady's lap, causing her to burst into delighted laughter.

Luke felt as if he'd been hit with the flat side of a sword. The music of her laughter stunned him. He'd never heard anything so provocative.

"Kit!" she exclaimed, kissing the black cat between its ears. "You found me!"

The animal's purr set the forest to vibrating.

"Is this your cat?" It was a stupid question, but he'd yet to recover.

"I'm his mistress," she corrected him. "Kit adopted me."

Luke watched her as she stroked the cat from head to tail. A disturbing thought flashed across his mind. How many nuns owned cats, anyway?

Running a hand through his hair, he sought his wits. Of course she wasn't a witch. She was an innocent woman who needed to be escorted to safety. The sooner he could do that, the sooner he could accomplish his mission and return to Arundel to be with his dying grandfather.

"Tell where you're from, lady, so I can take you home," he commanded, all business again.

She stroked her cat, stubbornly silent.

A tickle of alarm skittered through him. "You must have a home," he prodded.

"I had one," she finally said, "but they won't want me back."

"They who?" he pressed, glancing at Erin, who peered beneath the log for the missing knee guard. "Your family?"

She nodded, a frown creasing her forehead.

Sensitive to her sudden despondency, Luke asked gently, "How long has it been since they've seen you?"

"Three years."

"Much can change in three years," he offered, thinking she only needed reassurance.

She raised her eyes to him then, and he nearly took a step back at the fury blazing in them. "You ought to have let me burn!" she suddenly exclaimed. " 'Twould have been better for everyone if I'd died!" She bolted off the log with her cat, running to God-knew-where.

She hadn't taken five steps when she dropped the animal with a cry and crumpled to the earth, rocking back and forth over her injured feet. The cat returned to comfort her.

Luke and his squire shared a look of consternation. One minute the lady seemed out of her mind, the next in need of rescuing. Bent over as she was, Luke couldn't help but pity her.

"Mary," he said, bending at the knee to hunker beside her. "Perhaps you should put your feet in the stream."

When she looked at him, he was glad to see she wasn't crying. "My name isn't Mary," she said, her mouth curving into a bitter smile. "I wasn't named for the blessed virgin."

"What then?" he asked, thinking she had lied.

" 'Tis Merry, as in joyful." Her eyebrows took on a tragic tilt that made his stomach cramp.

He hesitated, remembering the beauty of her laughter. "Then I must contrive to make you smile again," he heard himself say. The offer startled him, given all that he had done for her already. *Jesu,* what was he thinking making such a foolish promise?

"I would like to put my feet in the stream now," she begged, betraying the pain she doubtless suffered.

He held his arms out to her, and she went to him with wary trust. Though exhaustion tugged at him, Luke found it scarcely taxed his strength to lift her slender form.

He picked his way around the sleeping men and headed for the stream where sunlight danced on the running water. The cat followed close behind.

Wading into the shallows, Luke placed his charge onto a sun-warmed boulder where she slipped her feet into the water. A hissing sound escaped her.

"Better or worse?" he asked, feeling for her.

"Better," she said, looking up. Amazingly, her eyes turned even greener as they absorbed the color of the forest.

"Are you hungry?" he asked, thinking she would resemble a wood sprite if she shed the black habit.

Merry shook her head, no. Her cat paced back and forth on the shore, as if wondering how to join her without wetting its paws.

Luke scraped a palm over his stubbled jaw. He was at a loss as to what to do now. His body demanded sleep, yet it seemed unwise of him to leave her in her present state.

"Go and take your rest," she invited, giving the appearance of calm. "I will sit and tend my feet. 'Tisn't as though I can run from you," she added mocking herself.

Weariness rushed through him, telling him he would be useless to his soldiers if he didn't seize this reprieve.

He gestured toward the bank. "I'll sleep close by," he answered.

She had already dismissed him, giving him her shoulder.

Luke called his squire away from his search. "Take your rest, Erin."

"But I still can't find the knee guard, sire."

"Then it's gone. You must have dropped it at the priory." He found his cloak and shook it out at the foot of an elm. Removing his boots, he left them to dry. Suppressing a moan for his aching muscles, he lay down on the makeshift bed, notched his hands behind his head and took one last look at Merry.

The cat had performed a marvelous leap and was now sitting in her lap. She held her pet, unmoving. Luke suffered a moment's qualm that something bad would happen if he closed his eyes. But the weight of his lids was too much to fight. He gave in to his exhaustion, his eyes falling shut.

Merry waited for the sun to thaw the place in her heart that had been frozen for weeks, possibly years. She called the entity despair. Mother Agnes would have said 'twas Satan's seed, planted in her on the night the devil took her soul.

A vision of Ferguson panting over her helpless mother flashed through Merry's mind.

Perhaps Agnes was right. Not even the sun could thaw her.

Neither could the smooth glide of Kit's fur soothe her soul. And yet, circumstances seemed to have turned in her favor.

Had she truly been rescued? By a man with no ulterior motive than to see her safely home?

She turned her head to look at him. It was nigh impossible to look away. His face was nearly exotic with its black brows, sharp cheekbones, and blade of a nose. She marveled that a man could look so . . . so manly and be so kind. *Then I must contrive to make you smile again,* he'd said.

Impossible. She'd forgotten how to smile.

Her gaze drifted down his warrior's body, over the broad, muscular chest, the plane of his abdomen, toward his powerful thighs. With his arms locked behind his head, his padded shirt had ridden up, leaving the swell of his manhood clearly delineated, even in mailed chausses.

Merry wrenched her gaze away, mortified that she had looked at him *there*. What did she think, that he wouldn't have the same weapon as other men?

It took several steadying breaths to clear her mind. What if he did take her home as he'd promised? What then?

For a moment, she indulged in the fantasy that her family would welcome her back. Her mother, Jeanette, would run to her with open arms; the peasants would swarm her with welcoming smiles. Her heart clutched with regret.

Nay, they wouldn't want her back, given what she'd been—a girl mad with grief. Ferguson had killed her father and the world had turned against her. Only Sarah, the local healer, had known what to do with her. She'd taken Merry under her care, making her an apprentice to her trade. And Merry discovered her gift for curing ills.

She'd found a reason to go on living.

All might have ended well, had it ended there. After two years of tyranny, Ferguson was gone, killed by her mother as he battled her sister's husband, the Slayer. Her family had survived his desecration. Hope for happiness returned.

But then, without any discernable cause, the infants began to die at Heathersgill. Peasants and villains turned their grief-filled eyes on Sarah and Merry, crying, "Witch!" and demanding justice.

If Merry's mother and sister, Clarise, hadn't whisked her to Mount Grace, she might have been found a witch sooner.

Merry roused herself from painful memories. The cat had fallen asleep on her lap. The heat of his fur, in combination with her black robes, was heating her scorched skin. She leaned over the water, craving its coolness.

The sight of her reflection appalled her.

Had her hair turned gray overnight?

Nay, it was sprinkled with ash, making her look like an old lady.

She glanced at the sleeping men. Who would notice if she slipped into the water and bathed?

Setting a disgruntled Kit beside her, she peeled off her nun's habit, leaving on the linen shift beneath. She scooted to the edge of the boulder, slipped in, and gasped. The cold made her bones ache. Her feet touched the pebbled bottom, and she winced.

After a moment, she grew accustomed to the temperature and let the current sweep her into deeper waters. She paddled toward the opposite shore where soapwort grew in clumps. Kit called her back, his tail twitching nervously.

Snapping off a stalk of soapwort, she crushed it in her hand, releasing the herb's properties, which she rubbed into her scalp, working the lather through her plaits as she unwound them.

This was more than a physical cleansing, she acknowledged. It was a cleansing of the spirit. The past was behind her. God willing, she would start her life anew.

She submerged herself for a final rinse.

From his perch on the boulder, Kit watched her disappear. He gave a cry of distress so loud the warrior on shore lurched to wakefulness.

# Chapter Three

LUKE stared at the spot where he'd left the woman. The cat stood alone, its back arched and bristling. Only the girl's robes remained in a black heap.

Stifling a shout, Luke leapt to his feet and splashed into the shallows, causing Kit to hiss at him and leap away. He raked his gaze up and down the shoreline. There was no sign at all of Merry.

Christ's toes, what had he been thinking to leave the lady alone? Already she had expressed a will to die. Now it seemed that she had drowned herself!

It was then he saw it: a carpet of bubbles floating on the water's surface some distance downstream. He cursed and floundered toward the sign, falling into deeper waters as the bottom gave away. Half swimming, half running, he arrived at the place where Merry had gone under. In that same instant, her head burst to the surface, her hair streaming into her eyes.

He must have startled her, for with a garbled cry she threw herself away from him.

"Hold, lady!" he called, catching one of her sleeves. He was immensely relieved to find her alive. He held her firmly, lest she slip beneath the water again.

She struggled to free herself, her eyes enormous.

"Be still, lady," he ordered her. "You will not take your life this way."

"Take my life!" she exclaimed, regarding him with amazement. "I'm not drowning myself; I'm washing!"

*Washing!* He realized she was serious, for there were still suds in her blazing, red hair. He knew an urge to shake her until her teeth rattled. "The current is strong here," he pointed out. "You could easily drown."

"Nonsense. I've swum here many times," she retorted.

He looked around. "Here?" He was certain she was lying. "Were you not confined to the priory?" The current threatened to carry her away again, and he grabbed her more firmly.

"Release me!" she cried.

Hearing panic in her voice, he put both hands into the air. "I'm trying to help you!" he explained, marveling at the fact that he was standing in the middle of a running stream holding a senseless conversation. A quick peek over his shoulders assured him that his men were sleeping.

"I am not in need of helping, thank you. I swim quite well." She rolled away from him, cutting lithely through the water. He could see she'd had plenty of practice. He could also see that she wore only her linen shift, and it was nearly transparent.

"You left the convent just to swim here?" Not only was their conversation senseless, she was practically naked.

"Only when the moon was full," she disconcerted him by answering. "Look." She pointed toward the shoreline. "There are herbs that grow here. I can use them for all sorts of things."

With an urge to clap a hand to his forehead, Luke glanced at the greenery where she pointed and realized she was serious. It was madness, a girl prowling about under a full moon in search of herbs. No wonder she was thought a witch! "What sorts of things?" he asked, fearing the worst.

"Medicines," she said. "The sisters came to me when they were ill." She treaded water before him, her white shift shimmering around her.

She struck him, then, as a mad sort of angel.

"You should come ashore now," he said, angry now that his sleep had been interrupted for naught. "Come, before you catch chill." He seized her hand and towed her along behind him, ignoring her attempts to pull free. He couldn't help but notice how tiny her hand was, how easy it was to overcome her resistance.

As they neared the boulder, he released her. She reached for the black habit she'd left behind and clutched it to her chest, belatedly realizing her state of undress.

Luke continued ashore, giving her time to cover what she'd unknowingly revealed. A cry of pain had him spinning around. He was treated to a glimpse of a perfectly rounded bottom before she turned and hastily sat.

"I'm all right!" she cried, coloring fiercely. She'd sat so quickly that the habit slipped sideways and now he was looking at one perfect pink nipple, clearly outlined through her sodden bodice. To think that the black homespun had concealed such perfection!

The breath tangled in Luke's throat. He ripped his gaze away and marched blindly ashore, stopping before the bundles of provisions that littered the ground. "Are you hungry?" he asked, seeing the food.

"I suppose."

He fetched a couple of rolls and a wedge of cheese and brought them to her. Seating himself on a boulder opposite her, he was relieved to find her swathed from neck to ankle in the nun's habit. At the same time he was perversely disappointed.

She began to eat, so he waited, choosing his timing with care. As the minutes passed, he fancied he could feel the grains of time slipping through his fingers. He had so little of it left and so much work to do. Meanwhile, his grandfather lay dying.

"Where do you live, Merry?" He prayed she would tell him this time. "Your family will want to know you're safe."

"They've not inquired about my welfare these last three years."

Her cool reply made him uneasy. "Mayhap the prioress kept their letters," he suggested.

She shrugged her narrow shoulders, unconvinced.

"Tell me where to take you," he insisted. "I'll deliver you anywhere you like."

She chewed so long he feared he would be stuck with her forever. "Take me to Heathersgill then," she finally said, her tone resigned.

"Is that your home, Heathersgill?"

"Aye."

"Where is it?" He thought it might be easier to pull teeth.

"It lies north of here and slightly east."

"Then it's close," he guessed, sounding—to his own ears—hopeful.

"Several hours' ride, I believe. What is it you do?" She shift-ed the conversation abruptly to him, fixing him with her frank, green gaze. "You said you were the prince's right arm."

"I serve His Majesty, Prince Henry," he acknowledged.

"Plantagenet?" She frowned at him. "But he's Matilda's son. Why isn't the king's own son the prince?"

Her question betrayed her cloistered existence. "Eustace died eight months ago," he explained. "He choked on a chick-en bone."

To his amazement, her eyes clouded with regret. "So . . . " she paused, giving herself time to assimilate new facts, "what do you do for Henry, exactly?"

He didn't want to discuss his present mission. "I'm an army captain. I keep the peace," he said tersely.

"I see." Her gaze skittered over him, taking him all in.

Her innocent awareness of him caused Luke to draw a breath. He was reminded of how she looked beneath that ugly habit. His mind went completely and utterly blank, save for the memory of her pink nipple thrusting out of the fabric of her shift.

"Is there a war?" Her eyebrows, darker than her hair, flexed with worry.

He recalled himself. "Not a war. Just various pockets of resistance. I have much to do," he added, taking command of the conversation—and his errant mind, "and I must therefore get you swiftly home. Does your father live?"

He had his reasons for asking, but seeing her stricken expression, he was instantly sorry he had.

"Nay," she said, on a heartbroken note.

"Your mother?" he pressed more gently.

"She dwells at Heathersgill. The last I knew she was going to wed a man named Roger. Sir Roger," she corrected herself. "He's the seneschal of Heathersgill."

"Then you have an overlord." He jumped on the informa-tion. "Who is he?"

By the look on her face, it wasn't someone she cared for overmuch. "My sister's husband," she drawled with distaste. "The Slayer, they call him."

Luke sat straighter. "The Slayer of Helmesly?" He couldn't hide his surprise. "Christian de la Croix is your brother-in-law?"

She gave him a look that said she wasn't happy about it.

"I met the man at Dunstable," he admitted, "where the barons gathered to protest the . . . " he'd almost mentioned his unpleasant duties.

"The what?" she pressed, eyes alert.

"The destruction of adulterines," he finished, incapable of lying.

"What are those?"

He groaned inwardly. "Structures built without the sanction of the crown," he said tersely. "Perhaps you should go to your sister for protection," he added. "I'll take you to Helmesly even though it's farther out of my way." He remembered the Slayer well. Big and fierce, with hair down to his shoulders, he was just the man to protect Merry from the persecution she would now inevitably face.

"Helmesly!" She uttered the word like a curse. "Nay, I'll not go there!"

Her vehemence gave him pause. "Why not, if your sister lives there?"

She looked down into the water, reflecting on painful memories if the look on her face was any indication. "The Slayer isn't likely to welcome me," she admitted.

Luke's eyes narrowed. "What cause did you give him?"

She glanced at him sharply, and he was struck by how witchy she looked with her mouth pinched tight. "I cursed his manhood on the day that he wed my elder sister."

Her confession did not shock him; after all, she'd cursed him in a similar fashion.

"I wanted him to think twice ere he struck my sister," she explained.

It was painfully clear that Merry had witnessed an excess of violence in her short life. He sought to reassure her now. "The Slayer doesn't beat his lady," he replied. "I spoke to the man at length. He talked lovingly of his wife and his children also. He has three of them now, which would indicate that he treats your sister well," he added, offering her a smile.

She put a hand up as if repelled by the thought of propagation. "Just take me to Heathersgill," she begged.

"You'd be safer at Helmesly."

An awareness entered her gaze. "What has safety to do with it?"

She was too perceptive to mislead in any convincing way. Luke decided to be frank with her. "The prioress may send a party looking for you," he admitted. "I had no right to steal you from a priory. The Church will likely want you back."

The color leeched slowly from her cheeks, making him regret his decision to tell her. He cast about for reassurances.

"You gave the prioress your name," she recalled. "Won't that get you into trouble?"

She was worried for *his* sake! The realization made her suddenly quite likable. He shook his head at her. " 'Tis you who must be kept safe. I'll not lie to you, lady. You will need to stay behind thick walls for some time to come—long enough for the prioress to forget you. Is it true you tried to kill her?" He couldn't decide if she was capable of outright murder or not.

Her mouth grew pinched again. "If I had meant to kill her, she would be dead," she answered, feeding a crumb to her cat. "She beat a novice to death with her whip," she added, "for no good reason."

He wasn't surprised to learn of the prioress's cruelty. It was Merry's toughness that impressed him. She seemed so vulnerable, so fine-boned and bedraggled with wet hair straggling down her back. And yet she'd taken on the prioress to defend her sisters. Again, she struck him as an angel gone mad.

"You would be safer at Helmesly," he reiterated. Suddenly he wanted to be *certain* nothing bad would happen to her.

But she shook her head refusing him. "I won't go," she said.

He considered taking her there by force then dismissed the notion with a sigh. Helmesly was farther out of his way, and he and his men were already pressed for time. To Heathersgill it was then. Her mother would have to defend her as best she could.

"As you will," he said, pushing to his feet. "We need to leave soon. You'll catch chill if you travel in that," he added, seizing his chance to rid her of the ugly black habit. He marched toward his sleeping squire to shake him awake.

Merry looked on, wary of the captain's intent. Erin's dark glower assured her that he wasn't pleased with whatever his lord was asking. He dragged himself up and fetched a bundle from his horse, handing it reluctantly over.

Sir Pierce came up on one elbow and shook his leonine head. "Shall I rouse the men, my lord?" he inquired groggily.

"Aye, sergeant. Instruct them to eat. We'll be leaving shortly."

"My lord," the man reminded his leader, "Iversly is but an hour or two northwest of here."

"We're taking the lady to Heathersgill," Sir Luke retorted, his tone brooking no argument. He returned to Merry bearing Erin's clothing. " 'Tis best for your feet if you go without shoes or hose," he advised, handing her the bundle.

Merry looked at the clothing, then back at him. The bank was now astir with soldiers, yawning and stretching.

Guessing her quandary, the Phoenix gestured for her to wait. He fetched his cloak from the shore and, shaking the leaves from it, held it up as a screen.

Merry eyed the expansive curtain, uncertain whether it concealed her completely or not.

"Kindly hurry," the leader prompted.

His veiled impatience caused her to strip without argument. For an electrifying moment, she sat completely naked on the rock. In three years, she had never been more aware of her femininity. She tunneled into the tunic, then struggled to don the boy's braies without dragging them through water.

"Done," she said, tugging the laces about her slender hips.

Sir Luke lowered the cloak and assessed her transformation. By the angle of his eyebrows, she guessed she looked nothing short of ludicrous. He kept his opinion to himself, however, turning away to stamp his feet into his boots.

"Ready to mount?" he asked briskly.

She reached for her balled, wet clothing.

"Throw them in the stream," he instructed, with a gleam in his eyes. "You won't be needing them."

With relish, Merry hurled habit and shift into the stream.

Turning back, she found a smile hovering on the warrior's lips. "Freedom," he murmured, as though guessing her satisfaction.

She *did* feel a sudden sense of exhilaration. In fact, she felt dangerously liberated in boy's clothing as the warrior lifted her in his arms. Through his padded shirt, she could feel every dense muscle of his chest and the flexing of his arms beneath her. His shoulders were impossibly wide, his neck too thick to span with both her hands together.

The mewling of her cat interrupted her inspection. "Oh, Kit!" she cried, peering over the captain's shoulder. "He wants to come with us."

The captain ignored her plea. Placing her firmly in the saddle, he strode away, but not before glancing once at the cat. Taking heart, Merry waited as he toured the camp and rapped out orders.

"Please, can we bring my cat?" she asked again, as he prepared to mount. "I'll carry him in my lap. He won't be any trouble; I swear it."

His hand was already on the pommel. He met her gaze with an inscrutable look.

"Please?" she repeated, sensing his capitulation.

He bent over and scooped Kit up, depositing him in her lap. Swinging into the saddle, he prodded Suleyman into a walk.

Despite Merry's assurances, the cat reacted in terror, sinking its claws into her forearm. "Ouch!" she cried, as the blood welled up quickly.

A hand seized Kit by the scruff and dropped him into a saddlebag. One tug on the drawstring and his head disappeared.

Merry didn't know whether to thank him or take offense.

Holding up her wrist, Sir Luke examined the wound on her forearm. "He's half wild," he uttered, disapprovingly. "You should have left him behind."

To her shock, he lifted her punctured flesh to his lips and sucked the upwelling blood from it. The hot suction of his mouth left her speechless. He released her almost at once, and she sensed by the sudden tension in him that he hadn't meant to do that. Glancing down at her arm where the blood still oozed, she fancied she could see the place where his lips had burned her skin.

The male species had long been a mystery to Merry. She assigned his strange impulse to the savagery characteristic of all warriors. Fortunately for her, this particular warrior was more disciplined than most. Still, it would pay to keep wary, lest he fall prey to his baser instincts again.

Looking up, she realized they had left the forest to cross the undulating moors. Out in the open, the sun beat down on their heads. Only the breeze, which brushed the wild grasses around them, hinted at the cooler weather to come.

Relaxing moment by moment, with no further discourse between them, Merry took to admiring the plants and the flowering shrubs about them. Sarah had taught her the properties of most: Heather, tansy, and milk parsley; carrot weed, succory, and wild clary—all modestly displayed on these lonely fells.

She found herself imagining how her family would receive her and whether the past would be forgiven. Suddenly she realized she had put her back against the man behind her. She stiffened slightly, then relaxed bit by bit, putting faith in the wary trust she felt toward him. No longer did she fear he might ravish her. Other than the brief moment when he had put his mouth on her forearm, he'd behaved with perfect propriety. Frowning, she was forced to rethink her opinion of men—warring men in particular.

In the few hours that she'd known him, the Phoenix had earned her grudging respect. He'd saved her life, and she had yet to thank him for that, though she had no wish to break the peaceful lull to do so now. He'd remained courteous to her throughout the morning, despite the fact that she'd threatened his manhood. And now he was going out of his way to deliver her safely home.

Never in her life had she imagined such a man existed: a chivalrous warrior. Her father had been a kind man, but he had been a scholar, not a fighting man. Sir Luke, on the other hand, belonged to a breed of men she'd associated with Ferguson: Men who shed blood for the sport of it, men who held no moral code higher than the fulfillment of their own lusts.

Yet other than the fact that he was trained to fight, Sir Luke bore little similarity to Ferguson. Whereas Ferguson had been crude and unrestrained, the captain was dignified and disciplined. Indeed, though he'd yet to don his armor, he seemed cloaked in nobility; but with a name like his, he was not a nobleman. How, she wondered, had he risen to such rank?

Her gaze drifted left and right, scrutinizing the soldiers traveling with them. Depending on the terrain, they rode two or three abreast, their movements artfully choreographed. Their armor gleamed, demonstrating pride of ownership. Weapons bristled from their backs and saddlebags. Two smart banners snapped at the head of the retinue, one with the device of the royal crown, the other displaying a golden phoenix on a purple field.

Sir Luke was clearly a fine military leader, so good as to become the right hand of the prince.

"Why do they call you the Phoenix?" she inquired, seeking a tactful way to ask her questions.

His rich voice rumbled in her ear, giving rise to a pleasant shiver. "I pulled Prince Henry and his brother from a fire," he said matter-of-factly.

*Ah,* she thought, adding the missing pieces. The phoenix was a bird that rose from its own ashes into new life. The prince must have felt he owed Sir Luke a debt. "Is that how you came to lead so many men?" she asked.

"In part. My grandfather is the earl of Arundel." This was said without a drop of arrogance.

She considered that a moment. "But you haven't the name of a nobleman," she blurted, wincing at her lack of tact. She hoped he wouldn't take offense.

"Is that how you judge nobility," he countered, "by one's name?"

To her relief he sounded unperturbed. "I suppose it shouldn't be so," she acknowledged, refusing to prod him further. Nor did he assuage her curiosity.

Disappointed, she sought to focus on her environment again, yet she couldn't seem to shake her awareness of the man behind her. His long limbs surrounded her like a citadel. His large, square hands gripped the reins loosely but with confidence. She was surprised to find his fingers sensitive in appearance, as if he might carry a stringed instrument in place of a sword.

Kit gave a pitiful mewl, drawing Merry's gaze to the saddlebag. "He's hot," she guessed. "Can we not let him out?"

"So he can scratch you again?" Nonetheless, Sir Luke loosened the drawstring, and the cat's head popped free. Kit stared at the landscape with a look of bewilderment but made no effort to struggle free. After a moment, he seemed to settle in, content to be a passenger.

They'd begun their ascent into the Cleveland Hills, and suddenly there was much to catch the eye. The land rose sharply on all sides, quilted in colorful flowers, and studded with misshapen rocks. Here and there, a yew tree cast its branches upward as if pleading for rain. A hawk tested the currents of a flawless sky, its wings scarcely moving. Merry took a deep breath, seeking the scent of her home. Her home—a place where no one would welcome her, save perhaps her younger sister.

Unbeknownst to her, the long strands of her hair feathered Luke's shoulders and caressed his face. Inhaling her clean, herbal fragrance, it was impossible not to think of her as a woman. Her small, supple body fitted perfectly against the curve of his. Luke had tried not to notice how sweetly rounded her shoulders were, how enticingly her breasts jiggled beneath Erin's tunic. By the stream, she'd looked so feminine in his squire's attire that he'd known a bizarre urge to kidnap her and keep her for himself.

For no reason that he could name, she appealed to him. He could not decipher why, exactly, for she was everything he was not: impulsive, illogical, and unrestrained. Yet there was something about her that tugged at him—her vulnerability, perhaps. Whatever the reason, his interest in the lady dismayed him, for in six months time he would be wed.

His thoughts ought to be entirely of his betrothed, Amalie. Yet the lady failed to rouse his ardor or stir his imagination. It wasn't that his betrothed was unattractive—quite the contrary. Many a noble had called her exquisite, expressing envy over Luke's good fortune. Yet Amalie was fair, with pale blue eyes and flaxen hair. In contrast to the woman before him, she seemed colorless. Or was it her haughty demeanor that gave him that perception?

While he admired Amalie's regal grace, she had never interested him, sexually. He'd assured himself that lust had no place in matrimony. He was a cerebral male, not a man driven by his appetites. There were more important reasons for their betrothal: things like power, land, security.

Yet, experiencing the brushstroke of desire for a woman he scarcely knew, Luke now regretted that his marriage bed would be cold.

The woman before him would never know of his attraction for her—he was scarcely willing to acknowledge it to himself. Yet he'd acted out of character already, putting his mouth to her forearm. The impulse had caught him utterly by surprise. One moment, he'd been looking at the drop of blood on her flawless skin, the next he was tasting it, as though driven by some primal impulse to drink her. He would pretend it never happened. Certainly, it wouldn't happen again.

She was a strange creature, nothing like the ladies of the court whom he truly ought to admire. Lifting her freckled nose to the air, she scented it in the same way that her cat did. Her fascination for plants and shrubs puzzled him. Tall plants, short plants, scrappy and unadorned plants—all of them drew her gaze to such a degree that she pressed her breast against his forearm, straining for a better look. Against his will, he imagined the weight of that breast filling the palm of his hand.

Her sudden lurch in the saddle startled him. She had reached out, groping for a tree branch as they passed beneath its shade. She might have been snatched from the saddle had Luke not caught her back. "*Jesu,* lady, what are you doing?" he exclaimed.

"Getting berries." She held up her catch for his inspection. Splitting the skin of a berry with her thumbnail, she touched it to the tip of her tongue.

Luke knocked it from her hand and sent it flying.

"Whatever did you do that for?" she demanded, whipping about.

"Do you mean to poison yourself?"

Understanding softened her outraged glare. " 'Twas meant to soothe the burns on my feet," she explained, turning back, her shoulders drooping.

He'd forgotten about the burns, so little had she complained. Feeling as unsettled as he had in the stream, Luke turned his mount around and returned to the tree.

"Thank you," she said in a subdued voice as she plucked another bunch.

She split the skin again. This time, Luke held the mount still while she applied the juice to her soles. She had to lean against him to do so, and he gave into the temptation to peek down the front of her gaping tunic.

The slope of her high, white breasts was nearly his undoing. She moved to the left foot, forbearing comment on the blisters rising there.

"Does it pain you yet?" he asked, ignoring the stirring in his loins.

"Aye," she said simply.

Her bravery impressed him. He wished he knew what comfort to offer.

"Done," she said, tossing down the pits and wiping her fingers on his squire's braies.

With relief, Luke kicked his mount into a trot, hastening to catch up with the others before he truly lost his senses.

The closer they came to the top of the hill, the lower the sun sank behind them, so that their shadows beat them to the ridge.

IT was nightfall when they arrived at Heathersgill. Its single tower loomed black against a cobalt sky. The sun had dropped into the valley, giving way to an autumn chill that leaked from the shadows and spread insidiously.

Twin torches illumined the castle's outer gate. Yet the road leading up to the gate was treacherous. Because of its steep ascent, Merry practically sat in Sir Luke's lap, unable to put even a finger's width between them.

The men had fallen silent as they guided their mounts in single file behind their leader. They hugged the inside of the road, fearing that a misplaced hoof might send a man plummeting to his death. As they came to what appeared to be the last bend, a shout went up near the end of the retinue, followed by a terrified whinny.

Luke brought his horse up short and leapt from the saddle. Merry lost sight of him as he sidled his way down rank and file to investigate.

She pricked her ears, catching snatches of conversation, spoken in accents of alarm. Kit gave a frightened yowl and she reached back to stroke his head, empathetic to his fear. By the time the Phoenix rejoined her, she deduced that a horse had taken a plunge off the side of the trail.

" 'Twas a packhorse," he confirmed, nudging her forward to make room in the saddle.

To her sensitive ears, he sounded angry. "Is it dead?" she asked, feeling somehow to blame. After all, Heathersgill was her home.

"I believe so. There are no sounds coming from below."

An unquiet feeling settled over her. What if the horse's death were a sign to her? A warning not to return? She felt her premonitions stir. At the same time, it became harder to breathe. Without fully realizing it, she shrank against the captain's broad chest, gaining solace from his warmth.

Too soon for her uncertain state of mind, they arrived at the gate where the torches had died to a mere whimper.

"Hail the gatehouse!" Sir Luke called. His assured voice echoed off the stone wall and into the valley behind them.

A taper flared to life, and a face appeared in the window slit. Merry recognized the irascible gatekeeper who had always controlled the gates. After her father's death, Edward had played traitor to keep his own head. He'd then guarded the gates for Ferguson. How he'd retained his position was something Merry failed to comprehend. She detested the man for bowing to her stepfather, and Edward returned the sentiment unabashedly.

"Who are you?" he growled now, squinting at the army below.

"My name is Luke le Noir. I would speak with your mistress right away."

Edward fastened his gaze on Merry. "Be that you, witch?" he bellowed in a surly tone.

The question prompted a startled silence, then a murmuring among the troops. Merry felt Luke's thighs tense, though his voice betrayed little agitation when he repeated his request for audience with the mistress of Heathersgill.

The gatekeeper made a face, then disappeared from view, presumably to fetch Merry's mother. Merry herself struggled for air. Her lungs seemed suddenly too tight to expand. She heard herself wheeze.

"Are you well, lady?" The Phoenix put a hand on her shoulder.

"Aye," she choked, but she was not well. Her heart hammered in her rib cage. Her palms felt sweaty. Would her mother welcome her home? Where would she go if she were not wanted here?

They waited for what seemed an eternity. Then suddenly the sound of running feet could be heard over the labored breathing of horses. The crossbar grated and the gates groaned inward, revealing nothing at first but a black rectangle.

Then a woman rushed into the torchlight, accompanied by a man with silver curls and an arm in a sling.

Luke knew the woman's identity by her resemblance to Merry. She wore her nightclothes already, her long chestnut hair falling down her back. But for the lines of worry that etched her face, she might have been Merry's sister.

"Mother!" whispered the woman in front of him.

"Merry!" cried the woman, tears glinting in her deep-set eyes.

Luke dismounted. Mindful of propriety, he lifted Merry from the saddle and put her on her feet, helping her to limp forward.

"Oh, Merry!" the woman cried again, stepping forward to throw her arms about her daughter. "My dear, you should not have come here," she added, whispering these words fervently in her daughter's ear.

Luke saw his young charge stiffen at the warning. His gaze then slid to the man who'd accompanied Merry's mother. The scarred warrior bore no resemblance to Merry. His face was a map of war wounds, including a scar by his mouth that gave him a perpetual smile. The Slayer's seneschal, Luke guessed, hailing him. "Luke le Noir," he introduced himself.

"I thought so," the man said heartily. "I remember you from Dunstable. I'm Sir Roger de Saintonge, husband of this lady and vassal to the Lord of Helmesley."

"The Slayer," Luke said with a smile. "I remember him well, but not you, I'm afraid."

Sir Roger nodded, as though that were a common circumstance. "You should come in," he said.

Merry's mother spoke up suddenly. "What of those who know of the reward?" she asked in a frightened voice.

Luke pricked his ears. "Reward?" he prompted.

Merry's mother released her daughter long enough to sketch him a curtsy. "I am Lady Jeanette," she introduced herself. "You must be the one who helped my daughter flee. I thank you for that, but it isn't safe for her here."

"How have you heard of this already?" Luke demanded, amazed that news of Merry's escape could have reached their ears.

The woman wrung her hands together. "A messenger arrived here but an hour ago, enjoining us to look for Merry, saying she might well return to us. I presume she has got herself in trouble, though the man wouldn't say." Jeanette cast a harried glance at her daughter.

Merry stared at her mother, speechless.

Luke spoke up on her behalf. "The prioress meant to burn your daughter for a witch," he said coldly. "Surely you won't refuse her a welcome."

Lady Jeanette's eyes filled with tears. " 'Tis not that I don't want her here," she assured him, including her daughter in her desperate look. " 'Tis just that I fear for her life. The Church is so powerful, and we've such a small stronghold!" Her voice cracked on the final sentence. She seemed paralyzed with fear at the thought of justice pounding at her gates.

Sir Roger stepped forward to put an arm around his wife's shoulders.

Merry had yet to say anything. Her stricken look cut Luke to the quick. He recalled his foolish promise to make her smile again, and he could see that he was failing.

"Where is Kyndra?" she asked, startling him with her sudden question.

"Your sister dwells in York where she attends the baroness Le Burgh," her mother answered.

Merry seemed to shrink in stature. "So, she's not here," she said quietly, looking down at the ground as if the last drop of life had been leeched from her.

"What shall we do?" Lady Jeanette whispered, turning to her husband.

"We shall let them in, of course," Sir Roger answered heartily. "Tomorrow we'll decide the best course of action. Come." He took his wife's hand in his one good hand and tipped his head, gesturing for Luke and Merry to follow. "Your men are also welcome," he added, "though our garrison is small."

With a rush of tenderness he refused to analyze, Luke lifted Merry off her feet, feeling tension in her small body as he placed her on the saddle. Taking up the reins, he walked his mount through the gates of Heathersgill.

Two emotions warred within him. The first was concern for Merry's fate and the mention of a reward for her capture. The second was sheer frustration. He had gone out of his way to return the lady to her home, leaving himself less time to complete his final mission. Now he had doubts that Merry's family would even take her off his hands. What would he do with her then?

At this rate, his grandfather would die ere he ever made it home.

# Chapter Four

LUKE swiped his face with a weary hand. Under lids that grated his eyeballs every time he blinked, he returned the gaze of the man sitting across from him at the writing table. Sir Roger's gray eyes were not without sympathy.

They sat, just the two of them, in a small solar situated off the great hall. After a quick repast of smoked ham and cheese in the company of Merry's family, Sir Roger had pulled Luke away, urging him to sample his best spiced wine. Eager to get the evening over with, Luke had willingly agreed.

Now he wished he hadn't. Sir Roger felt obliged to relate the tragic history of Merry's life. Luke learned that her childhood had been cut short by the siege of a Scot named Ferguson, a savage who slew her father and forced her mother into wedlock. Lady Jeanette, not surprisingly, had lapsed into a state of temporary madness, and Merry seemed to do so as well. She became like a wild animal, Sir Roger explained, wearing rags, keeping herself in filth, and heaping curses on any who confronted her, men especially.

"There was a woman who lived in the hills," added the knight, "a cunningwoman with knowledge of healing. She was the only one who could tame Merry. The girl had taken an interest in the woman's art, so Sarah made her an apprentice to her trade. The arrangement became more of a curse than a blessing when Merry learned that herbs could be used for harm. She tried several times to poison Ferguson, thereby planting the seeds of her later reputation."

The knight heaved a sigh. "Eventually, the Scot was laid low by my wife, Jeanette, who stabbed him in the neck whilst he did battle with the Slayer. Merry might have become whole as her mother did, but her fate was then linked to Sarah's, and when babes began to die at Heathersgill, both of them were blamed for the scourge. My wife removed Merry to Mount Grace, thus saving her from trial, but Sarah was not so fortunate. She was tried as a witch and drowned.

"It was hoped that Merry would rediscover her peace of mind at the priory," Sir Roger reflected, splaying his fingers. "Apparently she hasn't. The Church has named her a heretic. A reward of forty marks has been offered for her return. And the peasants here bear her little love. 'Tis only a matter of time before she is betrayed."

Concern and resentment twisted through Luke. He resisted the urge to rub his temples, disliking the manner in which he was being drawn into the dilemma. "She is your kin," he heard himself say. "Take her to Helmesly where her brother-in-law can guard her. I doubt there is anyone willing to wrest her from the Slayer," he added, recalling the intimidating aspect of that warrior.

Sir Roger let out a ponderous sigh. "Aye, you're right, and I would do so this very night if several factors did not conspire against me. The first is that most of my men-at-arms have already gone to Helmesly to serve my overlord. The second is this cursed arm of mine, which prevents me from wielding a sword, for I am sadly left-handed. Finally," he leaned forward, pitching his voice to a level of confidence, "I do not dare to leave my wife alone at night. She suffers horrible dreams from which she cannot wake. Nor is she able to leave the keep without similar attacks. 'Tis a consequence of her enduring so much."

Luke struggled to keep his scorn from showing. Surely a servant could be called upon to guard the mistress from her dreams. He briefly closed his eyes and pressed his fingers to his right temple. "What do you suggest?" he asked, summoning the last dredges of his diplomatic skill. He opened his eyes and skewered the knight with a look. "Shall we claim the reward ourselves and turn the girl in?" He knew his tone was biting, but he lacked the resources to smooth it out.

Sir Roger blanched, his perpetual smile taking on a sudden downward turn. "Nay," he protested, clearly appalled that Luke would even think it. "My lady adores her daughter. She would do anything to protect her."

*Save escort her to Helmesly herself,* Luke forbore to point out. "What is it you want from me?" he demanded.

Sir Roger gave him an uneasy look. "You could escort Merry to Helmesly," came the predictable answer. "Surely she is most safe under the royal banner, whereas I can only offer her feeble protection."

"Helmesly," Luke said, with clear articulation, "lies south and east, does it not? I go north and west to Iversly." It was as polite a refusal as he could muster.

Sir Roger sighed. "Then I must admit that only three men-at-arms remain here at Heathersgill," he said, confessing a shocking state of vulnerability. "I will not leave my wife to escort her daughter. Nor can I protect Merry here. There are too many who would sooner enjoy the reward money than her company."

The slight against Merry did not go unnoticed. Luke felt a spark of indignation on her behalf. "Who will defend her," he retorted, "if not her own family?"

Sir Roger looked away, acknowledging the question with proper shame. "My liege lord will protect her," he promised, "once she is safely within his walls."

Silence fell over the cozy chamber, interrupted only by the soft crackle from the brazier. Luke sat back, his gaze drifting over the simple furnishings, the serviceable tapestry, the clean rushes on the floor. He tried to understand what had happened in this tidy little stronghold to throw a family into turmoil. How had the middle child become so estranged that even her kin wished to wash their hands of her?

A sudden vision assailed him, reminding him that he'd once been in similar straights—an outcast among his mother's people, the son of a crusader who'd gotten a Saracen woman with child. If not for the Norman grandfather who'd searched for

Luke and found him, he would likely be living in Jerusalem still, stealing for a living. In those hard times, his grandfather had been the only person to stretch out a welcoming hand. What a difference that hand had made, taking him from street urchin to tenant-in-chief to the Prince of England!

Acknowledging the difference one person could make in the life of another, Luke realized he wouldn't turn his back, no matter the inconvenience. Merry was little different from the orphans he'd plucked from various villages throughout Europe since his transformation to a life of privilege. He would help her as he had helped them, thus keeping alive the spirit of hope his grandfather had inspired in him.

He raised his eyes to the man seated across from him. Sir Roger's allegiance was to his overlord to whom he'd sent a better part of his army. His next concern was for his wife whose frailty he protected. 'Twas not weakness he displayed, then, but faithfulness to duty. And duty, no matter how tormenting, was something Luke understood.

"Is the Slayer presently at war?" he asked, out of curiosity.

The knight shook his head. "He needed hands to rebuild Glenmyre, another of his strongholds."

"Ah." Luke felt beaten. Every muscle in his body ached with fatigue, so that he wanted nothing more than a pallet on which to lie. If it took an oath to escort the Lady Merry to Helmesly to be given a bed, so be it.

He thumped his palm on the table, causing Sir Roger to look at him questioningly. "I'll take her to Helmesly," he growled, pushing back his chair. He stood up abruptly, not caring if his actions were rude. These people had asked too much of him already and given him not a word of thanks for rescuing their daughter. Come to think of it, Merry hadn't thanked him either.

As Sir Roger led the way to the door, muttering at last a word of gratitude, Luke found himself wondering whether the Slayer would be equally reluctant to take the witch under his wing.


HE couldn't sleep.

Luke stared at the canopy of the narrow bed he'd been given

and fumed in silence. His body lay immobile, exhausted, yet his mind churned relentlessly as resentment bubbled in his chest.

Already he was pressed for time, and now he would be delayed several more days. He had risked much to save the lady from the stake; now was obliged to go out of his way for her. Meanwhile, his poor grandfather looked for his return.

He rolled to his side and punched up his pillow. A ribbon of moonlight slipped along the crack of his bed curtains, telling him the shutters at the window must have come ajar. Perhaps he would sleep better with the light blocked out.

Flinging back the linens, he shuffled toward the window, rushes crackling under his feet. Sure enough, one of the shutters had blown open. As he reached out to close it, a chilly gust blew across his chest, rousing him to full awareness. Out of sheer habit, he scanned the walls and the rooftops below and was just about to latch the shutter when a movement close to the keep caught his eye.

Luke pressed himself to the wall and peered down. His chamber was situated at the fourth level of the keep, with more bedchambers one floor below. Something white was being lowered out the window directly beneath his. A rope, he guessed, watching its descent. Nay, it was a sheet.

Intrigued, he watched until it stopped, just above the ground. Someone was intending to leave the keep through the window. Recalling the reward for Merry's capture, Luke felt his pulse accelerate. He stepped back from the window long enough to jam his feet into his boots and snatch up his sword.

Returning to the window, he wondered whether he should wait and watch or charge down the steps and confront her abductor. He would determine who the villain was, he decided, and assure himself of Merry's well-being.

Would she be conscious? Impossible. How could anyone convey a wriggling woman down a length of knotted sheets? Her assailant would have to have knocked her over the head first to ensure her silence.

With mounting concern, he waited, aware that his body no longer ached. In fact, he felt sharply awake, his senses alert to any sound or movement. Before too long, he was presented with the sight of two shapely legs, clad in braies and coming out the window. The sweetly shaped bottom that followed was unmistakable. A thousand possibilities sifted through Luke's mind as her head and shoulders appeared. A bundle of sorts was fashioned around her neck and dangled beneath her left arm.

As she inched onto the length of improvised rope, it dawned on Luke that no villain was forcing Merry out the window. She was leaving voluntarily, in the most daring and foolhardy fashion possible.

With belated horror, he thought of the knots that might slip and the fabric that might tear. Merry hung two and a half stories above the cobbles, sheets twitching below her like the tail of a cat. And speaking of cat, he thought he heard a muffled yowl coming from within her bundle.

On the point of calling out her name, he caught himself. Nay, he shouldn't distract her. Abandoning the window, he tore out of the room. Down a pitch-black hallway he sped, slowing only to negotiate the steps that twisted to the lower levels. He would go to Merry's chamber, and pull the sheet up himself.

Locating her door, Luke grabbed for the latchstring and gave it a shove, but the portal wouldn't budge. She'd secured it from the inside.

He would have to go down and wait for her, then. Sharp fear raked his spine. What if she fell before he got there? Would he find her broken body on the cobblestones? The image tormented him, making him reckless on the tower stairs, so that he nearly broke his own neck before bursting out of the keep.

He looked around, catching his breath. *God's eye*! He was on the wrong side of the building!

Sprinting to his left, Luke rounded the keep and drew up short. To his dismay, the sheet dangled like a slender ghost with no one on it. His gaze dropped to the ground, but neither was she there. In the few seconds that he'd spent racing down the tower steps, she had either climbed back up or shimmied down and slipped into the night.

With the sheets still dangling, the latter seemed more likely. Yet, as he cast his gaze about the cluster of buildings in the inner ward, he could see no sign of her.

Bearing his sword point down, Luke made his way across the courtyard, his breath rasping in the silence. For the first time, he asked himself where the lady thought she was going.

She had said she foraged for herbs by moonlight, but surely she wasn't expanding her herbal at this tenuous time of her life.

Instinct led him toward the castle exit. With caution a constant companion, he kept to the shadows, sensing danger in this midnight outing. Gooseflesh rippled across his bare chest, making him wish he'd thought to don a tunic.

Was it possible Merry was running away? She hadn't been enthusiastic about returning to Heathersgill, and her mother's welcome had surely been a disappointment. Remembering her stricken look, earlier, Luke took a sudden breath. That was it, then. She *was* running away, the little lunatic! Where in God's name did she think she was going?

He ducked through the shadows of the inner gate, not surprised to find it slightly ajar. He quickened his stride, intending to intercept her before she got too far. But then he reined himself in.

*Wait a moment.* Why should he go after her? It was because of her he was being asked to go to Helmesly. What if the Slayer were to reject her once they arrived? What would he do with Merry then?

Perhaps she had somewhere better to go. Perhaps she knew of a safer place outside the walls.

His wishful thoughts disintegrated in the face of reason. They were isolated in the Cleveland Hills with nary a neighbor for leagues in any direction. If she tried to live as a recluse, she would suffer from cold and starvation, subject to occasional hunts by those seeking the reward money.

Another thought nearly froze him. Mayhap she would take her own life before then. After all, she had expressed the will to die.

The sound of voices had him ducking behind a cart, parked a stone's throw from the gatehouse. Of the two wrangling voices, Merry's belligerant tone reached him clearly. "Stand back, Edward. I mean to leave."

The man being addressed responded with rough-timbered violence. "That's right, yer leavin'. It were your fault, witch, that I lost me only son. He died along wi' the rest of 'em." Luke recognized the voice of the gatekeeper.

"I didn't kill your son." This time Merry's voice was pitched on a note of regret. "Sarah and I did our best to save the infants. 'Twas a scourge that took them."

"Ye lie witch. I remember when ye put a curse on me—"

"That was for betraying my father!" Her pitch rose as sharply as it had fallen. "You bowed to Ferguson to save your miserable head. You betrayed my family—"

"And you took mine! Now I'll turn you over to the Church and ne'er regret it."

Luke decided it was time to intervene. He sprinted into the shadows of the barbican in time to see the gatekeeper reach for Merry. Her cat leapt from the bundle with a cry of alarm.

"Let her go," Luke commanded, bearing down on them. Too late he spied the dull reflection of an ax, and he drew up short.

"Stand back," the gatekeeper growled, "or I'll spill her bowels o'er the ground." He pressed the ax's blade to Merry's midsection.

Luke swiftly reconsidered his approach. "We'll get no money for her dead, good man!" he protested.

"What?" Edward sputtered.

"Aye, I'm after the reward money, same as you."

Edward glowered suspiciously. "But ye were the one what brought her here."

"True," Luke conceded, "I thought her family would pay to see her safely home, but they'll not give me a shilling for all my trouble." He lowered his sword. "I'd as like give her over to the Church. At least they'll pay me." He heard the lady's indrawn breath, and he knew a moment's regret for misleading her. "Mayhap you and I might come to an understanding," he proposed, keeping a sharp eye on the gatekeeper's expression.

"What do you mean?"

"If you disappear from here, everyone will know you took the lady. You won't be able to return. Let me take her when I leave tomorrow. If she's hidden in one of my packs, none will be the wiser. I'll give you thirty marks now and profit only ten."

The gatekeeper screwed up his face. "Have you thirty marks with you?" he asked mistrustfully.

"In my chamber. I'll fetch it straightaway. Come," Luke urged, "you've nothing to lose. Cry foul on me tomorrow if I don't pay you what I promised."

"Bastard!" Merry gritted suddenly. "I thought you were dif-

ferent!" She fought Edward's hold, mindless of the blade goug-
ing her belly.

Luke struggled to maintain a careless expression. "Lady," he
pretended to mock her, "I'm a mercenary by trade. You should
know that I only work for coin, and your family has offered me
none." He hoped she would recognize this as an outright lie, yet
her face reflected only betrayal.

He turned back to the gatekeeper. "Come, have we a deal,
Edward? Thirty marks for you and only ten for me."

Edward's face twitched with greed. "Deal," he said. "Go
and get the money. I'll hold the girl till then."

"If you prefer," Luke shrugged. He put his sword in his left
hand and extended the right one. "I thank you for catching her,"
he added with a congenial smile. "She nearly got away from
me."

Edward fell right into his trap. Dropping his weapon a
notch, he reached for Luke's handshake only to give a yelp as
Luke slung him in an arc. Edward hit the wall with a crunch,
the ax flying out of his grasp.

"Hold this," Luke requested, putting the hilt of his sword
into Merry's frozen hands. He pivoted just in time to meet the
gatekeeper's charge. With a roar, Edward barreled into Luke,
sending both of them crashing to the opposite wall. Luke raised
his arms above the man's bearlike grip and brought them down
hard, pounding Edward to his knees. An upper cut to the jaw
sent the gatekeeper keeling backward, where he slumped into a
dead faint.

In the aftermath of the struggle, Luke paused to rub his
aching knuckles. He squared his shoulders, feeling anew each
and every ache in his body. To his consternation, he found himself staring at the point of his weapon.

Merry held the sword before her, needing both hands to
keep it aloft. The point of it was aimed squarely at Luke's chin.
"There's no need for that," he said.

She trembled so badly that moonlight danced on the tip of
the blade. "I should kill you now," she answered through her
teeth.

He found her tense demeanor even more alarming. This was
the Merry who'd nearly skewered herself with his sword. "And

what would that serve?" he inquired, feeling out her state of mind.

" 'Twould rid the world of another war-loving brute," she replied.

"Ah," he said. "Well, kill me if you must. But then, there will be no one left to take you to Helmesly."

The point of the broadsword wavered. "You said you were turning me in."

"Lady, I am not a mercenary," he said simply. "This night I promised Sir Roger I would take you to Helmesly, and tomorrow I will take you there."

"But I don't want to go to Helmesly! I don't wish to go anywhere but up into the mountains to be left alone!"

His gaze fell to the bundle still secured beneath her arm. "You have what you need, then?" he inquired, dispassionately. "A heavy coat? Food enough to see you through the snows; a flint for starting fires, presuming wood is found. A bow and arrows for hunting, a sharp knife, a pot. Let's see, what have I forgotten?"

By this time, Kit had melted out of the shadows and was winding himself around Luke's feet. "Ah, yes, a cat. You must have a cat," he finished, dryly.

It was obvious that the bundle she carried held less than a fraction of the goods he'd mentioned. A hint of doubt creased her forehead. "Go, then," he said, waving her toward the gate. "Edward isn't going to stop you."

"What about you?" she asked, a hitch in her voice.

"What about me?"

"Won't you stop me?" Strangely, it sounded more like a plea than anything else.

He crossed his arms over his chest. "Nay, why would I? This will save me from having to convey you to Helmesly, which, as I said before, is not on my way." He felt rather mean for pointing it out.

"I see." she said. Her chin wobbled a moment. "I'll just go then and not bother anyone." She took a step backward, and he saw her wince. His gaze fell to the boots she had put on her feet to protect her burned soles. How far, he wondered, did she think she would get in such a sorry state? Uncertainty pinched him anew.

But then reason asserted itself. He truly had no time to convey her to Helmesly. Not when each passing day might make a difference in seeing his grandfather alive.

"Take your sword back," she said, lowering the blade and extending him the pommel.

Their fingers brushed. Feeling her slim, cold hands, he was reminded how pleasant it had felt to ride with her before him. He knew an urge to close his fingers over hers and not let go.

She withdrew her hand. "I have to go before they find me missing." She inched toward the gate. "Come, Kit," she called to the cat who still rubbed himself against Luke's legs. Kit hesitated then bounded after her.

Luke watched Merry struggle with the crossbar. At last he went to help her, pulling the gate open himself. The cold air of the valley rushed inside the enclosure.

She slipped through the opening without a sound, the cat at her feet.

Luke stood at the gate, watching her shape become a shadow as she headed down the cart road. Raking his hands through his hair, he knew he wouldn't sleep the remainder of the night, thinking of her stumbling about on the hillside. Surely there were wolves and cliffs and, worse yet, rogues and thieves skulking about. He didn't want to learn that she'd been ravaged, killed, or had taken a lethal fall.

"Are you sure you wouldn't rather live at Helmesly?" he called before he could stop himself.

She turned, throwing him her bittersweet smile. "I know when I'm not wanted," she retorted quietly.

He found he didn't like her answer. "Merry," he called again, making her stop. He could only see her eyes, luminous in the dark. "If you change your mind," he said, realizing suddenly that he hoped she would, "meet me along the cart road at dawn." As far as he knew, it was the only way off the mountain.

He thought he saw her nod. A tender moment blew between them, as fragile as a breath of wind. But then she turned away and disappeared into the inky blackness.

Luke stared at the spot where she'd just stood, struck by the realization that he'd just let her walk to her certain death or, at best, a lifetime of persecution.

He'd been thinking only of himself and his reluctance to

take her to Helmesly. He ran into the dark and called her back. "Merry!" But the wild, irregular hillside stood deserted. "Merry," he called again. "Come back."

His own voice was all that returned, mocking him on an echo for having encouraged her. Insects chirped in the tall grass. He stood there, disgusted with himself.

He began to go after her. But then the thrifty moon ducked behind a cloud, leaving the hills in preternatural darkness. Recalling the fate of the packhorse, he backed up to the gate again. The air outside the walls seemed sharply cold against his skin.

He was not equipped to chase after her. Besides, if he tried and came back empty-handed, the finger of guilt would point squarely at him. Better to pretend ignorance of the matter and return to his bed. At dawn he could then be on his way, delayed no longer.

If Merry's family suffered for not knowing where the lady was, it was every bit their fault for failing to look after her, he reasoned.

He slipped back into the castle, leaving the gate unlocked, should she change her mind.

Stepping over the unconscious Edward, Luke headed blindly toward the keep. He had always thought himself a man of integrity, but the bitter taste in his mouth proved otherwise.

With leaden feet, he retraced his footsteps. He kept his gaze averted, so as not to see the hanging sheets as he crossed the courtyard

Entering the keep by the same side door, he returned to his room. Through the open window, the fickle moon came out of hiding, then disappeared again. It seemed a symbol of Merry and the uncertainty that she would pass the night unharmed.

Luke kicked off his boots and collapsed onto his bed. Exhaustion pulled at him, and he lapsed at last into dreams filled with horrifying visions of Merry slipping on tumbling rock. He woke several times, bathed in sweat. He stalked to the window, sick at heart to see her makeshift rope still dangling.

*This is my penance,* he reflected, for until this night, he'd never broken a promise.

# Chapter Five

**H**UDDLED over the cat in her lap, Merry took comfort from Kit's guttural purr as she tried to warm herself. The bottom of her feet burned, not with warmth, but with shooting pangs that took her breath away. She'd put her back against a boulder in the hopes that its breadth would shield her from the wind that whistled down the hill and tugged at her meager clothing.

*What a fool I am*, she lamented inwardly. So much had changed in just three years, transforming the hills into a foreign country. The cold had caught her unawares. She had only her cat for warmth, not a cloak as Luke had wisely pointed out.

She realized how woefully she'd planned for her future.

Three years ago, these hills had been her refuge against Ferguson's soldiers. The rocky terrain had seemed safe when compared to the threat the men presented. Yet Luke was right to have called her back.

She'd watched him from behind a rock, a dark silhouette against the gate. She'd pretended for a moment that he desired her return, truly. Perhaps the sense of companionship she'd felt while sharing his saddle was something he'd experienced as well.

Only, he hadn't called her back. He was glad to see her go. As he'd said, he would not have to travel out of his way now.

Yet why had he challenged Edward, then, coming to her rescue like a bare-chested angel? What a novelty to be defended! Still, once Edward was subdued, Luke had been all too willing to let her go.

Betrayal spread through her, as bitter as wormwood. She shuddered from the cold, struck to the core by the depth of her isolation.

*Be strong,* she counseled herself. She didn't need her family— her mother whose fear for her was unsettling; nor Kyndra who'd been sent away like Merry, apparently too strong-willed for Sir Roger to manage. Aye, Katherine DuBoise, nicknamed Kyndra, was a wild spirit like her sister. Perhaps Merry should go to her in York, and the two of them could find a way to eke a living? But, nay, the presence of the Church was overpowering in York. She had no wish to drag her younger sister down into the fires of hell with her.

Only Luke le Noir seemed mighty enough to shield her from her persecution. Yet she didn't need him either. Come morning, she would seek out Sarah's rock-hewn cottage and avail herself of the goods that were hopefully still there—crude tables and chairs, cooking utensils, bottles of herbs and powders. She would strike a fire for warmth and make herself a home.

With a vision to give her courage, she closed her eyes and dreamed of her life to come.

She knew she was dreaming when Sarah stepped through the rocks and settled beside her, folding her in the warmth of her double-wide mantle. The scent of tansy, pine, and wood ash clung to her, making her presence seem real. *Merry, you mustn't try to live like me,* Sarah cautioned, her voice scratchy with age. *'Tisn't safe to remain here.*

Merry gloried in the warmth pouring from her mentor's cloak. *I want to be good like you, Sarah,* she argued. *I want to heal the sick.*

*And you will,* Sarah promised. *But not here.*

*Where then? My family doesn't want me. There's no place for me but the hills.*

*There is a place,* Sarah insisted. *Meet the one who saved you from the prioress. He will look for you at the cart road at dawn.*

*He doesn't want me either.*

*Mayhap,* Sarah conceded. *But he* needs *you, my child. Without you, he will surely come to harm.*

Suddenly there was no one beside her but Kit, who was rubbing against her, mewing loudly.

Merry started awake, her heart pounding fast. The silvery glow on the tops of the rocks surprised her. It was dawn already, the clear sky bringing promise of fair weather.

She rose on shaky knees, asking herself if her dream were mere hallucination or a sign pointing her toward her fate. The Phoenix coming to harm? She found she couldn't stand the thought, not when he'd risked himself to save her, not when she'd forgotten to thank him.

Making a sudden decision, Merry called Kit to follow and hastened in the direction of the ravine. The soles of her feet protested only mildly. Thank the saints, for if she meant to intercept Luke on the cart road, she would have to run without stopping.

LUKE scratched the back of his neck in a vain effort to appease the prickling there. Leaving Heathersgill without volunteering knowledge of Merry's whereabouts left his stomach on fire.

The distraught countenance of Lady Jeanette had nearly been his undoing this morning. He'd felt a confession burn repeatedly toward his tongue, but he'd swallowed it, saying nothing, even when the scouring of the castle, both inside and out, had failed to yield any sign of Merry.

It was assumed someone had claimed the girl for the reward money. Edward had been questioned, but though he bore a bruise that testified to some kind of scuffle, he remembered nothing of the night before. Nonetheless, he glowered suspiciously from his gatehouse window as Luke and his army filed out.

With his troublesome task out of the way, Luke put Merry from his thoughts. Still, as he led his men down the sinuous cart road, he peered hopefully around each bend. He eyed the sky in dread of buzzards, turned his head quickly toward the sound of rolling rock.

He clenched his jaw in self-disgust. Either he was glad to be rid of her or he wanted her back. Which was it? He could not make up his mind. The memory of her leaf-green eyes haunted him. The scent of fresh herbs clung to his shirt, tormenting him with the agonizing possibility that she was already dead.

*Forget her*, he commanded of himself. He had enough matters weighing on his mind without having to wonder whether a woman could survive in the Cleveland Hills alone.

Yet as they approached the foot of the great hill with still no sign of her, he failed to beat back his dismay. They'd passed beyond the point where Merry might still intercept them. Likely she was dead already. With fingers that shook, he rubbed his bleary eyes and tried to pull himself together.

He had just lowered his hand when the head of a horse came into view. *Not Merry*, he told himself, unable to squelch a flicker of hope. And yet as the rest of the road grew more visible, he realized that it *was* Merry, her hair disheveled and shot with grass. Her eyes shone with a light he hadn't seen before. Her cheeks were flushed as though she'd ridden hard to greet him.

Joy leapt up in him, unbidden. He kicked his own mount to a gallop and drew alongside her, trying to restrain the smile that seized the edges of his mouth. To his astonishment, the lady returned his grimace with a dazzling smile of her own, making her breathtakingly beautiful.

Where did you get the horse?" Stunned by her smile, he uttered the first thing that came to his lips. His soldiers were just catching up to them.

" 'Tis yours." She leaned forward to pat the mare's neck. "I found her in the ravine. She isn't hurt at all, save for a slight limp. I was sorry to have to ride her, but I didn't want to miss you." She bit her lower lip, then, as if dreading the possibility he might rescind his offer.

He should have recognized the animal's markings or at least the satchel on its back. "Sir Pierce!" Luke called, waving his sergeant closer. "Look, 'tis the mare we lost last night. The lady found her in the ravine."

A murmur of amazement rippled down the file of soldiers. The men pressed closer to have a look, more than a few raising their eyes to assess the rider also. Merry stiffened at the attention. A look of foreboding crossed over her face.

"She must be a witch to raise a horse from the dead," said one of the mercenaries.

Several soldiers chorused their agreement. "Aye, a witch."

Merry had guessed what the men would say. Offended on her behalf, Luke twisted in the saddle, leveling a glare at the guilty soldiers. "I will tolerate no such talk!" he thundered. " 'Tis by grace alone that the horse lives."

Absolute silence followed his declaration. The men stared at him in astonishment. Inwardly, Luke cursed his thoughtless reaction. It wasn't like him to rail at his men. He left that to Sir Pierce, while he himself remained their cool and levelheaded leader.

He turned toward Merry, abruptly in control again. "I'll send a rider back with news that you've been found," he clipped. "Your mother was sore distressed by your absence."

It was better to chastise her than publicly defend her. Yet her eyes darkened as if bruised, and he suffered immediate remorse. *Jesu*, what a cur he was to scold her when he'd been the one to open the gates for her!

He sent the vocal soldier back with news that she'd been found. "I have to go to Iversly," he added to Merry. "When I am done there, I will take you to Helmesly on my way south. Elsewise I go two days out of my way." He'd made up his mind instantly.

She nodded her understanding, the light in her eyes slowly returning. "Then you'll take me with you?"

"Aye, but time is important to me."

"I won't be a burden to you," she promised in a rush. "I'll stay well out of your way."

He hid his skepticism behind a bland nod. "You'll have to ride with me if that horse has a sprain," he said. "Erin, add the mare's bundle to your pack."

No sooner had he issued his command than he found Merry on her feet, extending a hand to him. He reached down and took firm hold of her, pulling her up before him. Immediately, his senses quieted from their restless seething. It took every bit of willpower not to fold her against him and bury his nose into her fresh-scented hair.

"Where's the cat?" he asked, scrambling for aloofness.

She cracked her bundle so he could peek inside.

"Ah," he said.

"Where's your armor?" she countered, resting her palm on his unprotected thigh.

The touch of her hand brought him to instant awareness. "Still missing a knee guard," he said, prodding his horse into movement. He needed to unleash his sudden energy with a vigorous ride. "Hold tight," he warned. "I mean to make good time." With that, he kicked Suleyman into a trot.

"Are you hungry?" she asked a moment later. She had reached into a bundle and pulled out a loaf of bread sprinkled liberally with cat hairs.

"Thank you, but I ate," he politely declined.

With a shrug, she picked off the hairs and bit into the bread with gusto. A comfortable silence fell between them, filled by the thunderous rhythm of the horse beneath them and the army behind. A swallow and its mate swooped by, catching insects in their open beaks. The sun burned away the last hint of chill in the air, leaving it fresh and warm.

A sudden heaviness against his chest brought Luke's gaze down. Merry had fallen asleep, crust still clutched in her hand. Her head lolled against his chest. Her absolute trust in him touched him somewhere deep inside. He slowed his pace so as not to jar her awake.

How like a child to fall asleep in his arms! Yet the sway of her breasts assured him she wasn't a child at all. Fortunately, Merry was sleeping and therefore unaware of her effect on him. Surely his decision to take her to Iversly wasn't motivated by desire for her? He frowned at the disturbing thought.

Nay, of course not. He was in a hurry to get to Iversly. Besides, he wasn't a callow youth ruled by his humors. He could find the lady desirable and never give in to the urge to caress her or to kiss her, though the thought of doing so quickened his pulse and brought a hot flush to his skin. He remembered how he'd put his mouth to her wound, and his self-confidence wavered.

What if he weren't as disciplined as he believed? Perhaps he'd best keep his distance from her.

So long as they shared a saddle, keeping his distance was impossible. The only alternative was to let her ride with another of his men. He discarded the option as quickly as it occurred to him.

Already, his soldiers thought her a witch. Superstition rode hand in hand with ignorance, especially for men so far from home. Her coloring betrayed her, and of course there was the matter of the cat and the horse she'd supposedly raised from the dead.

His men had yet to see that she was not a mean-spirited creature at all. Still, they could not have overlooked her puckish beauty, nor the sweetness of her shape in Erin's clothing.

Nay, Luke trusted no one with her but himself. He knew he could resist her charms. It was Amalie he wanted—not for her body but for her royal bloodlines, blood that would cleanse the taint of his illegitimacy, making it feasible for his grandfather's title to pass through him to his children.

He had only to keep his focus on his ultimate goal, and Merry would cease to tempt him. Once his work at Iversly was done, he would deliver her to Helmesly and into the care of the Slayer, forgetting her from that point on.

He wrapped his thoughts into that tidy mental package and stowed it away.

MERRY woke the same moment the horse beneath her stilled. She sat up quickly, bumping the Phoenix's chin.

"Shhh, be still," he whispered, touching a hand to her shoulder.

Her eyes widened at the warning. A quick sweep of the forest revealed that they were standing in a dense copse of trees. Hemlock pines surrounded them on all sides, shrouding them in shadow.

Had they stopped to water the animals? She strained her ears for the sound of running water, but all she heard was an eerie silence, punctuated now and then by the snapping of twigs, the crunching of pine needles.

Fear rippled through her as her imagination took hold. Any moment now, thieves and outlaws would step from behind the trees. Others would swing down from the branches overhead with the intent to attack the royal army. Hadn't Sarah's spirit warned her that the Phoenix would come to harm without her?

A sudden drum of hooves shook the forest. Merry gasped in alarm and gripped Luke's thigh. He looped an arm around her shoulders, but made no move at all to raise his sword. A hideous squealing rose above the thunder, and then a beast hurtled through the undergrowth toward them, tusks gleaming, eyes rolling with terror.

On legs that churned desperately beneath its rotund belly, the animal tore by. Five men on horseback followed close behind, the riders bearing spears.

It was a hunt, not a human massacre. Merry heaved a sigh of relief and slumped against her companion, her skin clammy.

The boar squealed and turned, tearing up the bed of pine needles as it retraced its path in a desperate bid to escape the wall of horses closing around it. One hunter leaned low as it passed and stuck the boar along its spine.

The animal gave a tortured scream and kept running. The spear went with him, wagging obscenely from his torn flesh.

Another hunter met the boar head-on and aimed his weapon with more care. As the beast darted by, the point sank deep into the animal's neck. A fountain of blood spurted out. The boar stumbled and regained its feet, squealing in agony and terror.

Merry watched, unable to look away. Blood pumped from the animal with every beat of its heart. It tried to run, but couldn't make its feet move. In defeat, it collapsed, snorting loudly.

Images flickered through her mind. Her father's body, lying in a broken heap, severed at the neck. The blood coming out in great spurts. And Ferguson, wiping her father's blood on her father's tunic, resheathing his sword. Raising greedy eyes to her ashen-faced mother.

"Nay," Merry whispered now, willing the memories to recede. Her stomach roiled, and bile started up her throat. She swallowed, hoping the moment would pass.

The second hunter dismounted. As he ripped the dagger from the boar's back, the sound of tearing flesh tortured Merry's imagination. She turned her head away, panting for fresh air. The stench of death hung thickly in the copse. She needed to escape it.

"Lady?" Luke's query seemed to come from a distance.

Merry shook her head. Moving too quickly to be stopped, she slipped from the saddle and dropped her bundle, deaf to Kit's startled cry. She dashed behind the nearest tree and retched up her meager breakfast. Gasping, she waited for the nausea to subside.

"Merry!" Luke called.

*God's mercy, he was following her!* Wiping her mouth, she hastily turned, realizing belatedly that the eyes of the entire regiment were upon her. Some soldiers looked perplexed, others sympathetic; and still others glowered with suspicion.

Luke approached her. With a frown of concern, he took her by the elbow.

She wished the ground would swallow her. She didn't like revealing weakness, having found that others were always quick to exploit them. "I must have eaten something that didn't agree with me," she said, tugging free.

Marching back to the horse, she kept her gaze deliberately averted from the carcass.

"We needed meat," the Phoenix explained, coming up behind her. " 'Tis rude to appear at a stronghold with fifty men and no way to feed them."

She glanced at him sharply. His searching look assured her that he'd guessed the source of her distress. She found his intuition both a comfort and a threat. Just how much did he see with those golden eyes of his?

He was helping her into the saddle when Merry overheard one soldier mutter to another, "The boar's spirit entered her body. 'Tis the reason she fell ill."

" 'Twas a demon possession," agreed his companion.

Merry pulled her shoulders to her ears, wanting to block the words completely. Why did others continue to think her a witch? She'd done nothing wrong for a long, long time.

From the corner of her eye she saw the Phoenix pivot. To her astonishment, he abandoned Merry's side and stalked toward the guilty soldiers. Grabbing the first man by the scruff, he hauled his face down level with his own. Merry strained to overhear what was said, but he spoke at barely above a whisper. She watched the mercenary pale and nod his head vigorously. Whatever warning Sir Luke had given him, the man appeared to take it to heart.

Yet, the moment his captain released him and turned away, the soldier sent a warning glare at Merry. She was given to know that he blamed her for his humiliation.

With a prick of fear, Merry looked away. How long could the Phoenix keep her safe? His protective wings extended only so far. And when he finally dropped her off at Helmesly, like an unwanted infant at the doors of a church, who would protect her then? The Slayer, whom she'd foolishly cursed?

She heaved a troubled sigh. Her future seemed so uncertain. And what of Sarah's warning that Luke would come to harm without her? Would that truly happen, or was it just a dream?

Sir Pierce had supervised the stringing up of the boar. Giving the call to move forward, Sir Luke swung into the saddle, and they were off.

"I'm sorry I'm a burden to you," Merry apologized, as they shot forward through dappled sunlight.

Her companion said nothing, though she was certain he had heard her. Her heart grew heavy. She'd wanted some assurance that she wasn't much trouble. Apparently, he couldn't give her even that.

An hour later, they stopped again to water their horses. Merry sought a private place in the woods in which to relieve herself. Distracted by a glen of wildflowers, she dallied a moment to wreathe herself a crown of chicory blossoms.

Turning back toward the horses, she stumbled quite by accident upon the mercenary who'd glared at her before. "Your pardon," she said, having caught him whizzing on a tree.

He drew his lips back in a smirk and stroked his member lewdly, enjoying her horrified look. Merry hastened her footsteps. She should not have wandered so far from the others. Ears pricked to the sound of pursuit, she began to run.

Her heart beat not only with the certainty that the man intended her harm, but also with anger that he continued to taunt her, despite the captain's warning. Everywhere she turned there were villains who preyed upon the weak. She thought of Ferguson and the prioress, and her anger grew until she was shaking with it.

She would warn the man as she'd warned the Mother. But what herbs did she have at her disposal? Toxic plants abounded in these woods, yet most of them required preparation and she had no time.

Her gaze fell upon a vine of poison oak. Snapping it from the trunk of a tree, she carried it swiftly toward the stream where the horses stood with their noses to the water. Soldiers milled aimlessly. Most of them made a point to avoid her, no doubt thinking of their captain's warning.

Sir Luke and his sergeant were bent over a leather map, determining the best route to Iversly.

Merry approached Suleyman and took an apple from her bundle. She ducked beneath his head and moved downstream to the mercenary's horse, finding the animal by its markings.

Lifting the flap of the soldier's saddlebag, Merry coiled the vine onto his cloak, careful not to touch the leaves herself. If all went as planned, the oils would leech into the wool and raise a rash on the mercenary's neck and elsewhere, especially if he used it as a blanket.

Satisfied that she'd done *something,* Merry fed her apple to his horse and waded back upstream. Ducking under Suleyman's head, she came face-to-face with the Phoenix. She stifled a gasp but failed to hide her dismay at coming upon him so soon.

His eyes narrowed as he took in her guilty expression. "What have you done?" he demanded without preamble.

His cold tone froze the blood in her veins. "Naught," she said, clutching his horse's neck for protection. "I shared my apple with the horses, 'tis all."

His gaze flickered toward the other mounts. He took a step forward, pinning her against his mount. With a huge animal at her back and an unyielding man before her, Merry's heart thumped with fear. "Lady," he warned, his voice low and lethal, " 'tis enough that I let you bring your cat with you. Do not make a mockery of me by doing something impulsive."

She tried to hold his burning gaze and failed. She focused instead on the deep tan of his thickly corded neck. A mysterious scent wafted toward her and she sniffed to identify it.

He took a quick step back. "Did you hear anything I said?" he demanded, frustrated this time.

A flash of anger gave her the courage to meet his gaze. "You're not the one they say is possessed!" she told him fervently.

Understanding warmed the coldness in his eyes. "Let it go," he told her, more gently this time. "I will protect you from men like Cullin."

She marveled again at his perception. She gave him a considering look, wanting badly to believe him. 'Twould be a marvelous thing not to have to glance over her shoulder in fear. Yet Sir Luke couldn't always be near enough to guard her. His duties would keep him away.

"Please," he said, surprising her with his sudden request, "do not inflame the superstitions of the men. You are not a witch, but a lady. Do you play that part, the soldiers will forget their foolishness."

She swallowed hard, thinking of the vine on Cullin's cloak. She knew a sudden urge to confess her guilt. But then the Phoenix would think worse of her, and she found she didn't want that. She offered up a nod, instead, keeping her transgression private.

Without warning, he lifted his hands to her head, straightening her crown of flowers that had slipped to one side. Merry held perfectly still, savoring the gesture . . . as what? A token of understanding? Then why did it have the power to suspend her breath?

"You look like a wood sprite," he said, snatching his hands away. With a sudden frown, he turned away and marched into the midst of his soldiers, calling for them to mount up. They would reach Iversly by nightfall, he swore.

As they continued west, setting a pace that rattled the teeth in Merry's skull, Luke's words echoed in her head, giving her much to think about. *Please, do not inflame the superstitions of the men. You are not a witch, but a lady. Do you play that part, the soldiers will forget their foolishness.*

Would they? She wasn't a witch, true enough. But she was a healer, and healers were sometimes mistaken for witches. 'Twas a hazard of the practice.

With the clarity of hindsight, she realized she should not have put the vine in Cullin's saddlebag. The Phoenix was right. If the soldiers guessed that she had done so, they would persist in thinking her a witch. Oh, mercy, would she never learn?

She was a healer, and healers inflicted suffering on no one, no matter how deserving of punishment. Henceforth, she swore to use her skill for good, counting on the Phoenix to protect her, as he'd said.

Her brow puckered. Yet what if he forbade her to heal at all, given the similarities between physic and witchcraft? Why then, she would have to defy him. She had been called to tend the sick, just as surely as he'd been called to lead men.

Perhaps, one day, he might rely upon her skills to save his own life. Given Sarah's warning, such circumstance seemed likely. If so, then the Phoenix would see for himself, Merry DuBoise was more than a lady.

*Chapter Six*

THE Baron of Iversly stood behind his closed portcullis gripping the iron grid with blue-veined hands. His white beard was all that Merry could see, for the sun had sunk behind a hill and the shadows of night had thickened and spread.

"So," she heard the baron growl as Luke and his sergeant approached the gate, "you've come." His tone was ponderous with doom, and Merry wondered precisely what the Phoenix did for the prince. His quiet reply frustrated her attempts to overhear.

"I cannot feed an army here," groused the baron through the closed gate.

"We brought a contribution to your kitchens." Luke indicated the dead boar, a grotesque shadow dangling between two horses.

Silence ensued until, at last, the baron called for the portcullis to be raised. It rumbled upward, revealing an even older man than Merry had first supposed. He was also very tall. Turning his back on the army, the baron led the way into his stronghold.

Once within the courtyard, Luke helped Merry to her feet. "My squire will look after your cat," he said, handing her bundle to Erin.

With reluctance, she acceded to his wishes. Likely there were hounds within the keep, and she was loath to cause a stir by bringing her pet inside. She hurried along beside him, her feet still tender.

The captain, his sergeant, and Merry followed the baron toward the well-lit keep, while the remaining soldiers were left to occupy the garrison.

In the evening dusk, the baron failed to notice Merry, whom he must have thought a squire. His wife who waited in the great hall, her hands knotted before her, was more observant. As they approached her for introductions, her curious gaze slid at once to Merry.

"They've come," said the baron curtly. "This is the legendary Phoenix and his sergeant, Sir Pierce. Gentlemen, the baroness, Lady Adelle."

The baroness sketched them a distracted curtsy. 'Who is this woman?" she demanded, her gaze locked on Merry.

"This is Merry of Heathersgill," Luke explained. "I'm escorting her to Helmesly."

The old couple noted her boy's attire with mute curiosity. When Luke offered no further explanation, they turned their attention back to him. The tension seemed to rise once more, and Merry wondered again at Luke's business here. Did he intend to inspect their ledgers?

The baroness indicated the high table with resignation. "Won't you join us for supper?" she suggested, her invitation less than warm.

"With pleasure," Sir Luke smoothly replied.

Lady Adelle preceded them to the dais. "Our sons have gone to tour the continent, so we do things simply now," she called over her shoulder. "Please, take a seat."

Trailing Luke to the table, Merry cast her eyes about the hall. Though neat enough, there were cobwebs in the rafters, and the rushes needed to be replaced. A sense of timelessness hung over the chamber, enhanced by the ancient tapestries and the yellowed linens.

Within moments of being seated, a page brought a bowl for them to wash their hands. A quick study of the handful of men below determined that the baron's vassals were as old as he

was. They looked incapable of defending their fortress should
the need arise.

Immediately, a trencher of grilled trout in herb sauce was
placed before her. Merry would share hers with Luke, seated as
she was to the left of him. She ate with gusto, finding that she
was suddenly quite hungry. Without comment, Luke gave her
the choicest portion of the fish and ate sparely himself.

Merry's impatience to hear his business rose, yet talk
remained impersonal. Reaching for her wine to chase down a
bone, it dawned on her that the Phoenix was leading the conversation. He did it so deftly and with such courtesy that it had
nearly escaped her notice. He was putting the baron and
baroness at ease, she realized, but why?

At last, when they'd all been served a measure of spiced
wine, and trays of raisins and nuts had been placed before them,
he put his goblet down with purpose. "You understand I have a
thankless job to do here," he began, his tone gentle. "Both the
king and prince have declared that structures built without a
charter must be taken down. I must ask to see Iversly's charter,"
he added apologetically.

*Taken down!* Merry reeled as Luke's purpose came to light.
He'd been sent by the prince to destroy illegitimate structures.
*Ah, yes, he'd called them adulterines. What a horrible name for
such a beautiful castle!*

Leaning in, Merry assessed the baron's reaction. His expression had darkened with resentment, but he was prepared for the
request. Crooking a finger at his steward, he took a rolled
parchment from the man and extended it to Luke.

The vellum was brown with age. For the sake of the old couple, Merry hoped that all would be found in accordance with
the charter.

Luke read the document in its entirety then carefully re-
rolled it. "This is the original charter," he summarized. "It was
signed by the king's grandfather and allows for a central keep,
an outer wall, and a gatehouse. Can you present a charter which
grants you right to build a garrison, to raise your outer wall, and
to construct a tower at either end?"

Merry's heart sank. She marveled that he had taken in such
detail on their way inside the keep. The baron's face flushed
with emotion.

"Now look here," he growled, gripping the arms of his chair. "Before you go and raze my walls, you should think about the safety of this country. For three score years I've deflected the Scots and the Welsh. I've kept the enemy out of England so that the pampered lords to the south can sit in their plush strongholds and drink Spanish wine!" This last statement was uttered with so much force that spittle flew from his mouth.

Merry's full stomach began to churn. She cast the baroness a worried glance and saw that the woman's face had gone white. Lady Adelle put a restraining hand on her husband's arm.

"Prince Henry will not leave you defenseless," the Phoenix swore. "I will carry your request for rebuilding straight to His Majesty and you will build again."

"Where is the wisdom in that?" challenged the baron, a vein appearing on his wrinkled forehead. "Destroy only to rebuild? It makes no sense at all. I've spent my life in service to the king and this is how he repays me?" The baron shoved back his chair in a show of disgust. "Fie on His Majesty, then," he said, standing. "Fie!" He shook a finger at the Phoenix. "Get out of my castle," he said suddenly. "Get out and take your men with you."

It was a ridiculous request, for the Phoenix had his orders, and his men were already established within Iversly's walls. The aging men-at-arms stood no chance of thrusting the younger soldiers out the gates. Sir Luke said nothing. He returned the baron's stare, enjoining him silently to be reasonable.

Lady Adelle tugged her husband's sleeve. "Ian, please!" she begged him. "Sit down and be reasonable."

The baron shook her off. "I will not be reasonable," he thundered. "The prince's terms are unreasonable. The marcher barons have never been given enough of a voice in the—"

He cut his words short and clapped a hand to his heart. His eyes widened, nearly bulging from their sockets.

"Ian?" Lady Adelle cried. The baron seemed not to breathe. The baroness pushed to her feet and put her arms around him. "Ian!" she cried again, panicked this time.

Merry had seen enough. "He's having an apoplectic fit," she

said to anyone who would listen. "He's going to fall," she added in warning.

Luke must have believed her for he jumped to his feet just in time to keep the baron from flying backward off the dais. The baroness screamed. Luke laid the unconscious baron on the platform, and Merry slipped from her chair to offer advice.

She had seen spells of apoplexy before. She knew the dangers it presented to the internal organs, the consequences that often resulted. "Give him air," she commanded of the baroness who practically lay atop her husband, pleading with him to rise.

Luke cast her a grim look, and in his eyes she read helplessness. Confidence rose up in her, for this was her forte.

"Be calm, Lady Adelle," she said to the baroness. "He is only sleeping. He must be made as comfortable and warm as possible. Is there anyone who can take him to his chambers?"

By now a number of men-at-arms, servants, and vassals were peering through the legs of the chairs to get a better look. Seeing their gray and white heads, Merry determined that the lot of them together would not be able to carry the baron up the steps.

"Sir Pierce and I will do it," said Luke, who must have had the same thoughts.

"Good," said Merry. "Then take him under the arms, but do keep his head low. Sir Pierce, hold his legs as high as you can."

Both men leapt off the back of the dais and slid the baron toward the edge, where they took him in their arms. Merry drew confidence from their obedience. Following the trembling baroness, they moved as a group in the direction of the living quarters.

"In here," said Lady Adelle. They had labored to carry the baron down a drafty hall, then up a set of twisting stairs. At last they arrived at the baron's solar, a chamber of vast proportion, lit by two oil lamps. A massive bed with drapes of an indeterminate color beckoned them.

Merry drew back the drapes and pulled the blankets down. Luke and Sir Pierce counted to three and deposited their burden in the center of the bed. Lady Adelle fussed frantically over her husband, making it that much harder to get the baron's limbs beneath the sheets.

Merry leaned over her patient, hoping to see his eyelids flutter. She was at the point of calling for a candle when the Phoenix took her arm. "Come, we will leave them now," he said.

Merry shook him off. "I've seen this before. I know how to treat it."

"We're going," he repeated in a tone he used on his men.

"But if I leave him now, he may die!" she whispered.

Overhearing her, the baroness wailed.

The hold on Merry's arm tightened. "*Now*, lady," the captain gritted. "You are not to draw attention to yourself."

Merry fought his hold. "You don't understand. I can help him. I know how to treat this."

"Not this time." Using his superior strength, he propelled her toward the door. She had no choice but to abandon her patient.

"Wait," called the baroness, dabbing at her eyes. "You must be given rooms."

"We'll sleep in the garrison," Luke answered more gently.

"A lady does not sleep with soldiers," the baroness retorted. "And I'm certain you'd prefer a feather bed." She unhooked the keys that hung on her girdle and called one of the servants in the hallway.

"Selwin," she said to the steward. "Kindly see that the lady is put in Ewan's chamber and the two men lodged in Edgar's. The boys wouldn't mind, I'm sure. It's been . . . so long since they've used their own beds." She handed him her ring, and as she turned away, she sent Merry an imploring look.

There was no mistaking the woman's look as anything but a plea for help. Merry's resolve doubled. She would placate the Phoenix and then return to the baron's solar to help the baroness.

The trio followed Selwin into the hall. "Go back to work," the surly steward bellowed to the lingering servants. "There's naught ye can do but pray. This way," he added.

He led them a short distance down the hall and thrust a key into the door. "This were Ewan's room which the . . . " he ran a dubious look over Merry's attire, "which the lady may use. Only don't touch nothin'," he warned, grabbing a torch from the hall. "The baroness wants everything to be the way it was when the masters return." He mumbled something under his breath as he entered the chamber and thrust the torch into a holder.

Merry forgot her resentment momentarily. As the light flared, she made out a handsome chamber with deep green drapes and matching tapestries. The odor of disuse greeted her nostrils as she waded deeper. Her gaze fell upon the dust that blanketed the wardrobe chest. "How long have Ewan and Edgar been gone?" she asked out of curiosity.

"We don't keep track o' the time here," Selwin replied.

"Open the window," Luke suggested to the servant.

Selwin did so, then marched out of the door, leading Sir Pierce to the next room.

The captain remained, his gaze sharp on Merry's face. "You're not to offer your services," he warned her again.

"Why not?" she demanded, her spine stiff with resentment.

"The Church has servants scouring the county for you, lady," he said darkly. "You're not to draw notice to yourself."

Down the hall came the groaning of a lock as Selwin opened the other door.

"My well-being pales in comparison to the baron's, don't you think?" Merry argued. "I have to help him."

He stepped close enough to put his hands heavily on her shoulders. "If you treat the baron and he dies, what then, Merry? You'll be blamed."

"But he won't die if I help!" she insisted.

He placed a finger on her lips, silencing her, and arguments frittered away like fireflies melting into darkness. "As long as you are in my protection, you will do as I ask," he said. "You may comfort the baroness if you wish, but no healing. Now give me your word."

She couldn't think, couldn't breathe for his finger was straying now across the fullness of her lower lip, leaving a trail of pleasure in its wake.

"Sometimes I think you are a witch," he muttered, drawing his hand away.

Merry's insides quivered. "You said I was a lady," she reminded him.

His gaze dropped to her breasts as he took a deliberate step back. "You would do well to remember that," he said, turning toward the door. "Rest well," he said, disappearing with a final, backward glance.

Once her heart resumed its normal beat, Merry realized she'd gotten away with not giving him her word. She listened for the sound of him entering the chamber next to hers. The moment she was certain he was sleeping, she would slip from her room to comfort the distressed baroness, promising her a tonic that would save her husband's life.

THE sound of shattering stone awakened Merry the following morning. She cracked an eye. The light beaming through the fragile seams of her bed drapes was already bright. *Jesu*, she had overslept!

She threw back the musty bedcovers and hurried to the washbasin.

The Phoenix had clearly begun his work of tearing down unsanctioned structures. He wasted no time, Merry reflected, scrubbing her face. The water was cold, unlike the steaming buckets that had arrived last night, along with a large, copper tub—a token of the baroness's gratitude.

Last night Merry had promised to brew a tonic first thing in the morning. Lady Adelle's relief was all she needed to defy the Phoenix outright. Yet the baroness had warned her that the castle leech had died a year ago. There were no medicines readily available.

With hasty fingers, Merry unraveled the plaits of her hair, causing it to fall into ringlets, still damp from last night's bath. She ran her fingers swiftly through them, and hastened to the baron's solar.

The baron's door flew open at her knock. "He's awake," cried the pale-faced baroness. "He tries to speak but is unable. He grows more agitated by the moment. We have to hurry!"

Merry found the baron propped against a mountain of pillows, a manservant hovering over him. When he tried to speak, only a gurgling escaped him.

"Keep him comfortable," Merry instructed the manservant. She took Lady Adelle's hand and said, "Take me to your herb garden."

Her hopes sank minutes later, for the herb garden resembled

a graveyard, complete with leaning headstones. The drought had killed most of the plants. "This won't work," she admitted. The thunder of pickaxes cast a pall of gloom over the enclosed garden. "We have to find a plant growing wild. Lead me to the outer ward."

Together, the women left the keep. As they crossed the courtyard, Kit leapt from a window slit in the garrison and bounded up to greet them.

"Kit!" Merry cried, scooping him up for a quick kiss. "I've missed you, too." At Lady Adelle's curious look, she put the cat down hastily and continued on their course.

Oblivious to his betrayal, Kit trailed happily behind.

The trio filed into the outer ward where the sun had already scaled the walls, infusing the air with summerlike warmth. Normally, this strip of land between the inner and outer walls was used for training. But at Iversly, weeds had besieged the practice field and taken over. The men-at-arms were all too old to hone their skills.

Merry glanced uneasily at the eastern tower. Though disguised by scaffolding and swarming with men, Luke was easy to spy upon the wall walk. He stood shirtless, his back to her as he directed his men. A metallic clamor filled the air, and rock pattered the earth not far away.

Fearing he would spy her and guess her intent, Merry hurried around the corner, with the baroness and Kit close behind. Once out of sight of the army, she fixed her gaze on the ground, and the hunt for a cure began.

They had reached the far side of the castle before she found what she needed. Hardy stalks of motherwort, with their tiny pink flowers, grew in thick clumps. "Here!" Merry cried, pulling several plants, roots and all, from the soil.

Motherwort was a member of the nettle family. Sarah had often used a powdered form to settle the wombs of pregnant women. Its warm properties calmed the heart and induced tranquility. It was the perfect remedy to counteract the baron's agitation.

Relieved to have found something, Merry gripped the long stalks in one hand. "Is there another entrance?" she asked the baroness.

Lady Adelle frowned at her, not understanding. "There is the postern gate," she admitted, "but we keep it locked."

"Don't you have the key?"

"Not I. The master-at-arms keeps it."

Merry swallowed hard. "We'll have to be swift, then," she said, offering no explanation. Keeping close to the wall, she led the way back to the main entrance, relieved that Kit, at least, was chasing crickets and had ceased to follow.

The sudden quiet warned her that the soldiers were resting. Peeking around the corner, she cursed her timing. The men had descended from the tower to gather round a barrel. Passing shirtless men was not a circumstance she would have relished normally, and certainly not now, knowing the captain would have something to say if he saw her. Swiveling on her toes, she determined to wait it out.

"What is it?" the baroness asked. A long wisp of gray hair had worked free of her headdress. Her blue eyes reflected suffering and bafflement.

Merry took immediate pity on her. She could not afford to be cowed by Sir Luke's demands. "If the Phoenix forbids me to help you," she said to the woman, "you must speak up for me, else your husband will go untreated."

"Why would he forbid it?" the baroness inquired. "Does he want my Ian to die?"

"Nay, nay, 'tisn't that!" Merry assured her. "He doesn't want me to be blamed, should your husband not get better," she answered, supplying Luke's excuse.

"But he must get better!" cried the baroness. She wrenched the stalks of motherwort from Merry's hand and marched around the corner alone. Merry had no choice but to hurry after her. She ran straight into the Phoenix, who had apparently set out to corner them.

She leapt back, even more dismayed to come face-to-face with him so abruptly. She had seen him shirtless before, but only in the dark. This morning, his torso gleamed with sweat; his muscles bulged. With his hair slicked back from his forehead, his eyes seemed sharper than ever, like an eagle's. The slight crease between his eyebrows caused Merry's stomach to drop. She was exceedingly grateful that the baroness held the motherwort.

"Good morrow," Merry said, forcing lightness into her greeting. "Lady Adelle and I were taking a walk."

He unpinned her with his gaze long enough to greet the baroness. " 'Tis rather hot for a walk," he commented, his tone laced with skepticism. His gaze flickered to the stalks of motherwort.

Merry glanced at the line of hair arrowing from Luke's chest to the waistline of his chausses. The sight of it caused her to lose track of the conversation.

"The heat is tremendous," agreed the baroness. "We must be heading in. Good day." She brushed by Luke with her shoulders squared.

He stepped to one side, blocking Merry's path as she made to follow. "Did I not make my wishes clear to you, lady?" he demanded quietly. Twin flames of anger flickered in his eyes.

Did nothing get by him? She jutted her chin into the air. "Do I tell you how to do your work?" she countered. "Nay. Go back to tearing down towers, then, and leave me to mine."

He reached for her arm, gripping it firmly. "My work isn't likely to kill an old man," he retorted. "If I cannot trust you to stay out of trouble, then I will keep you by my side."

She didn't believe him. She would be too much a burden to him trailing him about. " 'Tis your work that has made him ill in the first place," she replied, trying in vain to free herself. "I wager if you stopped your destruction, he would rally within a day."

The baroness returned just then, wresting her from the captain's grasp. "Excuse us," she cut in with an offended tone. "We were enjoying a walk." She tugged Merry forcibly away.

*Well done*, Merry thought. Relishing her victory, she couldn't resist a backward glance and was pleased to note a dull blush on Sir Luke's cheekbones as he glowered after them.

She realized with amazement that she'd enjoyed their confrontation. It made no sense that she would find pleasure in defying him. Not only was he a warrior, but she was also utterly at her mercy. He could do with her as he pleased—lock her in her chamber, punish her physically if he wished. Only she had no fear he would take such measures. He'd treated her well, up to this point, content to lecture her where another man might have struck her.

But more than that, she'd begun to realize a certain power within herself, something Luke was wary of. He was not unmindful of her wishes, she was certain. Just how much she could get away with she would have to discover for herself.

Meanwhile, the thrill of defying him fizzed in her blood. For the moment, anyway, she'd gained the reprieve she needed to treat the baron's malady. Whether Luke threw up his hands in surrender or fulfilled his threat remained to be seen.

With the sun beating down on his shoulders, Luke watched the pair flee, clutching their bouquet of ugly flowers like children pilfering sweets from the kitchen.

God's blood, the woman had defied him outright! The toss of her flaming hair was like the wave of a kerchief to mark the start of a tourney. He was tempted to chase her down right now and turn her over his knee! Only he'd never beaten a woman in his life, and he didn't intend to start, no matter how much the lady needed to be taught restraint.

There wasn't a man in his army who would have ignored a direct order from him! He'd made his wishes perfectly clear: she was not to treat the baron.

She'd be lucky if she didn't kill the old man with those ugly weeds.

He ground his back molars together. *Jesu,* at this rate, she'd be imprisoned for witchcraft before they even left Iversly! Her good intentions would count for nothing if the baroness turned against her. Yet for now the woman had put her faith in Merry, and it would seem heartless to wrest the girl from the older woman's side.

He would do it tomorrow, then. Before Merry found herself the scapegoat for an old man's demise. Recalling her parting words, he experienced a wrenching of guilt. If the man did die, it wouldn't be Merry's fault. In that, she was right. 'Twas the threat to raze his castle that had brought on the attack. Luke shifted his feet, uncomfortable with his conclusions.

Regardless of the cause, Merry would be blamed, he reasoned. He would find a means then to free her from the baron's bedside ere that circumstance occurred. He narrowed his eyes. Merry hadn't responded to an outright order. He would have to lure her by subtler means; make her think that she controlled her destiny when, in fact, she did not. He'd dealt with her kind before, though they were usually stubborn nobles, accustomed to getting their way.

He devised a plan. Simple enough. By this time tomorrow, she would be safe beneath his wings and out of harm's way.

He was turning back to work when an unsettling thought pricked his satisfaction. Was he truly thinking of Merry's safety or was he seeking ways to keep her in his company?

He'd not been able to wrest her from his thoughts that entire morning.

He shook his head, cursing his impulse to touch her lips last night. Discovering them soft and silky had only heightened his interest in her. Her soft gasp of pleasure had echoed in his mind ever since, thrilling him with each and every recollection.

He'd found himself wondering if she would taste the way she smelled—like fire, spice, and intoxicating herbs.

Nay, it got him nowhere to think such thoughts. With an imposition of his will, he rescued his mind from the dangerous exercise and sent a signal to his sergeant that the work should resume. Taking the tower steps two at a time, he swore to himself he wouldn't think of Merry until the day's work was done.

MERRY tucked a straggling tendril behind her ear and straightened. Her back ached from bending over the baron all day, yet she had finally persuaded him to swallow. If only he had drunk the whole cup! The infusion was so mild it would take more than a sip for the baron to improve.

Instructing the baroness to try again, she bid the lady good night and slipped from the lord's chamber, intent upon collapsing onto her own bed. Night had stolen suddenly upon them, and she'd had not a moment to herself all day.

As she closed the door behind her, a shadow detached itself from the wall. Luke had clearly been waiting for her. Recognizing his tall form, Merry suppressed a groan. She'd looked forward to testing her newly discovered power over him, but not now. Not when she felt like a well-wrung rag.

He stopped before her, his broad shoulders dwindling the width of the hallway. Even in the dimness, she could tell he had recently bathed, recognizing the fragrance of his soap. She had yet to identify the herb used to scent it.

"A word with you lady," he began, in his usual, courteous manner.

She eyed him inquiringly, struck by how handsome he appeared with the mellow light of a torch licking over him. His dark hair gleamed, just a hint of curl at the ends.

"I heard you made an infusion from those weeds you picked in the outer ward."

"Weeds?" she retorted, cutting short her inspection. "Motherwort is not a weed. 'Tis a benign herb with soothing qualities. And it isn't likely to kill him, no matter what your concerns. So if you mean to lecture me, you can save yourself the trouble."

He gave her a tiny smile, seemingly unperturbed by her prickly interruption. "Allow me to jump straight to my proposition, then. Your expertise is needed on the wall."

The air gusted out of Merry's lungs. She stared at him blankly. "Whatever do you mean?"

His eyes gave a gleam, and for the tiniest of moments, he seemed to be gloating. "Three of my men were injured when a portion of the wall fell on them this afternoon. Gervaise treated their cuts with a liniment that caused them all to swell."

Picturing the result, she couldn't help but wince. "Gervaise is just a barber," she said in his defense. "Likely he sets bones well enough, which I do not."

"Aye, he sets bones, but we require someone more adept at treating wounds." He tipped his head slightly to one side, waiting, watchful.

Merry sensed a trap. "What of the baron?" she asked, recalling their disagreement. "I can't just leave him."

"The infusion is made?" he queried.

"Aye."

"Then allow the baroness tend him. You've done more than enough."

*Was that sarcasm?* If so, it was cloaked in such blandness, she couldn't be sure. She narrowed her eyes at him. "If I refuse you?" she asked, testing him. Her blood began to bubble at the prospect of defying him again.

"Do as you will," he said, shrugging. "My men have survived cuts and scrapes before."

She considered how such wounds were prone to fester.

Nonetheless the baron's situation was far more tenuous. "I'm needed more here," she decided. "I will watch the baron until he improves." She lifted her chin a notch, challenging the captain to forbid her.

His expression remained perfectly impassive. "I can only point out the risk. You endanger yourself by treating him," he added.

"Nonsense." She found it immensely enjoyable to contradict him. "The infusion is so mild, I could drink it now and suffer no ill effect. If the baron dies of anything, 'twill be a broken heart." She gave him a pointed look. "And you will be the cause of that."

His expression did not change, but his eyes seemed to burn from the inside out. "I am under orders from the crown to do a job," he said succinctly.

"And I have a job to do as well," she countered, propping her hands upon her hips.

"Do it on the wall where your skills will meet with more success."

"What, have I failed already? I've scarcely begun to treat the baron and already you accuse me of failure."

"He is old, Merry. He is likely to die no matter what skills you may possess."

"I will not give up on him for such a reason," she avowed.

He took a sudden step forward, an abrupt movement that betrayed, at last, a slipping of his self-control. "You swore to me you would make no trouble, lady," he reminded her. "I ask now that you keep your word."

The planes of his face seemed harsher in the shadow. She sensed that she ought to be afraid of him. Instead, the racing of her blood made her reckless. She took her own step forward, angling her chin into the air to look him in the eye. "I will keep my word and stay out of trouble as I promised," she agreed. "But only on one condition."

It was his turn to look wary. "Speak it."

"No more interference. You must allow me to do my job, as you do yours."

He hesitated, a look of frustration entering his eyes. "Wounds and cuts," he offered. "You may treat those and naught else."

She threw her hands up in frustration. "Fine, then you may tear down just the towers and leave the wall and garrison intact."

He drew up to his full height. "Your role as healer has nothing to do with my work here," he growled, his temper on the rise.

Merry congratulated herself on cracking his self-control. "On the contrary. 'Tis your work that gave me my first patient." She knew she was goading him; she simply couldn't help it.

"Lady—" He grabbed her by the shoulders and gave her a single shake. "There are moments when I truly think you a witch. Do not presume to tell me how to do my job."

*Do not tell me how to do mine.* She longed to counter with those words, but they caught in her throat, frozen by her overwhelming awareness of his strength. If he were suddenly to unleash his anger on her. . . . Perhaps she had been unwise to test him.

His grip loosened slowly. But then his gaze fell to her lips, and with a low groan, he bent his head and pressed his mouth to hers.

Merry's heart suspended its beat. She braced herself for violation, yet she was paralyzed, unable to step away. His mouth was firm yet smooth. The pressure too light to be threatening, too real to ignore. He molded his lips to hers, and pleasure shimmered unexpectedly, spreading with the increased pressure of his lips, recalling her heart to beat once more.

His thumb pressed her jaw down, and she realized with a gasp that he meant to kiss her more deeply. Her lips parted, and his tongue sleeked in.

A languid caress ensued, stirring warmth inside her. Merry's eyes melted shut. His fingers on her chin were all that kept her upright, as her knees turned liquid.

She imagined him a sorcerer, stirring magic potions in a great, black kettle.

But then he severed the kiss abruptly, stepping back, and he was once more just the Phoenix, all cool composure and daunting self-control.

Without his support, Merry staggered backward, coming up against the wall. Her heart pounded with amazement. She gazed at Luke dumbstruck and disoriented.

He'd kissed her! He'd kissed her and she'd not only survived his kiss, she'd tasted pure magic on his lips. Who would
have guessed?

"I'll waken you at dawn," he said tersely, his expression
impossible to read. Swiveling on his heels, he stalked away,
disappearing into his chamber and shutting the door firmly
behind him.

Blood swished against Merry's eardrums. The kiss lingered
like a warm, disturbing dream. She stood there in the darkened
hallway, questioning the reality of what had happened.

The Phoenix had kissed her. 'Twas nothing like the sloppy
kisses she'd endured from Ferguson's filthy soldiers. Nor was
the kiss cold and practiced, as she might have expected the captain's kiss to be. Not at all. The savagery she'd sensed beneath
his stoic veneer had never been more evident than in that kiss.

Recalling the tingling of her lips, the magical ingredients
that swirled within her, she found she wanted to be kissed by
him a second time.

She laughed softly in the darkness—a laugh that was part
amazement, part relief, and part feminine intuition. *Mercy,* she
had more influence over him than she'd originally thought. Not
only had she gotten away with scolding him for his duties,
she'd provoked him to the point of kissing her.

She couldn't wait to provoke him again.

# *Chapter Seven*

MERRY lifted the heavy plait off her neck and prayed for a cooling breeze. Unlike the men, she could not strip off the tunic that she wore, and a constant stream of perspiration trickled between her shoulder blades and dampened her breasts. The sun glared down on the granite wall walk, making the crenellated shelves on either side too hot to sit on. So Merry stood, with nothing to do, as soldiers swarmed around her, surrounding her in a thunder of ringing metal and flying stone.

She felt she would be far more useful in the castle keep than out here with the men. She stood off to one side, out of range of the flying chips and shards. Just far enough away to be called upon if needed. To be forgotten until then.

Her mouth felt dry. Tiny grains of rock and debris had found their way between her teeth. She longed for a cup of water, but the Phoenix had yet to call a break. He and his men worked as she'd never seen anyone work before, hacking at the tower as if their lives depended on it.

Try as she might, she could not see the purpose of destroying the outer wall. What if Malcolm, King of Scots, suddenly got the notion to invade England? What if the Welsh decided to start trouble? How could Iversly defend itself without towers to volley arrows from or a means to pour hot oil over the heads of the attackers?

Surely the Phoenix could see the folly in tearing down the baron's stronghold. Yet he was bound by his duty. No doubt there were grave consequences for defying Henry's mandates. Thus he worked alongside the men, putting forth as much effort as they for a job that could be nothing but distasteful to him.

He seemed oblivious to the men's complaints about her presence. From the moment Luke escorted her up the tower steps, she'd been conscious of their glares. Clearly they feared some disaster now that "the witch" was among them.

Merry sighed and cast a worried look at the baron's chamber. Its windows were tightly shuttered. She hadn't had time to check on his condition before Luke roused her from a deep sleep. She prayed Lady Adelle had more luck than she in getting her husband to drink the infusion. What if she hadn't, and the baron died?

Luke was right. It took little imagination to see herself taking the blame for his demise. She had come to that conclusion herself, or she wouldn't be standing in the sun now, sweltering.

Tugging the tunic from her neck, Merry directed her gaze over the wall to the wild hills. A line of dark clouds scored the horizon, promising relief from the heat. Under her breath she murmured a phrase that Sarah had taught her to bring the clouds in faster. "Come rain to drench the ground, 'till all around the herbs abound."

The soldier nearest to her pivoted swiftly, his pickax suspended in the air. "What'd ye say?" he demanded, a wildly suspicious look in his eyes.

With an inward groan, Merry recognized Cullin. She gave him a neutral look, her gaze falling to the pink bumps that ridged his neck. "I wasn't speaking to you," she replied, experiencing a subtle vindication. The poison oak had done its work.

"Aye, ye did. I heard ye cursin' someone under yer breath. It better not've been me." He took a menacing step toward her.

She backed away from him, relieved to see Luke wending his way toward them.

"Is there a problem here, Cullin?" he inquired, giving the mercenary a dark look.

Cullin scratched his oily, sand-colored hair. Rings of sweat stained his undershirt just beneath the arms. "The witch here just put a curse on me," he muttered. "I don't like her up here."

Merry was surprised to see a flash of raw anger on Luke's face. "In the first place, Cullin," he replied in a voice as sharp as his blade, "she isn't a witch. Secondly, I don't much care whether you approve of her presence or not. She is here by my request. Henceforth you will call her Lady Merry. Is that clear enough?"

Through his stubby lashes, Cullin gave her a narrow-eyed glare. To his leader, he muttered a brief affirmative and turned his back on them.

Luke took Merry by the elbow and steered her some distance down the wall where she was less likely to incite Cullin's superstitions. "What did you say to him?" he demanded, frustration lacing his tone.

"Not a thing," she insisted. "I'm thirsty and I'm hot and I'm tired of standing here with naught to do but to sweat!"

His fingers curled about her elbow, making her all too aware of him. "Have a care in how you speak to the men," he advised her. "They're an uneducated lot, especially the mercenaries like Cullin."

"I tell you, I said not a word to him!"

"Lower your voice. The men are watching."

She wondered briefly whether it would gain her anything to provoke him now. Nay, she decided, his control would hold in the presence of his men. Still, she caught him glancing at her mouth, and a thrill chased through her.

"Stay away from Cullin," he repeated, taking a visible step back.

*Ah, so he was tempted.* She offered him a knowing smile then lifted her face to the breeze. There was something to Sarah's rain spell, after all, for the clouds had surged closer.

Luke scowled at Merry's profile. God help him, he wanted to grab her and kiss her right here, right now, regardless of their audience. She knew it, too, little witch, smiling at him like that.

*Fool!* He berated himself. Kissing her last night had been an impulse he immediately regretted. Somehow she'd provoked him into losing his temper—the same temper he claimed not to have. How dare she tell him to defy his prince and leave his work here undone! He'd kissed her just to silence her, to make it plain that her judgments were unwelcome and presumptuous.

Yet now he couldn't get the taste of her from his tongue, and he craved more of it.

The realization left him shaken. Merry was the last sort of woman he should find intriguing. She embodied all that was impulsive and emotional, two human tendencies he found disturbing. He, himself, had long overcome them. Yet, for no apparent reason, he could not banish the memory of last night's kiss. Nor could he deny his reckless desire to kiss her again.

*Jesu,* if he didn't know better, he would say she'd cast a spell on him.

"Stay well out of the way 'til you are needed," he ordered, frustrated by his errant thoughts. He swiveled away, questioning his decision to bring her on the wall in the first place.

He hadn't taken four steps when the shouts of his men wrested his attention. "Get that bloody cat off the wall!" one of the men roared.

It was then Luke spotted Merry's cat, darting among the feet of his soldiers as it headed toward its mistress. With a blistering curse, Luke went to chase it.

Finding himself pursued, Kit scurried between the feet of a soldier still swinging his ax. Surprised by the brush of fur against his legs, the man took his eyes off his tool. Luke saw the inevitable consequence. The point of the pickax slammed straight into Phillip's shin.

Merry screamed behind him.

A roar of agony split the humid air. The hulking mercenary from Poitiers doubled over, dropping his ax as if it were a venomous snake. With another roar of pain, he collapsed onto his back, clutching his knee to his chest and cursing profusely.

The cat bolted away from the horrendous noise.

Luke sprinted to the fallen man and went down on one knee. He quickly examined Phillip's leg. A bright, puddle of blood welled through the man's hose. Worse yet, a bit of bone stuck straight through the fabric, telling Luke that the break was severe. "Find Gervaise," Luke ordered one of his soldiers.

"Merde!" shouted the giant again. Beads of perspiration dotted his bald head as he ground his molars together.

"Please, let me through. Step aside."

Over the sounds of confusion, Luke heard Merry pushing her way through the crowd. The next moment she kneeled opposite him to lean over the invalid. Luke, like his men, eyed her mistrustfully. After all, she had practically been the cause of the accident. "Gervaise will be here shortly," he informed her, indicating that she need not tend to this particular injury.

Merry ignored him. "Someone fetch me an arrow or a stick!" she called. She glanced at Phillip's wound, and Luke saw the color drain from her face.

"Gervaise is coming," he repeated. "There's naught that you can do for him."

Phillip roared as agony broke over him in a fresh wave.

"I need a bloody arrow!" Merry shouted, frantic to put him out of his misery.

The men drew back, some of them crossing themselves as if to ward off evil.

Luke was about to drag Merry away when someone handed her an arrow with the point broken off. She bent over Phillip and put a tender hand on his cheek. "Bite down on the arrow, soldier," she commanded him. "Do it now."

Responding to the mixture of tenderness and authority, the giant opened his jaw a fraction, and she thrust the stick between his teeth, keeping him from grinding his molars to powder.

Several bystanders murmured their approval. Luke decided to let her continue.

Sweat still poured from Phillip's bald head. Merry pointed at another soldier. "You, find me a flask of wine, or something stronger if you have it. Go, hurry!" She waved him away, and the man, fearing she might put a hex on him, scrambled to obey.

Merry met Luke's gaze over the writhing body between them. "We need a large block of ice to keep the leg from swelling. Send a man to the kitchens to inquire," she suggested.

"I'll go," volunteered a soldier standing nearby.

At that moment, Gervaise finally joined them, huffing from his long trek up the tower steps. "Ah!" he cried, throwing himself down beside the wounded man. He inspected the break with something close to glee. "This will take some work," he stated. He thumped down a satchel that gave a metallic ring and began to fish inside of it.

"Not here!" Merry cried, bristling with alarm. "Mary's blood, this place is filthy! The man hasn't had any wine yet!"

Gervaise took immediate offense to her language. "You think you can tell me how to do my job?" he shouted back. "I've been setting bones since before you came into the world naked and screaming!"

"Gervaise!" Luke interrupted. He did not appreciate the mention of Merry naked, for he could see the sudden interest in the eyes of the men, who were no doubt picturing her naked right now. "We do as the lady says," Luke decided.

Just then a soldier handed him a wineskin, and he passed it on to Merry who took it with a quick smile of gratitude. He felt better for putting his faith in her.

Tugging the arrow from the giant's teeth, Merry assisted him to empty the wineskin. Phillip swallowed so eagerly that he scarcely spilled a drop.

"Give him another moment," Merry begged. She stroked the giant's chest, crooning words of comfort. She seemed oblivious to her audience.

Luke glanced up at his men, wondering what they thought of her now. He wasn't surprised to see the broad range of expressions on their faces, from hope to envy to wild superstition. She had the same effect on him.

At last Phillip's eyelids drooped. He ceased to shout profanities. With Merry's nod of approval, Luke appointed three men to carry him, and they levered him off the ground.

The giant came roaring back to life as they struggled to carry him down the myriad steps, all the way to his cot in the garrison.

"We must do something for the pain," Merry begged many moments later. They had peeled away Phillip's hose, revealing the extend of his injuries. Blood no longer leaked from the wound, thanks in part to the block of ice that was now propped against it.

"He's emptied two wineskins already," Luke pointed out. "He's a warrior Merry; he can tolerate the pain. Look at his right hand."

She noticed for the first time that Phillip was missing his ring finger. "Just get it done then," she begged, her gaze sliding to Gervaise. "This is your area of expertise," she informed the man. "Do it well." She stalked to the far side of the garrison hall, where a roaring fire burned in the fire pit.

Hugging herself, Merry fought to quell the tremors that seized her. Queasiness roiled within her, but she refused to succumb to it. Healers did not lapse into shock every time they saw blood. But Merry did.

She was grateful for the roll of thunder that drowned out the giant's moans as Gervaise worked to set the bone aright. The darkening sky caused uncertain light to seep through the narrow windows lining one wall. A similar disquiet settled over her as she waited for the hardest part to pass.

The soldiers had taken advantage of Phillip's accident and the approaching storm to spend the afternoon in idleness. Most of them reclined upon their pallets. Erin played chess with a black-haired mercenary. While the men ignored her for the most part, she felt their darting and accusing glances like pricking needles. She'd overheard one say that he would kill her cat if he found it.

Suddenly a voice rasped in her ear, so close that Merry leapt away from it. "So it was Phillip ye cursed wi' yer words, was it?"

She spun around and found Cullin leaning against a center beam next to her.

"Ye called yer familiar ta sneak up on 'im and make 'im miss his aim," the man continued.

"Don't talk to me," she muttered, stepping back.

"Why not?" he challenged, pursuing her. "Will ye do the same to me as ye did to Phillip?" He ran an insolent gaze over her boy's attire, and Merry shifted, disliking the sly look that entered his slate-colored eyes.

"I didn't curse Phillip," she replied. " 'Twas an accident."

"And the packhorse fallin' into the gorge and comin' out alive? Was that an accident, too?" he taunted. "And what of the blisters on me neck and back? I suppose ye've got nothin' ta do with that now, have ye?"

Merry glanced toward the far side of the room, hoping for Luke's intervention. A fork of lightning split the sky outside, lighting the Phoenix's handsome face for the briefest moment. He was bent over Phillip's cot, keeping close eye on Gervaise's work.

A crack of thunder shook the stones under Merry's feet. She kept her silence as Luke had asked, refusing this time to rise to Cullin's taunts.

"Ye'd better watch yourself, witch," he added in a silky undertone.

She glanced back at him, not liking the threat in his tone. "Stay away from me," she told him again, "else I *will* put a curse on you."

His lips pulled back in a feral smile. "Ye already have," he answered eerily. He might have been referring to the poison oak, but his gaze fell to her breasts, pushed higher by the arms she'd wrapped around herself to quell her trembling.

With a shiver of revulsion, Merry whirled away and approached the pair playing chess. She pretended to watch them a moment. But then Erin and his black-haired companion lifted hostile looks at her, and she moved past them toward the only refuge left in the garrison, under the wings of the Phoenix.

She found Phillip unconscious. The giant had passed out from the pain. Gervaise was busy at a washbasin, washing the blood off his myriad tools. Luke gestured to a pile of bandages. "Can you wrap his leg?" he asked her.

To her discerning eye, Merry thought he looked a little gray beneath his tan, but his expression was as unperturbed as always. "Doesn't Gervaise want to do it?" she asked, noting that the wound had begun to bleed from the tugging and reshaping of the leg. She swallowed hard and looked away.

"You may do it, lady," Gervaise called generously. It was clear that setting the bone was the only part that held interest for him.

Merry glanced from the bandages to Phillip's battered flesh. "I would like to make an ointment first," she said, lifting pleading eyes at Luke. "Surely you've heard of knitbone," she added. " 'Tis excellent for healing broken bones. There may be live roots in the castle garden—"

"No herbs," he answered shortly. He pointed at the bandages. "Do you want to wrap his leg, or shall I?"

What Merry wanted was to knock him on the head and shout that knitbone was a common remedy used in any household. He didn't have to fear that she would kill his soldier with a salve, by heaven!

She considered marching out of the garrison door and heading straight for the herb garden, ignoring his refusal. But the clouds outside had buckled, and rain pelted the cobbles in heavy drops. It would be difficult enough to locate the herb in the pouring rain.

Instead, she snatched up the bandages and wrapped Phillip's leg with a vengeance, grateful that the giant had swooned and couldn't complain about her rough treatment.

Moments later, she was surprised when the Phoenix squatted next to her. He nodded approvingly at her handiwork, then gave her a searching look. "You look pale, Merry. Are you well?" he asked.

She hid her trembling fingers in her lap and looked away. "Of course," she lied. She could feel the heat of his body, given his proximity. She knew an overwhelming urge to rest her head on his shoulder, to give over to his strength. The urge surprised her as much as his kiss last night. She had always relied on her own strength, not trusting another—certainly not a warrior—to comfort her.

He gave her knee a squeeze. "You kept your head when everyone else was seized with panic," he added, his eyes alight with respect.

Merry grew warm from the inside out. Suddenly she was no longer weary but euphoric. " 'Tis my job," she murmured, heat stealing into her cheeks.

"Come," he added, standing and extending her a hand. "It's been a long morning. Let us join Lady Adelle for the midday meal. You can inquire after the baron's health," he added kindly.

With a backward glance at the sleeping invalid, Merry slipped her hand into his, reveling in the heat of his palm, the firmness of his grasp. It wasn't only his kiss that pleased her.

THAT night her dreams were a tapestry of images, most of them gory. Toward the end, she dreamed of Luke, and the images of blood and bone gave way to better things.

He awaited her in the outer ward, standing on a bed of buttercups. He took both her hands in his, his eyes bright with

admiration. Then he began to whirl her round and round, until
they both fell breathless upon the flowers.

He tied a blindfold over her eyes. "Don't be afraid," he murmured. She was not at all afraid of him. "Lie down." She lay
back on the fragrant carpet, and he kissed her, not just her
mouth but her neck and her shoulders, even her breasts. She felt
suffused with warmth and pleasure. His mouth moved lower,
opening over the soft plane of her belly, which now lay exposed
to him. He lightly licked her hip, her thigh. She felt no qualms
about his slow seduction; instead, she opened herself, unfurling
like a flower.

Suddenly the blindfold was ripped from her eyes. To her
horror, it wasn't Luke looming over her but Cullin, the mercenary. He squeezed her breasts until they hurt. He bit her shoulder. As he thrust her legs apart, preparing to ram himself inside
of her, Merry jerked to wakefulness.

She scrambled to a sitting position, her heart thudding in her
chest. For a terrifying moment, she thought someone was in the
chamber with her. A cold sweat bathed her pores as she strained
her ears for sounds of an intruder.

Then she heard it, a scraping against her window.
Remembering the ill feelings harbored by some of Luke's soldiers, Merry rose trembling from the bed. She snatched up the
poker that was used to stir the brazier and gripped it until it cut
into her palm.

Very slowly, she approached the window. Reaching out, she
grasped the knob and flung the shutter wide.

Kit's black form was outlined against the blue-black sky. He
hissed and arched his back as she raised the poker against him.

"Kit!" she exclaimed, dropping the weapon. "How did you
get here?" She reached for him, lifting him into her arms. His
fur was damp and cool. "Oh, Kit, have they been chasing you?"

She cast a wary look out the window and saw no one. Kit
must have leapt onto the kitchen roof, then picked his way
along the narrow ledge, for she was on the second story.

Merry shut the window and carried the cat to her bed. The
moment she placed him on the blankets he began to purr contentedly. She slipped beneath the covers and stroked the lingering fear out of him. "Don't worry," she promised him. "I won't

let them harm you." With the throb of his purr in her ear, she fell asleep again.

"I'M lame and useless, lady. You shouldn't have to stay with me."

Merry glanced at the soldier whose feet stuck out over the end of his cot. She hadn't known he was awake. The others had followed their leader out of the garrison this morning, shortly after dawn. Luke had awakened her minutes before with the charge that Phillip would need his bandages changed.

From what Merry could tell, the sun had yet to surmount the horizon, and already the men were back on the wall, splintering the peaceful quiet with the sound of their blows. They'd left Phillip to rest and recuperate.

Merry put down her mug of watered beer and approached the prone figure. "Believe me," she assured him, "I would much rather tend a wounded man than stand on that wall feeling useless."

He grunted by way of reply, and she had just decided he had lapsed into sleep when he turned his head. A strip of light fell across his bright blue eyes. "Thank you for your care," he said gruffly. "Your touch is gentle."

*Another compliment!* She stood still a moment, overcome with joy. "Well," she heard herself say, "Gervaise set the bone for you. That part I couldn't do. You were in a great deal of pain," she added.

He lifted his disfigured hand into the air. " 'Twas worse when I lost my finger," he said.

She looked at the space where his finger used to be. "How did it happen?" she asked.

" 'Tis a long story."

She ran a dry gaze around the empty garrison. "Have you somewhere to go?" she countered.

Phillip gave a huff of laughter. "Nay. If you really want to hear the story, then I'll tell you."

Merry eased her backside onto one of the rough pallets—a mat of straw laid across a bench, supposedly out of reach of vermin that crawled in the rushes.

Phillip's cot crackled as he propped himself up on one

elbow. "You may not believe this," he began, "but I was born a fisherman's son!" He grinned so widely that his white teeth flashed in the semidarkness. "We lived in Poitiers, my father and I, and we fished every day beneath the cliffs of Chateaux Briand. In that castle lived the most exquisite woman I have ever seen—besides yourself," he added, gallantly, making her shake her head.

"Her name was Marguerite, and her father was the Count of Poitiers. On her sixteenth year, he decided to host a tourney to determine who should marry his daughter."

Phillip lowered his voice, conspiratorially. "I had seen the lady Marguerite many times walking the cliffs as I fished below. But I was not a warrior then, only a fisherman. Still, I told my father, 'Sell our fishing boat, *mon pere,* and I will win the lady!' My father believed in me, so he bought armor and a horse in exchange for our boat. For six months I trained. I learned by watching others fight. At last, the time came for the tourney."

"You're making this up," Merry interjected, though she was enchanted by the tale and the lively manner in which Phillip told it.

"Nay, 'tis true! I swear it by my sword. I gave myself a noble title and forged the necessary documents," Phillip continued. "You should have seen Marguerite, sitting with the spectators the day of the tourney. I can still remember: Her dress was silver and blue, her hair was gold. She was so beautiful that my heart forgot to beat. I swore she would be my wife, if I had to die to win her.

"I began to fight. Without even growing winded, I made it to the final round with the greatest knights in France. I felt confident in my abilities, for it had been easy up until that point to unseat my opponents. But then, the Duke of Orleans swept me off my horse, and I cut my forehead against my helm. There was so much blood in my eyes I could not see.

"Still, I fought, and the crowd began to cheer for me. The finger of my right hand was severed—*Mon Dieu* but the pain was terrible! I moved my sword to the left, which I continue to use to this day. I would not surrender, so much did I love my lady. But I am only a man and, alack, I fainted for loss of blood."

Merry sighed with dismay. "Then you didn't win her," she concluded sadly.

"Not I," he agreed, looking dismal for a moment. Then he brightened. "But the greatest lords in France had witnessed my strength and determination. Many offered to hire me on as a mercenary, including the count of Anjou, Prince Henry's father."

"So you went from being a fisherman's son to serving royalty!" Merry marveled. "That *is* a tale worth telling, Phillip."

" 'Tis all true," he swore. He gave a shrug. "So, here I am," he added, with a hint of irony.

Merry clasped her hands in her lap. "I'm sorry my cat caused you injury," she apologized, quietly. "He didn't mean to, truly. He was only looking for me."

"Do not fret, lady," the giant answered kindly. " 'Twas an accident."

Merry noticed then that the room was growing lighter. "You're a kind man," she said. Still, she did not volunteer Kit's whereabouts, lest the others come after him.

"Your turn to tell a story," Phillip said, with an expectant look.

Merry averted her gaze. Threads of yellow light now illumined the rough cots, the woodwork on the beams, the whitewashed walls. The only stories that came to mind were ones she didn't wish to relive. "I haven't got any story to tell," she equivocated.

The giant regarded her for a discerning moment, then nodded once. "No matter, for I have another," he admitted cheerfully. "And this story is even better than mine: 'Tis the tale of the Phoenix and how he rose from the ashes."

Merry's heart beat faster at this mentioning of Luke. She had been thinking of him all morning, thanks in part to the dream that had begun so pleasantly last night.

"Not too many people know this," Phillip began, his voice pitched low, "but he was born a bastard." He darted a quick look at the door as though wary of being overheard. "His father was a crusader from the First Crusade, when Jerusalem was captured. He did not return home after that victory, but remained with Godfrey and Baldwin, to protect the city from

the Muslims. He took a Saracen woman to be his mistress, and
Luke le Noir was born a short time later."

Merry was aware that her jaw had gone slack. At last she
knew why he lacked a nobleman's name! Instead, he was called
Luke the Black, the perfect name for one who was half Saracen.
Hadn't she remarked something foreign about him?

"When Sir Luke's father died of fever years later, the boy
was forgotten," Phillip continued. "He spoke the language of
the Saracens, he lived among them, yet he was treated as an
outcast. 'Tis said he was half starved when his grandfather, the
Earl of Arundel, found him on the streets of Jerusalem."

"Was his grandfather looking for him?" Merry interrupted.

"Aye, he'd been looking for some time. With the death of his
son, this grandchild was his only heir. Sir William brought the
boy to England and civilized him. He taught him to read, both
Latin and French. Of course, he speaks his native tongue as
well. During the Second Crusade in which the Holy City was
lost, he served as translator."

Marveling at Luke's colorful past, Merry considered his
diplomatic skills, no doubt cultivated during his adjustments in
early life. "Will he inherit his grandfather's title?" she wondered.

Phillip's eyes twinkled. "The laws prevent him, a bastard,
from holding the title outright. Yet it may fall to his heirs. Let
me tell my story and you may decide for yourself." He cleared
his throat for dramatic effect. "The earl of Arundel, being a sup-
porter of Matilda, fostered his grandson to her half-brother, Sir
Robert of Gloucester. My lord spent his adolescence in
Normandy as Robert of Gloucester's squire. 'Twas there he
earned his famous name."

Merry was aware that the castle could fall under siege, and
she would still demand that Phillip finish his tale.

"He was finishing his training at Castle Carrouges, where
Matilda dwelled with her three sons. Henry and Geoffrey were
the eldest, about ten and eight at the time. It had been a dry
summer like this one, and one morning, when the cooks had
retired briefly, the kitchens caught fire. All the fighting men,
myself included, were called to put the fire out, but it raged on,
despite our efforts.

"At the same time, rumor spread that the princes had last been seen in the kitchens and no one could find them now."

Merry knotted her fingers together.

"As the fire could not be overcome, we were told to stand back. The roof would collapse at any moment. But my lord ignored the warning. He went into the building, where we thought he would surely perish. It seemed a lifetime passed. The fire roared higher. Though the roof held, we were certain everyone inside was dead. Then suddenly, Sir Luke appeared, leaping through the window with his cloak on fire and a boy in either arm. He had risked his life to save them! If not for him, Henry would not be heir to the throne this day," Phillip concluded, thumping his hand upon the bed frame.

Merry marveled at the tale. Luke had mentioned something of his bravery, yet his version had been far more modest. "He changed the course of history," she reflected.

"Indeed, he did."

"And his sword, it has a phoenix on the hilt."

Phillip nodded. "The sword was a gift from Matilda. He was knighted that very day. Henry named him captain soon after. Sir Luke is his most loyal vassal."

Merry looked down at her hands, surprised to find them white-knuckled. Phillip's tale filled her with awe and pride and, strangely, regret.

"So you see," Phillip summed up, "my lord's first son will likely be an earl. He is betrothed, you know, to the prince's cousin."

Betrothed. She hadn't known. The news turned her cold, or was it that a cloud outside had blocked the sunlight? An emptiness she couldn't begin to name spilled through her and spread.

The captain was betrothed. To the prince's cousin. A woman whose royal descent would ensure the passing on of his grandfather's title.

But . . . he had kissed Merry just last night.

How could he, when his betrothed awaited his homecoming? Unless he'd kissed her just to silence her.

She drew a sharp breath. Had she misinterpreted the kiss entirely? Had she been the only one to enjoy it? What did she know of kisses, anyway? Very little, since she'd been the recipient of unwanted kisses forced on her by lewd and filthy soldiers.

The emptiness within her spread. "I should eat something," Merry muttered, using that excuse to leave Phillip's side and examine the foodstuffs strewn upon a rickety table.

She swallowed a wedge of cheese without tasting it. Feeling self-conscious, she looked down at the clothing she had worn since the day of Luke's rescue. Erin's braies were filthy at the knee. A layer of dust had turned the tunic gray. The elbow was rent where she'd leaned against the wall yesterday. She hadn't had time to comb her hair this morning.

She closed her eyes as shame burned a merciless path to her cheeks. How could she have thought, even for a moment, that she held sway over the mighty Phoenix? She was no more powerful than the roach creeping past the toe of her right shoe. Worse than that, she looked like a commoner, dressed as she was, and a boy at that.

"Phillip," she said, turning a worried look on the giant from Poitiers. "Would you be all right without me for an hour or so?"

He had locked his hands behind his round head. "Of course," he said. "I was going to take a nap."

"Is there aught I can get you before I go?"

"Just a jakes if you can find one," he muttered, flushing.

Merry fetched a jakes from the bathhouse. Phillip looked away as she put it down beside his cot.

Bidding him a restful morning, she slipped out of the garrison to dart across the courtyard. She would seize the opportunity to gauge the baron's response to his infusion. And then she would ask Lady Adelle for the gown the baroness had tried to foist on her two days ago.

Why the desperate urge to improve her appearance? There was only one reason Merry would acknowledge. She didn't want the grandson of the earl of Arundel to say he'd been kissed by a witch and lived to tell about it.

# *Chapter Eight*

LUKE followed his sweaty army into the garrison. Ignoring the rumbling of his stomach, he allowed them to hasten toward the trestle of food ahead of him. After all, he would dine in the main hall shortly. The men were hungry, as he had forced them to work through the midday meal, promising them an earlier finish.

He wondered at his motivation to end the work early, especially when the task before them seemed interminable and every day brought the possibility that his grandfather would die ere his return. Normally the castle population was called upon to help, but the elderly vassals of the baron could scarcely walk upright, let alone use pickaxes or carry stones. Thus with so little in Luke's favor, it made no sense that he would give his men the evening off.

He had to suspect what he didn't wish to suspect—that he was eager for Merry's company. He denied this conclusion with the argument that she would treat Phillip with all manner of vile herbs if he failed to keep an eye on her. He told himself she might slip into the castle and poison the baron unwittingly. He'd sworn to deliver her to Helmesly, and he would do so, alive and well, so long as he kept her out of harm's way.

Across the length of the garrison hall, he sought sign of her tending Phillip. But Merry was too short to be seen over the heads of his men. Luke skirted the trestle table where the men vied for seats. Rounding the fire pit, he came to an abrupt halt.

There she was, almost unrecognizable in a gown of forest green. Bending tenderly over Phillip, her hair was a silken curtain gilded with afternoon light. Her breasts swelled over the gown's square neckline. Her face a picture of concentration as she eased the bandages away from Phillip's swollen limb.

In that instant, Luke was shaken by the inescapable revelation that he'd been longing to see her the entire day. More than that, he wanted to clap blinders on the eyes of every man present to prevent them from ogling the tops of Merry's breasts.

God's truth, maybe she had put a spell on him! He swallowed heavily, seeking the cool poise that helped him keep his head when others lost theirs. It was nowhere to be found.

Floundering for his composure, Luke approached the pair. He paused at the head of Phillip's cot, disproportionately relieved to find the giant sleeping. As Merry glanced up at him, her cheeks flushed with color, and she jerked her gaze away almost at once. "Look at this," she commanded of him, moving so that Luke could see the giant's leg.

He saw that Phillip's shin had swollen to gross proportions. The edges of the torn skin were inflamed. Infection, the dreaded tormentor of wounded souls, had found the Frenchman.

"This would not have happened," Merry said, fiercely, "had I put knitbone on the wound!"

Luke looked into her stormy green eyes and found his tongue in knots.

"Now he is eaten up with fever," she added, warming to her indignation. "He has been like this all afternoon. 'Twill be your fault if he dies," she added, her eyes dangerously bright. "He is a good man, and I refuse to take the blame!"

Luke could not remember the last time he'd been chastised by a woman. Amalie had subtler ways to show displeasure. Merry hid nothing from him.

She began to pace the length of Phillip's cot, back and forth, back and forth, her arms folded across her chest so that the mysterious shadow between her breasts grew more pronounced.

Luke watched her, his mind unable to move beyond the fact

that she looked like a perfect lady wearing a gown. The scent of her hair seemed to fill the large chamber. He was so focused on her that he failed to notice the attention she was gathering.

She whirled on him suddenly. "Have you nothing to say for yourself?" she demanded.

With a start, he glanced at his men. He was dismayed to find them watching the exchange with amazement. Some of them had forgotten to eat. They gaped at Merry, many of them eyeing her as if she were a vision of some long-dead saint.

"All you think about is that . . . that wretched tower and tearing it down!" she added, gesturing in the direction of the eastern wall. "Have you no concern for your men?" She gestured now at Phillip.

"He has concern for us." It was Erin, rushing to his lord's defense. The youth leapt up from the bench bearing a shredded loaf in his hand, the other half in his cheek.

It was time to take their conversation outside. Luke laid a grateful hand on his squire's shoulder. "Thank you, Erin, but the lady was addressing her grievances to me. Come," he added, seizing her elbow. "Let us take a walk, shall we?"

She gaped at him in amazement. "A walk?" she repeated. "Your man has a fever and you wish to take a walk?"

"To the herb garden," he said through his teeth. He could not believe she'd made it impossible for him to refuse her. And yet neither could he afford to make himself look more of a fool.

Her pink mouth rounded into an O of surprise. She fisted the material of her skirt and strode briskly past him.

Her fragrance tantalized him as she wafted past. He trailed after her, every inch of his body thrumming with awareness. He eyed the gentle sway of her hips, and the thrum became an ache.

Once within the courtyard he caught her by the elbow and spun her about. There were fewer witnesses out in the open, only an aged manservant strapping a nag to a cart. "Merry," he began. His gaze fell to the dazzling white expanse of her bosom, and he nearly forgot what he meant to say. "You should not have made a scene before my men," he lectured.

She wrenched her arm free and notched her hands on her hips. "It seems the only way to get your attention," she tossed back.

Little did she know she'd always had his full attention. "Where did you get that gown?" he snapped, irritated that it undermined his determination to ignore her.

She tossed her hair over her shoulder. "Lady Adelle gave it to me. Which means—oh, yes—I must have visited the baron today. And I would have you know he is much improved," she informed him, her chin angled self-righteously. "In fact, he rose from his bed to stand by the window. I'm surprised you didn't see him."

Actually, Luke had seen the baron. He'd looked up from the wall at one point to find the baron at his window. The man had looked so much like his grandfather that, for a startled minute, Luke had thought he was looking at a ghost. The incident had so unsettled him he'd had to put his ax down.

He ground his teeth together, aware that she was taunting him. "Did you increase his medications?" he asked evenly.

"Indeed I did. Two cupfuls a day are needed for the infusion to have any effect."

"Then you disregarded my wishes once again," he concluded. A flaring of anger caused him to raise his voice above its usual limits. "Not only do you forget what is in your best interest, but you taunt me with your defiance. I waste my breath to caution you. Cure Phillip as you see fit, then," he challenged. "If you wish to be thought a witch, far be it from me to stop you. I am not your keeper!"

With that, he abandoned her where she stood and stalked to the forebuilding. It was either retreat at once or grab the woman and crush his mouth to hers.

She had made him lose his temper again! He couldn't recall the last time he'd yelled at anyone. Had she no concept of the dangers she heaped on herself by toying with herbs? All it did was corroborate the superstitions of his men. Now he had to worry one of them might abduct her and return her to the Church for the monies promised.

Not that he could blame them. He was nearly ready to do the same himself.

Nay, that wasn't true. He knew her not to be a witch but a stubborn woman, certainly. His fingers flexed with frustration, and at the steps of the forebuilding, he cast her a glowering look.

She stood exactly where he'd left her, her eyes enormous pools of green.

Christ's blood, he'd hurt her feelings.

Luke wavered. This was the side of Merry he'd glimpsed only briefly, the side that roused his protective instincts. As she lowered her gaze to the cobbles, her expression crestfallen, his anger crumbled into dust. Before he realized it, he'd retraced his footsteps.

"My concerns are for your welfare," he insisted, stopping before her. "I have heard my men talking, Merry. It is true that they mistrust you. 'Twould be better to let Phillip's infection take its course than to produce a salve for him."

She shook her head. "His fever is too high," she answered in a small, determined voice. "I don't care what your men think of me, Captain. Phillip is suffering. Who will help him, if not I?" At last she raised her eyes to him, the picture of a perfect martyr.

He was reminded of his early impression of her—that she was a ministering angel, gone mad. Yet when she beseeched him with such noble purpose shining in her eyes, he found it impossible to refuse her. He could see that nothing would sway her from tending to the sick. He had to admire that kind of tenacity. The only way to ensure her safety, then, was to openly support her. He scratched his chin and sighed. "Then you and I will work together," he decided, grimly. "Show me to the herb garden."

The smile that lit her face snatched his breath away. Its incandescence rocked him on his heels. And when she reached for his hand and led him swiftly toward the kitchens, he felt as if he were walking on a current of air.

Her hand in his forged a connection that both dismayed and invigorated him. They were cohorts on a common mission, now. He told himself he was only acting as her protector, and yet he found he delighted in the slender coolness of her fingers laced through his.

As they moved along a path too narrow for two to walk abreast, he put an arm around her rather than release her. And though he pricked his shoulder on the overgrown hedge, he was rewarded by the softness of her breast. With every sacrifice came reward, he realized.

"Here we are," she said, as they came upon an open area surrounded on four sides by the castle buildings. She slipped away from him. "The garden is in deplorable condition," she added, prancing down a walkway of crushed shells. "They shouldn't have let it come to this. And yet everything about Iversly seems old and unkempt. Have you noticed?" She threw him a puzzled look and continued to sweep along the rows of dead plants.

Luke muttered something to the affirmative. His gaze was drawn to the indentation of her waist, so neatly defined in the tight bodice. She bent over here and there, examining leaves, breaking off bits of dried stem, clucking under her breath.

He watched her, masking his fascination for her with what he hoped approximated an expression of patience. Her breasts threatened to spill from her bodice whenever she bent forward. Her hair slipped over her shoulder, a curtain of fire, and he discovered that each vibrant strand held a different hue of sunlight, from copper to sienna to brightest red.

"Aha!" she cried, digging into the dry dirt. "The leaves are dead but the root still lives." She teased an ugly little clump out of the ground and held it up for him to see. "Knitbone," she said, triumphantly.

Luke was not impressed. But moments later, when she led him to the kitchens and scrubbed the dirt from the snarled tendrils, he saw that the roots were indeed alive. And when she crushed them in a mortar, releasing the juices, he felt his curiosity stir. Could such a small thing truly help Phillip to mend?

As they hurried back to the garrison, like children bearing a bouquet of dandelions for their mother, Luke realized that he had gone from banning the use of herbs outright to aiding and abetting a woman wanted by the Church.

*So much for holding the line,* he mused.

MERRY breathed harshly in the dark box of her bed. A coat of sweat smothered her skin. Not even the heavy presence of the cat beside her could abolish the dream she had just dreamed.

She'd been tied to the stake again. The flames had come closer and closer, and she had cast her eyes to the crowd below, seeking desperately for Luke. The fire began to lick at her toes, and still he hadn't come.

She'd cried out his name. What would happen if he didn't come for her? She would burn alive, of course. She would watch her flesh ignite and smolder and fall from her own bones. She didn't want to die—not this time. What she wanted was to see his face, to hear his voice, to feel his hands spanning her waist, offering sanctuary.

The fire roared up, singing the flesh of her calves. She screamed in fright and agony. It was the sound of her cry that startled her awake.

She sat up in bed, her heart still pounding. What could the dream signify? Would the Church soon catch her and condemn her anew? Why hadn't Luke come to her defense?

*If you wish to be thought a witch, far be it from me to stop you. I am not your keeper!* His words returned to her, supplying an answer.

If he was not her keeper, then she was pitted against a terrible tyrant with no one to defend her.

Knowing now that he was betrothed to another, she realized just how vulnerable she truly was. Luke was not a talisman she could use at will to keep the wolves at bay. Eventually, he would leave her and return to his betrothed, the prince's cousin.

And who would guard her then? The brother-in-law whom she'd so foolishly cursed?

Feeling restless, she threw off the covers and crossed to the window. The moon was a flat, silver disk obscured by feathery clouds. The air smelled of wood smoke and dried grass.

Leaning onto the windowsill, she gazed down at the sprawling structures below her. Phillip was down there sleeping. What if his fever had returned? If he died, the soldiers would all blame her. She'd seen their looks of mistrust, their whispered comments when she'd put the salve on Phillip's leg. What would it take for one of them to betray her, revealing her whereabouts?

There was no other choice. Phillip had to get better, else Merry's own future was at stake. The dream seemed a warning to take immediate action.

She had no idea what time of night it was, yet Merry turned and sought the wrapper Lady Adelle had given her. Finding her slippers, she left her room. The torch in the hall gave off just enough light to speed her toward the tower stairs.

Moments later, she threaded her way through a maze of sleeping bodies. The cool air seeping through the windows did little to dispel the odor of dirty bodies. Merry wrinkled her nose in distaste as she honed in on Phillip's cot. The giant from Poitiers was sleeping on his side, a good sign as far as Merry was concerned.

She placed a gentle hand upon his shoulder so as not to startle him. Placing a hand on his forehead, she found it cool to the touch, thank the saints.

Despite her gentleness, Phillip lurched to wakefulness, grappling for the sword that wasn't there.

"Shhh," Merry whispered, " 'tis I."

"Eh?" He came up on one elbow, cursing at the pain the movement caused him. "What are you doing here, *petite*?" he asked.

She had grown accustomed to the nickname. Her fondness for him had likewise grown over the last few days they'd spent together. "I had a bad dream," she admitted. "I had to see if you were well."

"Aye," he whispered, "perfectly well. But you should not be here at night. 'Tis dangerous. Go back to your chamber."

"I will," she promised him. "I only wanted to be sure."

He patted her hands with his big, rough paw. "Go," he said. "Sir Luke would not approve."

Merry grimaced, imagining the captain's reaction. She felt foolish now for wandering into a garrison full of men, wearing only her nightclothes. She had no doubt Luke would blister her ears for such impulsive behavior.

Straightening, she hurried back through the crush of bodies. Her knee came into sharp contact with the end of a bench, and she swore, stopping for a moment to rub away the pain. Her outburst roused several soldiers. Most of them rolled over and went back to sleep.

One soldier in particular followed her progress as she hobbled toward the door. He waited a fraction of a second then slipped out of his cot and crept after her.

Merry nearly reached the exit to the courtyard when a hand stretched out of the darkness and clamped down on her shoulder. She spun around in terror. With the aid of the moonlight coming through the open door, she recognized Cullin's malicious countenance with dread.

"Now I've got ye, witch," he growled, clapping a filthy hand across her mouth. "Thought ye could put a spell on me an' not pay the price of it, didn't ye?"

The hand blocked her nose and mouth, stifling the scream that rose at once to her throat. Merry clawed at Cullin's grip, desperate to get away. At the same time, he began to drag her backward, down a hall that led to the communal bath.

It dawned on Merry that Cullin was drawing her toward an isolated area of the garrison. The realization of what he intended to do impaled her with terror. She had witnessed her mother's rape. The thought of such violence perpetrated on herself filled her with frigid denial.

Yet not even a burst of panic gave her the strength needed to overcome him. She raked her nails along Cullin's arm, drawing blood, and still he pulled her relentlessly down the hall, her feet dragging. At last, he shouldered his way into a room that was musty and damp. Rushes still burned in the rush holder casting an orange light upon the walls.

Merry had glimpsed the room before. This was where the men bathed. A stone ledge wrapped around three of the four walls, while the fourth was studded with pipes that brought water rushing from a cistern on the roof. The pipes were plugged now, but water still leaked, breaking in musical drops upon the flagstone floor.

Cullin lifted the hand from her mouth. As Merry sucked air into her starved lungs, he fisted her hair in a vicious grip. "I've got a surprise for you, witch," he growled. He thrust his groin hard against her pelvis.

A scream bubbled in Merry's chest, but her throat had closed with fear. She could no longer make a sound.

Cullin's free hand closed over the edges of her wrapper. She heard the silk material tear. He clawed at the chemise beneath. Remembering her nightmare of several nights ago, Merry lifted her knee in a sudden upward jab, and he doubled over with a stifled groan.

Finding herself suddenly free, she sprinted to the door and threw herself into the hallway, muscles screaming as she sought to outrun him. Still, she could feel him descending on her like a striking serpent. Halfway down the hall, her dash for freedom came to an abrupt end as he grasped a fistful of her hair and yanked her back. "Nay!" she cried, finding her voice. "Let me go!"

He lifted her off her feet, ignoring her flailing limbs as he wrestled her down the hall and back into the isolated chamber. Turning toward the nearest ledge, he slammed her abdomen against the hard stone.

With the air crushed from her lungs, Merry's cries were barely audible. With one hand, he pressed her skull against the cold stone, fumbling to lift the hem of her nightclothes with the other. She squeezed her eyes shut. Visions of her mother's rape blended with the awful inevitability of the moments before her.

She caught a breath just as the unwelcomed head of his manhood prodded her thighs. A full-throated scream erupted from her throat, shattering the nighttime quiet.

"Shut up, witch! Ye deserve what ye get." Cullin backhanded her cheek, causing bursts of light to streak across her vision. He pushed her into place again.

Suddenly there was a stamping of feet. A shadow sailed through the open door. Cullin's weight was lifted abruptly off her. She turned around in time to see a flash of steel. A garbled mutter of denial reached her ears. Then Cullin collapsed where he stood, hitting the flagstone floor with an ugly thud. The shadow turned, and Merry saw his eyes first.

"Luke," she croaked. She tried to say more, but her voice failed her.

He caught her as she stumbled blindly toward him. He held her rigidly at first, and she could feel the rage still quivering in his powerful frame. She burrowed her face into his chest and realized he was shirtless. His skin was hot and silky and dusted with crisp hair. At last, his arms enfolded her, sheltering her against the wall of his body. Merry melted against him, her knees scarcely capable of holding her upright.

"Take this body out of here," Luke instructed the men who hovered at the door.

Merry hadn't even noticed the others. She'd been too blinded with relief to see anyone beyond the Phoenix. He'd saved her again.

She heard the scuffling of feet, but no one spoke. They had dragged the body out the door before anyone dared to address their leader. "Er, where should we take him, m'lord?" inquired a brave soul.

Luke hesitated a moment. "Leave him outside the gates," he said. "Let the wolves and raptors eat him."

Merry shivered at the chilling reply. She kept her eyes closed, unwilling to behold his countenance. 'Twas the warrior in Luke speaking—a side of himself he'd been careful to conceal from her. Logically, she ought to fear him now, yet she didn't. She'd never felt safer in her life.

As the soldier dragged the body down the hall, Luke and Merry were left alone. An unknown stretch of time elapsed with no words spoken between them. It was a comfort to be held by him, to hear his thumping heart, feel his certain warmth. His skin smelled of the now-familiar scent of his soap. She longed to stand in the circle of his arms forever.

"How did you know where to find me?" she finally inquired. To her surprise, her voice sounded raw and tattered. She'd screamed herself hoarse.

The pressure in his fingers increased. "I heard you leave your chamber. I waited for you to return from the garderobe, and when you didn't, I went to look for you." The tension in him had increased with each sentence. "For Christ's sake, Merry," he blurted, "why did you leave the keep at night?" He held her at arm's length, glowering down at her. "What foolishness were you up to?" he raged, giving her a little shake.

Moisture sprang to her eyes at his reprimand. "I had a vision," she admitted, hanging her head. "I had to know if Phillip was well. If he wasn't, I would be blamed for his death." She shuddered, recalling the horror of her nightmare.

He cursed at length in a tongue she did not recognize, then he snatched her close again, rocking her as if she were a baby. Merry gripped him hard, thankful for his comfort.

"Tell me . . ." he hesitated, struggling to form the words. "Tell me he didn't . . ."

"Nay." She shook her head. Tears gushed from her eyes. She felt the moisture with surprise. She could not recall the last time she had wept.

"Merry," Luke said, with gentle dismay. He must have felt

her tears against his chest. With another string of foreign curses, he lifted her into his arms and carried her from the bathhouse.

Ashamed of her weakness, Merry hid her face in the crook of his neck. As he conveyed her down the hall and out of the garrison, the buzz of male voices followed them.

News of the incident had arrived at the main keep before them. The stairwell was ablaze with torches, as was the corridor to the bedchambers. Luke gave Sir Pierce an order to speak to the men, and the sergeant strode away toward the garrison. Lady Adelle awaited them at the top of the stairs, her plaited hair swinging to her hips.

"My child!" she exclaimed, as Luke's shoulders crested the stairs. "There you are. What an awful thing to have happened!" She hurried down the hallway before them. "I've ordered a bath to be brought up for you," she added, addressing only Merry, who had yet to look up.

The baroness bustled into Merry's chamber. She'd lit the brazier, which shed a golden light upon the bed curtains. Luke drew them back and lowered Merry to the edge of the mattress. As Kit called out a greeting, Luke started with surprise to see the cat. To Merry's relief, he abstained from comment.

As he straightened, she caught sight of his sword, still gripped in one hand. The scarlet stain on the blade brought the jarring reminder of Cullin's death. Merry blinked and looked away, but it was too late. Her stomach protested at the gory sight. She swallowed convulsively, combating the betrayal of her flesh.

Luke had withdrawn to the door. He paused there, regarding her uncertainly. "Merry?" he queried.

"I'm going to be sick," she managed to confess.

Lady Adelle fetched the washbasin with remarkable speed. "There now," she crooned, tucking Merry's hair behind her ear, holding the basin for her as she retched. "I'll see that she's cared for," she informed the Phoenix, who looked more indecisive than Merry had ever seen him.

When Luke continued to linger, the baroness leveled him a glare. Her look was meant to remind him that Merry had served her a good turn, and she would repay in kind. Luke, on the other hand, had done nothing but destroy her home.

With a nod, the Phoenix withdrew, shutting the door quietly behind him. Merry tamped down the urge to call him back. She didn't want him to see her in such a wretched state, did she? Already she had wept like a child when he held her. Her pride was shattered, her dignity in shreds. She thought of the noblewoman, his betrothed, who awaited him, and she moaned aloud at the realization of her shame.

She had dressed like a lady yesterday to encourage Luke's respect, but tonight she'd made it terribly plain she was still a source of exasperation. Hadn't it always been so? Time after time, she'd done her best to help others, only to have her intentions misinterpreted. Then, betrayed by her quick tongue, she'd been accused of all manner of wickedness.

Eventually, Luke would look back on this night and conclude she was squarely to blame. She had acted impulsively, skulking about the castle in her nightclothes. His disgust of her would grow until he couldn't wait to be rid of her.

With a clutch of regret, Merry savored the tender moments Luke had held her in the aftermath of violence. If only his gallant protectiveness would last, and yet she knew it wouldn't. She had been a scapegoat too many times to envision any other outcome. All too soon, the rumor would spread that she'd incited Cullin to unnatural acts. The soldiers would blame her for the death of their companion, and Luke would eventually take sides. She knew, with bitterness, he would choose to stand with his men.

Lapsing into silent misery, Merry submitted to the baroness's ministrations. Depression, dark and insidious, stole over her. The one thing she knew with certainty, the one thing that caused her heart to ache with regret, was the suspicion that Luke le Noir would never hold her tenderly again.

# Chapter Nine

LADY Adelle threaded her needle with the dexterity of a much younger woman. Seeing her companion occupied for the moment, Merry crossed the hall to one of the few windows and peered out. She and the baroness had enjoyed a late breakfast and would pass the day in idleness, giving Merry a chance to recuperate.

Outwardly, Merry seemed unaffected by the violence she'd suffered at Cullin's hands. The bruise on her cheek was the only testament to his brutality. Inwardly, she suffered more, certain that Luke would treat her differently the next time they met. She dreaded that painful inevitability, while at the same time experiencing an overwhelming need to see him again.

To her satisfaction, the window afforded a view of the courtyard, the inner wall, and beyond that a portion of the eastern tower. Merry strained on tiptoe. The breath caught in her throat as she spied Luke at a distance, toiling under the noonday sun. The autumn temperatures had made a blessed return, and she could see he'd donned a blue tunic. It flapped in the breeze, conforming to the shape of his powerful body as he wielded a pickax, bringing it up and down in fluid movements. Even from afar, he stirred an incomprehensible longing within her.

" 'Tis so pleasant having a young person here," Lady Adelle

remarked. Merry drew guiltily from the window and returned to the chairs that were set before the hearth, taking up her own embroidery ring.

It was not the first time Lady Adelle had commented on the pleasure of her company. Merry stitched a couple of threads, and the question that had burned in her mind since her arrival found its way to her tongue.

"How long have Ewan and Edgar been gone?" she dared to ask. She gave the gentle baroness a frank but sympathetic look.

The embroidery in Lady Adelle's hand began to tremble. She fought to keep her expression serene, but it crumpled abruptly, causing Merry to drop to her knees before her. "I'm so sorry," she rushed to apologize. "I've upset you. I do it to everyone. Please, forgive me."

Lady Adelle tried to smile, but her eyes were dimmed with tears as she met Merry's gaze. "They left over ten years ago," she admitted. The words sounded stilted, as though she had never dared to say them aloud before. "There's no use pretending anymore," she added, lifting her gaze to the cobwebs that dripped from the rafters. "They won't be coming home." She looked at Merry one more time and burst into tears.

Merry put her arms around the baroness. She was not surprised by the woman's answer, for she'd suspected that Edgar and Ewan had been gone a very long time. But ten years! Ten years without a word from them could only mean that they were dead.

Sorrow swamped her heart for the mother who'd lost two sons. She felt instantly ashamed for wallowing in her own sorrows, for not recognizing the depths of the baroness's loss. Not only were her only sons, the most important people in her life, likely dead, but her home was being destroyed and her husband in danger of dying, also.

Tears of empathy flooded Merry's eyes as she soothed the baroness, murmuring foolishly that it would be all right. How could it be? The lady had nothing to look forward to but the destruction of her home, the demise of her husband.

It was impossibly unfair!

Merry drew back, suddenly outraged on the woman's behalf. The baroness straightened and sniffed, embarrassed by her emotional outburst.

"I will speak to him," Merry said, her voice quavering with indignation.

Lady Adelle dabbed at her eyes. "Speak with whom? Sir Luke?"

"Aye," Merry insisted, growing more determined by the second. "He hasn't guessed your sons' plight. I'm certain if you told him, he would cease this terrible destruction and leave you in peace."

The baroness put a hand on either side of Merry's face. " 'Twould do no good, child," she said sadly. "I know what kind of man he is. My Ian is the same way. He does what he believes is his duty. He will do as the prince commands."

Merry shook her head, certain that Luke would have more compassion than that. "Nay," she protested, "he will do what is right. You must tell him. You must beg him to—"

Lady Adelle squared her shoulders and silenced her with a look. "I will not beg anything of him," she retorted.

Merry's eyes widened at the demonstration of blue blood running through the woman's veins. "Then let me tell him," she suggested, more humbly.

" 'Twill do you no good," Lady Adelle answered, thinning her lips.

"Only let me try," Merry repeated. "How can it hurt? He might be content with the damage done and leave you in peace."

The baroness's answer was to pat her cheek. "You're a good-hearted girl," she said.

Merry blinked several times, scarcely comprehending the compliment. For so many years no one had called her anything but a witch.

"Why don't you stay here with us when the Phoenix flies away?" added the woman, demonstrating the extent of her loneliness.

A sad smile curved Merry's mouth. "I thank you for your kindness," she replied, "but I will have to go." She doubted the baron, with his elderly vassals, could protect her should the Church discover her whereabouts. Only her brother-in-law, the Slayer, had that kind of might.

In the meantime, she would forget her own shame and misery and approach Luke about the plight of the baroness. Surely if he knew the extent of Lady Adelle's suffering, he would find it in his heart to have mercy on the woman.

LUKE rested the point of his ax at his feet and glanced for the hundredth time at the keep. He'd just seen Merry peering through a window. One second she was there, and the next she was gone. Her piquant face remained in his memory, however, tormenting him with conflicting emotions—relief to see her well; distaste for the violence he'd perpetrated while saving her; and an overwhelming desire to gather her close once more.

Checking on Merry that morning, he'd discovered that Lady Adelle had spent the night in her chamber. He told himself he was grateful to the baroness for her vigilance, but the feeling in his chest had felt like envy.

At the moment, he could not have said what he was feeling. His emotions seemed to shift with each beat of his heart. On one hand, he blamed Merry for having caused him to slay one of his own men, for the savage violence that made his men respond with predictable dismay. It would take a while to win their trust again.

On the other hand, it was the soldiers themselves who angered him, for they had judged Merry a witch without knowing her. Their quickness to blame her for last night's incident set his blood to seething. He had no patience for ignorance and superstition. The fear that one of them might yet whisk Merry away for the reward money haunted him.

He shuddered with an emotion he'd never experienced before. He told himself 'twas merely concern. After all, Merry was *his* responsibility. He'd promised Sir Roger he would deliver her safely into the Slayer's hands. He wasn't one to take his promises lightly.

And yet he knew it was more than that. The thought of Merry falling prey to any man shook him. The violation she'd nearly experienced last night left a taste in his mouth so bitter he knew an urge to spit.

On the heels of that confession came the confusing revelation that he wanted no man touching Merry but himself.

He staggered back a step or two, nearly losing his balance

where the low wall had been stripped away. One misplaced step and he might have plummeted to his death.

*Consider that a warning,* he thought, wiping sweat from his brow. He had no right to consider Merry his personal property. To do so could only cause harm—harm to Merry who would certainly expect more of him than a quick possession and a quicker farewell. Harm to him, also, for inflaming him with the taste of what he could not have. He'd betrothed himself to Amalie, a lady who would give him all he'd ever wanted: legitimacy and the Castle Arundel.

Reasoning this through, he hoped to ease the stirrings of his body. But the backbreaking labor had increased his stamina and swelled his muscles, making him painfully conscientious of his masculinity. The need to seek relief between a woman's legs throbbed in him more strongly.

Perhaps he ought to tup one of the castle's serving women. He toyed with the possibility, but it was a vision of Merry that came to him as he imagined sweet relief, her ripe breasts swaying beneath him. Lying with a woman now would only inflame him further. Better to ignore his needs and concentrate on his work.

That thought in mind, he turned to assess his accomplishments. The eastern tower had been leveled at least, so that only a great pile of rubble littered the wall walk. His men were busy heaving stones over the side where they tumbled downhill. Luke's job was to break larger blocks into pieces, making them easier to discard.

His men scuffled about in silence, picking up stones and pitching them over the wall without heart for their labors. Their faces were long, their brows puckered with thought.

Luke knew that the incident last night had taken its toll on their morale. Two mercenaries, Cullin's friends, had deserted Iversly last night, presumably to bury their companion, rather than leave him for the raptors as Luke had ordered.

They had not come back.

It was the first time Luke had ever lost men to desertion. The temptation to blame Merry rose up in him and then receded.

If anyone were to blame, it was he himself. He'd been the one to bring Merry up on the wall. He'd been the one to insist they go to Iversly and not straight to Helmesly. Had he taken her straight to her brother-in-law, he'd have fallen days behind schedule, but so what? Likely, he was going to be delayed in any event. The lethargy of his men and his own inability to focus had put them well behind schedule.

He lifted his ax to vent his frustrations. *Crack!* Shards of rock showered his calves as the blade glanced ineffectually off the heavy stone. Luke cursed his poor aim and tried again, splitting the slab neatly down the center. He moved to another block, catching a glimpse of movement in the main keep. He glanced up sharply, hoping to see Merry.

It was not the object of his obsession but, rather, the Baron of Iversly. As was his custom of late, Lord Ian had taken up post at his chamber window. Luke's ax felt suddenly too heavy. He put it down and met the baron's gaze.

*I am only doing my job!* He sought to convey his frustration across the space between them.

Perhaps it was the proud angle of his shoulders, but the baron looked more than ever like Luke's grandfather. From his chamber window, he regarded Luke with sad stoicism. Strangely, the words of Luke's grandfather, written in a summons over a month ago, returned to him. *I am dying, Luke. I will hold off death until your return.*

In disgust, Luke threw down his ax. Forty-six sets of eyes swiveled in his direction. "Take a break," he snarled, having gotten their attention. He began to stride toward the tower stairs.

"Should we eat, my lord?" Sir Pierce called after him, frowning at him under his shaggy brow.

"Aye, eat," Luke replied, though the sun was only nearing its summit.

He took the stairs two at a time. Normally he did not take his midday meal in the great hall, but today he would make an exception.


"WILL you walk with me, lady?" Luke asked, using the edge of the table linen to wipe his hands, as was the custom. "I have a matter to discuss with you."

Despite Luke's cool tone, Merry's heart quickened its beat. "If you wish." She too craved a moment in which to plead mercy on the baroness's behalf, to determine Luke's response to last night's drama. Throughout the meal, she'd sought and failed to guess his opinion of her. He'd remained civil but quiet. The expression on his face betrayed nothing, save for the leaping of muscles in his jaw. That telltale sign failed to spark hope in her breast.

Nonetheless, she had an obligation to defend the Lady Adelle, regardless of whether Luke now condemned her. And yet, her heart thudded with trepidation as she awaited judgment. To hear any denouncement of her character from Luke's lips would surely hurt her more than if it came from another.

They'd shared a bond of sorts, an understanding that had grown out of their differences of opinion. Regardless of the fact that they often disagreed, Luke had treated her with consistent kindness. He'd even kissed her, with a gentle intensity that still had the power to take her breath when she recalled it.

As Luke secured their dismissal from the table, Merry intercepted Lady Adelle's quick look. The baroness could not disguise her hope that Merry would intercede for her. Merry nodded back, determined to do so. Regardless of Luke's feelings for her now, she knew him to be a fair man. Surely he would take Lady Adelle's plight seriously.

"How do you fare today?" he inquired as he escorted her through the forebuilding. His tone was dauntingly formal, keeping distance between them, and yet she caught his quick frown as his gaze fell to her bruised cheek.

"Well, thank you," she answered, in the same polite tone.

He pushed open the door at the bottom of the stairs, and she preceded him through it.

"Let us walk about the outer ward," he suggested, squinting against the vivid brightness of the sun.

"As you wish." She took the arm he offered, wondering at the purpose of such a lengthy walk. Clearly he had something of importance to tell her. She wondered whether to hear him out first or bring up her own concerns.

The outer ward lay deserted. Merry shaded her eyes as she surveyed the ragged hole where the tower had been. There were no men working. "What takes you from your labors?" she inquired.

Rather than answer, he slowed to a stop and regarded her

from his superior height. "I've come to a decision," he said, a frown settling between his winging, black eyebrows.

She turned to face him, hopeful that he'd decided to cease the destruction. "What decision?" she asked.

"I'm going to take you to Helmesly."

The unexpectedness of his reply left her dumbstruck.

"I ought never have brought you here with me," he continued, his voice flat, without inflection. "I had no idea one of my men would—" he broke off his sentence, cutting his gaze to the bruise on her cheek. "I hold myself responsible for what nearly happened to you," he added grimly.

Her shock subsided, raking bitterness over pain. There was only one explanation for his decision. He blamed her for the incident last night, and now he was eager to be rid of her.

She had expected such a blow. And yet, the suddenness of his decision left her reeling. To be shuffled off so soon! How badly he must want to be rid of her!

She blinked at the ravaged tower, striving to appear unaffected. Pain ebbed and flowed in her, rising up one moment, settling down into bitter acceptance the next.

She was painfully aware of each indrawn breath the Phoenix took, the way his chest rose and fell as though agitated. He said nothing to soften the force of his rejection.

At last, she trusted herself to speak well enough to plead on the baroness's behalf. "Will you be returning to Iversly?" she inquired, looking up at him, her voice thin but steady.

His scowl deepened. "Of course," he said. "I have unfinished work here."

She nodded, swallowing the lump that expanded in her throat. "There's something you should know about the baron's sons, then," she continued, fighting to keep her tone strong. "Ewan and Edgar have been gone for more than ten years now. No one has heard from them in all that time." She paused a moment to let the implication take hold in him. "The baron has no heirs," she finished.

Holding his gaze while betraying none of the pain that welled in her was no easy task. Yet her problems took second seat to Lady Adelle's, and given Luke's haste to be rid of her, this might be her only chance to make him see reason. "Now her husband is in peril of dying and her home is being laid to waste. Don't you think it time you showed some mercy, Luke le Noir?"

He regarded her as if she'd gone suddenly mad. She tried to read pity in his brown-gold eyes and failed.

"Can you not tell the prince that you destroyed the illegitimate structures and leave the rest standing?" she suggested.

"You mean lie," he interrupted, firmly. "Lie to my prince?"

A surge of anger beat back the ache in her chest. " 'Tisn't lying," she insisted, "to withhold some of the truth. Who will suffer for it? How can you say that destroying this fortress is anything but sheer idiocy! The prince will need to turn around and strengthen it again. Where is the sense in that?"

"I've told you already, it isn't your place to question Henry's commands any more than it is mine." His voice fell to a dangerous note. "I gave the prince my word, and I have *ever* been obedient to his command." The muscles in his shoulders looked tense as he flicked his gaze to the western tower still awaiting destruction.

Merry shook with sudden frustration, her knees trembling at the unfairness of life—of the baroness's situation, as well as her own. She had thought Luke would at least show pity for Lady Adelle, yet he seemed as heartless toward the baroness as he was toward her.

His callousness sparked a sudden fury, making her long to hurt him in return. "You, Luke le Noir, are nothing but the puppet of a tyrant," she denounced, speaking through her teeth. "And I have lost all respect for you. Furthermore, I have no intention of going to Helmesly when I am needed here. What about Phillip?" she raged. "Who will care for his leg?"

"Gervaise has it well in hand."

"Hah! Gervaise doesn't even know how to bring down a fever! What if the baron should suffer another attack? Who will comfort Lady Adelle if her husband follows her sons to the grave?"

He crossed his arms over his chest in an implacable gesture. "The baroness is not your responsibility," he countered, his eyes glittering with resolve. "But you are mine. Clearly I cannot protect you here."

"I will not go to Helmesly!" she raged. "There is naught for me there but a lifetime of exile!"

"There is nothing for you here," he countered, unswayed by her argument.

A significant silence followed his remark. *You are here,* Merry's heart cried out. Pride prevented her from saying the words aloud, for she had no claim on him.

"I promised to take you to Helmesly," he continued, spacing his words carefully. "What difference does a matter of weeks make?"

What difference, indeed? She could only think that Luke might yet have need of her, not only to tend the wounded but to teach him a lesson in compassion. She studied him, then, committing his face to memory, wanting to carry it with her into her bleak future. He had been the only man, other than her father, to treat her with some semblance of respect, to show her some kindness, though that kindness had now been revoked.

Certainly, he'd been the only man to make her tremble with desire.

Now everything had changed. She'd become no more to him than a complication, a duty that required completion.

"For mercy's sake, don't look at me like that," he growled at her suddenly.

She blinked and averted her face, surprised to feel twin tears slipping over the rim of her lashes.

"Merry," he groaned, taking a sudden step toward her. She flinched with astonishment as he captured her face between his hands, cradling it with unexpected gentleness.

"Please understand that I do this for your sake," he rasped, his tone now urgent where before it had been cold. "Clearly, I cannot keep you safe here. You are better off behind the walls of Helmesly with your family to protect you."

He spoke convincingly, causing her conclusions to waver. Perhaps he wasn't as eager to be rid of her as he'd seemed. She swallowed hard, finding it difficult to speak over the blockage in her throat. "Will you at least consider Lady Adelle's situation?" she begged, finding that the only topic she could safely address.

Luke did not respond to Merry's request, but eased his thumbs across her cheeks, wiping away the moisture there.

She had done it again, he realized. She'd confounded his determination to remain aloof, first by calling his duty into question, meddling in affairs that were none of her concern. Her insistence on the subject infuriated him, for he was not a man to leave a job undone.

But fury transformed into admiration as she boldly championed the baroness. Putting aside her own uncertain future, she demanded that Luke consider the baroness's plight. She had done the same for Phillip, he realized. And before that, she'd defied the prioress to defend her fellow nuns.

Merry DuBoise was a crusader for the discouraged and the helpless. He recognized the mightiness of her spirit with reluctant awe. To trample it, to be the cause of her tears, summoned instant remorse in him.

He cradled her petal-soft cheeks, wondering how to comfort her. His gaze slid to her generous mouth, trembling ever so slightly with the force of her emotion. Did she think she could hide her hurt from him? It throbbed in her impossibly green eyes, making his own heart ache. He sought the words to make her understand.

"I've no wish to hurt you, Merry, nor the baroness. This is something that must be done. I must fulfill Prince Henry's wishes."

"You could defy him," she suggested, her green eyes earnest.

"You're a mad, little angel," he heard himself reply. He was grateful none of his men were about to overhear him. Yet, at the same time, he experienced a strange exhilaration at giving voice to his thoughts.

Her tawny eyebrows drew together with confusion.

"I've never known a woman to speak her mind so fiercely," he explained.

Her brow cleared as she offered him her bitter smile. "It isn't an attribute that has served me well," she admitted.

The twist of her lips beguiled him. God's blood, but he found her irresistible, from her strong-minded opposition to her fearless championing of the needy!

His fingers flexed, reveling in the softness of her skin. "You *are* a witch," he decided, recognizing a dangerous desire to slide his hands into the satin fall of her hair.

He shook, battling the temptation. 'Twould serve him nothing to give in to his urges, he reasoned. And yet he watched with fascination as his fingers sank into her fiery tresses. He tugged her closer, even as he cautioned himself not to. The softness of her breasts against his chest made him groan aloud.

Suddenly, he was kissing her, his mouth settling hungrily over hers. He crushed the soft fullness of her lips, wondering how he'd abstained this long without tasting her again. To his delight, she parted her lips to him, offering the sultriness of her mouth to his thirsty tongue.

He dove in, dizzy with delight, provoked to recklessness by her tiny sob of delight.

Circling one arm about her waist, he hauled her against him, desperate for her softness. Hunger roared in his eardrums, both dismaying and exciting him by its sheer force. His brain sought and failed to exert control over his impulses.

For the first time in his life, he was helpless to stop himself. Every fiber of his being was focused on the fusing of his mouth with Merry's, on the fullness of her breasts, the thumping of her heart against his.

"Stop!" she cried, twisting her mouth suddenly free. "Please," she begged in a high, worried voice. "Release me."

It took a moment for the meaning of her words to penetrate his fogged brain. He realized he was holding her in a possessive grip, his erect manhood hard against her hip. She struggled again, pushing at his shoulders.

With something like shock, Luke released her and stepped back. Reason took up residence in his brain once more and he realized with chagrin that if Merry hadn't called a halt to his ravishment, he might well have taken her right here in broad daylight.

She stood before him, her mouth red and swollen as she breathed in and out harshly. Her jaw worked for a moment, as if she had something to say.

For himself, Luke was speechless. He dragged both hands through his shorn hair, seeking to slow the rate of his heart. He realized he ought to apologize, yet he couldn't quite believe he'd behaved so rashly. Surely Merry was to blame for his behavior in part, if not completely.

"I will escort you to Helmsly at dawn," he grated, falling back on their previous conversation. His tone, he knew, was overly harsh.

Merry flinched and faltered back. He watched with help-lessness as the color drained from her cheeks. Her eyes flashed at him, a hot, furious green. Then, with a strangled cry, she fist-ed her skirts and whirled, running from him as if the hounds of hell were after her.

Wallowing in confusion, Luke watched her flee. Guilt bub-bled up, and he took a few steps forward, intending to call her back. But then reason exerted itself once more. What would he say to her, when he could not explain his own actions to him-self?

*'Twas her doing,* he reasoned, gritting his teeth. She had provoked him one too many times with her saucy mouth. She had begged for his kisses with her feminine tears.

If so, then why had she been the one to sever their ardent embrace?

He swallowed uneasily. If the answer lay with him, then he was not the logical and disciplined warrior he'd always believed he was.

MERRY slept fitfully. The brazier had died down to a mere whimper, and the air seeping through the cracked shutters was cold. Lady Adelle, responding to Merry's insistence that she would rather be alone, had retired to her own chambers. Kit, who had been with Merry when she fell asleep, had apparently slipped through the crack in the shutters to hunt by night. Merry was left alone.

She buried herself in the coverlet, seeking warmth and refuge from the dreams that plagued her.

She had lapsed into exhaustion when the creaking of the shutter wakened her. She stiffened under the blankets, telling herself it was only Kit, returning from his nighttime prowl. She waited to hear the soft patter of paws upon the rushes. Instead, heavier footfalls caused the rushes to crackle. There was some-one in the chamber with her, and he was creeping toward her bed!

Every hair on Merry's body stood on end. She peeked over the edge of her blanket at the opening in the bed curtains. To her horror, they parted abruptly, and there stood Cullin, his face dripping in blood. He grinned at her evilly. "Ye thought I was dead, didn't ye?" he asked in a gravelly voice.

Merry was too terrified to utter more than a high-pitched whimper. Cullin flung back the covers under which she lay, exposing her to the air streaming from the window. Merry tried to scramble backward, but he grabbed an ankle and pulled her toward him. "Now," he growled, "Let's finish this."

She fought him with the same desperation that she'd experienced nights before. She clawed at his eyes, at his bloodied face until he pinned her wrists to the mattress. Her legs felt strangely weighted, as though he'd tied them to the posts at the bottom of the bed.

Merry stared into the darkness, not understanding the superhuman strength he wielded. In the darkness of the boxed bed, it was hard to see his face, but the man above her had a beard and a full head of shaggy hair. Merry studied him in consternation, her eyes adjusting to the darkness. As she recognized the silhouette, a cold nail of fear drove straight through her spine.

It wasn't Cullin at all. It was Ferguson. The man who'd killed her father. The one who'd raped her mother. The devil who'd shattered her idyllic childhood and left nothing but ruin and despair.

"And now, Merry," he growled through yellowed teeth, "I've come back for you."

# *Chapter Ten*

"MERRY! Lady, wake up!"

"Sweet child, we're here. You're all right."

The sound of two voices speaking to her at once pulled Merry from her gripping nightmare. She lurched to a sitting position, suddenly free of the weight that had held her immobile a second ago.

Ferguson was gone. The flame of a candle danced before the worried visage of Lady Adelle. A large shadow sat at her feet, with a firm hand clasped about her knee. "Are you all right?" the Phoenix asked, sounding full of concern.

Merry sat up. She found her mouth as dry as a desert. "May I have a drink?" she inquired.

The baroness left the room to find her one. She took the candle with her, leaving Merry and Luke in the dark. "Just a moment," he said, moving away. She shivered at the sudden loss of his heat.

A second later, a torch flared to life. He'd stuck it in the coals of the brazier and placed it now in the torch holder by the door. He returned to the bed, standing beside her. "You were dreaming," he said, his voice rough from sleep.

Merry nodded, still trying to free herself from the vestiges of her terror. She pulled her knees up to her chin and locked her arms around them to stop from shivering. Her dream faded with the recollection of her conversation with Luke that afternoon. Recalling his passionate kiss, she shivered again.

"Are you cold?" he inquired.

"Aye," she said, though her thoughts were already warming her. "I left the window open for Kit."

He turned away to secure the shutters, muttering something about her cat, which she failed to hear. He added a peat brick to the brazier, and the flames leapt up, brightening the chamber still more.

Merry eyed Luke as he returned to her, standing awkwardly beside the bed. Just as he opened his mouth to speak, the baroness returned with a goblet.

"Here you go, my dear," she crooned. "This ought to warm you." She cast a frown at Luke as she hovered worriedly over Merry.

The goblet held wine spiced with ginger and a hint of cloves. It warmed Merry's stomach, but failed to ease the fluttering there. What had Luke been about to say? Would he apologize for the kiss that had left her flushed and more confused than ever? Would he express regret or blame her for enticing him?

"Would you like me to stay with you, my dear?" the baroness inquired. "It was too soon to leave you alone."

Merry hesitated. She didn't wish to be left alone, but it wasn't the baroness she wanted fussing over her. She shook her head to decline. "I'll be fine now, really. The room was just too cold."

Lady Adelle looked around, clearly hunting for an excuse to stay. "Are you certain? I wouldn't want you to suffer such dreams again."

"I won't," Merry assured her.

"Well, then." The baroness gave Luke a meaningful look. "I suppose we'll leave you to sleep. You have a long ride in the morning." She moved slowly toward the door. "I wish you didn't have to go," she added sadly. She waited pointedly at the door for Luke to join her.

With seeming reluctance, he followed her. He paused once, looking back at Merry as he closed the door.

She held his gaze until the door severed it. She wanted to

speak with him, if only to reconcile whatever misunderstandings were between them before beginning their journey.

In the shadows it was unlikely that he could read her thoughts—not that he would necessarily indulge her. Kiss or not, he'd made it plain that he intended to take her to Helmesly. She couldn't forget he had a future wife awaiting him.

Left alone, Merry clutched the goblet, overcome by intense isolation and living fear. Though the chamber was awash with amber light, she half expected Ferguson to leap from the shadows and resume his mauling. She sat in a ball, battling her private demons, longing for Luke to come to her, to rescue her just one more time.

She had lost track of how much time had elapsed when the door gave a low moan. Merry sucked in a breath, letting it out only when the white sleeve of Luke's nightshirt came into view. Her heart grew suddenly lighter. He slipped into the room and shut the door silently behind him, holding her gaze captive.

"Do you want me here?" he asked her with his back against the door. Frowning, he looked as though he'd wrestled with himself for some time.

Merry extended him the goblet by way of answer. She could only wonder why he'd come—whether to apologize or to explain. And yet, his return to her chamber had seemed inevitable, somehow. Perhaps he was drawn to her as she was to him, and no other explanation was needed.

As he closed the distance between them, she saw that he wore a pair of loose linen drawers beneath his nightshirt. He sat at the foot of her bed, causing the ropes to creak. As he took the goblet from her hand, their fingers brushed, magic leaping between them. Their gazes locked, asking questions, seeking answers.

He took a bracing sip. "You shouldn't have left your window open," he lectured, presumably finding that a safe topic. "Not even for Kit."

"I heard a soldier say that he would kill my cat," she defended herself. "What would you have me do? Abandon Kit to that fate?"

He considered her answer in silence then passed the goblet back. "You would never do that," he said, with resignation.

"Will you tell me what your dream was?" he added, giving her a probing look.

Shuddering at the recollection, she placed the goblet on her headboard. " 'Twas Cullin, at first. He came in through the window. His face was covered in blood. He tried to force me again."

Luke nodded, the muscles of his face taut. "And then?"

"And then he turned into Ferguson. Though I don't suppose you know who Ferguson was," she added, frowning.

Luke remembered the name distinctly. "Sir Roger mentioned him to me. He was the one who murdered your father and forced your mother to marry him."

With a faraway look, she nodded. Sitting as she was, with her knees drawn to her chest, she looked young and vulnerable. Luke knew he was a fool to have returned to her chamber. This afternoon's debacle had made it terribly clear that his desire for Merry exceeded the bounds of his self-control.

He'd convinced himself that he would comfort her then return swiftly to his own bedchamber. Hearing her cries had set his heart to leaping in a way he wished never to experience again. A part of him prayed he would keep to his resolve and not touch her. Another part of him hoped he wouldn't.

"He raped my mother," she whispered. "He took her to the upper chamber, and I followed him . . ."

"You don't have to tell me this," he softly interrupted.

She shook her head. "Nay, I have to tell you. My father's body was still warm. I took a knife from the table." Her words became punctuated as though she could barely push them from her throat. "I meant to stab Ferguson in the back, to kill him before he could do us any more harm. But he was . . . he was leaning over my mother, whose face he'd pushed into the pillow. He was doing things to her. . . ." she broke off, her face a picture of horror and disgust. "I could do nothing but watch him." She raised her eyes to him, her face ravaged with guilt. "I let him go on hurting her!" she cried.

He cast caution to the wind and reached for her. She required his comfort; so be it. The icy coldness of her skin beneath the chemise shocked him as he circled his arms around her. "Hush," he said. Putting his back to the head of the bed, he drew her with him, not surprised to find that she fit comfortably against his side. "Stop blaming yourself," he commanded. "Merry, that dinner knife would not have stopped him. Likely it would have angered him enough to do the same to you. Nothing would have stopped him. 'Twas out of your control. How old were you then?"

"Fifteen," she answered, in a tone that pleaded for understanding.

"So a girl of fifteen is expected to defend her home from a band of warriors? Is that not asking too much?"

She was silent a long while. " 'Tis a bit much," she conceded quietly.

"Aye, it is." He stroked her arm with sweeping motions, entranced by the narrow indentation of her waist, the slope of her hip. While she seemed to grow drowsy against him, he grew increasingly aware of her, nuzzled so close.

"I have dreamt many times that Ferguson did the same to me as to my mother," she whispered unexpectedly.

He felt like he'd been run through by a sword. *God's mercy, had the Scotsman raped Merry as well?*

"He was like the devil in our midst," she continued. "At my trial I was asked if the devil had violated me, and I told them perhaps he had. I couldn't remember." She rubbed her forehead as if the truth were locked inside. "But I condemned myself with that confession."

Luke swallowed, his mouth suddenly as dry as dirt. "Do you remember now?" he asked, though he really didn't want to hear it.

She gazed up at him, her eyes enormous. "I have dreamt it so often that it seems he did." She shook her head. "I can't recall."

Luke pressed a fevered kiss to her forehead. The thought of a filthy Scot putting his hands on Merry's flesh made his fingers flex with bloodlust. No wonder she had struggled in his arms that afternoon. She'd been locked in his embrace, assaulted by his hungry mouth, prodded by his arousal. "Oh, Merry," he heard himself lament. "I didn't realize. I wouldn't have held you so tightly this afternoon—"

She cut his apology short. "I've dreamt of you as well," she said.

He pulled back, disconcerted that she might have confused

the violence Ferguson had wrought with something he'd done. "What have you dreamed?" he dared to ask.

"That we met in a field of buttercups." A hint of a smile danced on her lips, seducing him. "You whirled me round and round and made me dizzy. I saw the flowers reflected in your eyes."

Her answer both reassured him and disconcerted him. "Is that all?" he asked gruffly.

The mellow light could not conceal her pretty blush. "You kissed me," she added, "as you did today. Only you kissed me everywhere." She lowered her lashes then, biting her bottom lip.

He ought to be used to it by now—her ability to catch him completely off guard, to reduce him to an instinctive male without any ability to reason whatsoever. Did she know what she was doing, flirting with him so openly? "Why did you flee from me today?" he inquired, aware that it was his male pride asking.

She squeezed his nightshirt convulsively. "I felt that I was drowning," she answered, flicking him an uncertain look. "Why did you kiss me?" she demanded, turning the tables on him.

He shifted his position, uncomfortable now that the subject of that kiss had been broached. "I haven't an answer for that," he admitted, finally. "Where you are concerned, lady, I seem to do a number of things for no definable reason," he added, mocking himself.

"You didn't mean to kiss me?" she asked, sounding disappointed.

"Nay."

"But you seemed to like it."

A chuckle broke free of him. "I must confess, I did."

He was aware that their conversation was having a quickening effect on his heart, shortening his breath, making him painfully aware of her woman's scent as she shifted closer to him.

"Is lovemaking as enjoyable as kissing?" Her innocent question aroused him further.

He took a bracing breath. "It can be," he said evenly.

"And at times it can be awful," she deduced, "painful and unnatural."

"You mistake lovemaking with forceful rape," he corrected.

"What's the difference?"

*Is she serious?* He frowned at her earnest face. "Surely you know the answer already," he replied, determined to stay neutral.

"Do I? Will I ever know?"

Her rhetorical questions puzzled him.

"What if I die before I'm ever wed?" she answered more specifically. "What if I'm hung for a witch or burned as I was meant to burn before. If so, then I will never know if Ferguson touched me, never know the difference between love and rape."

His heart thudded with sudden force. Surely she wasn't asking him to volunteer a demonstration. "You won't die a maiden, lady," he reassured her. "Tomorrow I take you to Helmesly to ensure your future. And one day you'll have a husband to satisfy your curiosity." Even as he spoke those words, he found he didn't like the idea of Merry lying with any man.

His gaze flickered down to where her nightdress had ridden up, exposing the length of her naked calf. Her skin looked as soft as buttered cream. Here she was, vulnerable and in his arms, querying him about the act of copulation. He couldn't believe he'd put himself in such a tenuous position. At the same time, anticipation thickened his blood.

"There isn't a man alive who would wish to wed me," she argued, pressing her breasts, unwittingly, against his side. "I'm too outspoken, too bold. Besides, I have no wish to marry. I'm going to be a famous healer one day. A husband would only interfere with my plans."

He smiled faintly at her confidence and found he preferred the thought of her a spinster rather than a wife.

"What about you?" she asked quite suddenly. "Will you take a wife?"

He realized the time to extricate himself had passed. Merry had pinned him with her green gaze, and there was no getting away without answering. "Eventually," he prevaricated.

"According to Phillip, you are betrothed, to a cousin of the prince himself," she charged, her voice taking on a stronger edge.

Damn Phillip and his flapping tongue! Luke felt his irritation surge. He had no wish to discuss the Lady Amalie, nor for that matter, the prince. Neither of them had any place here. And yet it was just as well that Merry knew, he realized, tamping down his disappointment. She would come to no conclusions this way, allow him no liberties. "I am," he acknowledged in a neutral voice.

"Is she beautiful?" she inquired, relentless in her quest for information.

Luke stirred. "Aye," he said shortly. "I should go now, Merry. You will need your rest for the travel ahead of us."

To his astonishment, she lurched to a sitting position and shoved him back against the pillows. "Nay, you'll not go," she bit out, refusing to let him rise. "I would have your apology first for toying with me."

"I never meant to toy—"

She cut short his protests by placing her palms on his shoulders and holding him there. "You lie," she answered back, her tone openly belligerent. "You talked to me as if my thoughts carried weight with you. You kissed me and taught me what it feels to know desire. How can you say you never toyed with me?"

He gazed up at her, tongue-tied. Looming over him, her plaits lying heavy upon her breasts, he found he understood her anger and even rejoiced in it. She needed this to exorcise her demons, to vent frustration over a life-altering event that had changed her forever. He was content to be the focus of her blame.

"Apologize," she demanded, tightening her grip.

"I am sorry, Merry," he said sincerely. And he was—sorry he'd betrothed himself to Amalie before meeting her.

His words failed to mollify her. "Nay," she shot back, moving her grip to his hair. "I would have you apologize with a kiss," she decided, a glint in her green eyes.

His heart skipped a beat then leapt to a gallop. "That would not be wise," he countered, using that portion of his brain that would soon become mute if she did not release him. Already, the other half of his brain argued that a kiss was exactly what she needed, not just a kiss but a complete lovemaking experience to help eradicate old memories.

"Wise?" she scoffed. She leaned abruptly forward, her lips hovering so close to his he could feel their petal soft caress. "What has wisdom to do with anything? 'Tis what I want," she insisted. "Men take what they want without asking. I should like to do the same."

The promise of her mouth, the daring threat of her words intoxicated him. Luke found that he was helpless to deny her, stuck like an insect in a web of her weaving. Though he said nothing to provoke her, neither did he seek to dissuade her, and when her lips crushed his, he could not restrain a groan of pleasure.

She kissed him with a wantonness that sucked the air from his lungs. He strained upward, desperate to feel the length of her body against him, delighted to give her what she clearly needed.

Merry's pulse beat fast and thready. She was mad to make demands of a man twice her size, four times more powerful. And yet she felt strangely invincible, keenly aware of her feminine power, a power that had grown steadily since her first encounter with Luke.

Driving her tongue inside his mouth, she heard a vibration of surrender in his throat, and she speared her tongue still deeper. He could not disguise his need for her. In heady triumph, she teased and receded with her tongue, just as he'd taught her. Instinct prompted her to rub herself against him, and she was rewarded this time with a stifled groan. His hands came up, capturing her aching breasts.

She felt no hesitation feeling his hands on her—she craved his touch. But when his thumbs circled the tender peaks of her breasts, eliciting sparks of pleasure, Merry drew back with a gasp. She placed her hands over his, seeking to remove them.

"Two can play this game, lady," Luke warned darkly. He drew his thumbs intentionally over the stiff peaks, sending arrows of pleasure straight to her loins. "Shall I stop?" he inquired, seeming very intent on what he was doing.

She was growing accustomed to the intensity. Nay, she didn't want him to stop. Recklessness goaded her anew. Her time with Luke was running short. With a defiant toss of her head, she grabbed the hem of her chemise, seeking to drag it off her torso.

Luke made a gallant effort to prevent her. "Stop, Merry," he commanded. "You need not do this."

Oh, but she needed to, most desperately. She shook him off, wrestling the material up and over her head, so that she was left completely naked, on her knees before him.

Luke's stunned expression kept her from crawling away in sudden shame. She had gone about as far as she dared. What came next was the stuff of her nightmares. She had no idea how to proceed. She knew only that she had to conquer what demons lay beyond this point, and Luke was the only man she trusted.

"Merry," he whispered, on a note of wonder. With a trembling hand that did much to reassure her, he traced the line of her collarbone, sweeping aside the plaits that hid her rosy nipples from view. "God's blood, you are even more beautiful than I'd imagined."

His praise brought a hot flush to her skin. She sat up on the bed then, trembling with trepidation and desire, wanting in her heart of hearts for Luke to claim her now, tonight, while there was still time between them.

Luke sat down next to her. With utmost gentleness, he placed a kiss on her lips. She sighed with relief, for it seemed that her fervent wish would come true. His lips slid softly to her jaw. He trailed kisses down her neck, causing gooseflesh to sprout everywhere, even on her thighs. Her head felt both light and heavy as she tilted it to give him freer reign.

His lips moved down inexorably toward her breasts. He lifted one to his mouth, and Merry gasped, her fingers flexing about his thick neck. His warm tongue lapped at the aching peak until she thought she would swoon.

"You taste so sweet," he muttered, sounding like a famished man as he transferred his mouth to the other nipple.

Suddenly, his arms closed around her, and he swept her toward the pillows, pressing her down on her back. Merry's hands flew instinctively to his chest to ward him off. "Wait!" she cried, fearful of the moment in which he would impale her.

"Shhh," he silenced her protests with a gentle kiss, deepening it bit by bit. She felt her muscles relaxing. The fingers she had brought up to his chest tugged at his nightshirt, seeking the silken skin beneath.

He obliged her by shrugging it off. Casting it to one side, he hesitated as he gazed down at her. "Are you certain this is what you want, Merry?" he asked her thickly.

In the amber light of the chamber, his face seemed to be cast in bronze. His eyes had darkened to a deep brown. The stain of color on either cheekbone betrayed his excitement, his eagerness to have her.

"I'm certain," she whispered, intrigued by his arousal. She would never trust another the way she trusted Luke. He *had* to be the one to initiate her, the one to bury her fears forever.

He regarded her for a solemn moment. "I can give you no more than myself, tonight," he warned.

It seemed more than she would ever need. And yet she experienced a clutch of regret at his words. "I understand," she said, and she did. She was a woman wanted for her crimes, while he was the Phoenix, the right hand of the prince. It was enough to know him, to experience a connection with him unlike anything she'd known before, or would know hence.

To her consternation, Luke rose up and pushed the material of his briefs down his hips, divesting them in a single movement that left him as naked as she. Merry's eyes flew wide. She had scarcely gotten accustomed to the sight of his naked chest, let alone his entire, splendid body. As he tossed aside his clothing, she riveted her gaze upon his chin.

"You may look at me, sprite," he invited with a hint of humor.

Her eyes flicked upward, wondering at the name that had tripped from his tongue so easily. *Sprite,* he'd called her. Was that not a wood nymph or another word for fairy?

She abandoned the question as her gaze sank inevitably to the dark hair at his loin. She'd seen a man's privates before, but none so magnificent that it roused her admiration. Luke's manhood jutted proudly from his body, sleek and copper-toned like the rest of him. The sight of it did not strike fear into her heart, until she imagined it pushing inside of her.

She raised doubtful eyes at him. "It won't fit," she informed him, solemnly.

His mouth twitched as if he knew an urge to smile. "Aye, it will," he said, "and nicely." Luke seized her hand and brought it toward him. "Touch me," he invited.

She was surprised to discover his weapon both as smooth as a baby and hard as a pike. As she stroked her fingers lightly over the tip and down its daunting length, it leapt at her caress. Luke's indrawn breath brought a forceful reminder of the power she wielded over him. With a reckless urge to expand her power, she closed her fingers over him firmly, stroking his length.

Luke gritted his teeth and shut his eyes, submitting to her will for just a moment. "Enough," he said, drawing her hand away. "Lie back," he instructed. "Let me make you ready."

She wondered how she could ever be ready for an invasion of such proportion. Tense and uncertain, she lay back as he'd instructed. He leaned over her, kissing her with a skill that eased her fears. His mouth broke free, traversing the length of her body. He suckled her breasts then trailed openmouthed kisses down the plane of her abdomen.

Recalling the dream she'd once had, Merry smiled with awe-filled pleasure. Luke's warm mouth seemed to melt the bones in her body. She felt herself relaxing, trusting him completely.

When his mouth settled on the inside of her thigh, she sighed, not at all alarmed to feel him there.

"Open for me, sprite," he rasped, nudging her legs apart.

She spread her legs with a flash of anticipation. She had touched herself there before. She knew what sort of pleasure she could awaken, and yet she'd never associated that pleasure with a man, never imagined a man doing that for her.

The thought excited her beyond bearing. Her chest rose and fell with anticipation.

To her delight, Luke's mouth was even more effective than her fumbling fingers. His lips nuzzled her crisp woman's hair, and she gasped. His tongue, warm and sure, found the center of her pleasure and flicking it, caused her to fist the sheets in delight. He increased both speed and pressure, probing her at the same time.

When his finger slipped into her opening, she tensed, but there was no pain. Working that finger back and forth, he ignited a friction that caused her to lurch toward his touch, wanting more. He inserted two fingers, pushed them deeper and hesitated.

She was disappointed to feel him withdraw. The sensations that had risen up were nearing a critical point. With regret, she eyed him as he crawled up and over her.

"Merry," he said, settling his weight comfortably between her thighs. He captured her face in his hands, his grave expression giving her pause.

"What is it?"

"Your maidenhead is firmly lodged. Ferguson never touched you."

She blinked at him, and when the significance of his words registered, tears of relief stabbed at her eyelids. "Thank you," she whispered, as a piece of her past seemed to fall away, never to hurt her again.

He regarded her closely. "This means there will be some pain," he added, "whilst I break the barrier."

Relief faded, to be replaced by worry. "Oh," she said.

"We can stop this now," he offered, surprising her. "You've learned what you needed to know. You're chaste, Merry. Why not save your maidenhead as a gift for your future mate?"

The depth of Luke's goodness shook her in that moment. Gazing up at his dark visage, she knew there would never be another mate for her. Luke was the one man equal to her strength, the one man capable of looking past her flaming tresses and seeing not a witch, but a woman worthy of respect.

"Nay," she answered him, pulling his head down for a feverish kiss. "I want this. I want you."

She felt him tremble then and realized just how much control he'd exerted in restraining himself. With a low moan, he took command of her kiss, devouring her mouth with a hunger that left her shaken, but not afraid. She felt the head of his manhood nudge her wet opening. The invasion was thick, but as yet painless. He moved in her, deepening his claim by the slightest of increments.

Merry's chest expanded at the heady feel of him taking over her body. Her heart thudded with anticipation. 'Twas not such an awful thing to submit to another's will.

With coaxing hands, he encouraged her to lift her legs on either side of him, and she knew the moment had come. With a look of regret, he lowered his mouth and kissed her, at the same time, driving his entire body forward.

Pain, sharp and quick, seared Merry and she screamed into his mouth. Just as quickly, the pain subsided. He lifted his lips, and she gasped for breath, drawing her fingernails away from his tortured shoulders.

"Is it done?" she asked, for he was holding perfectly still. She knew it to be a foolish question, for he was still inside her, stretching past repletion.

He seemed to have trouble focusing on her. "Nearly," he rasped. "Don't move."

She understood, then, that if she moved, he would spew his seed inside of her, finding his pleasure. Why, she wondered, would he not want to seek that fulfillment? Perhaps he was too selfless. Perhaps he had no intention of spilling his seed in her at all; after all, he was betrothed to another.

She hesitated but a split second before making her decision. Luke deserved reward for his gentle skill—she'd scarcely suffered a moment's discomfort. More than that, she wanted him to feel ecstasy in her arms, to remember *her* when he lay with his future wife.

So, rather than keep still as he'd cautioned her, she moved her hips in a sinuous motion that was entirely instinctive. To her surprise, the movement ignited a lovely, gripping pleasure deep inside of her. "Oh!" she cried, moving again.

Through the roaring of blood in her ears, she heard Luke curse, but rather than protest her movements, he joined her, thrusting himself deeper, adding to her overwhelming delight. As the moment of crisis came upon her, she scarcely recognized it. Her release was more shattering than anything she'd experienced alone. She clutched his shoulders in helplessness, legs splayed to him, as ecstasy crashed over her and dragged her along with it.

Luke's hoarse cry blended with hers. He buried his face against her jaw, thrust a few more times, and then collapsed, his weight suddenly much heavier, though she didn't mind at all.

As their ragged breathing subsided, a moment of bliss settled over them, as soft as a blanket. Merry closed her eyes, marveling at the beauty of lovemaking. God's truth, she'd had no idea it could be so earthy, so life-confirming, so pleasurable! Her heart still hammered in the aftermath. Though she felt a mite sore, she couldn't wait to experience such delight again.

Luke stirred. He lifted his head and gazed down at her, his unfocused eyes slowly clearing. The look he gave her sent a bolt of longing through her heart. No one had ever looked at her with such tenderness and awe.

Then, with a blink, those emotions fled, replaced by something sharper, something clearer. He muttered a curse in that foreign tongue of his and with a hiss, pulled out of her abruptly. *"Jesu!"* he added, mystifying Merry as he scrambled out of bed. "Where can I find a cloth?"

She came up on her elbows, fascinated by the sight of him completely naked and pacing her chamber. "Look by the wash-basin," she said.

Pouring water from the pitcher into the earthenware bowl, he snatched up the towel there, and with hurried movements, dipped it in the water, wrung it out, and brought it swiftly to her, his expression grim.

Merry drew away from him, confused and frightened by the scowl on his face.

"Wipe yourself," he growled, thrusting the towel at her.

She took the towel with sudden chagrin.

"Go on," he prompted.

Nay, she wasn't going to wipe herself in front of him!

He snatched the cloth away and pressed it between her thighs. Merry gasped at the cold contact and squeezed her legs together with shame.

"Listen to me, Merry." Luke's urgent voice broke over her confusion. "I spent my seed in you. 'Tis something I swore never to do—to beget a child on any woman other than my wife. We must remove as much as we can."

As she sat in stunned silence, he drew the cloth away to return to the washbasin and rinse it, but not before Merry caught a glimpse of her own blood staining it. She tested the tender spot with her fingers, finding herself still wet with seed and just a hint of maiden's blood.

Luke returned, and she took the cloth from him this time, pressing it to her. He sat on the edge of the bed, regarding her with a somber frown, his thoughts clearly weighty. "If you find yourself with child, Merry, you have only to send a note to me in West Sussex. I will see to the babe's welfare."

His words failed to reassure her. If anything, they sent a

crushing weight through her as they reminded her of her empty future. Once delivered to Helmesly, she was not Luke's problem anymore. The burden of her welfare fell to her brother-in-law.

But then she thought of something that rallied her spirits. What if Luke did get her with child? Then she would have a part of him to keep as her own, forever. That hope lit the bleak corridors of the days to come.

"I have only to consume a drop of henbane," she commented, wanting to ease his worries, "and your seed will whither ere a babe is formed."

He frowned at her solution. "Henbane is a poison, is it not? I forbid it, Merry. You'll do no such thing." He eased the towel from her again, and, apparently content that it had drawn away most of his seed, he tossed it across the room.

To Merry's surprise, he eased onto the bed, drawing her once more against him. Her senses leapt back to life at the abrasion of his flesh against hers. Beneath the crisp sprinkling of his body hair, his skin was warm and smooth, dense with muscle.

Propped up on one elbow, he gazed down at her, his expression inscrutable in the amber light. With his free hand, he traced a line from her shoulder, between her breasts, to her hips. "Did I hurt you?" he inquired softly.

Lulled by his tenderness, she longed to ease that frown from between his eyebrows. "Nay," she reassured him, smiling. "You were very gentle. 'Twas the most . . . remarkable experience," she added, unable to help her dreamy smile.

Against her hip, she felt his manhood stir.

He caressed her again, this time painting invisible circles about her breasts. They responded at once to the attention, peaking and flushing like tiny rosebuds. Merry's eyes melted shut. Contentment hummed in her throat. Her heart began to beat with the anticipation of making love once more.

Luke's manhood swelled more fully as he pressed himself against her hip. He brought his lips to Merry's temple, kissed the line of her jaw. She didn't hesitate this time, but turned to face him, pressing her breasts against his chest. Drawing his lips to hers, she kissed him hungrily, eager to explore her newfound source of pleasure. "Teach me everything you know," she begged him, throwing a leg over his hips and drawing him close.

"Naughty witch," Luke growled without recrimination. Threading his hands through hers, he drew them up and over her head to hold her captive. Assaulting her breasts with his teeth and tongue, he drew whimpers of pleasure from her throat.

"Sweet Merry," he muttered between licks and nips. "You make me forget."

"Forget what?" she panted in dizzy delight. She had never been happier in her life.

He rolled suddenly on top of her, adjusting himself as she spread her legs in hot anticipation. At the portal of her entrance, he hesitated, like one balancing on the edge of a precipice. "Who I am," he finished, his eyes glazing as he eased slowly but inexorably inside her.

They gasped with mutual astonishment as urgency stormed their senses. Merry arched her hips, demanding immediate surcease. He surged into her, responding with every muscle to the demands of her frenzied hunger. In no immediate danger of spilling his seed right away, Luke took Merry's charge very seriously. In the hours that followed, he taught her everything he knew.

With each new insight, Merry felt herself flowering into completion. Nothing in her life had ever felt so right as this merging of souls and bodies. She and Luke strained toward each other, inseparable, yet never close enough, arching, grasping, clawing, and tasting.

Hours later, as she lapsed into exhausted slumber, her body tender but sated, she realized with bittersweet nostalgia, that the best moment of her life was now behind her.

# *Chapter Eleven* 🪶

RAINDROPS struck Merry's face like tiny arrows, yet she hardly flinched. She scarcely felt the cold, wet wind billowing beneath the cloak Lady Adelle had given her as a parting gift. Nor did she complain about the ache in her back that came from riding from sunup to sunset the day before. She could feel nothing beyond the numb disbelief that Luke had spoken no more than a sentence to her since their journey began.

In lieu of his arms around her, she had only the comfort of a sodden, miserable cat, for she rode alone. Luke had donned his armor as a precaution against danger. Ten of his best soldiers, equally well-armed, accompanied them. As Luke had tersely explained to her yesterday, Suleyman could not bear the weight of another rider when he wore his mail. She'd been given her own horse, and the helm he'd jammed down on his head had kept them from even sharing eye contact.

It was not the bittersweet end of their time together that Merry had envisioned.

Yet Luke remained a courteous knight. She could not fault him there. Yesterday morning, she'd awakened alone in the bed they'd shared, saving her from disgrace in Lady Adelle's eyes, as the baroness had been the one to wake her. Throughout the long ride yesterday, Luke had looked to her comfort, stopping often that she might stretch her legs or relieve herself. And when the rain had swept down on them last night, he'd erected a tent for her, so she would not have to sleep in the wet outdoors like the rest of the soldiers traveling with them.

Yet he'd made no attempt to prolong their intimacy. He'd taken great pains not to touch her. In contrast to the warm bed she'd shared with Luke the night before, no place had seemed so cold and lonely as that tent.

She tried reasoning with herself to lift her spirits. Luke had made it perfectly plain that their night together was all he could give of himself. She expected little beyond that. But perhaps some regret, some tenderness, a token to carry with her—was that asking too much? Instead, she was the recipient of his distant courtesy.

He was not the friendly companion he had been on the road to Iversly. He was naught but an escort, so aloof that she felt she was already at Helmesly, locked behind its thick walls.

Rising to face the second day of their journey, Merry found herself wondering if he'd used her merely to assuage his needs. The way he treated her now, it was not impossible to envision him dusting his hands off as he dropped her by the gates of Helmesly, relieved to get his duty done.

Could it be that the best night of her life had meant nothing to him?

The possibility left her stunned and silent in the saddle as their journey ensued. Desperately, she replayed every moment of their intimacy, searching for evidence that his tenderness had been a farce. Perhaps she'd only imagined the hunger that had burned in his eyes and in his touch, making him seem so possessive. Perhaps she'd imagined his gentle restraint. If not, then where had those emotions flown?

Through the curtain of rain sweeping between them, she sought a hint of her lover in Luke's rigid posture. He rode at the head of the retinue as if he could not arrive at Helmesly soon enough.

Her heart ached to look at him. She lowered her gaze to her tightly clenched hands. Soon she would never see him again. She could scarcely get her mind to accept that thought.

When had he become so vital to her joy? Was it when he'd

made that promise, weeks ago, to contrive to make her smile again?

She shook her head in confusion. Nay, she had not imagined his kindness, nor his tenderness, nor his desire. So where were those traits? She could read no hint of them in the set of his shoulders.

'Twas as if the man who'd lain with her the other night was not the same man escorting her to Helmesly.

The rain picked up again, driving Merry deeper into Lady Adelle's mantle. Shivering with cold and wet, her regret turned inward where it smoldered into anger. She would never forgive Luke for this. He'd committed the ultimate betrayal: he had made her feel again.

She should not have given him so much of herself, she reflected, morosely. She should have kept to her accustomed ways, guarded her heart in isolation as she'd always done. At least, in that frozen state, she could not be hurt. Not even the prioress, who'd condemned her to death, had pierced the armor that Merry had worn for years.

But Luke had refused to leave her in her bitter shell. With his courtesy and his restraint, he'd won her trust. Though naturally attractive, he'd contrived to make himself irresistible. If only she hadn't let her guard down and given her feelings a chance.

Now, in addition to the life she was condemned to, she must also endure the reality that happiness was denied to her, not just because of who she was, but because the one who stirred such joy in her did not return her affections.

Wallowing in her troubled thoughts, Merry realized with a start that they'd come to the outskirts of a town previously shrouded in mist. The name of it, Great Ayton, was carved into a stone by the side of the road.

As they cantered into the town square, she saw that it was little more than a sleepy gathering of huts huddled around a central well. Certainly there was nothing great about it. On such a bleak September day, the muddy little square lay deserted. But the scent of roast pork wafted from a whitewashed building that had weathered to a dull gray. The sign outside, creaking in the wind, was too worn to read.

Luke gave the call to stop. He turned and eyed Merry. "Are you hungry, lady?" he inquired.

Coldly polite. She sought to read his eyes through the slits of his helm, but the mist obscured them.

"I am," she answered. This was, perhaps, her only chance to pry a word of regret from him, something that would bring relief to her aching heart. She had overheard him reassure the soldiers that they would arrive at Helmesly by nightfall.

"We eat here," he announced, addressing his ten men. He managed to dismount on his own, hitching his horse and hers to the posts. The others followed suit.

Finding Kit asleep in her saddlebag, Merry left him sleeping and slipped from her mare, unaided. All the men, except for the one designated to guard the supplies, tromped toward the door of the building. Ignoring Luke's silent offer to escort her, Merry followed Erin into the smoky dwelling. It took a moment for her eyes to adjust to the gloom.

"Over here," Luke said, tugging her toward an alcove away from the fire.

Her gaze slid longingly toward the hearth. Her cloak was damp and heavy from the showers that had drenched her. But the area before the hearth was crowded with young men. As they were dressed in green and touted bows and daggers, she assumed that they were hunters. They had apparently been drinking for a while, for the liquor had roughened their laughter and swelled the volume of their conversation, making the tavern noisy.

Luke indicated she should sit at the end of the bench, farthest from the youths. As he sat beside her, settling his helm in his lap and tugging his fingers from the gauntlets, her hopes for reconciliation rose. She resisted the urge to stare at him, to commit his profile to memory. Waiting for a word from him— any word, she pushed back her hood, unaware that the firelight found a reflection in the fiery length of her single braid.

After a while, a buxom barmaid came over to take their orders, and the young men who'd been ogling the wench finally took note of Merry. They elbowed one another until all of them were staring.

Luke slid a fraction closer, and pleasure bloomed in Merry's heart. Was he jealous? Protective? She glanced hopefully at his shadowed profile, but his jaw looked harder than ever, and his expression was still remote. He gave the barmaid their order then returned the stares of the youths who jostled for a view.

Merry's heart thudded with expectation. While not exactly private, the noise in the tavern allowed for at least a modest conversation for those sitting side by side. There wasn't any reason Luke could not speak to her as intimately as he'd done the other night. She imagined him apologizing for his cold manner, assigning his aloofness to his military demeanor.

As the minutes crept past, her hopes died a slow and painful death.

Anger flared with double vigor—anger at Luke for teaching her heart to feel again, anger at herself for wanting more from him than he could give. With a desperate need to relieve it, Merry pushed to her feet, drawing Luke's startled gaze. The light from the fire illumined her erect figure, and the youths across the room murmured their approval.

She glared at Luke, her knees quaking with an emotion too powerful to name. "I'm going to the bog," she informed him, her voice sharper than she intended. Stepping over the bench, she fled toward the rear exit, seeking the outhouse, any place private in which to squeeze out a tear or two.

At the end of a short hall, she found a heavy door and pushed through it into the mist. A quick glance over her shoulder revealed Luke's shadow, coming after her.

She lengthened her stride, running across the muddy yard to the ugly structure at the rear. The bog reeked despite the cool temperatures. Merry finished her business quickly and returned to the inn, hoping not to encounter him.

To her dread, he was waiting at the door for her. Nay, she would not give him the opportunity to lecture her on her petulance. Thrusting her chin into the air, she made to brush by him, but he caught her back. The door slammed shut, startling them both.

"Release me," she commanded, raising imperious eyes at him.

"Lady, don't be like this," he ordered in a low voice.

"Oh, it's lady now, is it? Suddenly you're unable to call me by my name." Nor by the pet name he had given her, she noted with a pang in her heart.

"Merry," he said, tightening his grip.

She wrenched her arm free of his grasp and bolted past him.

Luke pursued her down the abbreviated hall. A second later, he spun her around. This time anger hardened the angles of his face. "I told you not to expect anything from me," he ground out. "Now cease this tantrum and comport yourself like a lady."

Bitterness that had brewed in her for years boiled to the surface. The last thing she wanted from him now was a lecture on what she could or couldn't expect from life. "If I were a lady," she hissed at him, her face on fire, "then you would not be conveying me to Helmesly, would you?"

She wrenched her arm from his grasp and fled blindly into the inn's main room, straight into the arms of one of the youths.

"Well, well!" the young man cried, spinning her around. "What have we here?" He pulled her into the circle of his companions, who welcomed her warmly.

Bemused and bewildered, Merry let herself be led before the fire. She was trembling, wet and cold. The fire's warmth was a comfort, the friendliness of the youths a distraction from Luke's chilling remainder that he'd given her all he could.

Her anger left her, leaving her sick for having humiliated herself. He *had* warned her, it was true, that there would be no future between them. She had given herself willingly. More than that, she had practically demanded that he lie with her. It wasn't fair to expect anything else from him, not even regret.

The youths crowded around her, exclaiming their amazement at the color of her hair. One who had clearly drunk too much stretched a hand toward her bosom. Merry slapped it away, drawing chortles of amusement.

"Ah, she's a vixen, this one," one of them remarked.

"Now see here, lady," cried the drunkard, rubbing his sore hand and looking more incensed by the moment.

"We don't mean ye ne harm," cooed his sly-looking companion. "Likely we can please ye more 'n the knight what escorts ye." He nodded toward the empty portal. Luke had yet to appear, but his soldiers were sitting rigidly and indecisively upon the benches. They'd begun to murmur amongst themselves, yet none went out of their way to bring her back into the fold, she noticed.

"Have a drink," said another, pressing a wooden cup into her hand.

Merry scented danger in the air. The men were pretending to be friendly, but she sensed their animal intent as they crowded around her, eyeing her hungrily.

She sent an imploring look at Luke's soldiers, but they'd apparently decided she wasn't worth fighting for. Only Erin seemed uneasy as he glanced at the empty doorway, clearly hopeful of his lord's return.

A heavy hand settled on her shoulder, and Merry shrugged it off. "Say," cried one of the men, turning her toward the fire to have a better look at her. "Ain't ye the witch what's wanted by the Church?" he asked, bending closer.

Merry flinched from the sour breath expelled across her cheek. At the same time, her heart froze in fear at his observation. Her face fell under scrutiny as the other youths leaned in to study her.

"Who's got the missive?" one of them asked.

Another reached inside his vest and unrolled a wad of tattered parchments. Merry recognized them as public notices, the kind that were pegged up at crossroads, describing criminals on the run. She eyed the quantity of tubes in the youth's hand and realized with a shrinking of her skin that these men were indeed hunters, but not for game.

The one with the notices pulled one vellum free and unrolled it. "Says here the witch is a lady of nineteen years. Says her hair is red like the flames o' hell. She escaped a burning with the help of a knight claiming to serve the prince himself. There's a reward of forty marks for her return!"

The light of ambition cleared the drunken mist from their eyes as they regarded her over the top of the notice. "God's wounds," whispered one of them. "It must be she!"

"The lady is with me." Luke's authoritative voice cut through their murmuring like a blade through butter. "Kindly unhand her," he added.

When the bounty hunters failed to move fast enough, Luke unsheathed his broadsword and extended it in warning. Firelight skittered up the length of steel and shone upon the smooth links of his armor. Even his eyes seemed to reflect the fire's glow. He looked like a magical being. In that moment,

Merry knew she would remember him without bitterness, despite his treatment of her now. He was the most incredible man she'd ever known.

The one holding Merry gave a forced laugh. "Now, good knight," he cajoled, leading Merry cordially forward. "Of course this fine lady isn't the witch in question. We only jested with her, isn't that so, friends?"

His friends had frozen at the sight of Luke's sword. They seemed to rouse from their amazement and, with a few shared looks, gathered their belongings swiftly and hastened toward the door.

The sly one continued to address Luke. "Is this lady your wife, then?" he asked, his hand still on her elbow as he led her back to Luke.

"I asked you to unhand her," Luke reminded the man. At the same time, he signaled for his men to rise from their meal. They did so, drawing weapons as they rose. Merry held her breath, sensing a violent confrontation.

She blinked. The hand that was just at her elbow was now pressing a blade to her throat. "Move a thumb's width and I'll kill her," the youth warned, his voice transformed into that of conscienceless murderer. Merry was reminded of the night at Heathersgill when Edward had threatened Luke much the same way. Luke had used his words to save her then. Somehow she doubted any words would save her now. Panic caught up to her belatedly, causing the blood to drain from her face.

Luke's sword rose a fraction, and the dagger at Merry's neck broke the skin. She gave a cry at the stinging pain, felt a certain moisture trickle down her neck. For a horrible moment, she thought she'd been mortally wounded.

Luke took a startled step back and dropped his weapon. "Don't hurt her!" he uttered, looking terribly grim.

Her captor dragged her backward toward the door. "Do you make one move to follow us, I'll slit her throat completely. She's worth nothin' to you dead. Just remember that."

He shouldered his way out of the tavern then pulled her roughly into the rain. With a mighty heave, he tossed her face-down over the back of a horse, leaping into the space behind her. "Hah!" With a loud cry, the horse jolted forward. The breath was knocked from Merry's lungs, cutting short the cry of terror that broke free.

He was taking her away! Away from Luke!

She tried to push herself up, to relieve the discomfort of lying facedown across a saddle, but a relentless hand shoved her down, again and again. A blur of hooves, mud, and trampled grass streamed across her vision. Squeezing her eyes shut, Merry concentrated on breathing, for the pummeling saddle pushed the breath from her lungs with every lurch. She could not believe what had just happened.

Because of her temper, she had fallen prey to fortune-seekers. They must have done this sort of thing before. Not a word was spoken, and yet they were galloping toward a common destination. They had taken Luke, a seasoned warrior, utterly by surprise.

Thinking of Luke made her eyes sting with remorse, made her wail within. Likely she had ruined any hope of his coming after her. Why should he bother saving her when all he'd gotten for his efforts was her stinging rebuke? She didn't deserve to be plucked free of this debacle. She was naught but a witch of the worst sort, and she deserved to be punished for her pettiness.

LUKE waited for the miscreants to thunder out of the village of Great Ayton before he gave the signal to pursue. His men, sensing his cold fury, poured silently out of the inn behind him.

They stopped dead at the sight that awaited them. The soldier on watch was sprawled under the bellies of the few horses that remained, his throat slit. The majority of their horses were gone, stolen by the bounty hunters.

Luke swore in his Saracen tongue. It was now impossible for his band to give chase. Yet three horses remained and, miraculously, Suleyman was one of them. Eyeing a furious Kit upon the saddle, his fur still spiked, Luke had to wonder if the cat was responsible for that good fortune.

The other mounts were Merry's docile mare and Erin's bony nag, both overlooked for their lack of speed.

Luke glared at the retreating villains, now just gray silhou-

ettes disappearing down the same road Luke had come in on, a
cart road running north to south called Rutland Rigg.

Luke could take only two men with him, and as one horse
was too small to bear the weight of an armored soldier, Erin
would have to be one. Luke signaled for his best archer to take
the second horse. Lifting Kit off Suleyman's back, he handed
the spitting cat to his men and instructed them to await their
return.

Then the threesome took off after Merry's abductors.

Luke had no wish to test her captor's threat. He'd seen how
quick the man was to nick her vulnerable neck. He indicated
that they should abandon Rutland Rigg and forge across the
moor itself toward an irregularly shaped hill that jutted from the
field. The mist and the undulating terrain would keep them concealed until they could approach close enough to surprise the
bounty hunters.

Fury shuddered through him. How could he have let such a
thing come to pass? *How?* He'd been misled by the young ages
of the bounty hunters, forgetting that recklessness and youth
went hand in hand. He'd been distracted by the furious bewilderment in Merry's eyes, helpless to comfort her in any meaningful way. Yet that was no excuse for letting down his guard,
even for a moment.

He ground his teeth together, grateful that he'd at least had
the sense to don his helm and his gauntlets. The youths were
armed, but not protected by armor. Even with their higher numbers, he was confident of his ability to catch and wound them
all. Whether he could do so without causing Merry to be killed
was yet another question.

He cursed again, drawing Erin's wide-eyed stare. The rain
slanted through the slits of his helm. Suleyman slipped in the
mud then righted himself. How had everything spiraled so far
from his control?

Up to the moment Luke had snatched Merry from the fire,
his life had been neatly choreographed, a straight line pointing
him toward his goals. He was the prince's favorite. Despite his
tainted blood, the title of earl would pass through his loins to
his heir. Until his son was of age, Luke would have charge over
Arundel, the castle that had enchanted him from his very first
sighting of it.

Since his rescue of Merry, his ambitions had become unfocused, less clear. She had delayed the completion of his work. She'd called into question the purpose of his duties to the crown. She had lured him from his commitment to Amalie. She had wrecked his equilibrium.

Nonetheless, he would die ere he consigned her to the fate the bounty hunters had in mind for her. He had sworn to Sir Roger he would take her to Helmesly. And yet he knew it was not his promise that made him desperate to catch up to her. It was the violation she would doubtless endure at the bounty hunters' hands. Merry—*his Merry*—would never endure mistreatment again. He'd appointed himself her protector.

And yet, what a miserable protector he'd been, having taken advantage of her vulnerability to assuage his fascination for her! Ah, *Jesu!* If only he'd managed to speak with her at the tavern, to offer her what comfort he could. He knew that his impersonal demeanor had disheartened her. He'd not intended for his actions to have that effect. He'd simply known no other way to crush the feelings gnawing at his heart. 'Twas a ploy he used deliberately in battle, separating himself from his emotion.

Truth be told, his desire for her had in no way diminished after their night together and that knowledge terrified him. God's bones, he'd taken her so often that night she had begged him to desist. Self-control? It had slipped away beneath her spell.

What a fool to think he could stray from the straight and narrow and not lose his way! He ought never to have surrendered to his attraction for Merry. Not only had that night fractured his vision of the future, but it had bruised Merry's generous spirit as well. He knew her to be too selfless not to give a portion of her heart.

Yet he had no choice but to escort her to Helmesly and to leave her there. He'd toyed with the notion of making her his mistress. Yet his own mother had been mistress to his father, making her an outcast to her people. Merry deserved a better fate than that.

She would have a future worth living, he vowed, but he would have to rescue her first.

With grim resolve, he led his two companions toward the base of Roseberry topping. The strange hill could be seen for miles in the open moorland. Yet it would afford Luke a means of cutting off the bounty hunters without being seen by them.

He urged Suleyman up a narrow foot trail, guessing that it would eventually lead to the summit. He had no intention of going that far; instead he would root out the best place for an ambush. He fancied he could already hear the bounty hunters thundering up the main road. He and his companions would have to hurry if they meant to surprise them.

They scrambled upward, slipping on the wet sandstone. At last they came to a ridge halfway up the incline. Luke gave the signal for Erin and the archer, Cyrus, to dismount.

"Wait until you have a good sighting," Luke informed Cyrus. "Then aim for the one who has the lady. Be certain that you fell him without killing him. Pick off as many of the others as you can. I'm going down to engage them by hand."

"Aye, lord," the two men answered. They tied off their horses and threw themselves upon the muddy ground, crawling to the edge of the ridge. Erin gripped his smaller bow in a white-knuckled hand. With a twinge of compassion, Luke realized this would be the boy's first taste of battle.

Crossing himself for protection, he turned his horse about and forged his own descent through the skeletal bushes, his ears pricked to the sound of Cyrus hitting his mark.

Over the gentle patter of the rain that had started up once more, the approaching horses gave off a sound like thunder. Luke urged Suleyman down the face of treacherous rock, goading him to recklessness for the sake of catching his prey.

A sudden scream rent the silence, assuring him that Cyrus had struck his first mark. Luke burst around a stone outcrop and charged, his sword firmly in his grasp.

His only advantage—other than that of armor and hidden archers—was that of speed and surprise. The bounty hunters had been thrown into a state of confusion by the wounding of one of their men. The horses, spooked to begin with, failed to answer to the commands of their unfamiliar riders.

Peering through the slits of his helm, Luke sought the one who held Merry. He failed to see her in the crush of horses and men as they rode in tight formation. For a terrible second, he feared he'd surprised the wrong party coming down the road.

But then he recognized the bounty hunters' clothing, and he spurred his horse onward.

An arrow whistled through the air, and another man howled in agony, falling off his horse. As the young men struggled with their mounts, Luke tore into their midst, his sword swinging. He caught one man across the arm, crippling him. He knocked another off the saddle with the flat side of his blade. It wasn't his intent to kill them. They were young, after all, and still had time to better themselves.

Wheeling Suleyman around, his search for Merry was confounded as a brave youth met him headlong. Crossing blades with the boy, Luke thrust him from his seat, knocking him under the hooves of a prancing animal. The crunching of bone and the accompanying scream signaled one less foe to contend with.

Luke raked the muddy scene for signs of Merry. Spying her cloak in the ditch, he spurred Suleyman toward it, his heart in his throat. "Merry!" he called out, his voice strangely unfamiliar.

When she lifted a pale face to him, he went limp with relief. He drew his horse as close to the ditch as possible and stretched down a hand to her. "Take hold," he cried. "Hurry!"

Out of the corner of his eye, he saw a bounty hunter stagger to his feet. He recognized the lad as the one who'd laid his knife to Merry's throat, the leader. Another straightened in the saddle, preparing to hurl his dagger.

Wearing armor, Luke had little fear that the dagger would penetrate his iron links. Merry, on the other hand, was defenseless. "Hurry!" he repeated. His fingers closed over hers, and he hauled her upward, shielding her from the weapon as it whistled past, falling harmlessly into the mud.

Having concerned himself with protecting Merry, Luke realized he had underestimated the leader once again. Somehow the youth had laid his hands on a wooden pike. Luke had no time to even lift his sword.

The bounty hunter charged at him. Thinking he meant to cripple Suleyman, Luke hauled at the reins, a cue to his horse to rear up and trample the attacker. Merry lost her tentative seat and slipped from the saddle to the ground, landing safely on her feet.

Somehow the youth dodged the horse's flying hooves, his aim still true. The point of the pike made stunning contact with Luke's knee. He flinched in surprise, having forgotten until that moment that his knee guard was missing. The force behind the weapon drove it deep under the metal chausses protecting Luke's thigh.

Pain, as awful as it was unexpected, took his breath away. He let out a strangled cry as the pike ripped apart the flesh of his inner thigh. Blood spurted from the wound, soaking his hose and his armor in an instant. The attacker gave a final heave then yanked the weapon free, preparing to strike again.

With shock slowing his reactions, Luke struggled to lift his sword. A sound like the sea roared in his ears, telling him that the blood was draining from him at a deadly rate. His sword felt too heavy to wield.

With utter helplessness, he watched as the youth bared his teeth and readied the pike for a second plunge. Darkness hovered in the corners of Luke's eyes and began closing in. Yet he was still alert enough to see the bundle of fury that threw herself around the attacker's neck.

A dagger flashed in her hand—the same that the other man had thrown? Merry rammed it into the man's ribs, not hesitating to kill him.

Knowing unconsciousness threatened, Luke slipped a length of leather over his shoulders—a contraption devised to keep him in the saddle in just such a circumstance. He had scarcely succeeded in adjusting it when the darkness claimed him.

Merry shoved her captor away and watched him pitch facefirst in the muddy road. It was no less than he deserved, trying to kill the immortal Phoenix. She knew an urge to spit on him.

Lifting worried eyes at Luke, she found him still on his horse but leaning heavily over Suleyman's mane, his chin against his chest. What little she could see of his face was bleached of color. She realized then that the leather halter around his shoulders was all that kept him seated.

"Nay!" With a raw cry, she reached for him, attempting to waken him. He did not respond to her shaking or the crying out of his name.

Some of the men he'd wounded were beginning to revive.

Merry glanced fearfully around her. At any moment they would fall upon her and capture her again, killing Luke if he wasn't already dead.

With strength born of fear, she managed to mount the horse behind his slumped form. Wrapping her arms about his armored frame, she fought to keep him upright as she gripped the saddle horn and begged Suleyman to flee.

Turning from the bloody scene, she goaded the destrier into a quick trot, heading back to Great Ayton where Luke's army awaited.

The sound of horses in pursuit made her look back in fright. She found herself being chased, not by the bounty hunters, but by the horses they had stolen. The faithful mounts were accustomed to Suleyman's lead.

Merry could only pray that Luke's men would welcome her in their midst. They had done nothing to prevent the youths from grabbing her at the tavern. And she had little doubt they would blame her fully if Luke died now. Nonetheless, she would need their help to save him.

And they would need her, too, if they ever meant to see their captain alive again.

# *Chapter Twelve*

ERIN and Cyrus caught up with Merry at the outskirts of the village of Great Ayton. With their help and the aid of Luke's men-at-arms, they conveyed their leader inside the tavern, laying him on the very table they had eaten on just an hour before.

"Help me get his mail off!" Merry shouted, pushing through the men who'd gathered around the stricken Phoenix.

No one complied with her demand. All nine men stared dumbstruck at Luke, grappling with the concept of his mortality as though it had never occurred to them before.

"Damn you all!" she cursed, raising her fists to them in her frantic need to stop Luke's bleeding. "Listen to me! I need you to strip his mail off. I must bind his wound. He is yet alive and he will remain so if you let me tend him!"

They raised dull eyes at her. The mewing of her cat, now wending between their feet with loud, disturbed yowls was the only sound to fill the tavern.

Erin was the first to break the standoff. "Do as she says," he commanded in his reedy voice. "My Lord Phoenix cannot die! We must try to save him."

Clumsy hands went to work, parting Luke from the weight of his armor. They stripped him down to his padded undershirt and leggings. The sight of his mutilated thigh caused several men to fall back with cries of dismay and whispered prayers. Others lamented the absence of Gervaise, who'd been left behind.

With the help of the buxom barmaid, Merry ripped a linen tablecloth into strips. "What is your name?" she asked, turning to the taciturn soldier on her left.

"Hugh of Tyburn," he replied.

"Hugh, I need you to raise his entire leg while I bind it. Erin," she added, "hold the muscle together."

With these two assistants, Merry managed to bind the lesion enough to slow the bleeding. With her hands drenched in blood, she knotted the ends of the bindings and brushed the hair from her eyes, leaving a streak of Luke's blood across her forehead. "Now we convey him to Helmesly with all haste. The castle is near. My sister and I will care for him there."

Luke's men stared at her in dazed amazement. They scarcely saw the tremors that shook her squared shoulders. In the muted light of the tavern's fire, they could not remark the pallor of her skin, nor even note its clamminess. All they saw was a woman with straggling, red hair, flashing green eyes and a streak of their leader's blood across her forehead.

Her noisy cat continued its howling as it paced about their feet. They dared not argue with the witch, lest they fall under a spell of her weaving.

Nodding their heads, they went to work placing Luke upon a bier loaned to them by the undertaker across the square. It was just a simple pallet lain across four poles. With haste, they hoisted the contraption between their horses and pointed their mounts toward Helmesly. Not one of them went without the thought that they'd been plagued with nothing but ill fortune since plucking the witch from the fire.

"HOW does he, Merry?"

Merry looked up from Luke's bedside and found her sister, Clarise, leaning through the door. She hadn't even heard the hinges groan, so exhausted was she. The four torches in the chamber had burned low. Yet they were still bright enough to gild the gold-red tresses of Clarise's hair. She wore her night-dress, telling Merry the lateness of the hour.

"He'll live," she said, tipping her head to one side to relieve the kink in her neck. It was her standard answer, one from which she'd refused to deviate in the last three days. Her refusal to let Luke die seemed to be all that had kept him alive. She'd heard the rumor that his soldiers thought him dead, so pale had he been at their arrival. She'd let no one but Clarise close to him since, leaving the soldiers to bed down with the Slayer's men in Helmesly's vast garrison.

Merry had stood vigil over Luke in all that time, scarcely remembering to eat or sleep. She'd treated his wound with the finest herbs in her sister's garden, with crosswort, knotgrass, and Saint-John's-wort. She had bathed him, stitched him, and bandaged him. As the days crept by, she'd forced a nourishing broth down his throat. When his fever soared, she cooled his skin with a wet cloth. She didn't want to leave him now, but she was close to fainting with exhaustion. Time would have to do the rest.

Clarise closed the door quietly behind her and came to stand by Merry's chair. For a moment, they both watched the dark-haired warrior sleep. A coal-black growth of beard obscured the lines of his jaw. His chest rose and fell beneath a blazing white sheet. Except for the bandage on his leg, there was nothing about his appearance that bespoke the severity of his wound nor the amount of blood he'd lost. To Merry, he was still as striking as the day she met him.

"How is his fever?" Clarise inquired.

Merry put a hand to Luke's forehead, brushing back the silky, raven locks. "It lingers," she said, hearing the helplessness in her own voice. She had struggled to keep the humors of his body in balance, and yet the fever would not leave him, likely because he lacked the moisture to combat it. Her fingers feathered through his hair. She had enjoyed tending him, enjoyed the leisure of studying his dark beauty without guarding her fascination for him.

Clarise cleared her throat, and Merry snatched her hand back guiltily. She glanced at her sister and found herself the focus of Clarise's discerning gaze.

"You look like hell, Merry," she said with typical honesty.

" 'Tisn't any wonder the Phoenix won't arise. He'd swoon again to look at you. Come, I've drawn you a bath. Sleep tonight and you'll be rested tomorrow when he wakes." She began to pull Merry toward the door.

Clarise was a good bit taller than Merry and accustomed to getting her way. Merry relinquished her patient to God's mercy and let herself be dragged from the room.

The sisters went a short way down the hall to Merry's chamber. Clarise thrust open the door, revealing a well-lit room, complete with a boxed bed draped in purple silk. Candles studded the furniture, circling an enormous wooden tub full of water. Steam still rose from the filmy surface. A trace of rose oil scented the air.

Merry glanced at her sister dryly. For months after Ferguson's siege, Clarise had tried to catch her wild, little sister and make her bathe. Merry had been like an animal then; how different she was now, only too glad to take a bath!

Clarise smiled at her tenderly. "You look so tired," she said, touching Merry's cheek with sisterly concern. "Turn around," she added in her no-nonsense voice. "Let's burn this filthy gown and dunk you in the tub."

Letting her sister strip her, Merry felt a pleasant lethargy seep into her limbs. With Clarise, she could let her guard down, not watch her words carefully as she had with Lady Adelle.

Once naked, Merry stepped into the tub and sank into the water with a groan. Releasing her breath, she went all the way under, floating weightless for a moment before surfacing. Clarise began to lather her hair with scented soap.

"So," she said, massaging Merry's scalp, "you've returned the debt you owed the Phoenix by saving his life." It was an invitation to discussion.

"He hasn't yet awakened," Merry reminded her.

"He will," Clarise replied, calming Merry's spirits with her assertion. "You've done miracles with your healing of him," she added. "I've never seen a more skilled healer than you, Merry."

Merry flushed at the praise, her spirits reviving from the state of numb desperation in which she'd dwelled for days. "Thank you," she murmured.

"Sarah taught you much."

"Aye, she did."

An awkward silence fell between them. Clarise sat on the side of the tub and began to rub her with a cloth, starting with her ears and working down. Merry's eyelids melted shut. She let her head fall back.

"What's he like, this Phoenix of yours?" Clarise inquired after a moment.

Merry felt her lips curve in a dreamy smile she couldn't hide. "He's noble," she murmured, "despite the fact that he's baseborn. He's kind and brave." She could think of hundreds of words to describe him, yet saying too much would reveal her obsession for him. "Disciplined. He isn't like other warriors."

"Like my husband, you mean," Clarise said with irony.

Merry cracked an eye. "I don't know your husband well," she answered, "at least that's what Luke says."

The washcloth moved down Merry's arm. "Well said of him," she commented. " 'Tis a shame he wasn't around when you cursed Christian's manhood."

Merry sank deeper into the water. "That was four years ago," she mumbled, feeling suddenly like a child again. "I only meant to protect you."

"I know you did," Clarise soothed, her tone forgiving. "You thought him another like Ferguson. He isn't, you know. Christian is as tame as they come."

Merry pictured the Slayer in her mind's eye and snorted.

"Now tell me," Clarise continued persuasively, "what does the Phoenix intend with you?"

Merry hid her despair behind closed eyes. "He means to leave me here," she said. The task of hiding her despair was beyond her in her present state. "He believes that I'll be safe," she added, "that your husband will hold off the bounty hunters and even the Church."

Clarise's silence told Merry all she needed to know: that her sister had her doubts on that score.

"You may turn me in, sister," Merry added, opening her eyes to meet Clarise's tawny gaze. "If I have truly saved the captain's life, then my course here is run. 'Tis all I wanted to do."

Clarise's eyes flared with outrage. "Don't you say such things!" she scolded, rubbing the soap into the washcloth. "Stand up, if you will," she added shortly.

Merry was used to Clarise's bossy tone and came obedient-
ly to her feet. Her sister began to scrub her with a vengeance,
bringing a rosy glow to Merry's skin. "You became a woman at
the convent," Clarise remarked, her only comment on Merry's
femininity.

An old wound bled anew. "You might have known that had
you written me," Merry said quietly.

Clarise straightened abruptly. "What do you mean? Mother
wrote to you once a week. And I, after the birth of Rose, wrote
you nearly as often as that! 'Tis you who did not reply!"

Merry gazed at her sister's earnest countenance. Clarise had
shown nothing but concern for Merry since her sudden appearance. The love she'd showered on her since birth had in no way
lessened over the years they'd spent apart. Tears of relief rushed
into Merry's eyes. She should have known her family would
not have abandoned her. "The prioress must have kept the letters from me," she whispered, her face crumpling.

With a cry of surprise, Clarise dropped the washcloth and
reached for her. "Oh, Merry, how terrible for you," she said,
putting her arms around her. "We would never have left you
without word from us. Never! What a cruel thing for the prioress to do. What manner of woman is she?" She didn't seem
to notice that Merry was soaking her nightdress as she clasped
her firmly to her. "Leaving you there was the last thing we
wanted," she added. "You should have seen Mother and me
weeping all the way home. 'Twas the only way we could keep
you safe, don't you see?"

Clarise put Merry at arm's distance. "We'll keep you safe
this time," she swore. A look of determination crossed her
exquisite features. Merry had seen that look before when
Ferguson ruled their keep. To defeat their stepfather, Clarise
had found a champion in the unlikely form of the Slayer—a
warlord in his own right.

"I know about the crowd outside the gates," Merry admit-
ted, feeling the familiar grip of fear. "I know they want me."
For two days now, a throng had gathered on the other side of
Helmesly's moat, raising their voices in a chant, demanding
Merry be given to the Church.

"Well, they cannot have you," Clarise retorted firmly. "Now
sit and rinse the soap off. And then we'll dry your hair." With

that she dismissed the topic of Merry's uncertain future, to be discussed at a later time.

Sinking back in the water, Merry silently acknowledged that the Slayer was a powerful warrior. But he was not above the dictates of the Church nor the will of the populace. The people were disturbed to have a witch in their midst. They wanted her to be turned over. Now that she'd fulfilled her obligation to Luke, just as Sarah's spirit had predicted she would, it scarcely mattered whether she lived or not. She'd done her penance; she'd redeemed her sorry life.

"DID you hear me, Christian?" Clarise demanded of her husband an hour later. She lay reclined on their enormous bed, nursing their third child and second son, if one counted Simon, who was not of her blood but whom she'd raised from infancy.

Baby Chauncey, like his older sister Rose, was as red-haired as his aunt Merry. He sucked contentedly and paid as much attention to his mother's strident tone as the warrior across the chamber.

"Hmmm?" Christian leaned forward in his chair and marked the line in his text where he'd left off. At last he raised his head and gave his wife his full attention.

"She loves him," Clarise repeated, letting the magical words hang in the air a moment. "I never thought I would see the day that Merry loved a man, and yet it's obvious that she does."

Her husband stood up, and the seat gave a groan of relief. He stretched his powerful body, then sauntered closer, holding Clarise's gaze. "Did she say so?" he asked with doubt. " 'Tis hard to imagine Merry loving any man."

"How dare you say such a thing?" she retorted. "If you'd seen the terrible things she'd seen you wouldn't much like your own kind, either. She didn't say that she loved him, nay. But she didn't need to. I could see it in her face."

"Ah," said her husband, easing onto the edge of their bed. Going down on one elbow, he studied Chauncey's rhythmic sucking. "Greedy pup," he growled, giving him an envious glare.

"Listen to me," Clarise demanded.

Her husband dragged his gaze from the sight of her exposed breasts.

"My point is that she loves the Phoenix. Think about it," she added. " 'Tis the answer to everything."

The warrior gave her a mystified look. At last his expression cleared. "You mean we should offer Merry to him?" he guessed. "To be his mistress?"

"Oh!" Clarise punched him in the shoulder and came away with bruised knuckles. "Nay, you big oaf, as his wife!"

He arched an eyebrow and tried to keep his face impassive. "His wife," he repeated. "My love, do you know who this man is?"

"Of course I do," she retorted. "All of England knows who he is. But he's also a bastard. Let's not overlook that fact. My sister is every bit worthy of him. Why, she's the best healer in all of North Yorkshire!"

To her frustration, Christian shook his head. "Clarise, the throne will have plans for him."

"She could study medicine if she were his wife," Clarise continued, ignoring his comment. "There are universities outside of London. With his help, Oxford might be persuaded to accept a woman for a student. She could become the first female physician in England!"

Her husband made a face. "You go too far," he said, kissing her swiftly, silencing her protests. His son put a chubby hand against his chin and pushed him away. Christian reared back with a growl of mock outrage. "So you won't share, eh?" The baby ignored his father's blustering and went on nursing.

Defeated, Christian rolled away and stalked to the nearest window. The sight that greeted him brought a curse to his lips. Outside the gates of Helmesly torches still burned. The handful of bounty hunters that had shown up days ago to demand the witch's release had swelled to a horde. Villagers from the town of Abbingdon had joined them, raising their voices in a chant. It had not taken long for Aelred, the Abbot of Rievaulx, to come calling.

Thankfully, Aelred and Christian were friends. The two had held council in Christian's solar, where Christian appealed to his friend for assistance in combating Merry's condemnation. Aelred explained she was likely already excommunicated and condemned by the Holy See. All he could do was to seek an appeal. Another trial would have to be held, with the Prioress of Mount Grace testifying against her. There was every chance Merry would be found a heretic again.

Christian closed the shutter against the reminder of his predicament. He had seen this kind of mass hysteria before. The recent flood that had washed away crops was being blamed on the witch within his walls. The common folk were a superstitious lot, and they far outnumbered more reasonable souls. Something would give way eventually.

He'd already decided it was going to be Merry.

Though he had yet to broach the subject with this wife— God knew it would cost him weeks of sleeping in the guest chamber—he intended to hand Merry over to Aelred, knowing the good abbot would do all that was within his power to keep Merry from being seized. 'Twas the only way to appease the populace.

He wished there were another way. He did not look forward to the fury he could expect from the woman whose love he cherished above all things. If only Clarise's suggestion were possible.

Perhaps the Phoenix *could* find a way to absolve Merry of her crimes. Christian turned thoughtfully around and found his wife watching him.

"If anyone can protect her, it is he," she added, as though reading his mind. "Mayhap he can even gain the crown's pardon on her behalf."

Christian leaned against the window ledge and crossed his arms. "The crown would have to appeal to Rome, first," he said, hating to squelch the light of hope shining in Clarise's eyes. He knew her family meant everything to her. Her worry these last few days had become palpable, making him uneasy. He truly dreaded letting her down. "What makes you think the Phoenix would take her?" he asked, playing along.

Clarise's brow furrowed. "Well," she said, calculating earnestly, "for one thing, my sister is a beautiful woman. Her body could tempt a saint into dissolution."

He clicked his tongue at her irreverence. "That would make her a good mistress," he pointed out, "not necessarily a good wife."

It was a mistake to say so. Clarise's cheeks flushed a deeper color. Her tawny eyes flashed. "She has saved his life, by heaven! I would say that puts him in her debt. How dare you relegate my sister to the status of mistress! She's as much the daughter of a nobleman as I!"

Christian winced. The subject of mistresses was a sensitive one, as he'd once made the mistake of asking Clarise to be his mistress. "I meant no insult, truly," he said, returning to the bed. "But we are talking of the prince's tenant-in-chief, soon to be the *king's* tenant-in-chief with Stephen so ill. A man such as he would marry a duchess or a princess, not the daughter of a modest landowner."

Clarise saw reason in her husband's argument, yet she refused to back down. "There is a way," she informed him stubbornly. "Merry says he is noble, kind, and brave. If you were to insist that he owes her a debt of gratitude, then mayhap he would agree to marry her."

Christian sat heavily on the bed. " 'Tisn't that simple," he replied.

His wife heaved a sigh and worried her bottom lip between her teeth. "Perhaps if he got her with child," she added, raising her eyes to him slowly.

Christian felt his jaw go slack. "You're not suggesting what I think you're suggesting," he said.

She looked down at the plump curve of Chauncey's cheek. "I know he's made love to her," she said softly. "I could tell by her smile when she speaks of him."

Her husband made a choking sound. "It doesn't necessarily follow that she's with child," he pointed out, outraged on the man's behalf.

"It doesn't follow that she's not," she tossed back.

With a whispered curse, he fell back onto the bed beside her, startling his son. "I should love to get rid of her," he muttered.

His wife gasped out loud and punched him in the arm again. "I tell you she's changed," she insisted. "She isn't full of venom anymore. All it took was kindness from a stranger. She is every bit the lovely girl she was before Ferguson's raid. Now cease being vengeful and work with me on this! I want the Phoenix to marry her. His influence may be all that will keep her from condemnation. He is likely her only hope, and beyond that, she loves him, Christian! Or have you forgotten what it's like to be in love?"

He rolled abruptly toward her, leveling a scowl at her that at one time would have caused her to pale. "Forgotten?" he said, putting a hand behind her head. "Nay, I remember it well. It went something like this." He kissed her with such blatant sensuality that she couldn't possibly mistake his interest.

Chauncey gave a yelp before they remembered he was crushed between them.

"This boy belongs in the nursery," Christian ground out, breaking away. He plucked the baby from his mother's breast and marched with him to the door. Throwing it open, he bellowed the name of Chauncey's nurse.

Minutes later, a huffing Doris took the baby away, but not before throwing her mistress a saucy wink.

"Why do you have to bellow?" Clarise complained. "Everyone in the castle knows what we're doing when you do that."

He approached the bed, unbuckling his belt as he did so. "I don't care what they think," he countered, dropping it to the floor.

He remarked his wife's growing interest by the brightness in her eyes and the flush of color in her cheeks. With a growl, he crawled onto the bed, intent upon reminding her just what it was like to be in love.

"WHAT shall we do about my idea?" she asked many moments later as she snuggled against him.

He struggled to remember what they'd been talking about.

"About the Phoenix marrying my sister," she prompted.

Christian groaned. "Are you still thinking of that?" he demanded. "After what I just did to take your mind off the matter?"

"Pah," she retorted. "You should know by now that wouldn't work."

"You'll pay for that remark, lady," he promised. "In the meantime, I have a question for you." He caught a tendril of her hair and let it spill between his fingers. "Why must you meddle in this matter? This is serious business, not a matchmaking festival."

She batted his hand away. "You mean I shouldn't try to save my sister's life?" she asked, growing rigid.

He knew his chances of a second round were ruined if he didn't surrender to her. He released her hair and hung his head. In a contest of wills, his wife always won. "What must I do?" he asked with resignation.

From the corner of his eye he saw her satisfied smile. "I'll let you know when the time comes. For now we must leave them alone together. The rest will work itself out."

Christian muttered darkly under his breath.

Clarise locked her hands behind her head in a gesture she'd learned from him. There was a final twist to her plan, of course, but her husband needn't know about that until the time was ripe.

LUKE struggled to open his eyelids. He wanted to tell the woman bending over him that he was conscious, that he could feel every limb in his body and therefore *knew* that he was whole and on the mend. And yet his mind was slow to respond, his thoughts flowing into one another like a mudslide. He couldn't get his eyes to open nor his mouth to speak. He was caught in a web of some unknown element. If his guess was right, 'twas an herb of some kind designed to keep him resting and feeling no pain.

He soon realized Merry was going to bathe him. While he sensed that they had gone through this ritual before, given her quick and efficient hand, he had never been conscious during any part of such intimate ministrations. Feeling her pull back the blanket and expose his chest to the mild air made him suddenly aware of his nakedness. Somewhere along the way, she'd stripped him of his clothes.

He heard a splash of water, followed by the sound of soap against a washcloth. He leapt a bit when the warm cloth hit his shoulder, but she didn't seem to notice. She started bathing his chest with sweeping, circular motions.

Luke managed a peek beneath his heavy lids and caught a picture of her before his eyes crashed shut. Merry wore a yel-

low gown, the color of buttercups. It made him think of the
dream she'd shared with him the night they'd made love.

The memory of that night brought his body to even keener
awareness. He swore he could smell the scent of Merry's skin.
She smelled of mint and lavender, with just a hint of rose
beneath. Her hair was in a plait so it wouldn't tickle him when
she leaned over to tend him. He recalled how it felt, cool and
silky against his heated skin.

For the first time he realized his skin was on fire. A fever
would account for his inability to open his eyes and address her.
And yet his growing warmth seemed directly related to her gentle touch.

A sudden breeze blew across his chest, giving rise to a prickle of gooseflesh. Merry clicked her tongue and went to latch
one shutter. He held his breath, anticipating her return.

"Now you won't take chill," she said, speaking to him as he
suspected she had done from the beginning. He had deduced by
now that he was at Helmesly, having overheard another
woman's voice on two occasions. Given its resemblance to
Merry's, the voice had to belong to Merry's sister. He marveled
at whatever miracle had occurred to bring him here.

The last thing he recalled of the day he was injured was a
vision of Merry, hurling herself at his attacker. Had she freed
him from the bounty hunters and seen him safely delivered to
Helmesly? Surely she could not have done so much, not even
with the help of his men.

A drying towel fell across his chest, and Merry rubbed him
dry with it. Luke's heart began to beat a little faster. Having
washed his torso would she move to other regions of his anato-
my? His body seemed to know the answer.

She pulled the blanket to his chin then lifted the other end
clear to his waist.

Luke did his best to speak, to alert her to the fact that he was
conscious. He managed to swallow, to move his tongue. The
cool air was a blessing to his heated skin, and yet he imagined
himself on naked display before her, and the image both disturbed and excited him.

He heard her dip the sponge into the bucket and wring it out.
Then the textured sponge touched his right thigh. She stroked

his uninjured leg with sweeping motions that did much to relieve his mortification but not his intrigue.

She moved to the left side, careful not to disturb the stitches he sensed were there, given the tight, pinched feeling of his skin. The healing flesh itched him like mad. She seemed to know this, running her fingers lightly around the angry edges. It was both a relief and a torment to have her fingers dance upon his thigh, so close to his manhood that it was hard not to think of her touch as sexual.

He realized he was holding his breath, and he let it out, hoping she would hear the difference in his breathing and guess his plight. But she went about her business, tormenting him with her light massage. His sex continued to thicken and rise. Surely she would realize he was cognizant and would grant him some modesty!

At last her hand did still. He waited, expecting the blanket to be pulled down with all haste. He fought to lift his eyelids, but to no avail. The chamber fell unbearably silent. He could only wonder if she was looking at his cock or at his face. Again he tried to indicate he was awake.

"Are you dreaming?" she finally asked him.

He couldn't form his mouth around the word *nay*. All he managed was a brief vibration of his vocal chords. He awaited her interpretation.

She was silent for the longest time. Then he felt the sponge taken away and dipped in water. She resumed her task. He gave a mental shrug. He'd done his best to alert her to his wakeful state, and she'd ignored him. Very well then, he wasn't responsible for what might follow. He surrendered to her ministrations, determined to enjoy them.

She ran the sponge delicately over the network of stitches. Each stitch felt like a pinprick going deep into his thigh, and yet she was gentle enough to keep him from lurching. Discarding the sponge, she dried the wound with the toweling cloth then began to spread an ointment over it. Her touch was exquisitely light, even pleasurable as she massaged it in.

He told himself 'twas his imagination when her fingers brushed his privates. His breathing grew shallow. All his senses were focused on her touch. Had she touched him there intentionally?

Aye, she had. She was delicately tracing the skin of his scrotum, now, perhaps noticing how his flesh contracted and drew up. Hunger roared through him, converging at his groin. His sex, he knew, stood straight and rigid, begging for her touch.

If he could speak now, he would likely plead for relief. Perhaps it was good that he couldn't.

She did touch him! Her palm ran smoothly up the length of him, bringing him instant pleasure. She did this several times, heightening his anticipation with each stroke.

Suddenly something moist was applied to him. He realized it was the same ointment she'd put on his wound. Somewhat shyly, she banded his thickness with her hand and moved it up and down much like she had done that night at Iversly.

Did she know what she was doing? Ecstasy seized him, making the question superfluous. What matter if she knew or not? 'Twas a boon he could not refuse. His heart pounded with delight. Perhaps he *was* dreaming.

He managed to peek through his lashes and was assured it was no dream. Merry's look of intense concentration stayed with him after his lids sank shut. She knew exactly what she was doing. Her single-minded intent made him wild with lust.

Beneath the onslaught of her slippery palm, it would not take long before he spent himself. He wondered at her motives. Was she enjoying herself, enjoying her power over him?

He felt the pressure of his release growing near, building to unbearable proportions. A blistering orgasm seized him. He felt his seed shoot forth, scorching hot. She continued to stroke him a little longer, making him shudder. Then she carefully wiped him down, removing all traces of the mess he'd made.

Suddenly Luke found that he could slit his eyes. He did so, wanting to thank her for such a fine treat.

She whipped her face toward his and gave a gasp. "You were awake!" she cried, clearly horrified.

He could scarcely nod. He searched for his tongue, needing to assure her that he thought no less of her.

She gave a cry of mortification and turned away.

*Don't be upset, Merry. 'Twas a wonderful treat.*

Without a backward glance, she bolted from the chamber, slamming the door behind her as she fled.

Luke cursed his immobile tongue. Belated shame caused a

blush to sweep into his cheeks. Damnation, he'd confused her further. He recalled how bewildered she'd been at the tavern, clearly confused by the distance he'd put between them. Now he'd humiliated her beyond acceptance.

He spent the next few minutes regretting his response to her seduction. He'd made it plain to her that their one night in Iversly was an aberration for him, that it was all that he could give. And yet he'd betrayed his desire for her again, capitulating to her touch. 'Twould make his eventual departure more difficult to endure, not just for Merry but for himself, as well.

Again he considered the possibility of keeping her as his mistress. Imagine indulging in their passion without limit! He frowned, blaming his weak thoughts on the herbs she must have given him.

Where were the goals he had planted so firmly in his mind? Why did he struggle now to keep them in sight? Arundel was all he wanted or needed. The respectability he'd craved for a decade was nearly in his grasp. He could not allow his hunger for Merry to turn him away from his ambitions.

And yet as he relived her tender touch, her earnest attempt to pleasure him, his body betrayed him and his member stirred again, eager to relive the pleasure she'd so guilelessly given him. With a sinking of his heart, he realized he would never again be satisfied.

MERRY pulled her head out of the pillow long enough to notice that Kit had moved from the foot of the bed to curl about her head. He settled down, his purring loud enough to drown the noises from the courtyard and the more distant chanting at the gates.

*Mother of God!* She'd never been so mortified. She had thought Luke soundly asleep. She'd even asked if he were dreaming, and he'd said nothing to warn her. *Nothing!* She'd succumbed to her lustful fascination, never thinking he would know the difference. And he'd been awake the entire time!

She moaned again, shedding a hot tear for her shame. That was it. She couldn't bear to look him in the eye again. Surely he thought her a trollop now, a whore. No doubt his opinion of her had sunk a good deal lower, if that were even possible.

What would he say if she confessed that she hadn't been able to help herself? Seeing him roused by her touch, she'd wanted him to know pleasure again, if only in his dreams. He deserved reward for coming after her, for risking his very life against the bounty hunters on the heels of her rebuke.

Her noble knight. He'd come to her defense again and again, regardless of how little it gained him. She heaved a sigh for what he was and for all that he would become. It couldn't be easy being a man of honor and integrity, a dutiful servant to his prince.

No wonder he'd withdrawn from her after their night at Iversly. She could see his motives clearly now. The only way to protect her from foolish dreaming was to break away neatly. He'd had the moral courage to do so, and she'd mistaken it for indifference.

In his estimation, how much lower had she sunk for her recent transgression?

She could never speak to him again. She would send the maidservant, Maggie, to look after him. The thought alone caused her a sharp stab of envy.

Of course, Maggie wasn't to bathe him as Merry had done, only to deliver him food and tidy up after him. Luke was on the mend. He could bathe himself and apply the ointment to his own wound, even bandage it himself. He didn't need her anymore.

*He didn't need her anymore.*

The realization made her lift her head from the pillow, sobered. It was over then, truly over. Her debt to the Phoenix was repaid. She had no purpose left but to while away her days, exiled behind the walls of Helmsly, and that was only if the Slayer let her stay.

Very slowly, she lowered her head back onto the pillow. Kit had ceased to purr at her movements, and now she could hear the voices chanting at the gates. In a week's time, the crowd had tripled in size, their demands growing more violent. Some had begun to throw stones over the wall. One stupid fool shot a flaming arrow onto a thatched roof before the Slayer's soldiers picked him off.

'Twould be a miracle if her brother-in-law let her stay. Why would he, when he could not even open his gates? They lived as if in a siege, calling upon the goods in the storeroom for foodstuffs in lieu of fresh food from the fields. And it was all because of Merry, whom the Slayer avoided at all cost. Not that she blamed him.

She closed her eyes in defeat. Whether she remained at Helmesly or fell into the clutches of the bounty hunters and was given to the Church, she was doomed either way. Doomed to want a man she would never have. 'Twas time to accept her defeat.

The end had come. She found she could not regret the Phoenix's rescue. Because of him, she'd discovered that her family loved her still, that she could use her skills for good and find reward in it. Yet knowledge came at a cost, and the cost, unfortunately, was her heart.

For somewhere in the last fortnight, she had fallen in love with the elusive Phoenix. She could not have said when it was—whether 'twas the moment he'd plucked her from the fire or the first time he'd kissed her. Or whether her love had come later, when he'd taught her the difference between lovemaking and force.

She knew only that her heart was no longer in her chest, for the empty feeling there was absolute. It belonged exclusively to Luke le Noir, whether he wanted it or not.

# Chapter Thirteen

LUKE sat up in bed—the only courtesy he could muster, given his injured leg. The woman sailing into his chamber was not the maid, Maggie, who brought him his food or vessels of ointment and carried off his soiled bandages. Nor was the woman Merry, whose face he clamored to see, whose presence he'd requested a hundred times only to be given lame excuses as to why she couldn't come.

Still, there was no mistaking the resemblance of this woman to the one who tormented his thoughts, waking and sleeping. Lady Clarise was taller than Merry, her hair a friendlier shade of honey-red. It was caught up and pinned with a tortoiseshell comb. She wore a splendid gown of burgundy silk. An open shutter slammed at her entrance as if to announce a queen. Indeed, there was a roaring outside the window, as if a great crowd had gathered to hear royalty speak. He'd been meaning to ask about the noise.

"Good day," he murmured, feeling shabby in his tattered gray tunic. At least he'd taken to wearing his britches to avoid upsetting the skittish Maggie.

The lady did not deign to make a reply. She gave him a critical inspection then met his gaze with flashing, catlike eyes.

Luke struggled to stand, ill-prepared for battle.

"Please," the woman finally spoke, waving him down. "Don't bother. You'll rip your stitches open and bleed to death."

He eased back onto the bed. It sounded as if his death would please her immensely.

"You look well," she added, her gaze touching briefly on his thigh where his bandage was hidden by his drawers. "My sister has saved your life. I hope you're aware of that fact." Her clipped words did nothing to discredit her cultured tone.

"I presume you are the lady of the castle?" he replied, doing his best to hinge their conversation on a friendlier frame.

"I am Clarise, Merry's sister," she announced, moving away to lock the errant shutter, dimming the noise of the crowd outside. "I don't suppose you would remember me. You were only half alive when she brought you here." She turned and regarded him from the window. "Merry and I kept watch over you the first week. I was certain you would die." Again, she sounded disappointed that he hadn't.

Luke clung desperately to courtesy. "I thank you for your care," he answered carefully.

His cordiality finally had the effect he wanted. She heaved a troubled sigh, her shoulders falling. "Merry said you were a kind man," she admitted. "I was beginning to have my doubts."

"Oh?" His stomach clenched with worry.

"You must have said something to upset her," she finished, arching a tawny eyebrow at him.

Heat stole up the column of Luke's neck. "Upset her?" he repeated. Surely Merry hadn't told Clarise about that!

"She has locked herself in her chamber for over a week, refusing to come out, scarcely eating. I wonder what you said to her."

The lady might as well have thrown an egg at his face. There was no hiding his faint blush from her catlike eyes. She took a step or two in his direction, causing him to draw back, warily.

"You may be the Phoenix, Sir Luke le Noir," she informed him in a voice as hard as the links of his battle dress, "but as far as I'm concerned, you are just a man—a man as mortal and as subject to desires as the rest of mankind. My sister says that you are honorable. 'Tis my suggestion that you do the honorable thing and offer for her hand." She put her own hand up, forestalling the protest that leapt to his lips. "Until then," she added, "I will hold you personally accountable for my sister's health."

It took him a moment to digest her meaning and her threat. "Is she unwell?" he asked, feeling concern on the heels of his chagrin.

Clarise glared at him through narrowed eyes. "I told you, she scarcely eats at all. She has no will to live. 'Tis as if she gave up her life to save yours."

He swallowed against the dryness in his mouth. "Send her to my chamber," he suggested. "I'm not yet able to walk, else I'd knock at her door myself."

The woman tapped an impatient toe. "I'll do my best," she answered with pessimism. "I have pleaded with her until my voice is hoarse, yet nothing seems to lift her spirits. If you have in any way dishonored her, then you must make amends at once."

With a meaningful look, she whirled about, perfuming the air with lavender as she swept from the chamber.

Luke thumped back against his pillows. He hadn't even had the chance to ask about the crowd outside. The purpose of Lady Clarise's visit had overshadowed everything. *God's bones!* Merry was avoiding him for shame. Yet she had nothing to be ashamed of. She'd given him something he longed desperately to be given again. If anyone should feel shame, it was he, for lacking the will to stop her. *Aye,* it was his weakness that caused so much turmoil she dared not venture from her room. If only he could speak to her, he would put her doubts to rest.

Yet it was not just Merry's upset that worried him. Clarise had come to the conclusion that Luke had dishonored her sister. He doubted Merry had been the one to tell her, so how, then, had she guessed the truth? Was it feminine intuition?

Why, she'd demanded that he make an offer for her sister's hand!

The very notion was ludicrous. Even a lady from the country would realize that the prince would be the one to choose Luke's bride. Not that Luke would ever choose Merry to wed of all women!

He shook his head, toying a moment with what it would be like if he *did* marry her. He pictured her at Castle Arundel, dressed in the latest courtly fashions, with an amethyst girdle about her hips. She would amaze the servants by refusing a headdress and digging on her knees in the gardens. The orphans who lived with him would love her, for she was just the type to run amok with them and get into mischief. He wondered what his grandfather would think and realized he had no idea. Sir William wasn't one to play the field of politics; he did as he pleased. He had no fondness for Amalie, that much was certain.

Recalling Amalie, Luke released his fantasy with a peculiar shudder. He'd found the thought of Merry as his wife far less disturbing than he'd thought he might. Yet only Amalie's impeccable bloodlines were pure enough to cleanse the taint of his illegitimacy. Without Amalie, the prince was more likely to bequeath Arundel to his hunting hounds than to Luke.

Losing Arundel was not something Luke even wished to consider. His grandfather's castle was the only true home he'd ever known. From the moment he'd first laid eyes on it as a boy, he'd fallen in love with its magical silhouette. All his years of service in Matilda's court, his perseverance had been for Arundel. He'd fought for Prince Henry's father in Rouen. He'd saved Henry's life and pledged him eternal fealty. In return, the prince showered him with honor and burdened him with countless fruitless tasks, like that of razing adulterines. But the end would be well worth it, so long as Arundel was his.

And yet, his life was not his own. Of late, he'd begun to realize that. Henry foisted the most distasteful jobs on Luke, sending him off to the farthest reaches of Norman rule when he wanted more than anything to be at his grandfather's side.

Luke summoned an image of his distinguished, articulate grandsire, a man he respected even more than the prince. Once a tall and imposing figure, Lord William d'Albini was the pattern by which Luke sought to cut his own bolt of cloth.

His grandfather never scurried to obey his king. Indeed, he'd scorned King Stephen in support of Matilda and still managed to hold on to his lands through years of civil strife.

Luke hung his head. With a gathering shame, he realized he wasn't half the man his grandfather was. He didn't always follow his moral conscience; instead, he executed the commands of his liege lord, clinging to duty in morality's place. Was he no more than a mercenary? A prostitute?

He drew a sharp breath at the thought.

He considered the baron and baroness of Iversly who mourned the loss of their outer defenses, as well as the loss of their sons. His conscience decreed that he cease tormenting them. Duty demanded he finish his job.

He thought of himself with Amalie and how it would feel to consummate their marriage. The vision filled him with poignant regret as he recalled Merry's sweet responsiveness.

If at some point he did not assert himself, Henry would continue to treat him as something less than what he was, what he knew he could be.

Luke rubbed his eyes, exhausted by his train of thought. He'd had entirely too much time to think these last couple weeks. Yet he realized now that Merry had spoken with a grain of truth when she'd called him the puppet of a tyrant.

'Twas exactly what he was. Yet it didn't necessarily follow that he would always be. He could put an end to the destruction at Iversly, banishing the heart-wrenching image of Lord Ian at his window once and for all. He need not sacrifice his conscience for the sake of duty! He could defy his prince on that score and not worry overly much that Henry would strip him of his authority.

A great weight eased from Luke's shoulders. He took a cleansing breath. He would send a missive to Iversly at once, calling his men to cease their labors and to rebuild enough of the wall so that the fortress was not left vulnerable. That done, his men would join him here at Helmesly, and he could lead them home, hopefully to find his grandfather still alive.

Feeling his spirits revive, Luke reached for the parchment and ink he'd requested earlier to defray his boredom. But then he thought of Merry, and he hesitated. What to do about Merry's situation and Lady Clarise's demands?

Morally, he was not obliged to wed her. He'd explained his betrothal to her clearly. Merry herself had no expectations along those lines. Still, he couldn't leave her with the belief that she'd disgraced herself.

He would pen her a letter, explaining the situation, blaming his male weakness and the added potency of the herbs she'd given him. That should bring her out of her depression, he reasoned. Despite Lady Clarise's insistence, he owed her nothing beyond an apology.

Then why the bitter taste in his mouth? The uneven cadence of his heart?

He balanced the inkwell on the mattress beside him, careful not to stain the sheets. It irritated him to have no answer. He never had an answer where Merry was concerned. The woman had cluttered his life irreparably. He almost wished he'd never laid eyes on her.

Ah, but then he would never have known the upper limits of ecstasy. Never have realized how blindly he followed the prince's dictates.

Perhaps he owed her a small debt, after all.


MERRY resisted the urge to crumple the heavy parchment and hurl it out the open window. But then someone would read it and be privy to her most intimate secrets. She tossed it on her bed instead, gripping the bedpost for support as she gazed down at Luke's neat script. Even his handwriting was handsome and precise, damn him. There were no spots where the ink had bled into the parchment. No errors. No uncertainties.

> *I will be leaving Helmesly in a sennight. I thank you for your care of me. Save for an impressive scar, I will be good as new and left without a limp. You are indeed a healer of the finest caliber. My apologies for ever thinking less.*
>
> *I leave you safe in the care of your family, certain that your sister will defend you against any who intend you harm.*
>
> *Let your conscience be untroubled by what passed between us. Whatever it was, it has changed me for the better. Under the influence of your healing herbs, and transfixed by your beauty, I took advantage of your generosity. For my weakness, I beg your forgiveness. For the memories, I thank you.*
>
> *May you be at peace now, after all you have endured. Should you need my good word in an ecclesiastic court, you have only to summon me.*
>
> *Yours, Luke*

Merry stared at the letter until the words ran together. A spell of dizziness caused the walls to whirl, and she gripped the bedpost harder, her emotions falling one atop the other.

He'd begged her forgiveness. 'Twas unnecessary. She'd eventually realized that the herbs she'd given him for pain had prevented him from speaking. Falling in love with him had been entirely her own doing. He'd warned her from the first that he could offer her nothing. She was a fool to have hoped for more.

He was leaving. She'd expected his departure all along, yet it crippled her to discover the end so near. She'd hoped he would linger longer, recover more fully. A wound such as his required at least another month of bed rest. He risked re-injury to mount again so soon.

Her dizziness did not abate. Merry turned from the letter, desperate for air. Nausea roiled in her belly, warning her that what little she'd eaten would soon reappear. She teetered toward the window and hung her head out, sucking in gulps of autumn air.

As the buzzing in her ears receded, she heard again the shouts at the gate. After nearly three weeks, the crowd outside the walls had become a horde. Some had pitched tents within the fields to sleep there by night. Often their chants grew loud enough that she could discern the word "witch." Their cries made her skin crawl, made her grow cold, then hot. When the crowd grew too loud, the Slayer gave orders for his bowmen to disperse them, but they were always quick to reappear.

Merry stood on tiptoe and caught a glimpse of milling peasants. If she'd surrendered herself as she'd considered days ago, she would likely be dead right now. She would never have discovered the miracle that encouraged her to rise and welcome a new day.

She laid a gentle hand against her abdomen. Luke was leaving. Yet he'd left her a consolation, a reason to go on.

The realization had come upon her only yesterday. She'd sat up swiftly and calculated with her fingers. She was a week overdue. Two weeks before that, she and Luke had lain together.

The hope that she was pregnant left her breathless. 'Twas a miracle! 'Twas redemption of the most unlikely kind. She'd ral-

lied from her dark despair, thrown open the windows and called
for food. A short while later, she'd vomited it up again.

Luke was leaving. The father of her child was leaving.

Regarding the undulating hills before her, now the color of
wheat for the cooler weather, Merry asked herself if she should
tell him. Would it change anything? Nay, why would it? He was
still a tenant-in-chief, betrothed to the king's cousin. She was
still a fugitive being hunted by the Church.

Perhaps if something were to happen to her, she would send
her child to Luke, certain he would care for it as he'd promised.
God forbid that it should come to that, but she would not be a
burden to him, not again. She would not ask for what he could
not gladly give.

"Good-bye, fair Phoenix," she whispered, imagining him on
his horse, riding away. She recalled the passages in his letter:
*Let your conscience be untroubled by what passed between us.
Whatever it was, it has changed me for the better.* Her mouth
curved in a sad, ironic smile. It had changed her for the better
too. No longer was she angry with the world, mistrustful, longing for death. Aye, it had touched her deeply—whatever it was
that had passed between them.

"ON a quest for fresh air, Sir Luke?"

Luke gave a start of surprise and ceased his painful hobble
across the great hall. Just a moment ago, the hall had appeared
empty. How the giant could have remained hidden until now, in
broad daylight, mystified him. Clearly his instincts had grown
dull in his hours of idleness.

He realized then that the Slayer had been sitting in one of the
carved chairs before the hearth. He rose from it now, laying a
thick tome on his seat as he did so. With a look of friendly
determination, he bore down on Luke.

Luke thought of the missive that was tucked inside his belt.
There wasn't any reason for the Slayer not to know of his intent
to summon his army. Still, there was a danger in the giant
knowing too much. For one thing, he might tell that meddling
wife of his, who would then redouble her efforts to see Luke
and Merry wed.

"I thought a walk in the inner ward might do me good,"

Luke answered casually. In fact, he was headed to the garrison to hand the missive over to one of his soldiers.

"Excellent," said the giant. "Then I'll accompany you."

"Thank you," Luke said, setting his teeth. He took a halting step toward the exit.

"How is your wound healing?" the Slayer asked, falling into step beside him.

Luke grimaced. "I am told I should be dead right now, so I can't complain." That did not stop every nerve in his body from screaming in protest, however.

"Merry has a grasp for nature's elements, one must confess," his companion answered. " 'Tis a shame there are no universities in these parts. She would do well in the field of medical science with mentors to guide her."

Luke refused to be drawn into the subject of Merry's future. Though now that the Slayer had planted the seed, he found himself picturing Merry at Oxford, keeping company with young men dressed in cappas, studying at the feet of the great pioneers of medicine. Such a thing might be possible if he married her, but of course he would not.

Their descent down the steps of the forebuilding robbed Luke of the ability to imagine anything at all. Drenched in sweat, he paused on the bottom step and put his back to the wall. Through the open door, he could see the garrison, his destination.

The Slayer paused also, leaning indolently against the opposite wall. Luke found the man's gaze unnerving. The giant looked like he had something on his mind and was on the verge of sharing it.

Luke pushed himself off the wall and hobbled out the door. *Coward,* he mocked himself. Using the cane he had found beside his bed, he strove for a rhythm that would convey him swiftly and as painlessly as possible across the inner ward. But then the point of the cane slipped off the edge of a cobblestone, and Luke stumbled, testing the strength of his stitches.

The searing sensation nearly brought him to his knees. Bent double, he was nonetheless aware of the Slayer putting a comforting hand on his shoulder. At the same time, he grew conscious of the same shouting and chanting that had troubled him for days now. He'd decided there must be some sort of festival outside the castle, yet that made no sense, since the Slayer was clearly not in attendance. Nor had the skittish Maggie satisfied his curiosity. She'd stuttered a garbled explanation impossible to understand and fled, clearly overwhelmed by his attention.

Straightening inch by inch, Luke sought to determine the extent to which he'd re-injured himself. He felt a certain moisture on his hose, telling him his wound was bleeding anew. With a shuddering gasp, he drew to his full height and looked the giant in the eye. "Would you convey a message to my men for me?" he heard himself ask. Clearly the task of completing his errand was beyond the scope of his powers today.

"Certainly," said the giant, looking surprised.

Luke reached under his belt and drew out the parchment tube. He saw the warrior's curiosity and added, "You may read it."

The Slayer scanned the contents of the note then folded it again, looking relieved. " 'Tis a goodly notion," he said, giving his approval. "The sight of your army will scatter the protesters. We might even make it look as if the royal army has come to claim my sister-in-law."

None of this made sense to Luke. He shielded his eyes against the sun's glare and squinted up at the man. "Protestors?" he repeated.

The Slayer gestured toward the sounds. "The horde outside the walls are demanding Merry's release. Surely you've overheard them, though your chamber faces east," he added with a frown.

Luke was stunned by the answer to his nagging question, that the population had been stirred to protest.

"The night that you arrived here," the Slayer explained, "it rained so hard that the water carried off the peasant's crops. They've blamed their misfortune on the Witch of Mount Grace. Bounty hunters have spread the rumor that she's harbored here."

Luke swallowed against the uneasiness that swelled in him. *Poor Merry,* he found himself thinking. Would she always be hunted like a wild animal? He gave his companion a considering look. "You say my army might help disperse the crowd?"

"It should," said the warrior, "especially if you convey her from here, tied to look like a prisoner."

Luke took an involuntary step back, bringing on another flash of pain. "Wait a moment," he implored, "I said naught of taking Merry with me. I promised Sir Roger I would bring her to Helmesly, nothing more. You are her family," he insisted, feeling his temper rise in proportion to his pain. "She's your problem; for God's sake, do your duty to her!"

"You are one to speak of duty, Sir Luke," the giant answered with equal heat. "You have seduced the lady and put her casually aside."

"Is that what she told you?" Luke demanded, his resentment focused now on Merry.

"Nay," said the Slayer. "She's not said a word against you—neither to me nor to my wife."

Luke's anger deflated. "Then how can you condemn me?" he asked warily.

"Because she is with child," said the warrior succinctly.

Luke hoped to heaven he'd heard wrong. "What did you say?"

"You've planted your seed in her belly," replied the giant. "Now I find no pleasure in beating a man who is wounded. But I'll pound you into the cobbles if you fail to redress the wrong you've done."

Stunned, Luke could only stare at the man towering over him. Merry was with child? Then their exquisite night at Iversly had borne fruit after all, despite his belated attempt to wash the seed from her.

"Are you certain?" he heard himself ask.

"My wife is rarely wrong."

Memories of Merry's warm skin assailed him. Their relentless passion relived itself in his mind. A part of him smiled rather smugly. 'Twas befitting that a child should be conceived that night.

*A child! A son or daughter!* It seemed a sudden boon, a blessing from heaven! Nay, it wasn't! It was terrible. The result of poor discipline and lack of control. He'd known pregnancy was possible, yet he hadn't been able to help himself, pumping his seed deep inside her when he'd only had to pull out.

By Christ, this was a serious matter. He couldn't marry a nobody from North Yorkshire! He couldn't! Worse yet, how could he marry a woman wanted as a witch?

"Listen," demanded the Slayer, shifting on his feet, "if you convey her from here with your army, the peasants and villeins will think the law has come to intervene. They'll go back to their farms and forget her. Even the bounty hunters may be fooled. Who will have heard of her in the South of England? She'll be safe from persecution there."

Luke shook his head. He was furious with himself. Furious with Merry's kin for foisting her on him once again! "She'll be persecuted in other ways," he countered grimly. "Henry will not be pleased. I'm betrothed to his cousin, damn you!" He allowed the Slayer to see his outrage.

The giant gave him a menacing glare. "If you die here," he threatened in a low voice, " 'twill appear to all that you died of infection. I trust I make my meaning clear."

Stunned by the threat, Luke regained his self-control. A grudging smile tugged at one corner of his mouth. The Slayer was refreshingly honest with his threats. Luke had always liked that trait in a man. He only wished that matters were as clear in Henry's court where one was always casting glances behind him.

He drew in a deep breath. He would have to think this through from every angle.

On one hand, he had labored since adolescence to ensure his footing at Arundel. Defying the prince by breaking his betrothal contract was certain to put his inheritance in jeopardy.

On the other hand, he would never have to suffer Amalie in his bed but rather Merry, with her warm, soft skin pressed to his. Hadn't he just realized that Henry treated him more as a servant than a vassal? Did he wish to continue in that vein, or would he assert himself and become like his grandfather, a man of his own making?

Also, he knew what it meant to be born a bastard, the work it took to rise in rank by effort and not by bloodline. He'd prided himself on how far he'd come, from a street urchin to tenant-in-chief. Yet at what cost? At the cost of his dignity. Could he condemn his unborn child to similar uncertainties? Nay, how could he?

Let his conscience be his guide, then. Pray God it wouldn't cost him Arundel. Pray God, the prince would come to respect him more for his independence.

"Well?" pressed the Slayer, curling his hand into a fist.

Luke took a look at the giant's knuckles. He dragged his fingers through his over-long hair and sighed. "Call a priest," he said with resignation.

At the same time, he felt a sudden buoying of his spirits. For the first time he noted the impossible blue of the sky above him, the braided trim on the Slayer's tunic. The stones of the keep and the cobbles in the courtyard seemed to stand out in sharp relief. The scent of apple pastries wafted from the kitchen. He put a name to the giddiness in his breast and realized it was freedom.

At last he'd done what he'd been chafing to do for some time now: to defy his prince. To set his own course. Merry, the mother of his child, the object of his obsession, was going to be his bride! Farewell to Amalie and her disdainful glances.

'Twas a fool's decision if ever there was one, lamented his logic. Did he think there would be no price to pay?

He wavered. His sense of freedom fluttered downward and settled on a dead limb. If matters became truly messy . . . if he incited Henry's wrath, what then? What if he were made to choose between Merry and Arundel?

It chilled him to think along such lines. He could only face the consequences as they came.

## Chapter Fourteen

AELRED of Rievaulx's sonorant voice filled the vaulted chapel with dulcet words of everlasting commitment, honor, and fidelity. The mullioned glass in the crossloop behind him glittered with afternoon sunlight. Clouds of incense hung in the air, released from the box the abbot had swung from a chain just moments before.

"Do you, Sir Luke, swear by your honor and your sword to uphold Merry, to nurture her, to love and cherish her, so long as ye twain shall live?"

With her hands in his, Merry sensed a fine tremor in Luke's touch. She wondered if he still felt weak from his ordeal, or if he found this moment as terrible and wonderful as she? She peeked into his golden eyes, seeking an answer to the questions that plagued her.

Why had he agreed to wed her? According to Clarise, he felt he owed her a debt for saving his life. Her sister had sworn quite convincingly the captain harbored feelings for her. Perhaps she had just said so to ease Merry's fears.

Merry had tried to ask Luke herself last night, when she saw him for the first time since the episode in his chamber. With her own eyes, she'd seen that Luke had not been physically coerced. Though pinched with pain, his face was as darkly handsome as ever, assuring her that he hadn't been beaten to a pulp or stretched on a rack as she'd feared.

His gaze had sought hers immediately, a hint of dull color rising to his cheeks. He'd been seated immediately adjacent to her, giving them the opportunity to speak. Yet as she screwed up the courage to ask him whether he truly wished to wed, a trencher of boiled eels had appeared before them. Merry took one whiff of the fishy stuff, and she'd had to leave the great hall immediately. Nor had she felt well enough to return.

The following morning had marked her younger sister's arrival at Helmesly. Delighted to be reunited after more than three years, Merry and Clarise had passed the remainder of the day with their youngest sibling, exclaiming over her transformation into a young woman, recalling their tumultuous childhood with shared commiseration.

Merry had yet to recover from the sight of her baby sister fully grown. Despite the striking change in her appearance, Kyndra's hair was still a reddish-blond mane, her dimples still deep with mischief. Though the baroness Le Burgh had taught her the skills of a highborn lady, the propensity to utter droll remarks beneath her breath had not abandoned her completely. With an innate talent that had both elder sisters bursting into laughter, Kyndra regaled them with her imitations of the portly Lady de Burgh and her husband, the penny-pinching baron.

Merry would have been content to gossip with her sisters all day, but the afternoon was devoted to fittings. A wedding gown and trousseau had to be sewed in record time, with four seamstresses working through the night to complete it. Standing on a stool with her sisters offering words of encouragement, it was tempting to believe that her life was taking a turn for the better. The mighty Phoenix had asked for her hand in gratitude for saving his life. Her days of persecution were nearly over, for he would whisk her away to his fortress in the south, and she would begin life anew as Lady le Noir.

This morning, Merry had been wakened early to be scrubbed and buffed, oiled and perfumed. Clarise and Kyndra had persuaded her to eat in her chambers, but her uneasy stomach would keep nothing down. After the midday meal, she was draped in a gown of alabaster silk. Wearing a girdle of precious amber links, with a matching circlet on her head, she had scarcely recognized herself as she stood before her looking glass. Seeing herself transformed, it was tempting to believe that the Phoenix truly wanted her. With the amber circlet on her head, she looked as regal as a queen and nothing like the witch she'd been accused of. Still, she could not shake the suspicion that she was being lead by false promises.

Did the Phoenix truly desire her for a bride, or had her family found another means to shelter her from harm?

Knowing Clarise and her protective instincts, the question kept Merry uneasy. Why would Luke breech his betrothal contract with the Lady Amalie, taking a witch for a wife instead?

Gazing up at him now, she hunted for the answer to her questions. He wore a wine-colored tunic, no doubt lent to him by the Slayer. The saffron cloak and jeweled dagger on his belt, lent him a formal air, but it was the expression on his face—the soldier's mask—that made the answer impossible to discern. The tremor in his hand was the only indication that his nerves were as overwrought as hers. But what did that mean—that he dreaded every word coming out of his mouth? That he was as terrified of the future as she? Or, could it be, he was moved by emotion, to make her his?

Realizing it was her turn to speak, Merry repeated her vows in a voice as insubstantial as air. Under the bolts of French silk from which her gown was sewn, her knees knocked forcibly together. She suffered from the sudden worry that she would sink on the flagstone floor and vomit on Luke's boots.

But then he squeezed her hands, slowly, reassuringly, and the nausea passed. With gratitude and hope, her words grew stronger and she concluded her portion of the sacrament on a certain note.

The abbot enjoined them to kiss—a kiss that would seal their union forever. Merry suffered a moment's panic. Luke had not kissed her since that night at Iversly. Now that they were wed, she feared his kiss would suddenly repulse her.

He lifted a hand, laying his fingertips against her cheek. The gentleness of his touch eased her fears. Then he lowered his head, and her lashes fluttered shut.

The taste of his lips, the heat of them were so familiar that her eyes stung with sharp relief. He deepened the kiss, pressing his mouth to hers with a tenderness that closed off the air to her throat. A sense of wonder rose in her. She was tempted, oh so tempted, to believe what Clarise had tried to convince her of: that Luke had chosen her out of gratitude.

He lifted his head, gazing down at her with something like recklessness in his eyes. "You are beautiful, wife," he said, his gaze seeming to strip her as it raked her adorned figure.

*Wife!* Her heart doubled its beat. She heard a buzzing in her ears, and the light-headedness that had come with not keeping food down for two days stormed her senses. Merry grasped the material of his tunic to steady herself. But it was too late. With a strangled warning, she fainted dead away.

"HOW do you do, Merry?" Luke asked, apparently forgetting that he'd just asked her that seconds before.

Sitting with goose-down pillows at her back, Merry cupped the goblet of elderberry wine he'd given her, but knowing it to be dangerous to women with child, she only pretended to drink it. "Fully recovered," she assured him with a shaky smile.

She had awakened in the bridal chamber—a formal guest chamber festooned with garlands of lily and yellow roses. Luke's had been the first face she saw upon reviving. But much to her dismay, a gaggle of serving maids had shooed him out of the chamber and set to work stripping Merry of her bridal gown and dressing her in a nightdress of embroidered lace. It was not even sundown.

But Merry had declined to sup in the great hall where a feast was being laid. Her stomach was too uneasy to be assailed with such varied scents. She'd thought it best to rest. In truth, she mostly desired privacy with her . . . her husband. Mercy, but she could not believe they were truly wed!

He sat on the edge of the bed, watching her with a steady gaze that disconcerted her. She was flattered, touched that he would stay with her and not dine with the others. Perhaps it meant . . . but nay, she would not be so naïve. He was a man of reason, honor, duty. Surely he hadn't married her for love, though perhaps to repay a debt.

"This is a switch," she said into the silence that fell between them, "I, the invalid, and you, the healer."

He considered her remark without humor. If anything, the

tension in his jaw betrayed a brooding quality in him. She was struck with dread that he now regretted their recent marriage.

"I thank you for your good care of me," he said courteously. "You saved my life."

She could have wished for more warmth in that statement. "You're welcome," she replied, as formally as he. It was coming now, his reason for marrying her.

The muscle in his jaw flexed. "I hope your conscience doesn't bother you for having killed the youth who struck me," he added, unexpectedly.

The memory of jabbing a blade between the youth's ribs made her queasy. "I scarcely think of it," she admitted. "I would do it again, without question, if it meant saving your life."

The last words hung between them, too revealing of her tender regard for him. She wished immediately that she could recall them, waiting to hear his confession first.

"You are an exceptional healer." His tone was unrelentingly courteous. "I regret hindering your attempts to treat the Baron of Iversly and Phillip. My apologies."

Merry grew impatient with his formality. "Is that why you wed me?" she challenged, welcoming resentment to beat back the chill of courtesy. "For my skill?"

He avoided her gaze, looking down at the bedcover. "In part," he acceded.

She accepted his admission with a wrenching of her heart. "And the other part?" There was still hope for a confession of tenderness. Her heart thudded heavily as she awaited his answer.

He lifted his gaze but only as far as the bodice of her embroidered nightdress. She knew an urge to cover herself, certain her nipples could be seen through the pattern of fine stitches. But then he placed a hand on the plane between her hips, and her near-nakedness was forgotten. When he looked her in the eye, Merry's heart stopped altogether.

*He knew!* She could tell by the look he gave her. He knew about the babe. Impossible! She'd told no one, not even Kyndra or Clarise. It was Merry's secret, her private consolation.

"Your sister says you carry my child," he said. "I would hear the truth from you."

She swallowed hard. "But how could she know?" she exclaimed in confusion. "I never told her. I never expected you to . . ." She couldn't finish.

"To what?" he demanded, his eyebrows sinking.

"To marry me!" she added with a rush of bitterness.

Her answer drove him to his feet with a grimace of pain. He loomed over her. "You would let my child be born a bastard and never suffer a moment's remorse?" he demanded. The word bastard was uttered as if it were an anathema. He was angry now, though it was well controlled.

"That was not my reasoning," she replied, dismay twisting through her. "I didn't wish to be a burden to you—"

"A child is not a burden," he retorted, turning away to limp across the chamber. He stopped to stare into the brazier.

With the feeling that her breath had been crushed from her lungs, Merry eyed her rigid husband and acknowledged the bitter truth that he'd wed her for the sake of their child and nothing more.

"I never meant that the child was a burden," she corrected him, pushing the words through her tight throat. "You told me you were willing to support a babe if there was one. You said nothing of supporting me. I can only wonder why you bothered when it meant breaking your betrothal—"

He looked up suddenly, cutting her short. "A child should remain with his mother," he said. The rays of the descending sun slashed across his face. "And also his father. Do you not agree?"

"Yes, of course." She heartily agreed, and yet marrying her seemed overdone, even for Luke who took duty and honor so seriously. He'd given his prince his word as far as the betrothal to Amalie was concerned. Surely he would face Henry's wrath for violating their contract. "What will the prince say?" she dared to ask him.

He limped to her bedside, his expression inscrutable. "That is for me to deal with," he said grimly. "You shouldn't worry in your state. Are you certain you feel well?"

She took note of his evasive measures and resolved to bring the matter up another time. After all, Henry's reaction to their marriage would surely affect her future. "I'm fine," she said, though it was her heart that felt sick now, sick that she'd fooled herself, however briefly, into thinking Luke harbored some feeling for her.

She saw his gaze flicker once again to her breasts, and she balked at the idea of making love just now. Not only was it still daylight but he had hurt her with his chilling admission. Though he had every right to take her now, she didn't want to give herself to him. "I'm weary," she stalled, hoping he wouldn't press her.

"As am I," he replied, unexpectedly. With a groan, he dropped onto the bed beside her. The mattress dipped and she rolled helplessly toward him. He surprised her further by putting an arm around her, pulling her close. Their bodies came together like two halves of a walnut. Luke gave a grunt of contentment. Merry scarcely breathed. She was keenly aware of his hard body against the length of hers.

He would expect her capitulation eventually. This was their wedding day. Now that she belonged to him it was her bounden duty to please him in any way he requested. And though he'd closed his eyes, she could feel the quick thud of his heart beneath her hand, the rise and fall of his chest. She gazed down the flat plane of his abdomen, not surprised to see a bulge beneath his chausses. Though he'd made no proclamation of love, he desired her, certainly. That was some consolation.

It wouldn't kill her to offer him her body, so long as she guarded her susceptible heart, counseling herself not to love him too much.

He rolled abruptly toward her, pressing her onto her back. She steeled herself against his allure, but the hawklike look in his eyes caused her lungs to fill with air. With very clear intent, he lowered his lips to hers, as if daring her to protest. Her aching heart longed to deflect him, but her weak flesh kept silent, suddenly anticipating the heat of his mouth on hers.

He kissed her thoroughly, almost savagely. Second by second, she felt herself thawing beneath his heat, felt herself responding.

His hands fell upon the fullness of her breasts, teasing and plumping them, and she forgot her displeasure with him, thrilling in the feel of his fingers. He pressed his hips to hers, stealing her breath with the strength of his arousal.

Without a word, he reached below the hem of her nightdress, stroking and kneading her thighs. All the while he gazed down at her, ruthlessly silent. She longed for a word of tenderness, the kind of reassurance he had given her at Iversly. His taciturn seduction left her heart aching and her flesh trembling for more.

"Take off your gown," he requested, his eyes glinting with a predatory light.

She obeyed him swiftly, sensing an anger that simmered deep within him, well controlled and not a threat to her, but worrisome all the same. Rolling up on her knees, she placed her nightdress at the foot of the bed, feeling more vulnerable than she had in her life with him still fully clothed and her entirely naked.

"Hold," he said, as she made to sit. "What is that?" He tilted her onto one hip, his gaze fixed on the birthmark on her right buttock.

She realized he hadn't seen it at Iversly where they'd made love in the dark. " 'Tis my Devil's mark," she said with a quick, mocking smile. "I was born with it."

He raised flashing eyes at her. "You will never say such words again," he warned her. "In West Sussex no one will think of you as a witch, not even yourself." Looking at the mark again, he caressed it with the flat of his palm. "It looks like a half-moon," he added more gently. "It becomes you well."

The sweeping motion of his hand reawakened her desire. She leaned toward him, not surprised when he kissed her savagely, ravaging her mouth, her neck, her breasts. Looping an arm about her waist, he pulled her roughly to the edge of the bed. "I have a favor to repay you," he warned.

Prickling with awareness, she could only guess what it was. He went down on his knees, grunting with the discomfort his wound caused him. Very deliberately, he pushed her legs apart, and Merry closed her eyes, acutely self-conscious. Here she was, bathed in the light of the setting sun, with her legs splayed. Every fine hair on her body seemed to stand on end.

"Keep your eyes closed," her new husband exhorted. "You aren't to move or to make a sound," he said.

She realized he intended to do to her what she had done to him on his sickbed. Her heart beat with mixed anticipation and uncertainty. He reached beneath the bed for something, and she dared a peek between her lashes. "Keep them closed," he repeated in a more threatening tone.

She swallowed against the dryness in her throat, feeling almost insufferably vulnerable. "Relax," he added. It was then that she felt a slick wet substance between her legs. He applied it gently, yet liberally, and she knew without being told that it was some sort of ointment, sweet-smelling with a hint of rosemary. God help her, he really meant to see this through.

She made a whimpering sound, only to be hushed again. She fisted the bedsheets, trying to distance herself from the starkly sensual glide of his fingers as he slicked them along her sensitive flesh. He acquainted himself with her secrets, unmercifully intimate. He softened her like clay, stretching her with his long, hard fingers.

She quivered at her utter loss of control. She felt herself turn liquid, felt the pleasure knot itself tighter and tighter. Yet he was the one to determine the exact moment of her release, and whenever she neared that pinnacle, he backed away, causing her to gasp with frustration.

He did this to her repeatedly, until she thought she might weep.

"Now, sprite." His voice was thick with sensual intent. "Now you may have your surcease." He gave her what her body longed for, stroking her inside and out until she spasmed with helpless ecstasy.

No sooner had she regained her senses than he pushed down his chausses, grabbed her hips and entered her boldly. Merry gasped at the thick invasion, her senses immediately reawakened. Moving her with his hands, he pumped in and out of her with an intensity that stole her breath.

A part of her reveled in his savage possession, matching his lust with a desire that was just as desperate. Another part of her mourned the tender restraint he'd shown her at Iversly. Swept up in the rocking movements of his body, she climaxed helplessly. At the same time, he gave a stifled cry. He remained inside her, not withdrawing now that his seed had borne fruit.

After a dazed moment, the roaring of Merry's ears subsided and the vision of them locked in an erotic embrace sobered her. She knew an impulse to withdraw from him. With the heat of passion draining away, she felt exploited somehow, sullied. Her skin abruptly cooled. She waited for the first opportunity to free herself.

Luke lifted his head, a crease appearing between his eyebrows. With a muttered curse, he dropped his forehead between her breasts in an attitude of contrition. "Forgive me," he whispered, unexpectedly, kissing her damp skin.

She didn't know what to make of his apology. He hadn't hurt her, hadn't done anything truly wrong, except treat her as an object—so differently than the way he'd cherished her at Iversly. Yet, with his dark head upon her breast, she felt sorry for him. Poor Luke. He'd sacrificed so much to marry her.

"There is nothing to forgive," she answered, feathering his dark hair.

His head came up. His eyes were shadowed, difficult to read. "You were feeling ill," he said. "I should not have pressed you."

She had nothing to say to that, except to assure him that she was feeling better now.

With a nod, he eased away from her, cursing at the pain it caused him. She sat up swiftly, helping him to his feet.

He turned away at once and limped to the washbasin where he wet a towel for her. When he handed it to her, she was reminded of the futile attempt to draw his seed from her at Iversly.

That night had changed their lives forever, she reflected. She bent her head to shield her expression of regret from him. She would never rue the tiny life now growing in her, yet she wished their marriage was based on more than Luke's commitment to their unborn child. His offer of marriage and protection was more than she could turn down at this desperate time in her life. And yet, the regret within her lingered, reinforced by the savage, almost impersonal manner in which Luke had made love to her.

Reaching for her nightdress, she carried it behind the dressing screen, too vulnerable to dress in his presence. Luke spared her a brooding glance.

Behind a veil of privacy, Merry's emotions fell one atop the other, prompting a flood of warm tears to track down her cheeks. She sought to comfort herself. Perhaps, in time, Luke would come to love her as she loved him. She had much to be grateful for. No longer was she condemned to a lifetime cloistered within Helmesly's walls. And their babe would be born into the certainty of matrimony, his or her future secure.

In the meantime, she prayed that Luke would not regret having made her his bride, for nothing would pain her worse than knowing she was, once again, unwanted.

MERRY could scarcely breathe beneath the burlap sack covering her head. She'd have preferred a gag, loosely tied. Yet the sack, she'd overheard the Slayer say, was to prevent her from giving the "evil eye" to those who would witness her departure. Merry saw it more as a token of revenge. Her brother-in-law was not a man who easily forgave.

She sat on the back of a horse, her hands tied with a rope so thick and coarse that it chafed her wrists. Because of its sturdiness, the rope would not be overlooked by the crowd anticipating her seizure. Her hair had been left to hang down her back so that her identity would not be left in question. She would be flanked by heavily armed guards, the number of Luke's entire army.

Unable to see for the sack over her head, Merry gave a thought to the sudden appearance of Luke's soldiers. The remaining thirty-six men had descended on Helmesly yesterday, scattering the horde of protesters. Last night at supper, Sir Pierce had reported that the wall at Iversly had been left intact. Merry guessed, then, that Luke had halted the destruction prematurely.

Later that night, she'd tried to thank him for his kindness to the baron and baroness, but Luke had refused to discuss his decision to curtail the destruction. Did his reticence mean that he regretted his kindness as well as his marriage? Or had he simply not wanted to involve her in matters between him and his prince?

A certain fragility had overtaken Merry's heart. How was she to embrace her future with any confidence when Luke seemed so troubled by it?

" 'Tis time, Merry."

She roused to the present as he lifted the edge of the sack and peered up at her. "Remember that this will all be over

soon," he encouraged tensely. "Whatever happens, stay mounted. I'll be watching your back."

He looked as if he might say more, but then he pulled the
sack snugly over her head and walked away. Merry listened to
the sound of his retreating steps, a chill settling on her skin.

"Good-bye, sister!" It was Clarise and Kyndra, rushing up
to her at the last moment to clasp her hands. "I'll write you!"
Clarise promised.

"We'll visit soon!" Kyndra added on a tearful note.

Merry clung to her dear family, regretting that her mother
had not been able to conquer her fears long enough to visit. "I
love you," she told them, her voice muffled within the sack. "I
shall miss you both. Tell Mother I am safe and happy."

The horse lurched forward, tearing the sisters apart. The life
Merry had known was abruptly over. She was off to a new
place, with new possibilities, yet the future loomed ominously—a dark unknown.

The sound of the draw being lowered merged with her sister's farewell cries. The roaring of the crowd grew suddenly
louder.

The Slayer had broadcast a rumor that the prince's own
army had come for the witch, and many had gathered to witness
her seizure. Merry tried to envision what it was they saw,
whether her departure from Helmsly appeared to be a true
arrest.

Only the prince's device was on display, flapping crimson
and gold at the head of the retinue. Luke's banner had been
stowed out of sight, lest it be recognized by the bounty hunters.
The soldiers were resplendent in their armor. Every spear, every
bow, every sword was put in plain view to discourage trouble.
Merry sat in their midst like the most perilous of criminals.

As the drawbridge opened, the roar of the crowd rolled over
her. She felt herself approaching a wall of hatred. Curses and
denunciations grew distinct. Even with her head covered she
could smell the pungent, stormy stench of violence. Her stomach churned. Their voices rose in chorus, "Let her hang! Let her
hang!"

"Get back!" Luke's soldiers pressed their horses forward,
cutting a swathe through the horde.

Despite the guards that flanked her, Merry felt her panic

rise. What if the bounty hunters were bold enough to attack and somehow managed to abduct her again? Worse yet, anyone with a weapon might hurl it at her or loose an arrow in her direction. Her heart galloped in her chest. She gasped for breath beneath the stifling sack.

Something *did* strike her shoulder, igniting a spark of pain. As she flinched from the unseen object, she was hit again, a stinging blow to the forehead. Merry squeezed her mount with her legs, remembering Luke's caution to stay seated. She realized with alarm that the peasants were throwing stones at her.

A shout went up, and the horse beneath her broke into a canter. Wind billowed up the sack and carried it halfway off her head, allowing her to see out of one eye. To abate her rising fear, she craned her neck and sought Luke's helm. Just as she spotted him, he veered out of formation and charged into the crowd.

With his sword raised high, he challenged the individuals bearing stones. They dropped their weapons and scurried out of harm's way. The point of his sword shredded the blue sky. Having subdued the crowd, Luke pivoted his mount and raced to rejoin his army. A short while later, he drew up alongside her.

"Did they hurt you?" he demanded, his voice hollow behind his visor. He reached over and snatched the sack from her head.

She was startled by the fury behind his gesture. "I'm unharmed," she said, forcing a smile to reassure him. She touched a hand to her forehead and was glad to see no blood. *Is he worried for me?* she wondered, *or is it only the babe he thinks of?*

"We will stop every other hour," he informed her. "Tell me if you feel at all uncomfortable. Is there anything I can get you now?"

Catching his earnest gaze through the slits of his helm, it was tempting to believe he did care for her, even in the absence of such a confession. "I'll be fine, Luke. Did we fool them, do you think?" she asked, glancing back. Even at a distance, she could see the peasants dispersing and heading to their farms.

"Aye," he answered unequivocally. "Let your mind be untroubled. Henceforth you will have a new life." He put out a gauntleted hand, and Merry accepted it, acknowledging his comfort. If only it was his love he offered! Then she would have no worries in regards to this new life he spoke of.

She was not a fool. Though he tried valiantly to hide it from her, she knew that Luke fretted over Henry's reaction to their unsanctioned marriage.

She assured herself that the prince was a reasonable man. Surely, having married Eleanor of Aquitaine just a year before he would understand the motivation of love ... but then the love was purely on her part. For Luke, the only true motivation was the babe he'd planted in her womb.

An insidious weed was growing in the garden of her mind. Would Luke, under pressure from the crown, feel the need to put Merry aside?

SHE came out of the water shivering. Luke remained on shore, just close enough to keep watch and far enough to give her privacy—though in Merry's opinion, the darkness was sufficient to do that.

It was a clear October night, All Hallow Even, by her estimation. She could practically sense the spirits of the dead skulking through the forest around them.

With her teeth chattering and her fingers stiff, Merry struggled to put her gown back on, letting it dry her in the absence of a toweling cloth. She'd used Luke's final sliver of soap to bathe herself, braving the sharp temperature to wash away the dust and grime of travel. Tomorrow they would arrive at Arundel, after nine days on the road. She'd wanted to look her best, given the circumstances.

Luke approached her now, picking up her cloak and placing it swiftly around her shoulders. Taking her elbow, he began silently to lead her up the path.

Ever chivalrous, Merry considered darkly. Nothing about his behavior gave her cause for complaint. Since their departure from Helmesly, he'd showered her with concern. He handed her the softest portions of bread, served her the meatiest gravy. They stopped every few hours to dismount, so that Merry might relieve herself and stretch her legs. At every stream in which he bathed, he insisted the water was too cold for her, that she might catch chill.

Merry had had quite enough coddling. On this, their last evening on the road, she'd waited for the men to fall asleep about the fire, and then she'd risen from her bedroll. Taking Luke's last sliver of soap, she'd marched straight for the water without a word of explanation.

With all her heart, she'd hoped Luke would refuse to let her go. She longed for a reason to argue with him, to vent her bottled frustrations and fears. Instead, he'd maddened her by following in silence.

What did he think, that she could ride into Arundel looking like a peasant? She wanted the people to see her as Luke's wife, not as an oddity that he'd picked up along the way. And yet, a part of her acknowledged that she was exactly that. The people of Arundel, Luke's grandfather included, would likely faint in horror at the thought of having her as lady of their castle.

Luke had scarcely gone out of his way to assure her otherwise. In fact, he'd said very little about his home. Whenever she probed him for information, he lapsed into silence. The further south they traveled, the more reticent he became. Indeed, since news had come to them via a messenger that King Stephen was dead, Luke had fallen into somber reflection. His disquiet only served to heighten her fear that Henry—soon to be king—would condemn their marriage.

Despite his mental distance, Luke was ever at her side. She jerked her arm from his grasp now, his chivalry suddenly cloying. If he were a true gentleman, he would tell her she had naught to fear. If he loved her, he would promise to shield her from any unpleasantness. Of course, he didn't love her, which was precisely the source of her disquiet.

"You might trip on a root," he cautioned her, taking her arm again.

"If I do,. I'm certain you will catch me." Her reply was scathing, but she no longer cared to play the grateful wife. She stormed ahead of him, marching through the circle of sleeping men to warm herself. From the corner of her eye, she watched Luke approach their bedroll. Normally, they slept beneath a tent he erected to protect her from the elements, but tonight she'd requested to sleep beneath the stars and he'd acceded to her wishes. It was All Hallow Even, and the spirits seeking shelter

would want to enter hers. She'd rather sleep outdoors than risk
their company.

As was his custom, Luke had taken off his armor, which he
cared not to sleep in. It sat in a burnished heap some distance
from the fire.

Thinking of the night ahead, Merry hid a sigh. 'Twas impossible to share a bed with Luke and not recall that night at Iversly
when he'd held her as if he couldn't get close enough. Or even
their wedding day at Helmesly where he'd made love to her
savagely but completely. Now he slept beside her, scarcely
touching her at all. Not once since leaving her sister's castle had
he requested his marital rights.

The distance he imposed between them unsettled her. The
fear that she'd been led by false promises was now a constant
and abiding dread.

Satisfied that she was dry, Merry approached their bedroll
and kicked off her shoes. She settled onto her portion of the
blankets, aware of Luke's surreptitious glance. She'd gotten his
attention, at least, by insisting on a bath. He moved into place
beside her and performed his ritual of pulling the blankets up
around her, so she would not be cold. He lay down next to her,
their elbows scarcely brushing.

Merry turned her head and studied his profile. Despite her
confusion and pent-up fears, it comforted her to look at his
handsome visage, to tell herself that he was hers—at least for
as long as he endured her.

She had little cause to complain, really. Luke was cordial to
a fault. He rarely lost his temper. How many women were beat-
en by their husbands? How many would gladly trade their husbands for one such as Luke? Every one of them.

Still, she could scarcely tolerate the sense of disquiet in her
chest or the loneliness that was so profound it threatened to
drown her.

"What is the herb in your soap?" she asked, if only to coax
him to speak. She'd been wondering that very thing for some
time. With the scent of it clinging to her, she remembered to ask
him.

"Sandalwood," he answered. He turned and looked at her,
his eyes lit by the distant stars. " 'Tis native to my homeland."

"Then it doesn't grow here." At last she understood why its scent had eluded her.

"I have many oils at home that you've never smelled before," he admitted unexpectedly. "And herbs that I brought from the East."

She came up on her elbow, intrigued. "What sort of herbs?" she wanted to know.

He shrugged. "I know only the local names of most of them, not the English words. One is called liquorice. Another is opium, which comes from the seed of wild poppy."

"I'm well acquainted with poppy," she interrupted.

"Not this kind. In Jerusalem the flowers grow as tall as a man. Their seed can be toxic as well as medicinal."

Fascinated, she wriggled closer. "Will you tell me more of Arundel?" she begged.

He hesitated. "You'll see it yourself tomorrow," he finally answered. His tone became remote. "You'll know everything then."

It seemed a strange reply. "Who is there that I should know besides your grandfather?" she insisted. He'd told her only that his grandsire was ill. She attributed much of his silence to worry that the man might have died during his absence.

He hesitated again. "There are children," he admitted unexpectedly. "Four of them whom I found in various places. The orphans will like you."

This was the first time he had mentioned any children living in his home. She stared at him in amazement. What other secrets did her husband harbor? "What do you mean? You gave them a home?"

" 'Tis late, Merry," he answered. "I don't wish to talk."

She stiffened with resentment. Why was it he felt he owed her no explanation for anything? Did he gain some perverse pleasure in leaving her in ignorance? Or did he not wish to consider any type of future with her in it?

With a muttered curse, Merry threw herself away from him and sought the far side of the bedroll. She lay facing away from the fire and into the dark woods, where the spirits of the dead skulked about. Kit was out there somewhere, keeping them company. She wondered if the camp's fire was sufficient to help the spirits find their way home or if it would invite them

into the campsite. She'd asked Luke if they might place a candle or two along the roadside to encourage them along their
way. Of course, he'd denied her.

Somehow she doubted she would sleep a wink that night.

An hour later, she was still awake, her ears cocked to the
sounds in the forest. Without warning, Luke's arm stole about
her, pulling her into the curve of his body.

Merry caught back a gasp and then a sigh. His body heat
chased away the chill that had seized her; moreover, his
strength delivered her from the fear that some demon spirit
might suddenly surprise them. She was safe in Luke's embrace.
She closed her eyes and drifted toward oblivion.

Suddenly, his hand closed over her breast, causing her lids
to spring open. Did he know what he was doing? she wondered.
Very gently, he squeezed her fullness. Merry caught her breath.
He toyed with her nipple, making it instantly erect. Desire
thawed her from the inside out, and yet she could not forget the
awful silence he'd imposed between them earlier.

Perhaps he would lapse back into sleep, she assured herself.
But he did not. Instead he pressed himself against her, his sex a
thick column against her backside. She tried to ease away from
it. He nuzzled her neck. He murmured into her ear, his voice
low and sleepy, "You smell sweet."

Merry's resentment wavered under the heat of his ardor. Her
body was all too willing to submit to his possession, yet she
could not forget that, moments before, he had refused even to
talk to her. An internal battle raged within her. She was not at
all certain which would win: passion or pride.

He pushed her skirts up, sweeping the length of her thigh,
moving steadily higher. If she did not resist him now, she would
succumb to her desire and feel all the more empty for it later.
Thrusting his hand from her hip, she scooted away from him.
"Don't touch me," she ordered, returning to the far side of the
blankets.

An ominous silence followed her request. "I've every right
to touch you, Merry," he finally said. By the tone of his voice,
he was fully awake, and more than a little angry with her.

She was grateful to hear anger at last. It gave her the right to
be angry back. "Nay, you've no right," she argued, whipping
around to face him. "You've become like a stranger to me,

Luke. I will not make love with a stranger!" she whispered furiously.

She overheard his expelled breath of air. He rolled onto his back and stared up at the sky, visible now that the trees were bare. "You don't understand, Merry," he finally told her. "There is much that is weighing on my mind now." He sounded exhausted in the face of it.

Compassion took some of the heat out of her ire. "You're concerned for your grandfather," she guessed.

"Aye," he said shortly.

"I will care for him when we get home," she promised.

He turned his head, regarding her in the darkness. "Thank you," he said more kindly. He looked back at the sky, and a long moment of silence passed between them. "Do you see those stars right there?" He pointed upward suddenly, drawing Merry's gaze to the starry dome overhead. The stars seemed especially bright tonight, brighter even than the wan moon.

"Which ones?" She scooted closer to sight down his arm.

"Those there. Do you see the brightest one, the one at the top?"

"Aye, I see it."

"When I was a boy, my father showed me that star before he died. He said I had only to wish upon it, and my wishes would be answered."

He paused for a moment, giving her the chance to envision Luke as a boy, an angel with gold eyes and black curls. Her heart softened immediately. Would their babe look like him? she wondered, enchanted by the possibility.

"My mother and I were very poor following my father's death," he continued. "We lived on the outskirts of Jerusalem, where we'd been ostracized. My mother's people had threatened to stone her to death. As far as they were concerned, she had given herself to an infidel, and I was the infidel's spawn. I think my mother resented me for it, though she did her best to care for me.

"In any event, when I was ten, I recalled my father's words, and I climbed to the highest rock around to wish upon that very star that our lives would be easier."

Merry felt her heart swell with compassion. It struck her that she and Luke had something in common after all. They'd both suffered, both been persecuted to a similar degree. "Did your wish come true?" she wanted to know.

"Not at once. Perhaps six months later, a pilgrim appeared at our hut with a handful of men. He took one look at me and called me 'grandson.' He paid my mother a sum of money and took me home to England."

"Wasn't your mother upset to see you go?" she asked, unable to fathom a mother trading her child for mere gold.

"Not really," he said with equanimity. "She seemed relieved more than anything."

"Were you happy to go?"

"Delighted. My father had told me about England and how green it was. About castles and how grand they were. All I'd ever wanted was to see it for myself. Suddenly, I was going to live there with a man who looked like my father, a man who had money for food and horses. What more could a boy want? I went from rags to riches. To this day, I look at that star and I marvel at my circumstances."

Merry gazed up at the bright point of light. Because of Luke's story, the star seemed suddenly to outshine all the stars around it. Without a word to convey her gratitude—both to Luke for having told her something of himself and to the star for having heard his wish—she laid her head upon his shoulder and embraced him.

"Ah, Merry," he murmured, holding her close. He released a deep and troubled sigh.

She waited for him to resume making love to her. Now that he had given something of himself, she would relinquish her stubborn pride. Yet he made no move to do so. Instead he kissed the top of her head in a manner that struck Merry's hopeful heart as tender. And seconds later, she overheard his soft snores.

## Chapter Fifteen

### West Sussex, November, A.D. 1154

THE land of West Sussex was tamer than the wild moors of Merry's home. Copses of beech and maple, with only a few bright leaves left on them, splashed color on the soft, sloping hills. The valleys were divided into rectangles, all varying shades of brown and green. The fields had suffered no drought here, but gave every indication of a healthy yield. In one large plot, winter wheat rolled beneath the brush of the wind; in another, furrows of ripe turnips awaited harvest. A crystal stream trickled between willows on a quest for the sea.

"We're close now," Luke said.

Discerning tension in his tone, she glanced at him sidelong. He had taken off his helm, and as they rode through a copse of white oak, the shadows of the branches fell across his face in quick succession. His brow was drawn with worry. She knew he was thinking of his grandfather, and she wanted to give him the reassurance he needed, but life, she knew, was oft times unfair.

By contrast, the soldiers riding on all sides seemed cheerful, their faces wreathed in smiles at the thought of the warm arms awaiting them. On the long trip home, there had been no talk of curses or spells, no resentment, no whispering. Phillip had ridden beside her a good deal of the time, regaling her with tales of battles won and lost. Even Erin, who'd accepted without argument the poultice she'd given him for his pimpled cheeks, vied for her company, casting her secret glances and coloring fiercely whenever she happened to catch him at it. Already, his skin had cleared, making him confident and handsome.

Merry reflected that she had either won the soldiers' allegiance by saving their lord's life, or they deemed it wise to respect her, given that she was now their lady. In any case, it was they who had kept her from being lonely, for Luke had ridden more often at the front or rear of the retinue than beside her.

"There," he said suddenly, pointing to the horizon. "Look over the top of that hill."

Merry followed his finger and spied the outline of a rooftop, one with crenellations and merlons creating a pattern like a crown. "I see it!" she cried, straining in the saddle.

As they wound down through a valley and up the opposite rise, Arundel came into glorious view.

Merry felt her scalp prickle with awe. She had never seen anything so majestic in her life! The castle rose up from the banks of the River Arun, a sapphire cloak about its base. The curtain wall was immense, with a gatehouse accessed by a wooden draw. She could see nothing inside the wall, save the top of the castle keep, rising like a crown atop a throne. Neat little cottages with their own fenced gardens huddled at the base of the outer wall like loyal subjects paying court.

All told, the vision left her breathless and painfully aware of her humble origins.

As they passed through the quaint village, womenfolk and children ran outside to greet them. Most of the soldiers fell out of line, heading home. Merry, Luke, and the bachelors who remained clattered over the drawbridge.

Merry did not recognize the silvery stone from which the gatehouse was carved. " 'Tis Caen stone brought from Normandy," Luke informed her, at her query. "And Quarr Abbey stone from the Isle of White."

Once inside the walls, she was amazed to see that there was no outer or inner ward. Rather, the castle grounds were divided into two wards by an elevated walkway guiding them upward, toward the central keep. Glancing over the wall, she realized the keep had been built atop a motte at least a hundred hands high. She was struck with the feeling that she was going up to heaven.

Her gaze jumped to the many souls who waved and called their greetings from the wall, from the gardens, from the windows of the keep. She felt herself being eyed curiously, and her panic rose as she wondered what they were thinking. Did they take her for a peasant? The gown she'd worn had faded from a robin's egg blue to a drab gray. It was frayed and dusty from their hours on the road.

They passed beneath a raised portcullis, into a scaled-down courtyard in the belly of the keep. A band of children burst suddenly through one of the doors, tripping over each other in their haste to greet Luke first. *The children!* thought Merry, amazed by their robust energy.

"Look, my lord!" shouted a little blond boy, "I found a frog in Maddie's inkwell!" He held up a disgruntled black frog for inspection.

"I think you'd best put him in water," Luke answered swinging down from the saddle.

All the children tried to jump on him at once. "Sir Luke! Sir Luke!" they shouted, vying for his attention. "What did you bring us?" one brave soul asked.

Merry wondered how he kept from being overwhelmed. They were so *loud!* They were clearly a reflection of Luke's travels, for the smallest was as dark as a gypsy, two were blond, and the other a freckle-faced youth. Luke reached into his saddlebag, and Merry was amazed to see him hand each child a different gift. Despite his coolness toward her lately, her heart softened to see his generosity. She was reminded of the goodness she'd often remarked in him.

The dark-haired girl received a carved, wooden doll with a cry of delight; the two blondes who might have been brother and sister each got a bit of sugared ginger he'd bought on the journey home; and the eldest boy received a rough-hewn dagger—his first by the look of awe on his freckled face.

An old woman made her appearance then, calling them away and threatening to lock them in the classroom. Merry could see that she had no teeth.

"Have mercy, Maddie," Luke cajoled, causing the woman to abandon her stern countenance and smile at him broadly. "I haven't seen the children in four months. Besides, there's someone here I want them to meet, and you, too," he added, including the old woman. He approached Merry's horse and helped her from the saddle. "Everyone, this is my lady wife, Lady Merry. Merry, these are the children, Collin, Reggie, Susan, and Katey. Their nurse and tutor, Dame Maddie." All this was said in a neutral tone, making it impossible to say whether he dreaded calling Merry his wife or reveled in it.

Merry curtsied automatically, though her knees quivered as she awaited their judgment. The children had fallen utterly silent. Through eyes that were brown, green, blue, and hazel, they stared at her. Then suddenly they remembered their manners, tugging forelocks and curtsying with great flourish. Their faces split into smiles of delight, and they all began to talk at once.

Merry did her best to answer their breathless questions. She was grateful to Kit who stuck his head out of her saddlebag and distracted them. "Oh, a kitty!" cried the older girl, Susan by name.

Merry lifted Kit out for all to see. Susan seemed so taken with him that Merry put her cat in the girl's arms and said she could watch him for as long as Kit allowed. "He'll find me if he needs me," she assured the girl.

Luke put an end to the pleasantries. "The lady has had a long journey and needs to rest," he told the children. "Go with Maddie now and finish your lessons."

They all obeyed, though that did not keep Reggie from shoving his frog under Katey's nose to make her scream. Susan held Kit as if he were a baby, and they all retreated toward the door from which they'd come.

Merry opened her mouth to comment on their liveliness but was cut off by the appearance of a hunchback who engaged Luke in conversation about his horse. The man was curtly introduced as Ewan. Without a word to Merry, Ewan took Suleyman into the stables. The remaining soldiers were already at work rubbing down their mounts.

Luke surprised her by reaching for her hand. "My grandfather lives," he said sudden with urgency. "Come, let's go see him!" He pulled her toward a set of doors. Merry hurried to keep apace. At the same time, her feet felt leaden. She knew the opinion of Luke's grandfather would weigh heavily with him.

As they entered the great hall, her concern turned to dismay. The hall itself was beyond anything she had imagined. Ornate tapestries padded the walls. Instead of rushes, costly rugs from the Orient muffled their footsteps. A massive table dominated the entire north wall; a modern hearth took up the other. High, mullioned windows kept the autumn winds outside, while twisting stairs disappeared into the fourth wall, providing access to the upper levels.

Luke was immediately flocked by servants who abandoned their dressing of the high table to greet him. Merry's gaze was drawn to the exotic tapestries and the colorful urns gracing the dais steps. They looked like goods Luke might have purchased while serving the prince abroad.

He acknowledged the servants as a group, too hurried this time to introduce Merry as his wife. Instead, he tugged her toward the stairs.

At the last moment, she slipped free of his grasp and hung behind. "Perhaps you should go alone," she suggested, "and give him warning first. I'm happy to remain here." She backed up farther, unwilling to face the possibility of his grandfather's rejection.

The sound of footsteps interrupted Luke's protest. Merry looked up and spied a richly dressed woman descending toward them. Her silvery-blond hair was covered by a veil that matched her pale gown. She hesitated at the sight of Merry, then evidently dismissed her. "You're home, dear Luke. What a surprise. We weren't expecting you till Christmas."

A quick glance at Luke revealed a stunned expression on his face, an expression corroborated by the fact that he did not return the woman's greeting but waited for her to approach him.

She did so, holding out both hands, a cool and practiced smile on her narrow lips.

Merry felt a spurt of envy as Luke's strong hands closed over the stranger's. "Amalie," he said. There was more than a hint of concern in his tone. "What brings you to Arundel?"

Merry froze, suddenly unable to move. Even before over-hearing the woman's name, she'd taken an instant dislike to her. Perhaps it was her dismissive, icy gaze. Not even in her worst imaginings had she pictured meeting Luke's betrothed this soon—if at all.

"Why, I've been looking after your grandfather, of course," Amalie answered with mild reproof. "There was no one else to do it, poor man. I trust I didn't overstep my bounds. We'll be married in just five months," she added with a patronizing look.

Oh, heavens, 'twas even worse than she feared! Merry nearly staggered back as a sudden light-headedness assailed her. She had assumed Luke had written ahead to inform Amalie of their broken engagement. Clearly he hadn't. The lady had no idea he'd wed someone else.

Luke flicked Merry a quick, uncomfortable glance. She realized in that instant that he was reluctant to say who she was. Her sudden dizziness turned into a cold sweat.

"Who's this woman?" Amalie demanded, giving him no room to skirt the issue.

"Lady Merry of Heathersgill," he answered neutrally. "Amalie Plantagenet," he added, completing introductions. "I brought Merry here to tend to my grandfather," he added, with a warning glint that was meant to keep Merry quiet. "She is renowned for her healing. How does the earl?" he added, cutting short anything Merry might say to contradict his assertion.

Merry scarcely heard Amalie's reply that she had called upon the royal surgeon himself for advice. The woman seemed icily offended that Luke would bring a stranger in to replace her. She squared her shoulders with queenly indignation. "I assure you, if the royal surgeon cannot cure him, this woman certainly cannot!"

"We'll discuss the matter later," Luke determined, forestalling further arguments. "The lady would like to rest, and I should like to see my grandfather immediately." He gestured for Merry to approach him.

She wasn't at all certain how her knees carried her forward. Surely Luke would acknowledge her now. Surely he was waiting for just the right moment.

"I'll come with you," Amalie volunteered.

"I would speak to him alone," Luke insisted, reaching for Merry's arm. He pulled her close, giving it a silent squeeze.

She realized, then, that he didn't intend to make their marriage known. He wished to guard their secret. *For how much longer?* she wondered with sudden panic.

From the corner of her eye, she saw Amalie's eyes narrow as she drew her own conclusions. With a hot rush of outrage, Merry opened her mouth to correct her, but the pressure of Luke's fingers increased as he propelled her up the stairs.

As they reached the second level, Merry wrenched free of his grasp. "Why didn't you tell her?" she demanded, trembling with the force of her upset.

"Please, keep your voice down," he warned, pulling her swiftly down the hallway. At last he stopped and turned to her, his face pale in the shadowed corridor. "I'm sorry," he said, quickly. "You've every right to be angry with me, Merry. But I didn't expect to encounter Amalie so soon!"

"So soon! We've been wed for nearly a sennight! Surely you could have sent a missive telling her that circumstances have changed."

He rubbed his forehead, revealing the full extent of his tension. "Merry, that isn't the way things are done—"

She cut him short. "Nay, I can see that it isn't. The way it's done is to humiliate me. After all, who am I but a woman you were forced to wed?"

"That isn't true," he countered, quietly angry. "I didn't know Amalie was here, tending my grandfather. I had no intention of humiliating you, Merry. But neither could I have informed Henry of our marriage by letter. I must do so in person where I can gauge his mood and take measures to appease him."

She tried very much to believe him, tried to banish the betrayal that squeezed her heart.

"I am walking a thin line, Merry," he continued, sensing her struggle. "Be patient with me and let me work my way through it. 'Tis the only way."

His assurances could not abolish her hurt. "When will you tell her?" she wanted to know.

"Soon," he promised her. "Before the children and Maddie manage to do so."

She drew little comfort from his promise.

"Let me introduce you to my grandfather," he urged. "His room is just down this hall."

"I don't feel well." She wanted only to bury her face in a pillow and shed the tears that pressured her eyes. She had expected to be rebuffed by those at Arundel. And yet it was Luke who had rejected her.

He looked at her in silence. "Then I'll show you to our room," he said, properly subdued. "You can meet him after you rest."

He led her down a curving hall and stopped before a door.

As he pushed it wide, Merry took apathetic note of the elaborately carved bed and whitewashed walls. The turquoise bed curtains were made of heavy silk. Other items in the room included a great wooden chest banded with leather, a writing desk, a marble washbasin, and a flawless looking glass hanging above it.

"Make yourself comfortable," he invited.

This room was also a reflection of his service to the crown. Long-necked vases, pillows, and sculptures graced the furniture and filled alcoves. As she edged onto the Eastern carpet, she discerned the fragrance that was Luke's own. Sandalwood, he'd called it. It seemed to be coming from the chest.

"Will you be all right, Merry?" he asked, still hovering at the door. "Shall I call for water?"

She glimpsed a reflection of herself in the looking glass and flinched. Her gown was even more tattered and inelegant than she feared. Despite her bath at the stream last night, her face was streaked with dust. She thought of the exquisite Amalie and her insides seemed to shrivel.

"I'd like a bath," she said dully. Turning from the mirror, her gaze fell upon the enormous bed, and her heart plummeted with despair. Could she give herself to Luke after this betrayal?

The click of the door latch caused her to start. Luke was gone. He'd shut the door without another word.

The doubt she'd suffered during their wedding had become manifest at last. She *had* been led by false promises.


AT the groaning open of the door, Merry glanced up from the journal she was reading, expecting to see Luke. To her sudden distress, she recognized Amalie instead. Her limbs grew petrified beneath the sheets as Amalie pinned her to the bed with her icy glare. Stepping into the chamber as if she owned it, she shut the door behind her, her bosom thrust into the air.

Merry set Luke's journal carefully aside. Dressed in her nightclothes, she was prepared to sleep, not to face her antagonist without warning. She had lost track of time but knew it to be after supper, which she'd declined. She hadn't wanted to lay eyes on Amalie again, not until she was at least on equal footing with her. Apparently, she had no choice.

The lady approached the bed, her skirts rustling ominously in the awkward silence. The flames of the many candles gilded her silver-blond hair and caused her eyes to look like ice-covered pools. Given the curl to her lip, it was impossible to guess whether Luke had told her the truth yet or not.

When words finally formed on Amalie's pink lips, they were not what Merry expected. "You poor girl," she lamented with exaggerated sympathy. "You think yourself saved, don't you? A dark prince has rescued you from a life of despair and made you his princess. Am I right?"

Merry turned as cold as the marble washbasin. *How much had Luke told Amalie?* she wondered. Surely he hadn't mentioned she was wanted as a witch. She was too shocked to give any reply.

"Ah, yes, Luke mentioned that you saved his life. He extolled your marvelous healing abilities. But that isn't the reason he wed you, is it?" She gave another false smile.

Though her thoughts raced, Merry held her tongue. Amalie did not seem to require an answer.

"Let me guess," continued the woman, propping slim fingers on her hips. "Could it be he got you with child?" She fixed her sharp eyes on Merry's face and was apparently rewarded by the flaring of surprise in Merry's eyes. "That's it, isn't it?" She clicked her tongue and looked at her rival sadly. "How noble," she remarked. "But then, he's like that, you know. For years now, he's brought home waifs and misfits and given them a place to live. I knew he'd never marry a woman of your . . . coloring on his own volition."

Merry's heart had begun to thud against her breastbone. In her mind's eye she saw again the children, their toothless nanny, the hunchback. She realized that there was truth to what Amalie was saying.

"He's gone too far this time," sighed the lady. "Yet he must know Henry would never tolerate a marriage! Ridiculous." The woman made a gesture with her jeweled fingers. "Luke and I were betrothed already. Henry simply won't stand for it. An annulment is the only solution." She shrugged and offered Merry a sympathetic look. "Of course, Luke must have known that." Her eyes were as dead as a pond in winter. "So sorry to topple your ambitions," she added. She let her gaze drift to the nest that Merry had made within the bed. "Perhaps he'll keep you as his mistress," she added, mocking her.

With a swish of silk, Amalie walked gracefully toward the door and paused to look back. "I wish you the best with the earl," she added falsely. "In my opinion, he has long outlived his usefulness. The kindest thing you could do for him is to poison him." With those shocking words, she slipped from the chamber as slyly as she'd come in.

Merry stared at the closed door until the grains of the oak came into focus. She replayed every word that Amalie had spoken to her, then closed her eyes and pressed her hand to her forehead. Nausea rose up in her and then receded.

Her fingers trembled. Just how much had Luke told the woman? Had Amalie simply guessed that Merry was with child, or had Luke made known that circumstance in order to excuse his own actions? Had he even hinted she was wanted for a witch? After all, Amalie had recommended poisoning the earl, as if she'd known that Merry had tried to poison the prioress. Surely Luke would not have revealed her darkest secrets. Not when he'd promised her she would start her life anew.

Unless there was truth to what Amalie had warned her. Unless Luke had hoped all along that Henry would insist on an annulment, declaring their marriage invalid. Perhaps Luke wanted it that way. Having insisted he had done his best for her, he would shrug his shoulders and set her regretfully aside.

Stunned by the depths of such betrayal, Merry struggled to breathe. She gripped the journal she'd been reading, an account of Luke's travels to Jerusalem and his meetings with Saracen leaders. Just minutes ago, she'd felt close to him again. She'd believed in his integrity, his goodness.

Was it all an illusion?

Without realizing what she intended, she slipped to her feet and returned the journal to the chest where she'd found it, along with treasures of gold, strange figurines, blocks of soapstone, and vials of exotic oils. She put the journal carefully away and latched the chest with finality.

Just as thoroughly, she buried her naïve dream that Luke would one day return her love, that her life would change for the better. Rising, she turned back to the bed, slipped inside the sheets, and laid her head upon the pillow. Not a single tear fell from her eyes. A shield of frost had formed about her heart, and she welcomed the oblivion it offered, for the pain that came from betrayal was too excruciating to bear.

# Chapter Sixteen

LUKE gazed down at his sleeping wife, touched by the innocent way in which she hugged her pillow. In the light of his single taper, her hair poured molten flames across the bleached pillows. Her skin glowed in the aftermath of the bath she had recently enjoyed. The scent of jasmine lingered in the chamber, telling him she'd found the oils in his chest. It pleased him to know that she'd helped herself. Did she hold her pillow close, imagining it to be her husband? Somehow, given what had happened today, he doubted it.

With a troubled sigh, Luke placed his candle on the writing desk and turned toward the washbasin. Although he would relish a bath himself, he would suffice with a rubbing down so as not to waken her.

He stripped off his shirt, wincing at how tightly the muscles were banded across his shoulders. He shrugged to ease the tension, but with Amalie's threats still ringing in his ears, he could not relax. He stripped himself naked and began to rub himself with a cloth. Goose bumps followed the path of the cold washcloth. His mind churned uneasily, suffering uncertainties in the wake of Amalie's departure.

He had planned to dissolve their betrothal in such a way that it would not offend her queenly pride. He'd expected to have the leisure to do so in a precise and careful manner, much the way he had approached Saracen warriors to negotiate the release of hostages. Not once had it occurred to him that Amalie would be at Arundel. Now the damage was done. In her eyes, he had violated their betrothal and flaunted his new bride. 'Twould require a miracle to keep Henry from reacting as bitterly as Amalie had done.

Luke scrubbed behind his ears and admitted to the fear that gripped him. The price of violating his betrothal might be more than he could endure. The price might be Arundel, his inheritance, denied him for having broken a promise.

Was Merry worth the cost? He paused to look at her. The sheets draped over her shoulder emphasized the curve of her hip, the narrowness of her waist. She looked so slight that the urge to shelter her rose up in him. She carried his babe. He could not let anything jeopardize their future! Both she and his child belonged at Arundel as much as he did.

Yet the prince would not see it that way. He would see them as usurpers. Dread made his heart beat faster. Again he wondered whether he would be forced to choose between Arundel and his newfound family. What then? He needed them both. How could he possibly choose?

If only his grandfather were not in danger of dying, leaving open the question of who would inherit Arundel. Then Henry would have time to accept Luke's marriage, to grow accustomed to Luke's uncharacteristic rebellion. Yet it was never more obvious that the earl's hold on life was tenuous.

Sir William had shriveled to a living skeleton, faded into a mere shadow of himself. He'd clearly lost his mind, rambling without meaning. The most painful thing to Luke was that he didn't seem to recognize his grandson after all the worry Luke had expended on his behalf. Luke had never pictured the proud earl coming to so piteous an end.

Not even Merry could cure a man so far gone.

Wringing out the washcloth, he sought a towel. A movement from the corner of his eye drew his gaze to the bed. He found Merry awake and watching him. In the wobbling light of the candle, she reminded him of how she'd looked when they first met, when she was tied at the center of a pyre. Her expression was pinched and drawn, her eyes wide and lusterless.

"Sorry to waken you," he apologized, forgetting until then that he was naked. He drew a drying cloth off a peg and wrapped it around his hips.

She regarded him in silence, her eyes still dull.

"Are you well?" he asked, with sudden concern.

As he approached her, she shrank back into the pillows. He eased cautiously onto the edge of the bed. "You're still angry with me," he guessed. "I told Amalie at supper," he assured her. Suddenly he wanted nothing more than for Merry to forgive him, to invite his touch.

His gaze fell to her long, graceful neck, scented now with jasmine. If she could only understand the fear he suffered thinking of her future, then she would know why he'd been silent and remote these last two weeks.

Now that he needed her comfort, she'd withdrawn her warmth. 'Twas his own cursed fault.

"She came to see me," Merry said, tonelessly.

Concern jostled aside his self-absorption. "She? You mean Amalie? What did she say?" he asked, certain it would not be good.

"She said I was just another of your misfits," Merry whispered. "That you married me out of pity."

For a moment, he was struck dumb. "She knows nothing of why we married," he growled back.

"She knows I'm with child," she countered. "You must have told her to excuse your actions." Color brightened the pale alabaster of her cheeks, whether in shame or anger he could not say.

He shook his head, though he could not recall exactly what he had said.

"She said the prince will annul our marriage the moment he hears of it," she added. Her hair seemed to burn in the light of the taper. "Did you count on that when you wed me?" she asked on a wrenching note.

Luke had suspected Amalie was heartless; now he was certain of it. "Nay, I did not," he swore, though he clearly recalled entertaining the idea of annulment should Henry threaten to deny him Arundel. " 'Tisn't within Henry's powers to annul a marriage anyway," he reasoned, angry at Amalie for tossing out such heartless threats. "A bishop is the one to make such decisions." He remembered then that Henry had personally appointed the bishop of Westminster, and his heart sank with dread.

Merry searched his face with eyes that saw everything, eyes as dry and pain-filled as a desert. "Then it never entered your mind that Henry would not acknowledge our marriage? Can you say that?" she demanded to know.

He wanted to deny it utterly, but he found he couldn't lie, not when she implored him so directly. "Look, Merry," he said instead, "I took a risk in making you my wife, we both know that. But no one can force an annulment on us, can they?" He gave her what he hoped was an encouraging smile. For himself, he felt that the very stone under his feet was shifting.

She did not reflect his smile. "What do you need me for, Luke?" she asked him imploringly. Her green eyes were enormous in her face, bottomless green wells into which he felt himself sinking.

He longed to comfort her, but being a man of reason and logic, he lacked words of such emotional nature. "What do you mean?" he asked, buying time.

"Tell me why you wed me," she demanded, her voice rising to near panic. "What do you want from me?"

The words reached down inside of him, touching some vulnerable core he wasn't ready to acknowledge for the price it would cost him. He retreated to safer ground. "I want you to tend my grandfather," he answered reasonably, "to be the mother of my child."

Her gaze drifted off to one side, and he knew that he was losing her. In desperation, he searched for something to bring her back. "I want you for this, Merry," he added, leaning swiftly forward. He caught her lips with his, gaining the slightest of responses as he kissed her tenderly.

"And this," he added, sliding his lips to the sweet column of her neck and kissing the spot where her blood pulsed warmly. Her scent filled him with sudden desperation. "Don't deny me tonight," he whispered. "Don't turn me away."

He sank lower still and nuzzled the swells of her breasts through the fabric of her chemise. He heard her indrawn breath and took heart from it, seeking her nipples through the silken nightdress. The one beneath his tongue beaded instantly, goading him on.

"Why now?" she cried, tugging ineffectually at his hair. "You touched me only once on our journey here."

He raised his head to give her a look. The answer seemed obvious to him. "Before my men?' he answered. " 'Twould have disrespected you to do so."

"You disrespect me now," she answered fiercely.

Hoping to rout her resistance for good, he ran a hand up the inside of her leg, sweeping up the hem of her nightdress. He slipped his thumb into her soft woman's flesh and coaxed her passion to the surface. She tried to clamp her legs together, yet she could not conceal her body's responses. She grew heated and damp almost instantly. He pushed the nightdress higher, finding her breasts and suckling them.

She gasped for breath, a ragged sound that struck him more as a sob than a gasp of desire.

Though his blood pounded against his temples, though he craved her touch in a way that defied logic, that small sound drew his head up. Looking down at her, he found her gaze directed past his shoulders, eyes glittering with tears.

"Merry," he said, with dismay, for he hated more than anything to make her cry.

She brushed away the hand that he lifted to her face. Struggling to free herself, she rolled away from him, scooting toward the very edge of the bed, where she readjusted her gown in silence.

With a sharp sense of loss, Luke eyed her tense shoulders. An apology stuck in his throat, warring against the hunger that still clawed at him. "You are still my wife," he growled. The instant the words left him, he knew he'd made a mistake.

The silence following his threat was so deep, so wide, he wondered if it would ever be breeched.

At last Merry spoke, her voice surprisingly calm. "Tomorrow, I'll look in on your grandfather," she promised.

He dropped his head against the pillow with relief. Perhaps he hadn't ruined everything; after all, he hadn't forced her to accept him.

"This will be my last night in your chamber," she added, dashing his hopes into shards. "Tomorrow I shall move my things down the hall." She rose to a sitting position and lifted a pillow that had been cast aside. Drawing it to her chest, she settled into position once more, still presenting him her back.

Frozen by her announcement, Luke considered the pillow she clutched to her chest. She had not been thinking about him when she held that pillow. If anything, she'd made up her mind before he'd even entered the chamber that she would abandon their marriage bed.

Luke rolled out of bed to hunt for the briefs he would wear to sleep in. He felt sick to his stomach, his thoughts thrown in turmoil. Merry was, in a sense, leaving him. He found his shorts and donned them, seeking the mental aloofness he employed in battle, hoping to distance himself from his unaccustomed feelings.

Succeeding in part, he settled rigidly onto his own edge of the bed. The chill that came from Merry had him eyeing the dark patterns of the bed curtain wondering what he might possibly say to change her mind.

*What did she want from him?* he demanded, hoping to whip himself into righteous anger. Did she think her husband held sway over Henry's reaction? What right had she to be angry with him, when he'd done all that was honorable?

He punched up his pillow in frustration. Christ's toes, it wasn't the first time he wished he'd never met her! His life had been a straight arrow to the point that he'd saved Merry's life. He'd risked everything to wed her, everything! He owed her nothing more.

And yet, sensing her slight, withdrawn form only inches away, he felt nothing but loss at the thought of her sleeping elsewhere. Sometime in the weeks that they'd spent together, she had become as necessary to him as the food he put in his belly. Her mind was a mystery that kept him perpetually guessing. The contradictions she embodied of tenderness and ferocity stirred his admiration.

She'd always had his full attention.

Nay, he didn't wish to lose her, not to the chamber next door, not for any reason. And yet, if he couldn't give her Arundel, because it had been taken from him, what quality of life could he possibly provide? That of the wife of a mercenary, or, at best, of a master-at-arms. His power and his protection were what she needed most from him. Stripped of those traits, he had nothing to offer her.

"THIS isn't what Amalie gave me," groused Sir William. He glowered at Merry over the rim of his goblet, morning sunlight playing upon the white wisps of his hair.

Merry pulled back the other half of the bed curtain, flooding the remainder of the earl's box with light. The air coming through the window was crisp with autumn frost, but the snapping brazier beat back the cold, and the earl was swathed in blankets.

Unlike most of her contemporaries, Merry believed in the healing powers of sunlight and fresh air. Part of their daily routine was to expose the earl to both those elements. He'd been locked in a dark, dank chamber for too many months.

Three days ago, she'd been shocked to find him in a state of filth, his face unshaven, his linens soiled. The first thing she had done was to order the rushes burned. They had been crawling with vermin. Next she'd stripped his bed and drawn him a bath. The earl had resisted mightily, fighting the manservant who assisted her. Yet he was so frail that his protests could not prevent him from being dunked and scrubbed, nor from having his bristles shaved. She'd soothed his flea-bitten limbs with a salve afterward and left him sleeping betwixt clean sheets.

In just three days he had regained enough strength to defy her, at least verbally.

"Drink it all," she ordered him firmly.

"I want what Amalie gave me," he whined again, giving his chamomile infusion a disdainful sniff.

"Infusion of poppy is for coughs," Merry explained for the dozenth time. "You haven't got a cough anymore."

Contrary to her suspicions, she'd found the treatment Amalie had administered to the earl was appropriate to his afflictions. The earl had suffered an inflammation of the lungs, according to his manservant, and Amalie's poppy infusion had been a sound treatment. Merry would have done the same.

Yet it was not a simple cough that plagued the earl now; it was an infirmity of the mind. His behavior was so erratic, so unpredictable that Merry was uncertain of how best to treat him. At times he saw objects that were not present; snakes and daggers that tormented him in broad daylight. He was subject to fits and starts and sweated profusely. Merry had seen no illness like it. She despaired of making him better.

Though she did not see how Amalie was to blame for the earl's condition, the nagging suspicion would not leave her. The castlefolk swore mightily that the earl had been of sound mind before the woman's arrival four months past. Furthermore, the state in which Sir William had been made to live bespoke of negligence, not care. Amalie had clearly believed the earl had outlived his usefulness, and in Merry's opinion, she'd done her best to speed him toward the next life.

What if he did not recover? Merry swallowed hard at the question. Luke had said he needed her to treat his grandfather. If she failed him now, 'twould be that much easier to put her aside. She'd lived through persecution and the threat of death, yet nothing seemed so grim as a future without Luke.

For the hundredth time she doubted the wisdom of her self-imposed exile. In removing herself to separate quarters, she had set her pride above her vows. She had wedged yet more distance between them, so that in three days' time, Luke had shared scarcely a word with her. The distance was breaking her heart.

Yet the alternative, to sleep with Luke and to love him, was just as much a danger to her, if not more so. Already the future gaped ominously. How could she protect herself or her child when it was almost certain Henry would insist on an annulment?

Most hurtful of all was the fact that Luke hadn't denied that the thought of annulment had occurred to him. It was never more evident why he'd married her in the first place: To avoid being crushed by the Slayer, and to do right by Merry. Yet he'd guessed all along that the crown would not stand for it. He'd refused to acknowledge her as his wife when meeting Amalie. How could Merry trust him to defend their marriage to the crown? She could not.

"Who did you say you were?"

The question startled Merry from her bleak thoughts. There were times when the earl seemed almost lucid. She stepped closer, hopeful that this was a sign of improvement.

"My name is Merry," she reminded him. "I've come to make you well." She'd already decided to say no more than that. It was up to Luke to acknowledge her as his wife.

"You remind me of my Beatrice," said the earl. He frowned into his goblet. "She was a beautiful woman."

The tilt of the earl's eyebrows reminded her of Luke. Otherwise, there was little resemblance between them. The earl was as pale as Luke was dark. "Was Beatrice your lady wife?" she inquired gently.

"Aye." His blue eyes focused on her then, and she thought she saw a glimmer of irony behind their bleariness. "She was only sixteen when I wed her. And I was forty-two. She was my second wife. I loved her best of all."

These were the clearest thoughts the earl had shared since her arrival; still Merry found them disturbing. Would Luke ever have a second wife? she wondered, feeling stabbed in the chest.

"Is my grandson here?" the earl suddenly inquired. "Is he home?"

The question betrayed the man's poor memory. Luke had been with him just this morning. "He visits you every day," she reminded him. "Don't you remember?"

He scowled at her as if she'd lied to him. "Have him come to me then," he demanded, as if testing her.

She stepped away, hiding her sudden tension. "He isn't here," she answered him shortly. "He went to Westminster today to report to the prince." Her stomach cramped at the reminder. She'd been trying all day to put it out of her mind. Today she would know whether the prince meant to honor their marriage or condemn it.

"Still a prince?" muttered the earl. "Isn't he a king yet?"

She smiled at the earl's aside, again hopeful that his wits were returning. "He will be. The coronation is just two weeks away." This was one of the few pieces of information Luke had shared with her since her exile. "Drink your infusion," she reminded her patient. "Then I'll leave you." She wanted to take a look at the herb garden to gauge its potential. Luke had said he'd brought herbs back from the East. She wondered if any were growing still in this cold weather.

At last, Sir William emptied his goblet, and Merry left the chamber, calling upon a manservant to keep watch over his lord. Fetching her cloak from her chamber, she made her way toward the exit, braced for the November chill.

She was halfway across the courtyard when a chorus of voices heralded her. The children burst from the stable, their hair shot with straw, their cheeks rouged from playing outdoors. She smiled to see them, for their happy faces were symbolic of her hope that Luke would stand by Merry, no matter Henry's opinion.

"Mornin' m' lady!" called the oldest boy, as he jogged up beside her.

"Hello, Reggie. Have you seen your frog yet?" He'd admitted to putting his frog in the castle well.

Reggie grimaced and shook his head.

"Frogs sleep in the winter," she comforted him. "You'll see him again come spring."

"Where are you going?" Susan asked worriedly.

Merry glanced at the girl, not surprised to see Kit in her arms. He seemed to have forgotten Merry was his mistress. "To the herb garden," she gave reply.

"Can we come?" This time it was Katey who spoke. Her liquid gaze made it impossible to refuse her anything.

"Oh, you must," Merry answered sincerely. The children, at least, had made her feel at home at Arundel. She'd won their hearts by insisting on their presence at meals. Their animated talk had filled the silence at the high table.

"This way, then," said Reggie, taking up the lead.

Merry felt Katey's hand slip into hers. Tenderness caught at her heart. *Oh, to have all this!* she lamented inwardly. *To come so close to happiness, only to have it snatched away!*

Together they descended the long walkway that conveyed them toward the outer wall. "Down these steps," said Reggie, when they reached the end.

Merry gazed out over the western ward, all of which had been cultivated with trees and herbs. Most of the garden's furrows stood empty, the plants having perished in recent frosts. But the soil looked dark and rich, and come spring, a multitude of herbs would thrive there.

*Will I be here to see it?* she wondered.

Moving down the steps, she wandered among the remaining plants. Hardy stalks of shepherd's purse still thrived, impervious to winter's approach. Sowbread, a winter plant, boasted delicate pink blooms that belied their powerful purgative effects. She stepped over these, toward the bloodwort that had ceased to flower. There was no plant living that she failed to recognize. Luke's exotic herbs had either gone dormant for the winter or been dried and put away in the herbal storeroom. She would probe the storeroom more deeply at the first opportunity, having found just the usual remedies on her first inspection.

Lifting her head, Merry took in the rest of the open space. Beyond the garden stood an orchard of quince, peach, and apple trees. Arundel would be nearly self-supporting under a siege, she marveled.

A gust of air, redolent with the scents of rich soil and rotting fruit, chilled her cheeks. Her heart clutched painfully. She had always longed for such a garden. Today she might well discover if this garden would be hers or just a temporary refuge.

As had happened so many times to her in the past, her very life seemed to hang in the balance, her fate being decided by others.

"Do you want to play chase with us, Lady Merry?" Reggie called, pulling Merry from her reverie.

She smiled at them and gently declined. The tiny life inside of her was growing, stretching her womb with cramps that left her tender.

"Will you watch us, then?"

She nodded and found a bench close by, gathering her cloak around her.

Soon the shrieks of the children enveloped her in a temporary comfort. Gazing at the four urchins, Merry found some assurance that Luke would not put her casually aside, not even for his prince. Remembering the child he used to be, the one who'd wished upon a star to be snatched from a life of misery, surely he would not ignore his conscience, not even for his soon-to-be king. After all, 'twould be his own child he would ostracize, and he'd firmly expressed his opinion that a babe should remain with both its parents.

Yet the realist in her mocked her fragile hope. She had always known Luke was high above her, too high for one such as she. He had so much to lose: power and authority earned, the prospect of ruling Arundel. As for their babe, Luke did not have to be wed to Merry to look out for its welfare. Likely he would find Merry a cozy place to live, somewhere nearby that he might come to visit his child often. Such an arrangement would appease his code of honor as far as their baby was concerned.

With such a simple solution at hand, it was all too likely that Luke would set her aside. Yet another stubborn part of her burned with faith. He had saved her countless times before— from the pyre, from Cullin, from her own worst imaginings. Surely Luke would not abandon her now.

LUKE paced the length of the chamber, willing himself to remain calm. The prince was usually prompt with his appointments, often running ahead of schedule, making it wise to show up early. Yet the water clock in the corner showed him to be half an hour late. Luke had heard that Henry showed displeasure by making his courtiers wait. 'Twas not a good sign.

At last, the doors of the royal solar groaned open, propelled by two guards. Luke looked up to find Henry's clerk crooking a finger at him. With premonition prickling his nape, he entered the double doors.

The royal solar used to be the king's, but now that Stephen was dead, Henry had made it his. Luke was not surprised to see some of the lavish tapestries replaced with rustic scenes of hunts and hawking, for the prince's chief passion was the hunt. Henry stood at a window, his square hands locked behind his back as he took in the bare gardens of Westminster below.

Luke waited, sensing a dark current in the atmosphere. The double doors slammed shut, and Henry turned around. With the window at his back, his hair looked almost red—though nothing close to the shade of Merry's hair, Luke thought irrelevantly.

"Well," Henry commented, "the Phoenix has flown home." His tone was indecipherable. He sauntered forward, his legs looking muscular beneath his forest green hose. Stopping an arm's span away, he proffered his hand with the royal seal, and Luke bowed dutifully over it.

"My liege," he murmured. It wasn't until he straightened that he saw the fiery gleam in Henry's gray eyes. He knew, then, that Amalie had pleaded her case with credible outrage.

"Make your report," Henry commanded with his usual efficiency.

It was difficult to recall his mission when matters of a different sort weighed upon his mind. Still, Luke managed to summarize his accomplishments, keeping to those that reflected on his duties. He omitted his rescue of Merry from the priory and skirted the issue of Iversly's outer wall, the one he'd left fully standing.

Henry turned away, shuffling through documents on his writing table until he produced a length of parchment. "You wrote that you did not complete your duties at Iversly . . ." he looked up at Luke, "because you were injured, you say."

Iversly was a trifling matter, but Luke suddenly saw that the prince would use it as a platform for complaint, leaping from there to Luke's unsanctioned marriage. The letter he held was the one Luke himself had penned just before his wedding, explaining his injury and rehabilitation. "As my letter explained, Majesty, the adulterines at Iversly were all destroyed, save the outer wall. Such a wall might yet be needed to safeguard against invasion—"

"From whom?" Henry cut him short, throwing down the missive. "Malcolm the Maiden? That milksop is too busy keeping a handle on his own kingdom." A familiar vein appeared at Henry's temple, a sure sign of his darkening mood.

Luke attempted to humor him. "He should look to your grace as an example. I hear you subdued the Lord of Torigny handily while in Normandy."

Henry slashed a hand through the air. "Don't try to change the subject, Sir Luke. Your mission was to destroy all adulterines, not solely those of your choosing!"

Luke sketched an apologetic bow. "Your Majesty may recall from the letter that I was gravely injured. My injury necessitated a lengthy recovery and a quick return to West Sussex."

The prince narrowed his eyes at this exaggeration. "A ripping open of the thigh, was it?" he commented, as though playing along. "Yet you scarcely walk with a limp. Why is that?"

They had come to the heart of the issue now. Luke disliked these games intensely. It was clear the prince knew the answers to his own questions, and yet they would bat words around until the end result was as Henry wished. "I was treated by a healer of great skill," he neutrally replied. "She saved my life."

"Your life!" the prince scoffed. "Since when is marriage the outcome of gratitude? Amalie says you got the girl with child. Why not settle a sum on her and leave her as she was?"

"I chose to marry her," Luke answered stoically.

Henry stepped closer. Though younger than Luke by ten years and a full head shorter, he had inherited Matilda's gift of turning men to stone with a single, glacial look. " 'Twas not your decision to make," the prince hissed through his teeth. "You were betrothed to another—my cousin!" he added, jabbing a finger at his robust chest.

Luke noted the prince's passion with a mixed apathy and wariness. The Plantagenet temper was a dangerous entity, yet in truth he thought it little more than a childish trait. "Majesty," Luke calmly replied, "I have served you faithfully for more than twelve years. My marriage was not meant to defy you. 'Twas necessitated by special circumstances."

Henry glowered at him. "You dishonored the contract that was signed between us," he insisted. "You grieve my cousin with your outrageous actions!"

"For the dishonor cast upon her name and yours, I beg forgiveness," Luke replied. "I never intended to breech the contract. Majesty," he added, sensing the return of Henry's reason, "oft times there are obstacles in our path, which we cannot predict. I continue to pledge you my sword. My service to you is unquestionable. I beg you, cast a merciful light on what I have done and forgive it." He held his breath, awaiting Henry's decision.

*Arundel or Merry? By the rood, don't make me choose,* he silently begged. A cold sweat stood between his skin and his wool undershirt.

With a show of disgust, the prince turned away and stomped once more to the window. Luke eyes his broad back, awaiting an answer. His lungs began to ache, and he realized he was holding his breath.

"Explain to me these obstacles you mentioned," Henry demanded, looking out the window. "What made you marry this woman?"

Luke took heart. At least Henry was willing to listen. "I

promised to escort the lady to Helmesly," he began, omitting any mention of her persecution. "My work took us to Iversly first. But then after one of my men attacked her, I decided to bear her with haste to Helmesly, taking only ten men with me. We were beset by ruffians at a tavern who snatched the lady and took our horses. In the process of reclaiming her, I was mortally wounded. The last thing I saw before swooning was the lady stabbing my opponent in the ribs. She managed to convey me and my remaining men to Helmesly, where she nursed me back to health."

"Then she is brave," said Henry thoughtfully, "though not beautiful."

Luke paused. Amalie had likely described Merry in unflattering terms. To Luke, she *was* beautiful, alluring, maddening, a threat to his senses. "Her coloring is unusual," he replied. "Some might say she is plain, others beautiful."

"I've heard of Helmesly," Henry admitted. "Have I a baron there?"

"My lady's brother-in-law is the Slayer of Helmesly," Luke replied, realizing a sudden advantage that had not occurred to him previously. "He pledged you fealty at the signing of the Wallingford treaty. No doubt you remember him. He is twice my size," Luke exaggerated, "with strength and skill unseen among your barons. Your grace can count on him to defend the northern border." Luke laid it on thick, playing up his only political advantage. Surely the prince would recognize that an annulment of Luke's marriage could impact a part of the country that was, in many aspects, still renegade.

Sharp silence filled the chamber.

Henry spoke at last, his tone sly. "You would have me believe that you married for love then, Sir Luke. Why is it you don't sleep with your bride?" he asked, still gazing out the window.

Luke stiffened, thrown off balance by the sudden shift in focus. He'd quite forgotten that the prince placed spies among his courtiers, having never felt a need for secrecy before. He would have to guard Merry's history with care, lest wind of her past reach Henry's ears. "She prefers her own bed," he heard himself mutter.

" 'Tis said her tongue is so sharp it tempts a soul to cut it out," the prince added.

Luke clenched his fists, determined to flush out the rat and thrash him soundly. "She speaks her mind," he paraphrased. " 'Tis refreshing to hear what a woman thinks, rather than to be left guessing." He let the implied slur against Amalie hang between them.

Henry grunted an acknowledgment and folded his arms across his chest. "You've put me in an awkward position, Sir Luke," he finally confessed, turning his face to profile. "Amalie had her heart set on Arundel," he added heavily.

Luke's heart beat a fraction faster. *Don't take Arundel,* he silently willed.

"On the other hand, your service to me has earned the respect of my barons. They are willing to overlook your illegitimate birth. They support your right to your grandfather's lands."

Luke's hopes took wing. Henry had upset the barons enough with his razing of adulterines. If the barons sided with Luke, perhaps the title might still pass to his children.

"Yet what you have done," the prince continued, turning at last, so that his face was lost to shadow with the window behind him, "is unprecedented. No one in my service has ever defied me in so personal a matter."

Luke tried not to blanch. Henry favored strong language, yet his choice of words made Luke's crime sound paramount to treason. "What does Your Majesty intend?" he demanded, refusing to back down. To show fear now would send the prince into a killing frenzy.

Stepping out of the shadows, Henry's face revealed an expression of impatience. He gestured at his cluttered desk. "Do you think I have time to deal with the matter now?" he demanded. "In two weeks time, I'm to be crowned. My uncle has left me a country seething in chaos."

Luke kept silent as they shared a close, hard look.

"Bring your wife to my coronation," the prince finally decided. "I will determine then if she meets my expectations."

Again, Luke was thrown off balance. "You wish to know her better, Majesty?" he asked, sensing a trap.

Henry gave a dismissive shrug. "I wish to see her odd coloring myself. Not any woman is fit to be the wife of a tenant-in-chief," he added. "If the title of earl is to pass through your loins, then I insist that your wife be of noble birth. I would question her about her ancestors. Perhaps she'll impress me," he offered insincerely.

Luke's wool undershirt began to itch. The prince had no intention of being impressed. He would use the two intervening weeks to persuade the barons that Luke had dishonored him, thus ensuring no resistance to having Luke's marriage annulled.

The itch goaded his own temper into an icy rage. He drew himself to his full height, considering the words that burned a path to his tongue. *Aye,* he would have to speak his mind, else the prince would walk all over him. "Do not make me choose, Majesty, between my wife and my loyalty," he warned Henry.

The prince glanced at him sharply, his face a dull shade of red. "Do you dare to threaten me?" he demanded, his volume abruptly rising.

Luke flexed his jaw and held the prince's glare. He knew the cost of defying Henry, and yet Arundel was nearly lost to him anyway. "You have need of me, Majesty," he reminded his overlord. "It is I whom you call upon to complete the tasks that others find beneath them. Who will serve in my stead if I refuse?" he demanded.

Henry's complexion darkened to an alarming shade of red. "You pledged me your sword," he growled at Luke, his eyes turning a flinty gray. "If you withdraw that pledge, then you foreswear your oath!"

"I also vowed to love and honor my wife forever. 'Tis you who would have me choose between one oath and another, Majesty," Luke insisted.

"How dare you threaten me when I have given you all you have!" thundered the prince. "How quickly you forget where you came from!"

Luke said nothing at all to this remark. He waited for the prince to recall that Luke had saved his life so many years ago. As the silence stretched thin, Henry's flush deepened, as if he had just recalled Luke's bravery.

Luke spread his hands and said with forced calm, "All I ask is a bride of my choosing. Is that too much?"

"Get out," Henry raged, gesturing violently toward the door.

"I offered you the cloak on my back, my own name to take as your own, and you scorned my offer."

"As you will." Luke gave an ironic half bow and walked slowly toward the double doors. He knew the prince well enough to take his time in departing. Yet he was almost out of the door before Henry called him back.

"Sir Luke!"

He turned with relief, his heart thudding expectantly.

Henry had propped his hands on his hips. He was breathing harshly as though he'd run a great distance. "I won't insist on an annulment," he snapped, glaring at Luke resentfully. "You've made your choice. Go and live with your witch."

The word *witch* seemed to jump off the walls, startling Luke with the possibility that Henry had heard of Merry's past.

"Bring her to my coronation," Henry reminded him. "I would see for myself whether she is plain or beautiful."

*Nay, Henry couldn't possibly know,* Luke reasoned. He'd called Merry a witch on the basis of her coloring and the sharp tongue he'd remarked on. Yet with nagging doubt, Luke bowed deep at the waist, showing Henry the deference he deserved for having made the right decision. "Your humble servant, Majesty," he muttered, straightening.

Henry made a face that bordered on comical. "Harrumph," he grunted. "Leave me in peace." He jerked his chin, gesturing for Luke to depart.

Luke slipped quietly through the exit, aware that his feet scarcely seemed to touch the flagstone. By heaven, he'd gone head to head with the prince and won! His marriage had been grudgingly blessed. It was all Luke could do not to break into a run down the lengthy hallway.

*Merry!* He couldn't wait to tell her. *Merry, the prince has accepted our marriage. Let there be no more talk of annulment. Come back to my bed and let me love you!*

His step faltered. Of course, he meant *love* her in the physical sense. Anything more was . . . well, it was sentimental. He liked her, certainly. She amused him with her outrageous honesty. Her bravery was more than he'd seen in most men. But his hunger for her was physical, was it not? So potent, in fact, that he felt himself stirring at the mere thought of her soft arms going around him.

What a lucky man he was! A bastard whose first son would
be the earl of Arundel! More than that, he had a feisty wife to
warm his bed and a child on the way!

It had been a gamble to defy the prince, yet he was glad he'd
done so. The resentment that had been growing steadily over
the last year had required a release. What a relief that Henry's
need of him outweighed his disappointment over Luke's marriage. He was the puppet of a tyrant no longer! He pushed
through the exit, making his way swiftly to the stables. He
couldn't wait to relate his news to Merry, to coax her back into
his bed.

If only his grandfather were well enough to understand what
had just transpired. Then the sky above would be truly cloud-
less.

# *Chapter Seventeen*

MERRY laid the cool cloth on the earl's forehead, soaking up the sweat that glistened on his brow. She had thrown back the blankets to make him as comfortable as possible. The fire in the brazier had been doused, so that the room was now cold. Still the earl continued to sweat profusely. Nor did she trust the peacefulness into which he'd lapsed, for any moment he might start violently from the pillow, crying out against unseen demons.

Merry allowed herself a sigh of weariness. It was late into the night. Out of pity for the manservant who had been with Sir William all day, she had ordered Egbert back to his pallet in the corner of the chamber and kept watch over the earl herself. That was hours ago. Her limbs were now leaden with exhaustion. More than once she'd had to pin the earl to the mattress to keep him from bolting out of bed. He'd fought her, his attempts feeble but powerful enough to sap her strength.

He seemed calmer now, rambling in such a way that finally brought him comfort. Merry caught herself listening to his words.

"Ah, Bea, sweet Bea! Your smile is like the sun; it warms my heart. Why did you leave me, Bea? I never thought you would die before an old man like me." His face crumpled into grief as he broke into sobbing.

Merry's heart wept along with him. *Must love be so painful?* she asked herself. *Why does it bring despair, both in life and death?*

As the earl drifted off to sleep, she shed a tear for his loss and for her own. When would Luke return? He'd been gone all day and most of the night. Her nerves were now so badly frayed she felt she was held together by a single thread.

A creaking of the door caused her to glance up swiftly. At the sight of Luke standing in the doorway, her energy flowed back into her, making her tense in expectation. The candle by the earl's bed seemed to brighten at his approach.

In contrast to Merry's frazzled state, Luke appeared larger than life and intensely handsome in a fawn-colored tunic. His hair was ruffled from a long ride, his eyes alert and focused. Without a word, he stopped before her, his gaze fixed on her face. He greeted her with intensity. "Merry," he said. But then he caught sight of a tear still clinging to her lashes and he frowned. "What's happened?" He turned to his grandfather, waiting to catch the rise and fall of the earl's chest before turning back to her. "Have you been here all night?" he asked.

She nodded, too entranced by the power he exuded to recall many details of the evening. "He's suffering one of his spells," she managed to say. "The worst is over now. I think he's sleeping." She drew the cloth away from the earl's forehead. The old man gave a whiffling snore but did not waken.

"Have you found anything to soothe him yet?"

She dreaded admitting defeat. "The chamomile helps a bit," she exaggerated.

"Then you still don't know what ails him?"

The truth froze in her throat. "I will soon," she promised, afraid he might cease to have need of her. "He . . . he had a racking cough which Amalie treated with a poppy syrup. These symptoms started soon after, according to the servants I've questioned."

"Poppy!" Luke's gaze jumped to hers, and the dark center of his eyes seemed to flare.

" 'Tis a common remedy," Merry assured him, "though I

was certain Amalie had done something amiss. She neglected your grandfather in most respects."

Luke seized both her arms, his grip jolting her. " 'Tisn't red poppy that grows within these walls," he whispered urgently. " 'Tis opium poppy! Remember, I told you I'd brought the seed vessels from the East years ago and had them planted in the garden."

Dread rushed up Merry's spine as the words of that conversation returned to her. "I should have realized earlier," she cried in dismay.

Luke's mouth was grimly set. "The juice of the plant is poisonous," he recollected, turning to gaze at the old man. "It causes the very symptoms my grandfather suffers. I should have noted it before!" He swore fluently in his foreign tongue.

"Why did you plant it if it's poisonous?" Merry wondered out loud.

"The seed eliminates pain and induces sleep. I've seen it give relief to the dying. I've seen surgeons remove arrows and limbs without causing the patient any distress. 'Tis a marvel if it's used right."

"And if it isn't?" she said, dreading the worst.

" 'Tis addictive," he admitted darkly, "and it will kill. I wrote the details in my journal . . ." He gave Merry a searching look then glanced at his grandfather. "Can we leave him alone now?" he asked.

"I think so. Egbert will hear him if he wakes." She glanced at the manservant who had lifted himself from his pallet and was watching them solemnly.

"Come with me," Luke said, reaching for her hand.

Merry could think of nothing beyond his warm, sure grasp. There was something different about Luke, something resulting from his visit with the prince. As she rushed to keep pace with his long strides, she felt certain that he bore good news. The earl's health, however, took precedence to the needs of her heart.

Luke pushed wide his chamber door. His room was dark, save for the low-burning brazier the servants had left for him. Releasing Merry's hand, he stabbed a candle into the brazier's embers, and the room brightened abruptly. Merry dashed to the chest, releasing the buckles with quick fingers.

When she'd last closed Luke's chest, she had closed her heart to him as well. Would her heart break free of its prison tonight? It swelled in her bosom, eager for release.

As the candlelight licked over the contents of the box, Merry located Luke's journal and pulled it out. She laid it on the carpet at their feet, and Luke kneeled beside her, placing the candle next to them. Leaning over the book, he began flipping quickly through the pages. "Where is it?" he murmured, narrowing his search, but without success.

Merry glanced at him sidelong. His midnight hair blended with the shadows behind him. His eyes blazed as brightly as the flame shining on his handsome face. Having been apart from him for three days, she had forgotten the quiet energy that radiated from him. She found she couldn't tear her gaze from him. The symmetry of his brow, his nose, the determined angle of his jaw kept her spellbound.

" 'Tisn't here," he said, meeting her gaze with a puzzled frown.

They stared at each other, the train of conversation briefly forgotten.

" 'Tisn't there?" Merry echoed.

"Look," he said, pointing to the volume. "A page is missing. It's been cut out."

Someone had taken a sharp knife and cut the parchment close to the binding, so that its absence was not immediately obvious. Merry drew a quick breath. She felt Luke's gaze on her face, and she reared back, putting a hand to her heart. "Nay, you don't think I did it?" she asked, horrified.

Disbelief transformed his features. "Of course not," he retorted. "The one thing I am certain of, Merry, is that you would sooner harm yourself than an innocent soul." Both his voice and his eyes warmed considerably as he said so. But then his brow creased in confusion. "Who would have done this?" he asked. "And why?"

Merry licked her dry lips. "Perhaps 'twas Amalie," she ventured softly. "She once said to me that the kindest thing I could do for the earl was to poison him."

Luke stared at her with a dismay that quickly turned to horror. "You said she treated him with a poppy syrup," he recalled.

"Aye, but she may not have known it was the eastern poppy. I'd forgotten so myself."

"Nay, she would have known it," he retorted, clearly searching his memories. "She took special interest in this chest when it first arrived, especially in the cosmetics, the kohl and the henna that I'd brought with me. I told her about the power of the poppy seed. She seemed fascinated to hear of its effects. God have mercy," he added, wiping a hand over his eyes.

Merry realized it must be a shock to Luke to discover that his own betrothed may have been killing his grandfather. "If she knew," Merry wondered aloud, "why would she have done such a thing?"

Luke shook his head, unable to answer, shock still fresh upon his face.

"Perhaps she thought it would heal him faster," Merry ventured, "or take away his pain." She didn't believe either to be true, but her opinion was likely colored by her dislike of the woman.

Luke shook his head and offered grimly, "The page that is missing from the journal describes the process of creating opium. The dosages for poisoning and death are clearly written as a precaution. Someone took the page. 'Twas most likely Amalie."

"But why?" Merry asked, unable to comprehend the woman's motives.

Luke heaved a sigh. "Henry said today she had her heart set on Arundel," he admitted heavily. "As long as my grandfather remains in health, he rules it. He was never fond of Amalie, and took no pains to hide that fact."

"So she took steps to weaken him," Merry guessed, still reeling at the thought of such cold-bloodedness. "What will you do?" she asked, lifting her gaze at Luke's angry face.

He turned his head slowly, his gaze warming as it lingered on her. "Nothing," he said after a moment's silence.

"Nothing!" Merry gaped in disbelief. "She might have been trying to murder your grandfather, your own flesh and blood, and you'll do nothing?"

"Merry, listen." He reached for her, taking hold of both her arms and turning her to face him. "Henry was distressed at the news of our marriage, having heard it first from his cousin, you know that."

She nodded slowly, bracing herself for a crushing blow. What was about to come from Luke's mouth had the power to catapult her into misery or free her from despair.

"He was sore displeased when he spoke with me today, but I managed to talk him into reason."

Merry swallowed hard. *Reason?* "What did you say?" she asked, her hope nudging upward.

"It doesn't matter now. What matters," he added, his voice becoming low and urgent, "is that he's willing to accept our marriage. He gave me his word, Merry."

Blood roared in her ears, like the surf rushing onto the shores of happiness. "Then you . . ." she wanted to ask what Luke intended now, but her throat closed up with the sudden urge to weep. Until that moment she hadn't realized the depth of her anxiety. Relief crashed over her. She threw her arms around him and promptly burst into tears.

"Ah, *Jesu,* don't cry," he gently begged. "Hush now, Merry. Did you think I would let Henry tell me what to do?" He slid his palms up and down her back. "I told you, no one could force an annulment on us. I would never let that happen. Never." His words were a balm to her soul. She wished he had told her so earlier.

Mastering her emotions, Merry pulled away, panged with sudden misgivings. "Might the prince yet refuse to grant you Arundel? Might he, out of spite?" she asked, wiping at her tears.

Thoughts shifted behind Luke's eyes, and he swiftly concealed them, looking down. He took her hands in his, brought them to his lips and kissed them one at a time, with a tenderness that made her heart melt. "It won't come to that," he promised. "He gave me his word."

Her first reaction was that of relief. Luke clearly believed in Henry's word. On the heels of her relief came belated self-pity. Luke could have told her he'd rather have Merry for a wife than Arundel for a home, only he hadn't. 'Twas only when he had both that he seemed satisfied.

Perhaps she expected too much. Passing on his grandfather's title was his life's ambition. She could not compete with such dedication, nor should she want to. She buried her selfish thoughts once and for all.

"Merry." Luke recaptured her attention as he slid his palm over her shoulders. He caressed her skin just above her neckline, a simple caress that made her shudder with need. "Come back to my bed," he added, his voice a rough whisper. "We are husband and wife. No one can take that from us." His fingers glided up the column of her neck and sank into her hair. Cradling the back of her head, he gave her a moment to deny him if she wished. Not a word came from her lips. With a brief smile, he lowered his head and kissed her.

Merry held perfectly still, her senses focused on the lips fitted warmly over hers. *No words of love,* she noted with regret. And yet he kissed her so tenderly, with such single-mindedness that there was no question he desired her. He pulled her closer, gathering her gently, molding her to him with hands that cherished her. This was the Luke she'd known at Iversly.

A fresh wave of tears stung her eyes. His kiss deepened, as if to claim her very soul. She kissed him back with all the love she'd held in store for days, for weeks, for months. Feeling him shudder, she gloried at the effect she had on him. He turned fiercely hard against her belly, making her melt with longing.

"Sweet Merry," he breathed, breaking away to rain hot kisses on her neck. His hands went behind her, fumbling with the stays that held her gown in place. A moment later, it slid from her shoulders to pool about her hips. She wore nothing beneath, having leapt from bed earlier to tend to the earl.

With an appreciative murmur, Luke admired her in the candlelight. Because of her pregnancy, her breasts had grown fuller and rounder. He cupped them reverently. "Merry, my wife," he murmured, his voice rough with desire, "I think you the most beautiful woman in the world." He looked into her eyes, convincing her of his sincerity.

The compliment amazed her. She, beautiful? With her shocking hair and freckled nose? Yet he seemed so sincere, she couldn't help but believe him. "Luke le Noir," she replied with utmost certainty, "I know you to be the world's handsomest man." Her throat tightened as the added confession forced its way free. "And I have loved you," she admitted, "since the day you plucked me from the fire."

His look of stunned surprise was worth the worry her confession cost her. "Is that why you nearly skewered me?" he
asked her, lightening the solemn moment with dry humor. "The
day I rescued you?"

She laughed despite herself. "I was afraid," she explained.

He bent his face closer, his humor usurped by more pressing
desires. "Are you afraid now?" he whispered, his lips scant
inches from her own.

*Yes,* said her heart. "Nay," said her tongue.

He claimed her then, branding her with a kiss that seared her
to her toes. Merry clung to his broad shoulders, delirious with
the passion that coursed her veins. It was only a matter of time,
she assured herself, that he would put into words what his body
was telling her.


"GOD bless you, Majesty, for granting me your ear."

The woman throwing herself upon the dais steps in an attitude of abject servitude had the voice of a man. Out of curiosity more than interest, Henry lifted his gaze from his cluttered
desk and frowned down at her.

The woman had been introduced as Agnes, Prioress of
Mount Grace Priory, North Yorkshire. Henry had heard the
name so often in the weeks since his return from Normandy
that he finally agreed to see the woman, if only to spare himself
of hearing her name again. He could not imagine what an
eremite from the north of England would want of him.

Her hands, splayed atop the steps were large and powerful
with short, buffed nails. "Rise," said Henry, curious to see her
face. She did so, and he found himself looking at a long, narrow face with a beak for a nose and flat, gray eyes. She called
to mind a blackbird, a most annoying creature, in Henry's estimation. Blackbirds were wont to gather after the hunt, waiting
for the fat to be trimmed from the kill. "What is your complaint?" he snapped, eager to return to the piles of ledgers
awaiting him.

"Majesty, I have something that belongs to a captain who
leads your army, le Noir," said the woman, rousing his curiosity again.

He glanced up. "You mean the Phoenix?" he said. "You

have something that belongs to him?" It irritated him to think of Luke just now. He'd suffered Amalie's tirades for a dozen days straight.

*Have you done nothing yet to reprimand him?* she'd demanded just this morning.

*What can I do that will not offend the barons?* He'd given her his standard reply. *I tell you, cease fretting over Sir Luke and set your sights on another courtier.*

*Luke!* she'd scoffed. *I care not a fig for that Saracen bastard. 'Twas Arundel that I wanted. Am I not the cousin of a prince? What good does it do to be your kin if you cannot even give me a castle of my own?*

*I will,* he'd promised her. *Have patience.*

It irritated him beyond measure that Luke had laid him over a barrel, he nearly a king! And yet Henry depended on Luke more than he cared to admit. The Phoenix was a soldier at heart. His leadership stirred loyalty in the hearts of commoners and barons alike. Christ's toes, he'd saved Henry's life! How would it look to deny Luke's right to Arundel, to refuse the title to his heirs? It would cost him not only his finest vassal but would set the barons against him for years to come.

He was weary of Amalie's seething bitterness. He would gladly ship her back to Normandy or foist her on the next unsuspecting courtier. Yet she would have none of them. Her sights were set on Arundel.

The prioress shifted, reclaiming Henry's attention. Reaching under her voluminous robes, she produced a knee guard, the straps of which had been neatly girded. She leaned forward and placed it faceup on the dais so that it resembled a steel-backed turtle.

Henry looked down at the armor. It was marked with the insignia that Luke's blacksmith carved into all his armor: the outline of a bird, its wings flared wide. There was no mistaking it for anyone else's. "And what do you want in exchange for this item?" he inquired. Surely the prioress didn't think it worth anything.

"I have a complaint against le Noir," she answered, surprising him. "He vaulted the wall of my priory and abducted a witch who was condemned to burn at the stake, who was even then being cleansed by the flame."

Henry felt as if he'd been struck by lightning. *Impossible!* *Luke had done something wrong?* Trembling with eagerness, he commanded the woman to tell him everything. She repeated her tale, elaborating the details.

Certainty pulsed through the prince. The woman could not be lying—she was a nun. Aye, and he knew Luke had a habit of rescuing social outcasts, an eccentricity that Henry had overlooked for a good number of years. Yet if the Phoenix had entered a sanctuary by force, then his crime was a grave one.

By heaven, it was the answer to his prayers! "Describe this witch," he commanded, struck by a sudden thought. "What did she look like?"

"Her hair is red like the flames of hell for which she is destined. I have heard a rumor, Majesty, that he brought her south with him."

"And her name?" Henry prodded, careful not to jump to any conclusions.

"We called her Sister Mary Grace, but her given name was Merry, Merry of Heathersgill."

*Perfect!* The prince reeled away to hide his glee. Ah, God was good to him! He strode to the window, rubbing his hands together. Luke le Noir had married a heretic, a woman condemned to burn! He forced himself to see the heroism involved. *How noble.*

Yet there was little Henry could do to protect his vassal now. The matter fell squarely into the domain of the Church. He shook his head. 'Twas a lamentable shame the marriage would have to be annulled, the woman condemned. Of course, if the Church had condemned her, then no doubt she deserved her punishment.

The glory of it was that Luke, no matter how outraged, would have no reason to blame the crown for her demise. 'Twas strictly a matter of ecclesiastical concern. Henry's hands would remain unblemished, pristine!

With a chuckle in his chest, he looked out over the Thames, glinting coldly under a December sky. *'Tis good to be a sovereign ruler,* he reflected. Even God Himself seemed subservient to his will. "Where are you staying?" he asked the prioress over his shoulder.

"At the Convent in Whitefriars."

"We will be in touch with you," he promised, his mind already plotting busily. A detailed plan was, even then, forming in his head.

The prioress took her leave with a rustle of robes and a surprising lightness of step.

MERRY clung to Luke's hand, fearful of losing him in the crush of people vying to enter Westminster Abbey. The enormous stone structure loomed over them, darker than the clouds that smothered the smoky sky. Folk from every walk of life thronged the abbey steps in the hopes of witnessing Henry's coronation. However, only nobles and those in positions of authority were admitted through the heavy wooden doors, guarded by the king's personal soldiers.

There would be no mistaking Luke for anything but a peer of the realm today, Merry considered, glancing at him sidelong, as he guided them through the crowd. In lieu of armor, he wore a long black tunic, belted at the waist. A costume sword hung at his hip, its jeweled scabbard peeking out from beneath the hem of his cape. The great, golden cloak protected him from the interminable drizzle.

And yet, more than his attire, it was the set of Luke's shoulders and the steadiness of his gaze that bespoke of his authority. He'd sworn just this morning that he was eager to introduce her to his overlord. It was his sheer determination that allowed them to make any progress up the steps as the crowd jostled and blocked their way.

Merry longed for just a portion of Luke's confidence. Beneath her own cloak, she wore a wine-colored gown, sewn from so many bolts of silk that it had cost a small fortune. Cut with a high waist, it hid the slight protrusion of her belly while revealing the porcelain perfection of her neck and shoulders. To downplay the vivid hue of her hair, her long tresses had been coiled elaborately on the top of her head and fixed in place with mother-of-pearl combs. She wished now that she had covered her head with a headdress. She feared at any moment the combs might be plucked from her hair by the milling masses. Keeping as close to Luke as possible, she saw that they were making progress. The bells tolled terce overhead, telling her they were right on time.

"Excuse us. Let us pass, please," Luke called, causing merchants and beggars alike to give way before his presence. At last they reached the double doors of the abbey and the soldiers who guarded them stoically.

"My lord," bowed the soldier, recognizing Luke. He gave Merry a peculiar look, and uncertainty assailed her. Aye, she should have worn a barbette and kept her hair out of sight.

The door was unlocked for them, and Luke ushered Merry in. As she stepped into a hushed narthex, she was awed by the height of the soaring ceiling. Blessedly quiet and lit with multiple torches, the room offered reprieve from the damp and noisy crowd outside. Shaking the moisture off her cloak, Merry glanced back at Luke who palmed the guard a coin before joining her.

Through the open doorway before them came the harmonious chanting of monks. The coronation ceremony was just beginning. Anxiety assailed her anew. What if the new king took a disliking to her? What if he changed his mind about accepting their marriage?

As if sensing her disquiet, Luke paused before her and tilted her chin with a notched finger. "You're the brightest star in the sky," he assured her charmingly. The kiss he dropped on her lips chased away lingering doubts.

How she loved him! As he guided her toward the open doors, she reflected on how beautiful life had been in the two weeks since his return from Westminster. She had never been so happy before, not even in her idyllic childhood.

In the nave, which was festooned with more torches and candelabras than she had ever seen in one place, the brilliance chased the gloom from the high, narrow windows. The floor was packed with elegantly garbed lords and ladies, standing elbow to elbow as they strained to see the high altar. No doubt Henry was seated on the raised, ornamental dais, though Merry couldn't see him over the heads of the crowd. Luke paused at the door, looking for a place to stand where his wife might see.

A scuffling sound drew their attention to two monks who appeared from an alcove on the right and intercepted them. One of them was as broad as he was tall. "My Lord le Noir?" whispered the smaller man, his eyes shifting nervously to Merry.

Luke was just at the point of leading Merry into the crowd. "Aye, what is it?" he asked impatiently.

The monk glanced down at a parchment in his hand. "We have notice from his holiness the bishop of Westminster bidding us to collect your wife," said the man. "She is to come with us now."

Merry glanced at Luke in confusion. Darkness seemed to gather around him as he focused on the man more closely. "What business has the bishop with my lady?" he demanded. "She is here to meet the king."

"Th-this is an e-ecclesiastic matter and has nothing to do with the king." Daunted by Luke's demeanor, the man began to stutter. "Sh-she must come with us right away, order of my lord b-bishop."

Luke's grip on Merry's arm became bruising. His other hand sought the hilt of his sword. "She stays with me," he retorted evenly. "I will speak to the bishop in person the moment the coronation is complete."

"I'm afraid you have no choice," countered the cleric, with a spurt of bravado. "Boris here has orders to restrain her."

"Then I will draw my sword against him," Luke replied, his voice now thunderously quiet. Merry wondered if his costume sword could even harm the hulking Boris.

"Violence per-per-perpetrated on clerics is a crime punishable by death," reminded the rattled monk. "Would you make a scene here, my lord, with all your p-peers bearing witness?"

Luke glanced toward the crowd. Already a handful of noblemen and women were gawking at them, their attention drawn to the stir at the doorway. Luke took note of their interest, the muscles in his jaw leaping as he considered his options.

His eyes blazed with fury as he redirected his gaze at the smaller monk. "Tell me this was not arranged ahead of time," he accused. "Come, Merry, we're leaving." He swiveled abruptly, pulling Merry along with him.

"The guards have orders not to let you out, my lord," the monk cried out behind them. He and Boris chased them out into the narthex. "Do you attempt to flee with her then you will be judged a party to her crime!" the small man added.

"Stop, Luke!" Merry begged. Recalling the heavily armed guard outside the door, she was loath to put her husband in harm's way. "Let them take me," she whispered.

"Never, Merry!" he rounded on her, his expression fierce. "I'll not let them take you. You know what this means."

"Nay, we don't know yet." She turned back to the monk. "What is this crime you speak of?" she demanded, her voice breaking with tension. She was vaguely aware of a voice droning in Latin in the nave. The coronation was well under way.

"You are wanted for a witch, madam," the man countered, stiffly.

She took a quick step back. Nay, it couldn't be! She'd been telling herself that this was some harmless matter—a whim on the part of the bishop to meet her. She gave a choked denial as the implications crystallized. The past had caught up with her after all! She felt the blood drain from her cheeks.

The sound of Luke's sword ringing free of its scabbard brought her swiftly to her senses. "Don't!" she cried, urging him to put his sword down. He pulled her behind him, out of range of his blade. Boris stepped threateningly forward. "Stand aside, monk," Luke warned him, "or I'll skewer you." He edged toward an archway on their left, pulling Merry with him.

"Luke, please!" Merry begged. Tears began to blur her vision. Oh, God, this was more terrible than anything she had ever imagined! To save her now, Luke would have to wound the two monks, and the punishment for that crime was too severe. "Stop!" she begged. "You can do more for me by acting reasonably. Negotiation is your strength, Luke. Fighting them will only bring more trouble!"

He hesitated, glancing back at her stricken face.

"Please, my love," she added, a knot forming in her throat. "You can help me more with your words than with your sword. Put it down. Let me go." She came out from behind him.

To her added torment, she saw his brow furrow as the weight of his decision crushed him. He went white about the mouth. Very slowly, the tip of his sword descended. Then he flung an arm around her and kissed her temple fervently. "I'll do all that I can for you, Merry," he whispered roughly. "I won't let them hurt you."

She took comfort from his promise, embracing him one last

time before stepping free. Swiftly, so as not to make their parting any more painful, she surrendered herself to the monks, her
chin held high. "Take me now," she commanded. Every one of
her senses screamed for her to turn around, to run to Luke's
arms, to run to safety.

They gestured for her to precede them toward the alcove
from which they'd come.

With his heart in his throat, Luke watched Merry walk away
like a martyr. He could not fathom how quickly she'd been torn
from him. One minute he was eagerly awaiting his opportunity
to introduce her to the king, certain that Henry would remark
the traits in Merry that made her extraordinary; the next she was
seized by the bishop's men.

His heart struggled to keep beating. A sensation like nothing
he'd experienced in battle, no matter how grievous the loss,
twisted through him. Panic and confusion stormed his senses.
All the contentment he'd experienced in the last two weeks
drained through the gaping hole that she alone had filled.

What could he call out now that would give her comfort?
Dare he admit the words that he'd guarded close, scarcely
admitting them even to himself? All this time, he'd known the
truth, known the love that burned in his breast for her alone. Yet
he'd guarded the words close in order to shield himself from
vulnerability.

It wasn't himself he wished to protect now. If words of love
would comfort Merry in the hours to come, then they were
worth uttering. "Merry!" he called, causing her to glance back
at him. Her pain-filled eyes snatched the words easily from his
chest. "I love you, Merry!"

Her eyes flared with surprise and gratitude, even as her steps
faltered. Then Boris shoved her abruptly into a shadowed hallway, and she was gone.

# Chapter Eighteen

MERRY paced the length of her windowless cell. She could take six steps in one direction and five in the other before coming to a wall. Her comforts consisted of a pallet of straw, thankfully raised off the floor, a crude table, and a hole in the corner, reeking of waste and soiled straw.

Though she knew it to be late at night, she could not sleep for her emotional distress. Her stomach rumbled with hunger, in no way sated by the meager offerings of bread dipped in grease. Placing a hand over her belly, she wondered how her babe would live if they starved her any longer.

Though it was too dark to see more than the outline of her skirts, she feared her appearance was more in keeping with that of a witch than a lady. The gown she'd worn to Henry's coronation was filthy. One sleeve had been rent by the rough handling of a monk. The material was soiled and creased. The mother of pearl combs had been seized with the excuse that they were vanity. In their place, she wore a coif of brown homespun that hid her flame-colored plait from sight—a blasphemy against God, they'd said. She told herself it was for the best.

A priest—Father Bartholomew by name—had come to see her twice. He'd explained that his concern was for her mortal soul and that she was to make confession to him. Although he seemed to be telling the truth, Merry had kept silent in his company.

"I would like to help you, lady," he'd urged her on his last visit. "But I cannot, not if you won't speak to me."

"How do I know this is not a trap? Bring my husband to me, and I will speak with you then," she'd demanded.

He'd left without a word, giving her no hope that he would contact Luke.

*Luke!* She felt as though her very bones were hollow without him. Where had he been? Why hadn't he come to visit her yet?

To comfort herself, she recalled the look on his face when the monks had led her away. His confession of love had kept her hopeful for a while. Yet, as the days passed without word from him, her hopes turned brittle and crumbled to dust.

Though this matter was made to appear an ecclesiastic one, Merry sensed it was more political than not. The king had given Luke his word that he wouldn't seek to annul their marriage. He must have known he wouldn't have to. He must have known she was wanted by the Church, an entity Luke was powerless to influence. His might was purely political; he held no sway over the religious leaders.

Exhausted by the weight of her burden, Merry sank onto her pallet, drawing her feet up for warmth. Did Luke even know a new trial was being set? Even now, witnesses were being sought and brought to London. She prayed her sisters would be among them. What would she give for Clarise and Kyndra's comfort!

If only she could wake and find that it was all over! Yet there was no solace even in that, for there was every chance she would be found a heretic a second time. Father Bartholomew had warned her that the sentence would likely be hanging.

The crunch of feet outside her door brought her head up swiftly. She did not trust the monk who brought her bread by day.

With trepidation, she listened to the scrape of a key in the lock. The breath froze in her lungs.

As the door gave a moan, Merry's eyes, already adjusted to the dark, told her she was looking at Father Bartholomew. She released the breath she held. Yet why would he visit her now?

"My child," he said softly. "Are you awake?"

"Yes, Father," she answered, catching a glimpse of another man behind him.

The priest stepped into her cell, and so did his companion. Merry's heart tripped over itself in its haste to beat. It couldn't be Luke, yet the second man was of equal height and breadth as Luke, and his presence gave reason for the priest's visitation.

The cell door closed with a muffled thud. "Merry!" cried the shadowed figure.

With a smothered shout, she scrambled off her pallet and into his arms. It was Luke! Oh, what a miracle! Surely she was dreaming! Within the circle of his arms she found sanctuary at last.

He returned her embrace fiercely, nearly crushing her brittle bones. "Merry!" he whispered raggedly, "I have been trying to see you every day, but they've refused me." He cupped her face, holding it still as he sought her features in the dark. "Have they been treating you well? How's the babe?"

She had lost the capacity to speak. With a nod of her head to signify that the babe still clung to life, she wept in silence. He clasped her to him, stroking her back to comfort her. "My God, she's thin!" he muttered to the priest. "Why haven't they been feeding her?"

"I'll look into the matter," Bartholomew promised. "We haven't much time," he added nervously.

"Bartholomew has risked much by letting me in to see you, Merry," Luke explained, setting her slightly away from him. "Swear to me that you will put your faith in him. He is doing his best for you, as am I." He squeezed her arms earnestly. "Not everyone in the coming trial is convinced of your crime. Bishop Tousaint knows me well. He trusts my testimony and will let me speak on your behalf. We have gathered witnesses to discredit those who would testify against you, including the prioress of Mount Grace."

"Not her!" Merry cried in dismay.

"Don't fret about her overmuch," Luke assured her. "Her testimony is the easiest to discredit. Not only did she fail to notify the Holy See of your last trial, she did not call upon an impartial jury of good men."

"This time the jury is impartial," added the priest. "I have helped to collect the *bons hommes* myself. The seven men are above the influence of bribery. Your chances are good. You must take heart, lady."

"Now promise me you will confide in Father Bartholomew," Luke urged her. "To prove you innocent, he must know what kinds of allegations are likely to be brought against you. But you have to understand that he can't openly defend you. Instead, he will pose questions that suggest your innocence."

"Then I won't be allowed to speak," she guessed. It had been the same at her other trial.

"Only in answer to a question." He gave her a reassuring smile, one that nonetheless betrayed his fear for her.

"Let us be on our way," urged the priest. "All will be ruined if we are caught here tonight."

Luke hesitated. "I'd like to stay with my wife awhile, Father. If I am discovered, I will not reveal your part in helping me."

The priest answered the request with dubious silence. Merry's heart leapt with joy. Oh, for a moment alone with Luke. Already, she could feel the warmth seeping back into her limbs. "Do not stay long," Bartholomew finally cautioned. "It will not go well for either of you if you are caught."

Luke promised, and as the cell door closed behind the priest, he led Merry to her pallet, gathering her onto his lap. Luke cradled her in silence, his body a citadel against evil. She realized he had no more words of consolation to offer. "Have you seen the king?" she whispered.

His fingers flexed about her waist. "I have tried many times, sprite. He refuses to see me."

For the first time, she heard weariness and worry in his tone. "Perhaps you could send him a letter."

"To what end? He will deny any involvement. My only hope is to prove that Amalie was poisoning my grandfather. I have informants working for me, seeking evidence. If I had reason to sue the king's cousin, then Henry might be willing to strike an agreement."

"But you just said he holds little sway over my fate."

"He might do something if his image is at stake. I have yet to prove Amalie's perfidy, however."

Merry heaved a sigh. It seemed too far-fetched, too removed from her circumstances to become a likely solution. With defeat, she laid her head on Luke's shoulder. Images of their lovemaking, of those tender days before her arrest, flickered through her mind. What if this were the last time she would ever be held by him?

"Will you marry another when I am gone?" she asked.

"Hush," he commanded, tightening his hold. "You aren't going anywhere."

"I want you to be happy, Luke, to be lord of Arundel, to go on with your life."

She felt him shake his head.

"Your grandfather loved his second wife best. Did you know her?"

"Merry, cease this talk of death!"

She realized then she was distressing him. "I'm so hungry and faint, I don't know what I'm saying," she apologized.

"By God, they will feed you tomorrow!" he swore. She felt his muscles bunch beneath her. "How can they treat you so in your state?" he asked savagely.

"If I am made to hang," she interrupted, harking back to the subject she'd just sworn to desist, "surely they can wait until our babe is born? Surely the Church would not take the life of an innocent—"

"*You* are innocent, Merry," he cut in fiercely, capturing her face between trembling hands. "You will not be made to hang, I swear it!"

"You mustn't swear!" she cautioned, seeing a glimmer of tears in his eyes, even in the dark. " 'Tis not within your powers to determine if I will or won't. You have made my life worthwhile," she added, sinking her fingers into his short, thick hair. "You said that you love me," she marveled aloud. "Will you tell me again, so that I may know I did not dream it?"

She heard a sob in his chest as he rasped, "I do love you. By Christ, I would not want to live without you!" He clutched her close, then, saying nothing more. Putting fears into words made them somehow more likely. Silence was better.

Moments later, he shifted, lowering Merry onto the pallet where he came down alongside her. "Sleep now, my love," he encouraged. As he draped a tattered blanket over her, she was reminded of the nights they had slept outdoors on their way to West Sussex. She had feared, then, that Luke might put her aside. How humbling to learn of his desperation to save her now. Truly, she did not deserve him.

"I love you, Luke," she whispered, yielding to her exhaustion, to the sweet luxury of his heat. With his strong arms about her, her pulse slowed to a restful beat, and her thoughts merged, then blended to naught.

LUKE stared into the ale at the bottom of his mug. His vision swam, not so much from the quantity of drink he'd imbibed, but from exhaustion. He had spent another two days playing cat and mouse with Henry's guards. But they were ever on the alert for him, and with their superior numbers, they managed to keep him at bay, though not without injury to themselves, for he had drawn his sword on the last occasion.

Phillip and Erin had begged him to storm the abbey and whisk Merry away. Yet stealing Merry from yet another house of God was not the answer to her dilemma—at least not yet. Not while hope for righteousness remained.

He applied himself to securing her innocence, instead. Visiting a number of nobles who were close to the king, he'd explained Merry's circumstances and persuaded them to pressure Henry. He'd sought the council of various abbots and priests. He was even granted a ten-minute audience with the bishop of Westminster.

As he'd told Merry, Bishop Tousaint was a reasonable man. He had listened to Luke's tale of a woman wrongfully condemned. He'd promised to give the matter thorough scrutiny, assuring Luke that a sentence of heresy was not a foregone conclusion. He'd generously agreed to let Luke testify on his wife's behalf. Then he'd soundly dismissed him, ordering him not to show his face until the trial.

Luke turned his energies toward exposing Amalie. His informants, two servants who worked in the palace, had come up empty-handed in their search of her quarters. They'd discovered no suspicious herbs or writings in her possession. Luke had come to an impasse. Without proof, there was nothing he could use to bend Henry's arm. Merry would have to save herself.

With the trial steadily approaching, he'd returned to Arundel

to look in on his grandfather, collect some much needed clothing, and money to tide him over throughout the trial. After this
night, he would be staying in London, at the home of a friend.

Seeking comfort in a deep mug of ale, Luke found it did little to numb his devastation. There had been many times in his
military past that, despite his efforts to negotiate peace, war was
inevitable. Unavoidable. He had tasted the bitter gall of defeat
before. Yet never had the matter been this personal, this close
to his heart. He had never blamed himself so bitterly for failing.
He had never felt so afraid, so useless, in his life.

Luke pushed to his feet. What time was it? Only a single
torch remained, illumining the stairwell that would take him
from Arundel's great hall to the bedchambers above. The servants had long since retired. Luke, too, should have slept, for
he had a long ride in the morning, followed by nerve-wracking
hours through which Merry would endure rigorous questioning.

Yet he'd known he would not be able to sleep for thinking
of her plight and lamenting his attempts to ease it. After supper,
he'd sent the children off to bed, unable to bear their long faces
and disillusioned eyes. He had failed even them. They could
not understand why, with all his vast resources of power and
wealth, he could not free Merry from the superstitious zealots
who held her.

Plodding up the stairs, he was hounded by the echo of his
footsteps. Arundel, with its cool gray walls and lofty ceilings,
struck him as empty. For all its beauty and grandeur, it was not
a home without Merry. Halfway up the steps, he stopped, struck
by the depth of his loss.

She was the source of Arundel's warmth. She was its hearth
fire. If something were to happen to her, he would not want to
live here, haunted by her ghost. Haunted by the aching emptiness he was already beginning to feel.

His own liege lord, Henry II, by that name, was responsible
for Merry's persecution. How could Luke ever pledge his
sword to him again? How could he accept Arundel when it had
cost him Merry's life?

He could not. He would not.

Without Merry, he wanted nothing to do with this place.
'Twas an empty consolation. It was Merry he wanted, vital and

alive. He would rather live the life of a mercenary, relying on his sword for income, than to live in Arundel alone.

In the dimly lit stairwell, Luke took a ragged breath. His knees gave way suddenly, and he sat heavily on the steps, doubled over by the pain in his chest. He pressed the heels of his palm against his eyes to keep the tears from coming.

*Ah, Merry!* He lamented. *Why must I realize now what you mean to me? I have failed you more than I have failed anyone. Please forgive me!*

He wiped the unaccustomed tears from his face and sniffed. And then, because he knew that lamentations would accomplish nothing, he pushed himself to his feet and continued up the stairs.

As his head cleared the second level, he spied a line of light shining at the base of his grandfather's door. Luke had visited the earl earlier that evening. He had found that, without Merry, the old man was once more lost to his illness. A light in his room could mean only one thing: he was suffering another one of his bouts.

Luke hurried down the hall to see if he could help. As he thrust open the door, the earl's manservant pivoted with a gasp. He'd been standing by the earl's bed, spooning a liquid into his mouth. His expression of guilt and dismay were so evident that Luke bore down on him, snatching the cup from his hands.

"What is this?" he demanded, peering at the milky contents.

"My lord's infusion," said the manservant, backing away from him. "L-lady Merry left instructions for me."

Luke gave the cup a sniff and recognized the bitter perfume of opium. "This isn't chamomile," he growled, masking his fury as he glanced at his grandfather. The old man had already slipped into a drugged sleep. With cold rage, Luke placed the cup on the earl's nightstand. He turned back to the manservant who was edging his way to the door.

Luke struck like the cobras of his native land. In the blink of an eye he grabbed Egbert by the scruff and slammed him against the wall. "At whose bidding do you poison my grandsire?" he thundered.

Egbert blanched and sputtered, unable to make a sound.

Luke slammed him against the wall a second time to jar his

memory. "Say it, man, and I won't hold you responsible. Keep silent and I'll kill you."

"The Lady Amalie!" blurted the manservant. By now a sweat had broken out on his brow.

"Why do you serve her?" Luke demanded. "Have you not served my grandfather for two score years?"

Guiltily, the man shook his head. "That were my brother," he admitted. "I was sent to replace him."

"Then you're the king's informant," Luke guessed, releasing the man so abruptly that he collapsed to the floor. "Stand up," he commanded, jerking him to his feet again. The moment he was standing, Luke plowed his fist into Egbert's stomach—nay, not Egbert, but his twin, by the look of him. The man doubled over, gasping for breath. "*That* was for saying my lady has a sharp tongue," Luke growled, finding great satisfaction in delivering the blow. He'd looked forward to this moment.

He waited again for the man to recover. Then he clamped a hand over his throat and pinned him to the wall. His cold fury had begun to thaw, causing his blood to flow freely. He welcomed its warmth and energy. Hope began to pulse in him once more. Perhaps this was not such a terrible discovery. Perhaps it would help him save Merry!

"What is your name?" he demanded.

"Nevil," gasped the man.

"Well, then, Nevil. Explain to me why Amalie still wants my grandsire dead? What could his death gain her now?"

The man stared back at him, wide-eyed. "She said he might recover and bear witness to the fact that he was poisoned," he replied. "In the beginning, the earl resisted."

"Did the king have anything to do with this?"

Nevil's small eyes darted wildly. "I don't believe so. 'Twas Lady Amalie that wanted him dead."

"Did she tell you why?"

"She said . . . when she became the marquess, she would grant me riches and a manor o' my own."

Luke tightened his hold threateningly. "If you swear to speak out against her, I will promise you just as much," he said. "If not, I will kill you."

The man began to whimper. "She will have me killed in any event," he cried, truly frightened.

Luke eased his hold. "You will remain safe in my protection," he promised. "Have you any proof other than your word that she meant to poison my grandfather?"

Nevil thought hard. "There is a . . . a bit of writing that she gave me, directions for brewing the poison."

"The page from my journal," Luke guessed. "Can you read and write, then?"

"Aye." He gave Luke a curious look.

"Then you will pen the king a missive yourself," Luke informed him. As in the second breath of battle, the hope of triumph exploded in his breast, giving him renewed strength. "You will tell Henry exactly what you have told me: that his cousin ordered you to poison the earl of Arundel. Moreover, I am apprised of the plot and together we will report Lady Amalie to the authorities."

The manservant swallowed nervously, his Adam's apple bobbing. "Do you mean to blackmail the king, lord?" he squeaked.

"I have nothing to lose," Luke countered.

By the man's expression, it was clear he thought otherwise. He could not know what Luke had already realized: that Arundel was an empty prize without his bride. That life itself meant nothing without her.

"Come," he ordered, thrusting Nevil before him out into the corridor. He marched him to his own room, resisting the urge to run. This was just the hidden weapon he required to best his king. But was it enough to procure Merry's freedom?

Finding a flint and taper, Luke lit the candle on his desk and pressed the manservant into the chair. He laid a sheaf of parchment before him and unstopped the inkwell. "Now write," he said, extending him the quill.

Fingers shaking, Nevil took the quill. Luke paced the chamber, listening to the man's hesitant scratches. He longed to dictate the letter himself, but it was crucial that the missive rouse Henry's anxiety. It was equally important that the king recognize it as authentic and not a hoax.

At last, the hand at work stilled. " 'Tis done," said Nevil.

Bending over his shoulder, Luke read what he had written. It dismayed him to think that Merry's future could rest upon such faint, spidery scrawl. Nonetheless he was certain its contents would rouse Henry's concern. If delivered at dawn, then by afternoon the same day, the king might be willing to work a deal.

"Take yourself to bed," Luke ordered the man. "Do not think to leave Arundel or you will lose your life. The guards at the gate will not hesitate to run you down."

"Aye, s-sir," answered the man, bowing as he backed out of the door and fled.

With swift and precise movements, Luke rolled the parchment into a tube and secured it. After a short rest, he would leave Arundel before dawn and bear the letter straight to Westminster. Merry's trial would occupy the rest of the morning. Pray God he would have acted in time to affect its outcome.

With a long, shaky breath, Luke closed his eyes in a moment of silence. He was not a devoutly religious man. Yet at this point he would have sold his soul to ensure Merry's freedom. *Please, God,* he prayed. *Keep her safe long enough for Henry to come to his senses.*

# Chapter Nineteen

❧

"THE time has come, lady," growled the monk.

Merry staggered to her feet and lurched to the door. It was odd that she had eaten nothing yet felt as though she'd swallowed a stone. Luke's promise of food had not been realized. Since his visit three days ago, she'd subsisted on the daily offering of bread and watered ale.

"Hold your hands out," the monk commanded.

By the evil glint in his eyes, it was clear he hoped she would resist him. She offered her hands to him meekly, and he wound coarse rope around them, pulling it taut until she winced. Satisfied, he tugged her out of the cell.

She was led along a maze of stone corridors, blinded by sunlight each time she passed a crossloop. At last, they came to a set of double doors. The monk threw the doors wide, and the noise inside dimmed to a curious buzzing. Merry was thrust into a chamber filled with people. They lined the benches of what appeared to be a refectory hall. Thankfully, thick leaded glass muted the sunlight at the windows, dappling the floor and walls with colored flecks.

*Luke must be here!* she thought, her pulse quickening. She scanned the many faces, yet every one of them was unfamiliar. Clerics, scholars, and nobles alike had gathered at this well-publicized trial to learn the fate of the Phoenix's bride. But there was no sign of Luke nor of her sisters.

At the front of the room stood a dais, draped in vermilion silk. A cross hung ponderously upon the wall behind it. Directly below the cross, on a throne that surely rivaled the king's, sat an austere, bald man gazing down at her. He wore a stole proclaiming him to be a cleric of some stature. *Bishop Tousaint,* she decided.

To the right of the dais was a table where a scribe was busy scribbling. Behind him sat seven men, each of them dressed in robes, though they did not bear the look of clerics. These, she realized, were the *bons hommes,* laymen respected by the community. These would be the jurors.

She was led to a bench to the left of the bishop, likewise facing the crowd. As the monk pressed her into her seat, the volume in the chamber rose, prompting the bishop to hold up a hand for silence. "This session is called to order," he announced. "Will the charges against the accused please be read?"

An expectant hush fell over the chamber.

The scribe at the table rose and read from a scroll. "For the propagation of curses and spells, for the unnatural application of herbs under the guise of healing, for the attempt to poison a member of a holy order, for bringing a dead horse back to life, for exciting the lust of innocent men, for causing injury and loss of crops, the Church accuses Lady Merry le Noir of malefaction and heresy."

A crowd murmured their amazement. Scanning the shadowed faces of the audience, Merry searched for Luke. Where was he? She felt adrift at sea, lost without him.

"How do you plead to these charges?" the bishop demanded, dragging her attention back to him.

She looked at the *bons hommes,* seated behind the scribe, and then at the crowd. Was there no one to guide her through this? Then she caught the eye of Father Bartholomew sitting directly before her on the first row of benches. He gave her an encouraging nod, prompting her to say what he'd advised during their sessions together.

"Not guilty," she said, wishing her voice held more substance.

A Bible was thrust suddenly before her. "Place your hand upon the Holy Word," said a monk at the bishop's behest. "Do you swear on the four gospels that you will tell the truth throughout these proceedings?"

Merry swore it.

"Summon the first witness," commanded the bishop. "Father Moreau, you may commence the questioning."

The priest next to Bartholomew leapt to his feet, and Merry's fragile hopes disintegrated. The man was a stranger. His little eyes burned with religious zeal. She sensed he would do his best to cast her in the ugliest light possible.

"The court calls Friar Matthew of Heathersgill," he said with relish.

Merry's mouth went dry as the parish priest of Heathersgill was brought before her. So, they intended to start at the beginning. The prosecution had been thorough in their research.

As the parish priest of Heathersgill shuffled into the open space before the dais, he cast an uncomfortable glance at Merry and looked away.

"State your name for the court," Father Moreau exhorted after swearing him in. "How long have you known the accused?" he added.

"Since the day she was born," admitted the friar.

"Can you tell us what she was like as a child?"

Matthew looked down at his feet. "She was a model child until her father was slain by the Scot who then married her mother."

"And then?" prompted Moreau.

A hint of color stained the friar's cheeks. "Then she lived in the hills with the cunningwoman, Sarah, learning the properties of herbs for healing."

"Did she use herbs solely for healing?" Moreau continued.

The friar hesitated. "Not always," he reluctantly admitted. "On occasion, in order to . . . to distance the men from her, she would curse them and sicken them. She carried a number of powders, which she threw at the youths who teased her. But you should understand that these men were soldiers, Scots that her stepfather—"

"Tell us what happened to the cunningwoman who tutored her in the herbal arts," interrupted Moreau.

At last the friar lifted his solemn gaze to Merry. She sensed him apologizing in advance for what he would have to say. "Sarah was drowned for a witch," he admitted.

A murmur rippled over the throng.

"And was this lady also thought a witch?" Moreau asked, gesturing to Merry.

The friar looked away. "She was only a child," he equivocated.

"Answer the question," exhorted the interrogator.

"Some folk at Heathersgill were set against her," he admitted. A flash of defiance entered his eyes as he lifted them to the bishop. "But she was just a child whose father had been slain before her eyes. She had good reason to be bitter—"

"So you suggested she be taken to the priory of Mount Grace, did you not?" interrupted Moreau.

The friar nodded.

"Where she was to turn her heart toward godly devotion," continued Moreau. "Thank you for your testimony," he added, gesturing for the friar to resume his seat. "The court calls the next witness. Mother Agnes of Mount Grace, kindly step forward."

Nausea swept through Merry as the prioress shouldered her way to the front of the room. The triumphant look she cast at Merry's bench drove a chill straight through Merry's spine. It was the same expression she'd worn when delivering her verdict at Mount Grace several months ago.

After swearing her in, the priest enjoined the prioress to tell the jury of her experience with Merry.

The prioress struck a pious pose. "I am the Prioress of Mount Grace," she said, softening her tone artificially. "This girl first came to my priory three years past. Knowing her history and the trouble she had engendered using herbs, I refused to allow her in the priory's garden."

The mother went on to describe in detail the difficulty Merry had displayed in memorizing the prayers and attending devotions. "Despite my precautions and gentle guidance, it was soon apparent I was wasting my breath. Mary Grace, as we called her then, was oft found digging in the gardens. The other sisters came to me and admitted they had seen her scaling the priory's wall *at night*," she tacked on dramatically. "It was then that I realized she had been led astray by dark forces. No doubt she was slipping over the walls to copulate with the devil himself. I tried to counsel her, but her defiance only worsened.

"One day, I discovered her secret herbal in one of the priory's storerooms, and I removed the collection of vile substances she had brewed. In retribution, she poisoned me, meaning to kill me. Three days and nights I did hover on the brink of death. Through piety and prayer, I survived her spell."

Father Moreau addressed his first words to Merry. "Is it true you tried to poison a woman of holy orders?", he demanded with sincere outrage.

Merry could not deny it. "My intent was to punish her for whipping a novice to death," she admitted, hoping the man would ask what she meant.

"Have you not read that vengeance belongs to God Almighty?" he said instead, his eyes alight with righteousness.

Merry waited for the murmuring to die down. "If that is so," she steadily replied, "then why am I here?"

Chuckles of approval rippled away from her.

Moreau tried again. "Has the prioress given accurate summary of your crimes or not, Lady le Noir?"

To her alarm, the priest's ears began to shift from side to side. She blinked, trying to clear her vision. "Mother Agnes has lied on several accounts," she answered.

"You call me a liar—you who thrive by deceit?" the mother railed, her poise slipping.

The priest looked startled by her sudden volume. "Only the bishop and I may address the accused," he reminded her. He turned back to Merry. "How has the prioress lied?" he demanded.

"She said I left the priory to copulate with the devil. In fact, I went to find herbs, specifically Saint-John's-wort, which grows in wooded copses."

"Wherefore would you require Saint-John's-wort?" he predictably asked.

"To make an ointment soothing to cuts and gashes, such as those caused by a whip. I did not sicken Agnes for destroying my herbal," Merry added. "I punished her for beating to death a novice who had done nothing more sinful than speak aloud at the supper table."

A thoughtful silence descended over the refectory.

"She lies!" shrieked the prioress, her tone bearing no resemblance to the gentle piety she had shown before. She turned to address the bishop. "She's a heretic. She'll say anything to save herself from purification. I am the prioress of Mount Grace. I will not suffer to be maligned by a godless girl."

"Calm yourself, prioress," urged the bishop, frowning at her fiercely. "Bring up the next witness," he advised Moreau.

Muttering to herself, the prioress stormed back to her bench, and the Abbot of Jervaulx, Agnes's cohort, was called forward.

In the aftermath of that excitement, Merry grew alarmingly light-headed. She could scarcely focus on the little man who had witnessed her first trial and condemned her along with Agnes. If anyone were to corroborate the mother's story it was he.

"Then you believe the accused intended to kill her victim?"

Merry realized she had lost track of the conversation. Panic rose up in her. It was vital that her mind stay sharp, and yet it seemed a fog was seeping into her brain, detaching her from her own thoughts.

"It was clear she meant the prioress to die," the abbot answered earnestly. "I saw the girl's herbal for myself. 'Twas filled with vials and ointments, salves and powders. I helped my colleague to destroy them all."

"In your mind, is there any question that this woman is a witch?"

"Objection," the bishop interrupted, testily. "I'm not interested in this man's opinion. He is here to bear witness to facts."

Merry threw the bishop a grateful look.

"Have you any testimony to offer that has not yet been said?" Moreau rephrased.

The Abbot of Jervaulx put his fingertips to his lips, his eyes shining with zeal. "Aye, under sworn oath, she said that she had given the devil dominion over her."

The crowd responded with gasps.

Moreau turned to her eagerly. "Lady le Noir," he said, "let me remind you that you have sworn under oath. Did you testify at one time that the devil had dominion over you?"

Merry's heart beat faster. "At one time I did say so," she replied, licking her dry lips. "But I was mistaken."

"You mean you lied under oath?" he countered, pouncing like a ferret. "How can we believe your testimony now?"

"I did not lie," Merry said, cutting him short. "I believed my stepfather was the devil, and for a brief time in my life he had dominion over me. But now he is dead, and the devil is said to be immortal."

A confused silence followed her words. It seemed no one had followed her logic, including Father Moreau. He turned back to the abbot. "Is there anything else you would share with the jury?" he inquired. "Something else that was discussed at her previous trial?"

"Objection," interrupted the bishop sternly. "There is to be no mention of a previous trial, Father Moreau. I thought I made that quite clear."

"Apologies, excellency. My mistake." Moreau clasped his hands together in a posture of repentance.

"Proceed," said the bishop darkly.

"Have you any more insight into the character of the accused?" Moreau asked the abbot.

"She does bear the devil's mark upon her backside," the abbot added with a flush of excitement. "There is no mistaking its distinctive shape."

*Nay, not that!* Merry looked down at her hands in dread. The eager murmurs of the crowd washed over. She saw that her knuckles shone white through her fair skin.

"Permission to have the mark displayed as evidence, your grace," Moreau petitioned the bishop.

Merry held her breath. She had already told Bartholomew how she'd been forced at her previous trial to hike up her skirts and reveal her birthmark to her persecutors. If she were forced to endure the same humiliation now, she would rather die. Bartholomew knew it, only he was sitting silently on the bench in front of her.

"Your holiness, first another witness from the priory."

Merry glanced up sharply. It was Bartholomew, standing now and addressing the bishop. He must have read her mind! Relief made her weak. Why had he waited until now to act?

The bishop glowered at him. "I've heard enough witnesses from the priory. What will one more contribute?"

"A second witness to the mark would make a display unnecessary," Bartholomew reasoned.

"But there are no other witnesses from Mount Grace," Moreau interjected.

"I took the liberty," Bartholomew admitted, with an apologetic smile. "Your grace?" He turned back to the bishop.

Tousaint gave him a probing look. "Proceed with the questioning," he decided, nodding at Bartholomew.

Merry's heart beat faster. She'd been warned that Bartholomew could not reveal his sympathies toward her. If he meant to discredit the previous testimonies, he would have to be subtle.

Bartholomew called forth Sister Magdalena of Saint Frideswide's. With pleasure, Merry recognized her former roommate, a soft-spoken girl who had been a novice at Mount Grace until last winter.

After swearing to tell the truth, Magdalena introduced herself as a nun who'd recently transferred to Saint Frideswide's.

"Sister, is it true that the accused has a mark on her backside?" Father Bartholomew began.

Magdalena's hazel eyes touched sympathetically on Merry. "She has a brithmark," the nun admitted reluctantly.

"What sort of birthmark?" Bartholomew pressed.

"It looks like a crescent moon," the nun said, gazing at the floor. " 'Tis rather pretty, actually," she added unnecessarily.

"Sister, have you a birthmark?"

Magdalena raised startled eyes at the priest. "N-nay," she said, looking frightened.

"Have you any marks on your back?" Bartholomew persisted.

A tense, little silence followed as the nun paled. "I do," she finally admitted. "I have several marks."

"What manner of marks are they if not birthmarks?" Bartholomew looked puzzled.

"Father, where is this line of questioning leading?" the bishop interrupted, mystified.

"Her answer will be relevant, your grace," Bartholomew assured him. "Please answer the question," he enjoined the girl. "What manner of marks are on your back?"

Sister Magdalena nodded slowly, as though finally understanding the reason for her torment. "Scars," she said simply.

"How did you come by them?" Bartholomew gently inquired.

The young nun's gaze strayed toward the prioress of Mount Grace, sitting like a raven on a nearby branch. "The prioress laid twenty lashes on my back," she whispered.

Benches groaned as the audience leaned forward to catch her answer.

"Such stern punishment," Bartholomew reflected. "What was your crime?"

The nun looked down at her twisted hands. "I misspoke the prayers at compline. I was weary, and I recited them incorrectly, so she beat me. 'Twas Mary Grace who tended my wounds with a salve." She lifted grateful eyes at Merry. "I might have died of fever had she not cared for me so kindly."

"I see," said Bartholomew, casting a look of chagrin at Father Moreau. "I am through with this witness, your grace," he told the bishop solemnly.

Amazed by his acting ability, Merry tried not to look at him as he resumed his seat. She looked down at her hands again, sending him a silent message of thanks. As Luke had reassured her, the prioress's testimony had clearly been cast in doubt. Hope was a chrysalis.

"Proceed with the questioning," ordered the bishop.

Moreau sprang to his feet. "Lady le Noir," he began, pacing back and forth before her, "on the basis of the testimony we have heard, you were thought a witch even before you entered Mount Grace Priory. Then at Mount Grace, despite the attempts of the prioress to wean you away from them, you continued to dabble with herbs. Will you tell the court why that was so?"

Merry fixed her gaze on the dark heads of the audience. Moreau's pacing made it difficult to order her thoughts. "Herbs are not evil, Father. They are heaven's gift to mortals, a means to soothe our physical ills." Those were words that Sarah had canted to her many times.

"Then you admit to leaving the confines of the priory at night?" Moreau prompted.

"I openly admit it. The mother forbade me to enter the gardens. I had to go elsewhere to find what I needed."

"Such as poisons?" he interrupted. "Did the poison you used against the prioress grow within the convent or outside its walls?"

Merry took several deep breaths. "Outside," she said shortly.

"And what is the name of that poison?"

"Henbane." Her throat was so parched with thirst that her voice cracked.

"How much is required to kill a living soul?"

"Clearly more than two leaves, which is what I used."

"How did you know to use only two leaves?" he pressed.

"There is a mathematical formula for such things."

"Was it the witch, Sarah, who taught you the formula?"

"She wasn't a witch. She was a gentle healer."

"Answer the question," the priest exhorted. He resumed his pacing, then, swimming in and out of Merry's focus.

"Sarah taught me the antidote. The formula I learned myself."

"And why would a girl experiment with poisons?"

Merry hesitated, but having sworn on the gospels to tell the truth, she did so. "To avenge the man who killed my father and raped my mother," she answered, her voice strained.

"Vengeance is the Lord's," Moreau shot back. "But then you confessed to giving the devil dominion over you."

Merry opened her mouth to set him straight, but he cut her short, calling Owen of Ailswyth and Donald of Tees forward to bear testimony.

Stomach cramping, Merry recognized the unkempt men stepping forward as the mercenaries who had disappeared with Cullin's body, rather than leave it to the raptors. *Worse and worse,* she thought. They would say anything to avenge their friend's death.

With a great black dread rising up in her, she braced herself to face more questioning. Already she had withstood about all that she could endure. *Oh God, get me through this,* she prayed, feeling the tremors that racked her body. *Where is Luke? I need him now!*

Again, she scanned the darkened faces for any sign of him. Scooting slightly to her left, she was able to see around a column, which hitherto had blocked her view.

It was then that she saw him.

He sat in the fifth row, his dark head clearly visible above the others. As their eyes met, pleasure illumined his face. He'd clearly been as frustrated not to see her as she had been not to see him. *Here I am,* his burning gaze conveyed. *I am as close as your heart.*

Merry held his gaze, letting his love sustain her. While nothing could ease her dread, Luke's presence eased the shivering that shook her limbs. She knew he had done everything within his power to affect the outcome of the trial. Before today, he had saved her from circumstances equally as precarious. She pinned her faith on that simple truth. He would save her again.

The witnesses were being asked to describe the manner in which Merry came among the soldiers. She listened to them, hearing their voices as if from a distance. She felt adrift from her environment, separated by a growing mist.

"It were clear she were a witch from the first," said Owen, scratching his chest. "She owned a black cat what followed her where'er she went. The moon till then had been full an' round, but the night we took her to her home, the moon stayed hid . . ." His voice faded completely for a moment, then swelled in volume, ". . . heard it scream as it fell. No animal could've survived such a fall, yet there she was the next day sitting astride it, with the horse bearing naught but a limp. She brought it back to life, she did."

"An' then," continued Owen's companion, "it were one bad thing after another. On the night of our arrival at Iversly, the baron sickened and was carried to his chamber. . . ." Donald of Tees became scarcely audible. ". . . She came up on the wall where we were busy at work . . . the cat brushed up against his leg . . . she put Cullin under a spell . . . he was inflamed wi' lust fer the witch . . . grabbed her one night . . . she had asked fer it . . ."

A buzzing noise replaced the sound of muffled voices. The refectory began to turn, first slowly and then more swiftly, whirling around the witnesses who spouted their tales of superstition to a riveted audience.

Merry fought to orient herself. She could not afford to faint now. She had to defend herself from these ignorant fools. But the flecks of colored light were bleeding one into the other, so that the room turned a murky gray. As the refectory grew dimmer, the voices became more distant. She felt herself falling but could not break her fall with her hands tied. The last thing she felt was her skull hitting the hard floor.

# *Chapter Twenty*

"MERRY!" Luke surged to his feet in horror.

The thud of her head against the stone flagging echoed in the sudden silence. She'd fallen with enough force to loosen the coif she wore, so that everyone was treated to a glimpse of her flame-red plait.

All Luke could think was that she'd killed herself or dislodged the babe in her womb. He tripped over the benches before him, desperate to reach her. But he was not the only one. Nearly every member of the audience had risen from their seats to rush forward, crowding around her.

Luke elbowed his way through them, not caring whom he jostled or how hard.

"She's lapsed into a trance!" said someone before him. "Wait'n see if the devil makes her talk now."

Furious with the comment, Luke peeled away a few more bystanders and arrived at Merry's side. He dropped to one knee, alarmed by the ashen color of her face. "Get back!" he commanded as people pressured him, making the air thick. "She needs to breathe. Move away!"

They obeyed, but only minimally. "Merry!" Luke cradled her head to discover the extent of her injury. A knot had begun to swell, but thankfully her skull was intact. By the steady pulse at the base of her neck, he could tell that her heart was beating rhythmically. *And what of the babe?* he wondered, sliding a hand to her belly.

He saw, as though detached from himself, that his fingers were shaking. Worry, helplessness, and lack of sleep had left him out of sorts this morning. From the corner of his eye, he saw someone nudge Merry's thigh with the toe of his boot, perhaps hoping to rouse the demon within her.

*That's it.* Luke laid Merry's head carefully on the floor and sprang to his feet. He fully intended to pick up the guilty man and hurl him across the room. But then he recognized the narrow-faced scribe who'd scribbled down every word that had been uttered throughout the trial. "Apologize to the lady," he growled instead, "for touching her with your shoe."

The scribe paled and faltered backward.

Luke was vaguely aware that two monks were coming to collect their prisoner. Bartholomew had caught him by the elbow and was tugging him back. The bishop thundered over the crowd for all to retake their seats.

But Luke was focused on the pitiful creature who'd dared put his boot against his unconscious wife. He would kill the man if he did not apologize.

"Move aside. Out of the way." It was the ugly monk who guarded Merry's cell. He stepped around the scribe, blocking Luke's view of the man, and without any consideration for Merry's condition, hauled her up by the arms. The other monk reached for her feet.

Luke forgot the scribe. "Have a care!" he snarled, redirecting his fury. He stepped threateningly toward the monk, only to find Bartholomew in his path, his eyes flashing a warning. With a sharp breath, Luke reined himself in.

The second monk picked up Merry's feet more cautiously. Then the two conveyed her toward the door. Luke followed close behind, breathing down their necks. He was not so intent that he missed the whispered remarks of the crowd.

"Isn't that the Phoenix?"

"Aye, looks like the witch has him firmly under her spell."

Luke ignored the gossip. He held the doors for the monks to keep them from ramming Merry's hip into the door frame as they carried her from the refectory.

"Sir Luke, you cannot follow them." Bartholomew chased him halfway down the hall and jumped in front of him again.

"How can I trust those idiots not to drop her?" Luke demanded. Seeing the priest's solemn face, he lowered his tone. "I'm sorry," he added, searching for a shred of self-control. "Can you go after them? *Please!*"

"I will," Bartholomew promised. "In a moment."

Luke understood. The priest could not afford to show too much concern for the accused. He took a ragged breath, fighting for normalcy. Never had any event spun so far from his control.

"Tomorrow it will go better for her," Bartholomew promised, casting a nervous look about them. "I have taken the measures I mentioned earlier."

Luke nodded. He owed the priest already for casting the prioress's testimony into doubt. Nonetheless, the second string of witnesses had managed to depict Merry as a strange and vengeful creature. Owen and Donald's tales had stirred the imaginations of the crowd. Their absolute conviction that Merry was a witch was dangerously contagious. Perhaps it was a good thing she had fainted, putting an end to their testimony.

"You should rest," said Bartholomew, regarding Luke with fatherly concern.

"Nay, there's something I must do. Thank you," he added, putting a hand briefly on the man's shoulder. Then he stepped around him, heading toward the exit. His steps slowed as he recognized the threesome bustling in.

The Slayer of Helmesly had to duck to keep from hitting his head on the lintel. His wife, looking unusually unkempt in a practical traveling gown, hurried before him. The youngest sister, Kyndra, followed behind with her nephew, Chauncey, in her arms. They all spied Luke at once, giving him a silent inspection as they neared each other.

"We came as quickly as we could," said the Slayer, his deep voice resonating in the passageway. "I'm sorry we're late."

"Tell us what's happened," Lady Clarise demanded.

Luke apprised them of the circumstances, and, for a moment, all four of them stood in silence while people squeezed by them, speculating aloud that the witch would be made to hang.

"So what now?" Lady Clarise demanded, her face pale, her eyes flashing with determination.

"I'm going to see the king," Luke answered. "A certain matter has come to my notice. It may persuade Henry to act in Merry's behalf."

"Why have you waited until now!" Clarise demanded, her color returning. Her husband put a restraining hand on her forearm.

"Believe me, I have not rested since your sister was snatched away from me," Luke assured her. "I have spoken to the bishop, the priests, and all the barons living nearby."

Mumbling her apologies, she looked away from him. An uncomfortable moment divided them.

Luke suddenly realized they were uncertain of his allegiance to Merry. After all, he'd been forced to marry her; this would have been a convenient means to rid himself of an unwanted wife. "I would have you know that I love your sister every bit as much as you do," Luke startled himself by admitting. "I would move heaven and earth to see her acquitted, and I still mean to do all that I can."

To his surprise, Clarise smothered a cry and threw her arms around him in a sisterly embrace. To his added consternation, Kyndra did the same, and he found his chin drooled on by baby Chauncey who thought it might be edible.

"Oh, it pleases me to hear that!" Clarise told him, her countenance transformed from disapproving to radiantly accepting as she squeezed him close. "I knew you loved her! I knew 'twas not a mistake to ask you to wed her."

"She will make you happy," Kyndra added, surprisingly outspoken for a girl of fifteen years.

"Da!" said Chauncey, slapping Luke on the cheek.

However startling the women's embrace, their sudden acceptance was comforting. He felt as if he'd just become a member of a large and loving family. "I have to go," he said, extricating himself.

"Would you care for company?" the Slayer offered. He looked eager for action, having been confined to horseback for at least a week.

Luke was more than grateful. "I would," he nodded. "Have you found a place to stay yet?"

"Aye, we're at the Blue Inn at Charing Cross."

"We had to go there first to change the baby's napkins. I couldn't leave him behind; he won't take a wet nurse," Clarise explained. "I hope Merry will forgive our tardiness."

Thinking Clarise had good reason to look unkempt, Luke sought to reassure her. "She'll take comfort from your presence tomorrow," he promised. "The session will begin as it did today, at terce."

"Was it cut short? 'Tisn't yet midday," Clarise observed.

"She fainted for lack of food," he tersely replied. " 'Tis a matter I intend to rectify at once."

"Let's go," said the Slayer. As a man of little talk and much action, he'd grown impatient with their loitering.

Luke led the way out of the abbey, his newfound family trailing behind. Nearly everyone else had already dispersed.

A short ride down King Street took them to the palace. Clarise and Kyndra continued with an escort of men-at-arms to the inn where they were staying. Luke and the Slayer halted at the palace gates.

"I've been turned away a dozen times already," Luke warned him.

"Do we fight our way in, then?" The Slayer reached eagerly for the helm that was balanced on his pommel.

Feeling a resurgence of confidence, Luke nearly smiled. "Nay, I've a feeling we'll be welcomed this time."

The Slayer threw him a curious look.

As Luke predicted, the guards who'd been conferring, swung the gates suddenly wide. The twosome trotted up the path of crushed shells toward the royal stables then made their way up the many steps to Henry's solar, escorted at a distance by several more guards.

Luke seized the opportunity to explain the circumstances of his grandfather's poisoning. The Slayer had nothing to say in response, but his lip curled in scorn, and a dangerous gleam entered his eyes. By the time the two were led into the king's private quarters, Luke felt invincible. They would accept nothing less than Merry's freedom and a signed apology from the bishop himself.

Henry was waiting for them, dressed today in a russet tunic that suited his coloring well. He took one look at the towering

Slayer and stepped hastily upon his dais to be at eye-level with him.

Luke made introductions, which Henry waved aside, saying he recognized the Slayer from their first encounter, when the giant had pledged him fealty. "State the purpose of your visit," Henry commanded, locking his hands behind his back.

To Luke's practiced eye, the king looked tense this morning. "Your Majesty must have received by now a missive from your informant at Arundel?"

The king gave him a shuttered look, saying nothing.

"I'll not mince my words, Highness," Luke continued. "Your cousin has been poisoning my grandfather. I'm sure you want no public speculation on the matter."

Henry's color rose in proportion to his lowered brows. "Sir Luke, you presume too much!" he blustered. "I am not a pawn to be positioned at will. I am your sovereign king, by God, and you will show me the respect that I am due!"

Luke refused to back down under Henry's blustering. "I have naught but respect for you, Majesty," he countered, "for I know you to be a fair and just ruler. Your cousin, however, is a scheming murderess, and I will expose her plot if you do not redress the wrong that she has done."

Henry set his jaw. He turned and paced the length of his dais, his boots thumping heavily on the wooden planks. "What would you have me do?" he demanded, pausing again before them. "Think you that this matter with your wife involves me at all? 'Tis an ecclesiastical concern and one over which I have no say."

"You appointed the bishop, Majesty," Luke reminded him.

"That gives me no right to tell him how to do his job!" the king thundered. "I tell you I have no authority where this trial is concerned."

"Your Majesty can send in a witness."

"A what?" Henry asked, thrown off kilter by the odd suggestion.

"A witness, Majesty, who will help dispel the notion that my lady is a witch."

The king glowered suspiciously. "Whom did you have in mind?" he asked.

Luke had every confidence that Merry could redeem herself

if given the chance. "Your physician," he answered. "Send Sir Guy of Gascony to the bishop with instructions that he is to question my lady on matters of healing. He is to be honest in his questioning," Luke warned, "else I will expose his part in the poisoning of my grandfather."

Henry looked at him as if he'd gone mad. "My physician?" he repeated.

"Aye, 'twas his recommendation that Amalie use a poppy syrup to treat my grandsire's cough. He knew well enough that any poppy grown at Arundel was of the Oriental sort, highly poisonous. 'Twas possibly even his suggestion."

Henry had lost some of his color. The participants of that crime were perilously close to him. "Very well," he finally agreed, his gray eyes watchful. "My physician will testify. I hope you expect no more of me," he added.

"If my lady is relieved of the charges, Majesty, then nay, I expect no more. If by chance she is still condemned, then I will enjoy dragging Amalie through the courts of law your grace is in the process of reforming. I trust, at such a time, Your Majesty will not interfere."

Henry drew himself up, his cheeks ruddy with ire. Yet he couldn't conceal the gleam of admiration shining in his eyes. "I need your sworn fealty, Sir Luke," he admitted, as though Luke's bravery reminded him of the strengths he valued in his vassal. "Your service to me is irreplaceable."

Luke returned his gaze impassively. "My fealty is not as yet withdrawn, Your Grace."

An awkward moment passed between them. "Nor is my offer of Arundel withdrawn," Henry countered, clearly sensing the need to offer more, in order to ensure Luke's cooperation. "Consider it yours, with the title going to your heir. No more stipulations."

Luke sketched the king a bow. He had been waiting to hear those words for over thirteen years. How ironic that he would have to qualify his acceptance now. "Your generosity befits you well, Majesty," he replied. "But if my lady is not at my side to enjoy Arundel, then I will refuse it. Arundel is not a home without her."

He had the satisfaction of seeing Henry's jaw slacken.

Beside him the Slayer made a choking sound as if he could not believe his ears.

Henry searched visibly for his tongue. "Christ's toes, I don't believe I heard you aright!" he roared.

"Your Majesty has excellent hearing," Luke assured him.

Henry gaped at him, clearly mystified by the workings of Luke's mind. "You dare blackmail me!" he roared, pointing a finger at Luke and shaking it. "You who swore your fealty? You would go back on your oath?"

"I gave Your Majesty good warning," Luke retorted. He knew he should be quaking in his boots. He was talking of surrendering his power, his influence, and the future of his offspring. Yet he felt nothing but satisfaction in rattling Henry's cage. In proving the king had no authority over his heart.

His heart belonged to Merry, his queen. She could not accuse him of playing puppet to a tyrant now. He warmed at the thought to the point of smiling.

"Get out!" Henry thundered, gesturing to the door.

This was the second time he had been tossed from the palace on his ear. Sharing a rueful look with the Slayer, Luke bowed at Henry's boots. Then he and his companion made their way to the door. The giant clapped a hand to his shoulder, sending a silent message to the king as to where *his* loyalty lay. Henry risked losing two mighty leaders, not just one.

Luke left, certain the king would send his physician to the trial. And if he were as judicious as Luke knew him to be, Henry would ensure that Guy of Gascony was impressed by Merry's knowledge.


THE first thing Merry did was to seek Luke's face in the crowded refectory. There he was, seated on the same bench as before but this time in the company of her sisters and the Slayer. Her heart leapt with joy to see them—aye, even to see her brother-in-law whom she had at one time cursed.

Meeting Clarise and Kyndra's worried gazes, Merry fought for a reassuring smile. Her sisters looked tense and ravaged by sleeplessness. Clarise nodded encouragement to Merry, her jewel-like eyes burning with love. A sharp tug on the rope pulled Merry away from the trio toward the bench that awaited her.

Merry gingerly took her seat, then stared at Luke's face to calm her erratically beating heart. *Did he know something?* she wondered, sensing a confidence in the steadiness of his gaze, the set of his shoulders. Would things go better for her today?

They could scarcely go much worse. In her mind, her faint yesterday had only corroborated Owen and Donald's testimony. She'd been weak, overcome by dark forces that robbed her of her own will.

*Not today,* she vowed to herself. Though she suffered a headache from yesterday's fall, she'd been revived by the food that was brought unexpectedly to her chamber: cheese, meats, pastries, even dried fruit. She'd eaten until she felt she might split then saved the rest for this morning.

Her full belly churned uncomfortably. Sitting in her appointed place, with the muted sunlight affording little warmth, Merry wondered who would bear witness against her today. Glancing at the crowd, she recognized a villein who worked the lands near Heathersgill. He had been instrumental in bringing charges against Sarah, for his babe had been one of the infants to die that fateful year. Merry's optimism faltered. The matter of the dead babes was not one she was prepared to deal with— she had told Bartholomew as much.

Where was Father Moreau? The bells of terce had already tolled, yet Bartholomew sat alone on the counselor's bench. The bishop had taken his seat on the dais and was drumming his fingers impatiently. A sense of expectancy grew as the proceedings were delayed.

At last Bishop Tousaint called for the session to begin. "Father Bartholomew, you will have to take Father Moreau's place. I cannot imagine what is keeping him."

Merry's gaze flew to the priest's closed expression. Had Bartholomew engineered Moreau's absence? If so, it was a prodigious sign for her. Her heart beat faster.

"Lord Bishop," said Bartholomew, coming to his feet, "we call upon the next witness to this case, Pierce of Cringle Moor, a villein. Please stand and approach the bench."

Pierce, the villein, did not appear to understand. Summoned, he rose from the bench and hobbled toward the center of the chamber. The man was bent nearly double from the arduous life of farming. He squinted at Merry through his one good eye.

"Tell the court your name and your relation to the accused," the priest invited, after eliciting his oath.

Pierce pointed to himself. He began to speak in the Anglo tongue, drawing snickers from the audience.

Father Bartholomew raised a dark eyebrow. "Have we anyone who can translate?" he inquired, looking around.

The room was filled with courtiers, gentlemen, scholars, and a handful of merchants. Everyone looked at one another, and though the merchants surely spoke English, none of them wished to confess to such lowly knowledge. Clarise, whom Merry knew to speak fluent Anglo-Saxon, kept notably silent.

Merry touched her tongue to her upper lip. "I can speak his tongue," she admitted, recalling now that Bartholomew had been impressed with that fact during one of their discussions.

His reaction now was one of exaggerated surprise. "You?" he said. "Why is it that you, a lady, speak the tongue of the commoners?"

She swallowed uncertainly. "My teacher was Anglo-Saxon by birth. She taught me while I was still young, so that I could speak with the peasants whose ills we treated."

Pierce, the farmer, began to speak at length in a language that no one but Merry professed to understand. He pinned her to the bench with his one good eye. " 'Tweren't natural fer so many babes ta die," he ranted. "Ye and Sarah laid a black spell on the babes fer it to happen."

Merry shook her head. "Nay, Pierce," she soothed. " 'Tisn't so. I would never have done such a thing, even if I had the power. 'Twas a scourge, an infantile disease—"

"Stop this nonsense!" interrupted the bishop. "This is certainly no way to conduct official proceedings. Father Bartholomew, we must dismiss this witness. The accused cannot be asked to translate for him. How would we know if she spoke honestly or in her own behalf?"

The priest hung his head, pretending—Merry realized with the urge to laugh—to look disappointed. "Very well, My Lord Bishop," he replied. He gestured for Pierce to return to his seat. "The court calls Phillip of Poitiers and Erin McAdan."

Merry was surprised she hadn't noticed the hulking Phillip,

who rose from a bench under the window. He limped to the center of the chamber, trailed by Luke's squire, looking nervous in a pea-green tunic but extremely handsome with his cheeks unblemished.

At Father Bartholomew's behest, they swore to tell the truth, then they restated their names and made it known how they'd come by Merry's acquaintance.

"What was your first impression of Lady le Noir?" the priest asked the pair.

Erin went first. "I thought she looked much like a witch," he said in a voice that had deepened to an impressive baritone. "Her hair, her eyes, the sharp manner in which she spoke seemed to me unladylike."

"Did you believe her responsible when the horse slipped into the ravine on the approach to Heathersgill?"

Erin nodded gravely. "I did then," he said.

"Then?" the priest prompted.

"But the next day when she appeared riding the mare and it was standing there good as new and happy to be alive, I thought to myself, she can't be all that bad. Then Phillip here, he sliced his leg with his own ax, and I saw how kindly the lady tended him. He was in bad shape, Phillip. He would not be walking if not for my Lady le Noir."

Merry's heart had softened and warmed throughout McAdan's testimony. She gave him an encouraging smile, causing him to blush to his hairline.

"And you, Phillip of Poitiers, is Lady le Noir a witch in your estimation?"

"A witch, hah!" said Phillip in his thick dialect. "She is an angel of mercy. When I burned with fever, she made a salve that took the fever away. Her touch is gentle, her soul is kind—"

"See here," said the bishop, leaning forward. "The object of this court is not to laud the accused but to investigate her crimes. I've heard enough from these lovesick fools. Dismiss them," he added, glowering at the priest.

Bartholomew darted Merry an apologetic look. "As you wish, Your Grace. Then I must call forward the renowned physician, Guy of Gascony, who will clear up the matter of the lady's skill. Lord Guy?"

A thin, elegant man with swarthy coloring stepped forward.

As Bartholomew swore him in, the doctor looked down his narrow nose at Merry. His look was decidedly patronizing.

"Please tell the court your occupation and who it is you serve."

"I am the royal physician to His Majesty, the king," intoned Sir Guy, his manner disdainful.

"Then you are, naturally, among the best of Europe's physicians," Bartholomew elucidated.

Lord Gascony smiled thinly. "Naturally," he said.

"Perhaps you might answer some questions that have come forth in these proceedings. Are you familiar with any spells that might result in the death of many infants?"

The royal physician looked offended. "I am a scientist, not a sorcerer. I don't deal in spells," he said shortly.

"Is there any powder or herb that might be forced into an infant that would cause it to die with no outward symptom of disease?"

Sir Guy considered. "I have heard of none," he replied. "However, there are diseases that may steal over a population, killing only the infants and leaving the adults to live. These are not instigated by witches, but are propagated by foul air and by water."

Father Bartholomew paused to let the *bons hommes* digest this information. "Well, on to other matters," he said briskly. "Could you determine the extent of Lady le Noir's knowledge in the use of herbs by questioning her?"

"Of course," the physician said, haughtily.

The priest gestured for him to begin.

Sir Guy approached Merry's bench and circled it once for good measure. "How would one treat excessive bleeding of the mouth?" he finally asked her.

Merry thumbed through the pages of her mind and answered with confidence, "The leaves of blackberry rubbed against the gums will bind the bleeding therein."

Sir Guy paused and cocked his head to one side. "What about colic?" he asked, resuming his orbit of her stool.

"How old is the patient?" Merry answered. "Does he suffer from any other ailments?"

"The patient is an infant, two months old."

"I would sugar the stalk of Angelica root and have the infant suck it until he find relief."

Sir Guy began to stroke his narrow beard. "Common household remedies," he answered, as though to dismiss the success of her answers. "The patient suffers inflammation of the lungs as well as a fever. He suffers nervous complaints, headaches, trembling, and palpitations of the heart. What will you give him?"

Merry thought longer this time, and the bishop settled back in his great chair with a narrowed gaze. To the spectators, it appeared that Merry had been stymied at last. Speculative murmurs filled the refectory. Merry sensed Luke's sweating anxiety. His stare was so steady that he seemed not to blink.

"Valerian," she said at last, her voice cutting through the whispers. "The entire stalk must first be dried and an infusion thereof be made with one pinch powder to every pint of boiling water."

Sir Guy ceased to pace. He looked to Father Bartholomew for guidance.

"Ask her about poisons," the priest recommended, giving the doctor a tight smile. "She confessed to poisoning the prioress of Mount Grace. Ask her if she knows the antidote."

Sir Guy looked at Merry and gestured to the priest. "You heard him," he said simply.

"The antidote to henbane poisoning is goat's milk, honeyed water, and mustard seed," she answered.

"And did you have this antidote on hand when you poisoned the Prioress of Mount Grace?" Bartholomew cut in.

"Yes, I did," she replied. " 'Twasn't my intent for the Mother to die, only to suffer as she made others suffer."

Bartholomew hesitated, his gaze drawn to the door, which had just creaked open. Merry followed his gaze, as did Guy of Gascony, and then the rest of the audience. A husky young man in a fur-lined cloak entered the refectory in the presence of two guards.

An urgent whisper riffled through the room, and everyone came respectfully to their feet, including the bishop. With awe, Merry realized the king had come to her trial. She struggled to her feet also, though she'd been told to remain seated.

"Your Majesty!" said the bishop, looking stunned.

Henry gave a negligent wave of his hand. "Please," he said. "Continue." And then he strode with his guards to the rear of the room, throwing Luke a challenging look as he did so.

Merry sank slowly onto her bench. What did the king's attendance mean? she wondered weakly. She was relieved to see a smile playing at the edges of Luke's mouth. The message in his eyes was clear. *All will be well, my love. Do not fear.*

It took Bartholomew a moment to gather his thoughts. He turned his attention back to the royal physician. "Sir Guy of Gascony, given your expertise in the field of medicine, what can you tell the court regarding this lady's knowledge and use of herbs?"

Sir Guy's dark eyes were still disdainful. Yet he glanced toward the rear of the room where the king awaited his words, and he pinched his lips together as if he found his answer distasteful. "It is premature for me to give a thorough answer. That would require hours of discussion," he said slowly.

More murmurs broke out, causing the bishop to thump his chair and call for silence.

"But," added the physician, the words seemingly torn from him against his will, "if I were to be struck suddenly ill, I would prefer . . . that this woman tend me in lieu of . . . any of the leeches here in London."

The words had been uttered grudgingly, and yet they could not be taken back. With sudden insight, Merry guessed that Luke was somehow responsible for Sir Guy's testimony. After all, the man was the *royal* physician, and the king himself had come to lend credence to his testimony. Had Luke convinced Henry to send his doctor to speak on her behalf? Then he *must* have found proof that Amalie was poisoning his grandfather, else he could not have persuaded Henry to do so much!

Once more the chamber was astir with commentary. The bishop thumped his chair. "Bring your next witness," he called.

"The court calls upon the Lord Ian, Baron of Iversly, and his wife."

Pleasure bloomed in Merry's chest. She inhaled a shuddering breath, even as she glimpsed Luke's broadening smile. As the baron and baroness of Iversly made their way slowly forward, Lady Adelle's blue eyes flashed with the same determination Merry had remarked in her before.

Father Bartholomew questioned them, casting scathing aspersions on Merry's character in order to reestablish his role as prosecutor. Yet the priest's criticisms carried little weight, for the couple depicted Merry as a healer in their midst; a lady who not only restored the baron to good health but also brought light and life into their stagnant world. The tension in Merry's shoulders eased. Her heart beat regularly for the first time that morning.

By the end of the old couple's testimony, the *bons hommes* were regarding Merry with respect and confusion, as if they did not know quite what to make of her.

"Are there any more witnesses?" the bishop inquired of Bartholomew.

Bartholomew wavered. "Er, my Lord Bishop. There are no more witnesses, per se."

"Then you're prepared to give your closing remarks?"

The priest cleared his throat. "As Father Moreau was the one to give the closing remarks, Your Grace, I request that that honor be left to Sir Luke le Noir, esteemed tenant-in-chief to His Majesty, the king."

"Husband of the accused," the bishop added, looking baffled.

"Aye, that too," Bartholomew relented.

The bishop frowned. The request was highly unorthodox, and yet he had promised Luke he would allow him to bear witness at the trial. He sought Luke's face in the crowd. "Are you prepared to address the jury, Sir Luke?" he inquired.

Luke's voice rang out confidently. "I am, Your Grace."

The bishop threw his hands into the air, signifying amazement with the entire proceedings. "So be it," he decreed.

Merry had been waiting for Luke to speak from the first. Her heart rose toward her throat. She gripped her fingers together, unable to look away from her husband as he approached the front of the room.

The buzzing that had erupted at the bishop's decision died a quick death as Luke strode forward, commanding attention by his mere presence. Dressed in a deep green tunic, with his muscles so defined beneath the combed wool, it was impossible not to admire his warrior's build. Yet when he opened his mouth and spoke convincingly of his reasons for scaling a priory's walls, it became clear why the king had chosen him as his personal representative in so many tenuous situations.

His remarkable voice soothed the crowd. Like the many foreign officials whom he'd nudged toward peace, the crowd sensed his integrity, his straightforwardness, the qualities that Merry had remarked in him from the first. The nobles, scholars, clerics, and merchants nodded their heads whenever he paused.

Merry felt the last vestige of fear slip away. At the very least, he would save their unborn child from death. Her heart wept with relief.

"Good sirs," he added, turning to the *bons hommes* who seemed bedazzled by his presence, "you have put the wrong soul on trial here," he admonished gently. "If anyone should be sitting there, it is I," he added, pointing to Merry's bench. "I was the one who scaled the wall of Mount Grace and cut this lady free from a burning pyre. She was willing to burn, not because she suffered remorse for any wrongdoing, but because the world had been unnaturally cruel to her." He had already summarized the trauma she'd endured at the hands of others.

"A priory is a place of peaceful reflection. How can one find peace when one is hunted as prey?" He turned and regarded the prioress, who seethed with rancor on the far side of the chamber. "The prioress of Mount Grace, without permission of the Holy See, prosecuted and condemned an innocent to die. Moreover, she intended for her to burn within the walls of her priory, hiding the ugliness of her vengeance from the public eye. That is what I saw when I beheld Lady Merry tied to a stake. Because the crime against her was so blatant, I took the condemned into my custody, escorting her to safety.

"We have heard divisive testimony regarding the true nature of the accused. Consider those who believe her a witch. Owen of Ailswyth and Donald of Tees are ignorant men, uneducated mercenaries whose tales stir the imagination, but are, nonetheless, mere stories. The truth has been told by more esteemed witnesses, those who have benefited from this lady's skill, those who have known her personally and found her pure of spirit.

"I count myself among the latter," he added, including the bishop in his sweeping gaze. "This remarkable woman taught me to do right, not for duty's sake, but out of compassion.

While escorting her to Helmesly, we were beset by rogues. This lady," he gestured to Merry, "saved my life. I would surely have perished if not for her bravery and skill."

He paused, groping for the poise that now threatened to abandon him. His voice quavered with heartfelt emotion. "How could I not desire such a remarkable woman to be my wife?" he inquired of the crowd. "For all that she has endured, she has retained something I lost years ago—her humanity. For the sake of that humanity, it is your duty to liberate her from the charges brought against her. Given her condition, she is deserving of an apology for the starvation and humiliation inflicted upon her." He bowed at the *bons hommes* and then to the bishop. "May your own humanity be your counsel now."

As he straightened, someone in the rear of the room began to clap. Heads swiveled and necks craned, including Merry's. It took a great deal of gall to clap in a courtroom, especially in support of an accused witch. She recognized the perpetrator at once. It was Henry himself who lauded Luke's closing arguments. Others joined him at once, as he, of course, expected.

Soon the chamber thundered with applause.

"Silence!" called the bishop, scowling at the impropriety of it. Yet his eyes, hitherto murky and mysterious, had cleared with something like relief.

Merry caught the eye of one of the *bons hommes,* an older man who'd watched her carefully throughout the trial. He gave her the tiniest of smiles. She knew then, without having to wait for the verdict that Luke had done it again.

He'd saved her with his words.

# Epilogue

MERRY shifted the baby on her lap so that little Isabel le Noir could watch the older children playing. A crisp autumn breeze ruffled the baby's dark curls and stirred the fruity scents wafting from the orchard.

Collin, Reggie, Susan, and Katey were taking turns tumbling down one of the little hills that formed the tiered garden. Head over heels they rolled, fascinating Isabel who watched through wide green eyes.

With a rush of tenderness, Merry kissed her baby's cheek and breathed her sweet scent. What a gift to see life anew through her daughter's eyes! On the day that Isabel was born six months ago, Merry had vowed that her tiny, perfect daughter would never suffer the travails that she had suffered. Within the protective walls of Arundel, Isabel would grow safe and serene, thriving under the devoted eye of her parents, who loved her to distraction.

The children in the castle had latched on to her with awe and devotion. She would never be lonely.

And God willing, she would never lose the father she adored, even though Luke was often called away, mostly to Normandy as an emissary for the king.

Luke's long absences would become less frequent once he

was needed at Arundel. Though Merry had no desire to hasten Sir William's demise, she looked forward to the day when Luke would come home to stay. Any day, now, she expected her husband's return from his latest voyage to France. He'd been gone nearly a month, negotiating the release of hostages. And though she kept busy herself, studying medicine under the tutelage of a physician from Oxford, the days seemed to creep by without Luke to cheer her.

The sudden blare of the trumpet caused her to start with expectation. Could it be Luke? she asked herself, even as she stood with the baby in her arm and tidied her hair.

The sound of a horse preceded any vision on the walkway. When the silvery head of the earl came into view, Merry had to swallow her sharp disappointment. Her wildly thumping heart grew still again . . . waiting. Yet she smiled and waved a greeting.

Sir William looked hale and hearty on his great black steed. She remarked no lingering effects of his illness, save a tendency to be weary. Even from a distance, she could tell he'd enjoyed his morning visit with his tenants. Over the distance between them, he grinned and, turning in his saddle, waved a second rider forward.

A knight in full armor appeared at the gate. Merry gave a cry of recognition as Luke took off his helm. With her daughter clasped to her bosom, she ran to greet him.

He vaulted from the saddle and they met at the base of the garden steps where Luke took her in his arms and whirled them both in a full circle.

Merry laughed openly, her love for him overflowing. He kissed her, his face rough with whiskers he hadn't shaved in days.

"My beautiful wife," he said. "I'm home. Now, let me see you." He gazed at her tenderly, his gaze sliding eventually to the baby who regarded him solemnly. "Oh, my pearl," he said, clearly awed by Isabel's porcelain perfection. "Look how big you've grown! Come to Papa?" he asked, holding out his arms.

Isabel looked politely away, as if unwilling to deny him, but frightened nonetheless by his scruffy appearance.

"Do you think she's forgotten me?" he asked on a worried note.

"Of course not," Merry comforted. "She feels you need a bath, 'tis all," she teased. "Oh, she can sit now, darling, on her own! And she rocks back and forth on her hands and knees. She'll be crawling any day now."

"Then I'll be here to see it," he said with satisfaction. He returned his gaze to Merry. "How I missed you, sprite. Next time you must come with me. Isabel will be old enough to travel."

Merry nodded in agreement. "Though not anytime soon, I hope," she said.

"Nay, not for a while. Normandy should be quiet for at least a few months. Henry and I whipped the rebels soundly." He took a step closer, his mouth by her ear. "It has been too long since I felt you pressed against me," he murmured. "I'm in bad need of you."

She lifted a hand to his tangled locks, gazing at him with soft invitation in her eyes. "There is nothing now that requires my immediate attention," she informed him.

"Oh, but there is," he corrected her, his eyes gleaming with intent. "Perhaps we should work on another pearl," he suggested.

She pretended to consider. "Would you like a brother or sister, Izzy?" she asked her baby.

Isabel looked puzzled by the question.

"I suppose we could try," Merry determined, unable to control her flush of anticipation.

Taking her hand in his, Luke led her toward the keep.

They tried all that afternoon and again deep into the night. The effort itself was most rewarding. Yet the result came nine months later in the form of a boy, the next earl of Arundel.